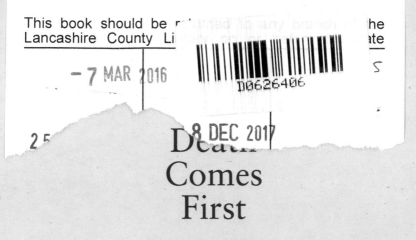

Death Comes First

Hilary Bonner is a full-time author and former chairman
of The Crime Writers' Association. Her published work
includes eleven previous novels, five non-fiction books:
two ghosted autobiographies, one biography, two com-
panions to TV programmes, and a number of short
stories. She is a former Fleet Street journalist, Show Busi
ness Editor of three national newspapers and Assistant
Editor of one. She now lives primarily in the West of
England where she was born and brought up and where
most of her novels are set.

BY HILARY BONNER

Fiction

The Cruelty of Morning
A Fancy to Kill For
A Passion So Deadly
For Death Comes Softly
A Deep Deceit
A Kind of Wild Justice
A Moment of Madness
When the Dead Cry Out
No Reason to Die
The Cruellest Game
Friends to Die For
Death Comes First

Non-Fiction

René and Me (with Gorden Kaye)
Benny: The True Story (with Dennis Kirkland)
It's Not a Rehearsal (with Amanda Barrie)
Journeyman (with Clive Gunnell)
Heartbeat: The Real Life Story

Death
Comes
First

HILARY
BONNER

PAN BOOKS

First published 2015 by Macmillan

This edition published 2015 by Pan Books
an imprint of Pan Macmillan
20 New Wharf Road, London N1 9RR
Associated companies throughout the world
www.panmacmillan.com

ISBN 978-1-4472-7210-6

135798642

A CIP catalogue record for this book is available from the British Library.

Typeset by Ellipsis Digital Limited, Glasgow
Printed and bound by CPI Group (UK) Ltd, Croydon, CR0 4YY

For Adam
With thanks for the inspiration
you never knew you gave me

Prologue

The letter lay on the table before her. It had arrived in the morning post: two sheets of A4 paper, covered with her husband's distinctive spidery handwriting, each word loosely formed in black ink. For the last half hour Joyce had been sitting in her chair staring at it, transfixed, unable to move. Her head felt hot and the back of her neck was clammy.

She'd read it twice yet still couldn't take it in. Not while her brain was reeling from the shock.

A letter from Charlie. But Charlie had died six months earlier.

Ever since then, Joyce had been trying to come to terms with the loss, with his absence from her life, from the children's lives. It had been so hard, consoling their three children, struggling to fill the void, but the worst times were when she was alone. Once the two youngest children went off to school the house seemed unbearably bleak and empty; even when the children came home there was so much less noise than there used to be. For their sake, she'd forced herself to carry on, to make plans for a future without her husband.

Little by little the sense of desolation had begun to lift. Until she'd read that letter.

Joyce reached out to touch it, wanting to read it one more time to try to make sense of it, but pulled her hand away as if afraid it might burn her fingers.

Perhaps if she never looked at it again, if she tore it up and threw it into the bin or flushed it down the toilet, perhaps if she did that she could forget all about it and life would continue as normal. Or as near to normal as would ever be possible after Charlie's death.

Back in her university days she'd had a friend whose father had left her a 'letter from the grave'. Having been ill for years, he'd come to terms with death and had written to his daughter to console her and help her deal with her grief. There was no consolation in Charlie's letter. Far from it. His words had left her feeling threatened and bewildered, undermining the very foundations of her world.

Tempting as it was to destroy the letter and try to carry on as if nothing had happened, Joyce knew that would be impossible. She would never be able to put Charlie's words from her mind. Then again, perhaps she had misunderstood. The only way to find out was to read it again.

She could read the first page simply by inclining her head slightly. She took a deep breath and did so.

My dearest darling,

If you are reading this then I am no longer alive. More than anything I want to tell you how much I love you. You, and our children, mean the world to me, even though it may not always have seemed that way. I want you to believe that, and to go on believing it, regardless of any bad times in the past, regardless of anything you may hear in the future.

I will never forget the first time I saw you. I know it's a

*cliché, but I really did spot you across a crowded room. A
young student, like so many others – except you were
nothing like the others. Not to me. Our eyes met. And that
was that. For me, anyway. For ever. Do you remember that
moment?*

Joyce remembered. She felt near to tears. But she was too
shocked and confused to cry.

The next two paragraphs continued in a nostalgic vein,
with Charlie recalling special moments they'd shared and
assuring her of his abiding love for her. Joyce skimmed over
those. It was what came later that had left her stunned and
shaken.

*I wanted to tell you all this, I needed to tell you, but most
of all I needed to warn you so that you can protect
yourself and our children from the dangers that face you.
I am so sorry that I have failed you. I have been a weak
man. You may not have realized this. Or then again, maybe
you did. But even if you suspected it to be the case, you
can't have known just how weak I have been. I have
followed paths I would never and should never have
chosen, but I was too weak to look beyond the easiest
option. I am so sorry, my darling.*

*My biggest mistake was to allow myself to become
immersed in your father's world. I couldn't bring myself to
destroy your illusions, so I kept things from you, thinking
I was sheltering you, but I see now that what I was really
doing was living in denial, dodging my responsibility to
protect my family. Now that I am gone, I'm afraid that
responsibility falls to you.*

It is probably already too late for Mark. But you must protect Fred. Whatever you do, please don't let your father get his hands on Fred . . .

Joyce's hand reached out to turn the page, but still she couldn't bring herself to touch it. Instead she sat there, heart pounding as she thought of her eldest boy, now twenty-two but young for his age, thanks to a sheltered upbringing in the closeted environment of Tarrant Park, the exclusive gated development midway between Bristol and Weston-super-Mare which was home to the Tanner and Mildmay clan.

The previous year Mark had joined his father and grandfather at Tanner-Max International, the import–export agency set up by his great-grandfather Edward Tanner with his wartime friend Maxim Schmidt in the late fifties. It was all Mark had ever wanted to do. He would have started work in the family business the moment he left school if it hadn't been for Joyce insisting that he at least go to university first. Her hope had been that Mark would immerse himself in student social life and be tempted to spread his wings a little, but it soon became clear that he had no desire to fly the nest. He had refused to consider any campus beyond commuting distance, ultimately securing a place at his second choice, Bath, to study business and management. Bristol had been his first choice, of course. In the three years he was there he'd shown no interest whatsoever in pursuing a social life with his fellow students. Instead he'd rushed home to spend his evenings and weekends at the office with his grandfather, learning the ropes in readiness for the day he would take his place in the firm.

Henry Tanner had been delighted, rewarding his grandson's loyalty by buying him a brand-new top-of-the-range Mini Cooper for the commute to Bath. And when Mark announced that he needed his own space and wanted to move out of his parents' home, it wasn't because he'd succumbed to the lure of independence. He merely migrated up the road into a newly converted self-contained apartment above the garage at his grandfather's place.

Mark had always been close to his grandfather, perhaps excessively so. All the same, Joyce could not understand Charlie's warning. Henry Tanner was famously controlling and a fearsome chief executive, but when it came to his family he'd always been a benign patriarch and a doting grand-parent to Mark and his siblings: fifteen-year-old Molly and eleven-year-old Fred. Without the support of her parents, Joyce couldn't imagine how she'd have survived the last six months. How could her father be a threat to her children's well-being? It made no sense.

Releasing the tissue she'd been twisting to shreds in her lap, Joyce moved the top sheet of A4 to one side. She took a deep breath and steeled herself for what was to come.

The second page began with more reminiscing and protest-ations of enduring love and devotion.

Do you remember the dreams we once had? I cannot tell you how much I regret abandoning the plans we made when we were young. I should have listened to you, my gorgeous, free-spirited girl, my fellow dreamer, my soul mate. It breaks my heart to remember how you pleaded with me to run away with you, how desperate you were to escape the gilded cage your father had made for you. You thought I was the man to help you, and I believed that too, my darling, I truly did. And for a time I tried to be. But then it all changed, and even now I cannot tell you why that happened. Why did I allow myself to be sucked

*into that world? Some days I barely recognize myself as
the man I used to be. And the thing I hate most about
myself is that I connived in dragging you along with me,
and our children.*

*Forgive me, my sweetheart. And try to believe that I did
what I did because I thought it was in your best interests.
I took what I believed to be the only option. My love for
you has been the one constant in my life, to the end, even
though I know only too well that I have frequently given
you reason to doubt.*

Joyce reached for the mug of coffee standing on the
kitchen table alongside the letter. She took a sip, then spat the
bitter dark liquid back into the mug. It was stone cold. Of
course it was. She had made the coffee before the postman
had called, and put it down on the table when she heard the
rattle of the letter box. Strange how life might now never be
the same again following such an insignificant, routine occurrence. The daily mail delivery.

Joyce forced herself to read on, though her mind was in
utter turmoil. Charlie hadn't been an easy man to live with
the last few years, and she couldn't remember the last time
he'd confided in her. So she couldn't begin to understand
what might have happened to make him write to her in such
a manner, in a letter she was only to read after his death – a
death which had come as a shock to everyone that knew him.
He'd been a fit and healthy man, only forty-three years old
when he died as the result of an accident while sailing off the
North Devon coast in his boat, the *Molly May*.

*I want you to take the children and go somewhere Henry
will never find you. Remember the Shangri-La we dreamed*

of? Still dreamed of, even after we settled in Tarrant Park,
even after it faded to nothing more than a pipe dream. I
want you to realize that dream with our children. Find our
Shangri-La, Joyce. It will be possible. Get our children
away from Henry for ever. He won't be interested in Molly,
but she'll be so much better off without him in her life.

Joyce paused and wiped the back of one hand across her
mouth. Her lips were dry. Her head was starting to ache.
There was a relentless dull thud somewhere in the middle of
her temples. She had been shocked the first time she read the
letter. Shocked to the core. It seemed even worse the second
time. But she made herself read on.

Empty all the bank accounts you have access to. There
should be enough for you to start again. Leave everything
else behind. Just walk away.
Above all, don't confide in anyone, not even Stephen.
You know how manipulative Henry is – you must not tell
a living soul . . .

Ordinarily, Stephen Hardcastle would have been the first
person Joyce would have consulted for advice. Not only was
he the family solicitor, he was one of her closest friends.
They'd known each other since university, and he'd been best
man at Joyce and Charlie's wedding. But that was before he
became company secretary of Tanner-Max International.

The letter, with Joyce's name written on the front, again
in Charlie's handwriting, had arrived inside another envelope bearing a typewritten address. Inside was a note from
Stephen's PA, apologizing for the delay in forwarding the

letter and explaining – rather lamely, Joyce thought – that this had come about due to a clerical error.

Joyce picked up the inner envelope, lying alongside the letter, and examined it to see whether it might have been opened before reaching her. She didn't think so, but as soon as she had recognized Charlie's writing on the front she'd been in such a hurry to get to the content that she'd ripped the envelope apart. She studied what was left of the seal beneath the flap. It didn't look as if it had been tampered with before her own careless attentions, but she couldn't be sure.

Realizing she was shivering, Joyce pulled her thin cardigan tightly around her, though the underfloor heating was on and the kitchen was perfectly warm. She couldn't remember ever feeling so alone and so unnerved. How could she contemplate uprooting Fred and Molly, robbing them of stability at a time when they needed it most? And what of Mark? He might be twenty-two, but he was still her son. Was she supposed to walk away from him without a word? How could she leave him to face this unnamed threat alone?

And the worst of it was, she had no idea what she was supposed to be fleeing from. All she had to go on was Charlie's evidently genuine conviction that they were in danger and their only hope was to run away – from her own father. If that were the case, she would have to act on it, even if it meant severing all ties with her parents. But how could she leave Mark?

Not for the first time she was consumed with anger at Charlie. Why did he have to die? Why had he delivered this warning in a letter instead of discussing it with her while he was still alive, so that they could take whatever action needed to be taken together? He must have known the distress and bewilderment it would cause. But then, that was typical of the man her husband had become. What did he care – he was dead. He was out of it. For a fleeting moment Joyce wished she was too.

She tore her eyes from the letter and looked out at the rainswept garden. Late May and half-term only a week away, but there was no hint of summer's impending arrival in the dark clouds and sodden greenery. Until the postman had called, Joyce's big worry of the day had been what she was going to do with her two younger children if the weather over the holiday proved to be as bad as was forecast. The two tall Douglas firs from which the Mildmay family home had drawn its name stood like sentinels either side of imposing electronic gates at the end of a wide drive. Water dripped from the lower branches on to shiny paving. Beyond, it was just possible to make out the private road linking the homes of the privileged residents of the gated community. There were no signs of life; it was rare to catch a glimpse of any of the neighbours.

Apart from her time at university, Joyce had spent her whole life in the confines of Tarrant Park. The home she'd grown up in, Corner House, was a hundred metres from where she sat now. Built to Henry's own specification, it was easily the most dominating and imposing house in the development. Ever since she could remember, the Tanner family's social life had revolved around the gated community's tennis club, golf course and swimming pool. As a child, her playmate had been her adored brother, William, two years her senior. It wasn't that visits from school friends were prohibited or discouraged, more that outsiders didn't seem comfortable in Tarrant Park. She recalled one girl describing it as 'seriously creepy'.

Sitting at her kitchen table with her dead husband's letter spread out before her and only designer green nothingness to be glimpsed through the windows, Joyce felt an overwhelming sense of eeriness, as if by opening the envelope she had unleashed some evil genie. And now that it was out there, she could not afford to ignore it, to pretend it did not exist.

For the sake of her children, Joyce was going to have to establish the precise nature of whatever danger faced them and determine how to react. Easier said than done, with her mind running riot from the possibilities of what it might be.

She got up from the table, poured away her cold coffee, and made herself a fresh cup, which she carried into the conservatory. She needed to think, rein in her imagination, be rational. The wording of the letter made it sound as though Charlie had been aware of this threat, whatever it was, for years. It seemed incomprehensible that he would have kept it entirely to himself; perhaps he had alluded to it in some way, but she'd chosen to ignore it, burying the recollection deep within her subconscious.

Once more Joyce's coffee grew cold as she sat dredging her memory for clues.

One

The business activities of the men in Joyce's life – principally her father, then her brother and husband, and now her son too – had long been a mystery to her. Wives and daughters were not privy to the workings of Tanner-Max; while male progeny were expected to join the family business, Henry clung to the outdated notion that a woman's role in life was that of wife, mother, home-maker. Joyce's mother, Felicity, had been a seventeen-year-old newly qualified typist on her first job with a temp agency when she met Henry, but the moment they became engaged her working life ended.

Not that Felicity seemed to mind. Far from it. They had married when she was only twenty and he twenty-two but even after forty-seven years of marriage they gave every impression of being a devoted couple, both of them content in their traditional roles. While Felicity stayed at home, raising the children, Henry provided for his family's every need – and did so lavishly. Despite periods of recession and financial austerity, under his leadership Tanner-Max had gone from strength to strength with profits steadily rising year after year. In part this was due to the fact that he was not only an astute businessman but a natural leader. There was something about him that commanded respect. Certainly he had great presence, and he made sure he always looked the part, holding himself stiffly upright and dressing in tailored suits and handmade shoes. He reckoned his shoes were worth every extravagant penny because they lasted for ever, and he bought a new pair only once every five years. At sixty-nine he remained a handsome man, with a full head of white hair that complemented his tanned skin (courtesy of a passion for all-weather golfing).

It occurred to Joyce that, beyond the fact everyone deferred to him and appeared to be in awe of him, she had little idea what Henry was like outside the home. He certainly believed in sharing the fruits of the company's success: whatever wealth the business brought in, he made sure that Tanner-Max employees were amply rewarded and that his family shared in the benefits. In return, however, everything had to be done his way. Charlie might have been a partner in the company, but Joyce doubted that he had ever done anything to warrant his generous salary. There was no question who ran Tanner-Max, quite autonomously, and would continue to run it until he dropped.

It was the same at home. Though Henry had been a good, caring father and she had never been given cause to doubt his love for his family, Joyce couldn't help but think of him as a benevolent despot. Growing up, she'd always known he would give her anything she asked for – except the thing she came to desire most: her freedom.

She had pinned her hopes on university as the means of achieving her escape from the confines of Tarrant Park. Predictably, Henry had been opposed to the idea. It had taken Felicity's subtle and patient intervention to bring him round, but even then he'd insisted that Joyce should apply only to West Country universities, making Bristol her first choice, and Bath her second. Playing the dutiful daughter, Joyce assured him that she was happy to remain in the West of England. Privately, unlike her elder son many years later, she was determined not to spend the next three years of her life commuting between campus and home. So she ignored Bristol and Bath in favour of Exeter. The old Devon county town was only an hour and a half's drive from Tarrant Park. Henry gave his approval on condition that she would return home every weekend, and that he or his driver would chauffeur her.

Joyce had accepted the terms with alacrity. In the Tanner household that was a result.

Regardless of the restrictions imposed upon her, she'd felt she was well on her way to achieving her greatest goal: to be free to live her life in her own way. But the reality was that, apart from one fleeting exploratory fling, she ended up spending most of her first year buried in her studies – she was reading history, which had captivated her from early childhood – and in sport, at which she was rather good. She played tennis for the university and golf during her weekends at home, which remained rigidly implemented. Joyce didn't mind. Not to begin with anyway. It was as if she needed to learn how to deal with freedom. Though she would never have admitted it, she welcomed her weekly break from her new world. It suited her to return to the closet at regular intervals.

And then everything changed.

It was the beginning of her second year at university. The new intake were gathered in the central hall. It was the usual meet-and-greet session with the principal and other members of staff. Joyce happened to be passing in the corridor outside. Nosily she sneaked a look through a glass-panelled door.

Across the room she saw Charlie. He seemed to stand out

from the others, like a character in an arthouse movie, projected in vibrant colour whilst everyone else was in black and white. Charlie was standing by a window, side-on to Joyce, the light silhouetting his profile so that she could not see his face properly. It was clear that he was tall and gangly, with long limbs that seemed to have outgrown the rest of him. And he had unruly fair hair that skimmed the shoulders of his crumpled blue denim shirt.

She found herself staring at him. Then he turned and looked straight at her. Had he felt her eyes upon him? Neither of them had ever been sure.

He was far too thin for her taste. He had a long bony face and a crooked nose that looked as if it had once been broken. The signs of a nasty outbreak of teenage acne still lurked around his chin. He was by no means the best-looking man she'd ever seen. But when his eyes, surprisingly dark for one so fair, met hers, Joyce had felt a shiver run down her spine. And it had been a very pleasant sensation.

Then he had smiled. A small, uncertain smile. And she'd smiled back. Much the same way.

Charlie always said it had been love at first sight. And even though the sensible half of Joyce did not believe in such a notion, she supposed it must have been that. Or something damned near to it.

At the time she merely told herself to get a grip, and hurried off for her afternoon's lecture.

When she emerged two hours later Charlie was waiting outside the lecture hall. She couldn't understand how he had known where she would be.

'Sixth sense,' he'd said, beaming at her.

Long afterwards he confessed that he'd noticed she was carrying a copy of H. A. L. Fisher's *History of Europe*, and upon making enquiries had discovered that there was only one history lecture taking place that afternoon.

Whilst their relationship had begun almost at once, it was several weeks before they slept together. Charlie and Joyce, perhaps unusually amongst students, became very much an item in every other way before embarking on the physical. Sex came second. They began to go everywhere together, do everything together, and were rarely seen apart. Around the campus they became known simply as JC. They were a unit. Everything they did, they did as one. Charlie was studying politics and liked to draw and paint in his free time; Joyce began to do so too, while Charlie took to reading Joyce's history books when he had a spare moment.

Charlie's political beliefs were far left and idealistic. In 1989, the year he arrived at Exeter, he was still a committed member of the Communist Party of Great Britain, even though communism was in steep decline throughout Europe. Joyce, whose interest in politics had hitherto been purely academic, found Charlie's conviction magnetic. She joined the Party too, allowing herself to be swept along on the tidal wave of his philosophy, determined to embrace his grand vision.

As a committed Marxist, Charlie was never quite sure if he wanted to change the world or hide away from it in a garret somewhere with his easel. Joyce dutifully – like a good Tanner woman, she later reflected – went along with his whims, regularly attending Party meetings with him, although she didn't share his conviction. She could see no harm in it; after all, communism in the West was over, whether or not Charlie was prepared to admit it.

The Berlin Wall fell in November 1989, two months after Charlie's arrival at Exeter and his fateful meeting with Joyce. But Charlie seemed to be the only person in the world oblivious to the significance. Looking back, Joyce could see that Charlie had behaved like an ostrich, blocking out this epic event because it didn't suit his notion of how the world should be. At the time, Joyce hadn't minded; in fact, she'd been vaguely amused. But that was before she discovered that Charlie would display a life-long predilection for denying the existence of anything which did not fit into his own scheme of things.

Charlie lived off campus on an old wooden sailing boat, the *Shirley Anne*, which had been left to him by his grandfather. Or the nearest thing he had to a grandfather. His parents, about whom he seemed to know very little, had been killed in a car crash when Charlie was three, and he'd been fostered by a childless North Devon couple who later adopted him. Their family became his family, Charlie always said.

The legacy from his adoptive grandfather had included an extremely convenient River Exe estuary mooring at Topsham, just outside Exeter. Charlie made the daily commute to campus aboard a rickety Lambretta motor scooter. It wasn't long before Joyce moved in with him, keeping her new living arrangements from Henry and Felicity.

She continued to travel home at weekends. But not every weekend. And by train, having managed to persuade her parents that this was the swiftest and easiest form of travel between Exeter and Bristol, thus avoiding any inspection of her living arrangements by Henry or his driver.

With or without Joyce, Charlie spent his weekends scraping and patching the old boat, in order, he told her, to make it seaworthy for a voyage around the world. Joyce joined in, when she could. She met Charlie's adoptive parents, Bill and Joan Mildmay, when they came to visit, bringing a picnic and wine. They seemed easy-going and totally accepting of her.

She wondered if she would ever have the courage to introduce Charlie to her parents. She would have to, sooner or later, that was for certain. Because Charlie had already told her that, whatever he ended up doing with his life, he wanted to share it with her. And she felt the same.

Of an evening they would sit planning a gap-year odyssey aboard the *Shirley Anne*. They would allow the winds to take them where they willed, said Charlie one night as they sat on deck, oblivious to the cold, sharing a spliff.

Joyce thought it was the most romantic thing she had ever heard.

Since Charlie was a year younger than her and a year behind in his studies, Joyce intended to extend her time at university either by studying for an MA, if her grades were good enough, or a teaching qualification. That way they would leave Exeter at the same time and take off on their travels, roaming the oceans like the free spirits they were.

Living on the *Shirley Anne* was not easy. They had to contend with a cantankerous gas water-heater, which would provide hot water for the one sink only when it suited it. There was no shower, let alone a bath. Thankfully the university locker rooms provided those facilities. The boat was connected to mains electricity, in a Heath Robinson sort of way. If you overloaded it by plugging in more than one device at a time, the entire system was liable to blow. So the sole electric heater which warmed the old vessel had to be used with extreme care. On top of that the place reeked of damp, and mildew was rife. All Joyce's shoes turned vaguely green with a persistent mould at which she resolutely scrubbed each time she wore them, although it never seemed to make much difference.

Their first winter in the leaky aft cabin was a cold and wet one. Joyce had never known what it was to be cold, and it amazed her that Charlie didn't seem to feel it or be affected by it. She shivered and coughed and spluttered her way through until spring, but it didn't faze her. Only one thing mattered: she was with the man she loved, living his dream.

Charlie was unlike anyone she'd ever met. With hindsight she wondered whether that was why she'd been drawn to him. He couldn't have been more different to her father. In those days, anyway. To his daughter, Henry Tanner seemed an utterly conventional man, to the point of being boring. Whereas Charlie was wild and free, bursting with dreams, like a throwback to the sixties, when young people had been obliged to rebel, in their dress and appearance if nothing else. Joyce's father had been a teenager during that era. She'd seen photographs of him, resolutely suited and booted in his classic style. He'd allowed his hair to grow a fashionable inch or so longer, but that was the extent of his rebellion. Even as a teenager, he'd refused to bend his ideas or principles to fit the times.

Charlie, on the other hand, declared that rules were made to be broken. He had an unruly nature to match his unruly hair. He loved and lived exactly as he pleased, and he carried Joyce along with him on a jet stream of youthful enthusiasm.

Joyce had known from the start that Charlie was unlikely to meet with the approval of her parents. Particularly Henry. Nevertheless a meeting was arranged. And the head-over-heels-in-love Joyce took her beau home to meet Henry and Felicity. Henry's offer to send his car and chauffeur was, of course, spurned by the free-spirited pair. And since Charlie said he couldn't afford train fares and wasn't going to take charity from anyone, they ended up trundling their way to Bristol aboard Charlie's Lambretta.

While it was obvious to Joyce that Henry Tanner did not share her enthusiasm for Charlie, he behaved with courtesy and was a warm and generous host. But during the course of the evening, when Charlie needed to use the bathroom and Joyce showed him where it was, she returned in time to hear her parents, unaware that she was in earshot, discussing her romance.

'Don't worry about it, dear,' her mother reassured her father. 'She's so young. He's her first serious boyfriend – they're sure to grow out of each other.'

Joyce knew better. And her mother's remarks incensed her. She burst into the sitting room, bristling with indignation.

'Little do you bloody know,' she began, pointing a forefinger at Felicity.

'Don't swear at your mother,' said Henry.

'I'm not,' said Joyce. 'I'm swearing at both of you. How can you be so bloody stupid? Don't you know the difference between casual sex and proper love? You should do – you've been married long enough.'

Henry looked poleaxed. Felicity blushed. Sex was never mentioned in the Tanner household. Joyce sometimes thought her parents hoped that she and her brother believed there had been a double immaculate conception.

'There's no need for that sort of talk, dear,' said her mother.

'Oh for goodness' sake,' said Joyce, as a bewildered Charlie re-entered the room. 'Look, you two met each other when you were younger than either of us, and you're still together. Anyway, you may as well get used to it. Charlie and

I are going to be together for the rest of our lives, aren't we, sweetheart?'

It was Charlie's turn to blush.

Joyce nudged him in the ribs with her elbow. 'Aren't we, sweetheart?' she repeated, a tad edgily.

'W-well, yes, of course,' stumbled Charlie. 'Of course we are, darling. I just don't want to upset your parents, that's all.'

'Do you know what,' said Joyce, finding a courage she didn't know she had. 'I don't give a damn whether they're upset or not.'

And with that, leaving her parents dumb with shock, she led a spluttering Charlie from the room, out of the house and aboard the Lambretta.

Naturally, she telephoned to apologize. Throughout her life she seemed to have been torn between wanting her freedom and being afraid to grasp it. But she wasn't about to give up Charlie for anyone.

Joyce's mother later told her that she and her father had remained convinced the relationship would not last. One thing came out of the otherwise disastrous meeting, however. Having seen the Lambretta his beloved only daughter was travelling about on, Henry Tanner presented her with a new Mini Cooper. Just as he ultimately would his eldest grandson.

Charlie muttered something virtually incomprehensible about the moral dilemma of accepting lavish gifts from wealthy parents, particularly if you were a paid-up member of the Communist Party. But, for once, Joyce ignored him. And his conscience did not prevent him from spurning his rusting scooter in favour of riding with Joyce in her shiny new Mini at every opportunity. Particularly when it was raining.

If she hadn't been head over heels in love she might have

noticed the ease with which Charlie abandoned his principles, she thought, as she sat at her kitchen table so many years later, with that letter before her, desperately seeking to make sense of the senseless. But she'd been blind to such things back then.

Immersed in her new life, she'd continued to spend the occasional weekend at Tarrant Park, but her visits were nowhere near as frequent as Henry and Felicity would have liked. They raised no objection though, perhaps because they were still getting over the shock of Joyce's 'sex' outburst. The Cooper made the journey to and fro both easy and fun, and more often than not Charlie accompanied her. While unfailingly polite in Charlie's presence, Henry would invariably find some pressing reason to spend much of the weekend in his city-centre office or tucked away in his study at home, emerging only for meals. And Felicity would try, usually without success, to lure her away to the golf course or on a shopping trip, in order to spend time with her apart from Charlie. But her parents soon learned that if you wanted Joyce you had to take Charlie. They were, after all, JC.

If Joyce had thought about it at the time, which again she didn't, she would have realized that her father was trying to drive a wedge between her and Charlie. He knew better than to confront his daughter directly, so instead he attempted to bribe her with solo treats such as a session with a top tennis coach in Spain, or getaways with one or other of her parents to London, Paris or New York. She turned down all his offers: no Charlie meant no Joyce.

Then, at the beginning of Joyce's third year at Exeter and just as her parents were reconciling themselves to the idea of JC, tragedy struck. Her brother William was killed by a hit-and-run driver as he crossed Bristol's busy Victoria Road right outside the Tanner-Max office.

The whole family was devastated. After the funeral Henry went into deep mourning and shut himself away for a month. The running of the business was left to his father, Edward, who came out of retirement to hold things together. Although well into his eighties, he was not the sort of man to sit in a fireside armchair while the business he'd created descended into terminal collapse through neglect.

After that month Henry re-emerged and once more took over the reins, conducting himself as if it were business as usual at Tanner-Max. But if anyone presumed to express their sympathy over William's sudden death, or if William's name cropped up in conversation, Henry Tanner simply purported not to hear.

Joyce was perplexed by his reaction. Felicity at least made no attempt to hide how devastated she was at the death of their only son. Every time Joyce saw her she seemed to be either in tears or red-eyed as if she'd been crying. But both parents seemed indifferent to getting justice for William. Their response to Joyce's demands to know what the police were doing about finding her brother's killer left her dumbfounded and dismayed.

'I'm sure the police will let us know if they find out anything,' they told her. 'Anyway, what does it matter? It won't bring him back.'

It mattered a lot to Joyce. She wanted to see her brother's killer brought to justice. It became, for a time, her foremost motivation in life. She badgered the police on a daily basis, and at one point even attempted to conduct her own investigation.

In the end her father took her to one side.

'You know, sweetheart, the longer this goes on the more upset your mother is going to get,' he said. 'I'm afraid she may be heading for a breakdown. Her only hope is to move on. William is dead and nothing can change that. If you persist in what you are doing you are only going to bring her more grief. Every time you talk about it you open the wound, just when it's starting to heal. Let it go, sweetheart, let it go, for your mother's sake.'

With considerable regret, Joyce did as her father asked and let it go, though for her the wound could never heal while William's killer walked free.

Six months after William's death, Henry suddenly expressed a desire to spend time with Charlie alone. He invited the younger man to join him for lunch at the country house hotel just outside Bristol which he habitually used for business entertaining.

Predictably, Charlie was not keen.

'You must go,' urged Joyce. 'This is Daddy's olive branch. It could mean he will accept you at last. You are the two men I love most in the world. Hey, the *only* two men I love in the world. It would be so great if you could be friends.'

Charlie had been unimpressed. 'I reckon your dad's more likely to make friends with a boa constrictor,' he said.

'Don't think he couldn't if he set his mind to it,' countered Joyce.

'Is that supposed to make me feel better?' enquired Charlie.

He agreed to the lunch, for Joyce's sake, but made it clear that he had absolutely no desire to spend time alone with Henry Tanner. Neither had he any wish to lunch at a staid and achingly conventional hotel, the kind of establishment he had always despised. And his reluctance turned to alarm when Joyce informed him that there was a dress code.

'Formal jacket and tie, I fear,' she said.

'Well, that's the final straw,' said Charlie.

'What's the matter, don't you have a proper jacket?' enquired Joyce, who had never seen him wear any such thing.

'Course I do,' muttered Charlie. 'Somewhere. If it still fits me. I don't have a tie though.'

'Well, I think we could run to buying one of those, don't you?'

'I just don't understand what your father could want,' Charlie sighed.

'He doesn't want anything,' said Joyce. 'He's trying to get to know you, that's all. He's finally come round to the fact that I'm determined to have you, for ever, and so there's nothing left for him to do but accept you. I think it's fab – now stop whingeing and let's go buy you a tie.'

And so the appointed day came and Charlie set off to Mendip House in his one and only formal jacket, which turned out to be the top half of a suit that had been bought for him on his eighteenth birthday by his mum, Joan, who had apparently been determined he should go into adulthood with at least one presentable suit in his wardrobe. The plain but good quality navy-blue jacket had only been worn on a couple of occasions; although a little tight across the shoulders, it looked quite smart once a light dusting of mildew on the collar and sleeves had been dealt with.

Joyce knotted for him, over an old but honourable and very nearly white shirt, the subtly patterned silk tie in varying shades of blue, which he had reluctantly allowed her to purchase at Exeter's Debenhams. Then she eyed him up and down approvingly. His hair, murky yellow or dark blond, depending on the light and how recently he had washed it, remained as unruly as ever and was even longer than when she'd first met him. It curled untidily over his shoulders, a bit like an avalanche of dirty snow. Joyce liked it. But she knew her father didn't. She reached out to touch Charlie's hair with one hand, wondering whether he might be persuaded to allow the lightest of trims around the ends.

Charlie read her mind.

'Don't even think about it,' he said.

It had been arranged that Henry's driver would pick Charlie up at Topsham, take him to the Mendip Hotel, more than an hour away, then drive him home afterwards. That way he could have a drink if he wanted, said Henry.

Charlie had muttered dissent, telling Joyce it was against his principles as a communist to ride in a chauffeur-driven car. But he said nothing of this to Henry, meekly accepting the arrangement.

Joyce spent an anxious afternoon awaiting his return. It was a sunny autumn day and there were any number of jobs on the boat she could have been getting on with, but she was too restless to settle to any task. Instead she threw a blanket on to the well-worn deck, lay back and tried to concentrate on the modern espionage thriller she was reading whilst enjoying the sun. But she was on edge. She so wanted this lunch between her two men to be a success. Maybe she was getting things out of proportion, but she couldn't help feeling her whole life depended on a successful outcome.

It was well gone six before Charlie appeared, weaving unsteadily along the tow path. She waved a greeting. Charlie managed a half wave in response, gave her a weak smile, then lurched to his left and was sick in the water.

'Good lunch then,' Joyce remarked, more to herself than to him.

'Oh God, I feel terrible,' mumbled Charlie as he staggered towards her.

'I should have warned you about the flow of booze at Dad's lunches,' said Joyce.

Charlie groaned.

'Well, aren't you going to tell me what happened? I want to know all about it. Are you friends for life or what?'

Charlie responded with another groan, his body swaying precariously as he stepped on to the gangplank. Convinced he was going to fall, Joyce hurried towards him, grabbed a flailing arm and pulled him on to the boat.

'Come on,' she said. 'Let's get you to bed – I can tell I'm not going to get any sense out of you until you've slept it off.'

She'd never seen Charlie so drunk, but Joyce remembered that, far from being unhappy at the state he was in, she'd taken it as a good sign. If things had gone badly with her father he would have returned much earlier and stone-cold sober. And what she wanted more than anything was for the two of them to become friends. Lunching and drinking buddies had to be a good start.

Impatient for Charlie's account of the lunch, she'd hovered close by as he descended to the lower deck after throwing up spectacularly over the rails. Then she'd climbed into the double bunk alongside him, but he fell instantly into a deep sleep and showed no signs of waking. Resisting the urge to wake him, she told herself she would have to be patient and wait till morning.

But when the morning came and Charlie emerged with a major hangover, he was no more forthcoming.

'You know what, Joycey baby, I got so pissed I can't

remember a thing,' he told her, running long fingers through his unruly hair.

No matter how much Joyce pressed him, Charlie persisted in dodging the issue. He remembered what he had eaten – seafood platter and roast beef – but next to nothing of the conversation.

Joyce couldn't understand it. She had been to any number of parties with Charlie where the pair of them had drunk far too much, and on sobering up afterwards he'd always seemed to have total recall. Sometimes embarrassingly so.

Joyce called her father. Henry Tanner was equally evasive.

'Oh God, darling, I don't know what we talked about. This and that. Told me all about that blessed boat he lives on . . .'

Henry paused. As far as Joyce knew, her father was unaware that she too lived on the *Shirley Anne*. She wondered if he suspected, and whether he'd grilled Charlie on the subject.

'Oh, and how much he cares for you,' Henry continued. 'But then I knew that, didn't I?'

'Come on, Dad, you can do better than that,' Joyce urged, trying to make her voice light and teasing. 'I want to know exactly what the two men in my life have been plotting. So come on. Spill!'

'We haven't been plotting anything,' Henry answered quickly. Perhaps too quickly.

'Trust you to be so bloody nosy,' he laughed. 'I can tell you, however, that I think you have a fine young man there.'

Joyce did a double take down the phone.

'You've given every impression you couldn't stand the sight of him from the first time I brought him home,' she said.

27

'Rubbish,' responded Henry. 'Like I said, I just needed to get to know Charlie a bit. And, anyway, I couldn't be sure in the beginning whether or not he was going to stick around, could I?'

There was, Joyce realized, some truth in that. She told herself she should stop being such a control freak – a trait which ran in the family – and be thankful that a friendship appeared to be blossoming between the two men.

But over the next few days Charlie became progressively more withdrawn. The Charlie she had fallen in love with had been an energetic young man with a lively and active mind, who never stopped talking, and was seldom capable of sitting still for more than five minutes. Following the lunch with Henry, it seemed to Joyce that he'd become uncharacteristically quiet and introspective. And instead of seeking out every opportunity to be with Joyce, as he had always done before, he seemed to seize upon any excuse to be apart from her.

No longer did he hover outside her lectures, ready to whisk her off for a coffee or a chat. No longer did he study alongside her. A couple of times he ate alone in the refectory while she was busy studying, something he had never done before. And when they were together aboard the *Shirley Anne* he contrived to be on deck while she was below and below deck when she was up top.

They still slept together. They still had sex. Satisfying sex. But – and Joyce had never been able to explain this to herself – it wasn't the same. Even in their most intimate moments, they were no longer really close.

JC, it seemed to Joyce, was no more.

Naturally she'd confronted Charlie. Told him she was hurt and puzzled. Asked him what was going on.

'You're imagining things,' he responded, kindly enough. But he wouldn't give her a straight answer or say anything to put her mind at rest.

Meanwhile Henry began to take Charlie out to lunch and dinner on a regular basis. The Mendip Hotel was their usual haunt, but there were also trips to London venues like the Savoy and the Ritz. Once the two men stayed over – at Henry's club, they said.

Joyce continued to be surprised, because her father and her future husband didn't seem to have much in common, apart from her. And both were frustratingly unforthcoming when asked about their meetings. She was accustomed to her father keeping his nearest and dearest in the dark; talking things through was not something Henry did. But Charlie was different – or so she'd thought.

There were other changes too. Charlie suddenly announced that he was giving up smoking; not just cigarettes – he had a fifty-a-day habit – but marijuana too. Though she knew she would miss the mellowing and sometimes aphrodisiac effect marijuana had on them both, Joyce was glad. She didn't mind the odd spliff but had never cared for cigarettes.

Then, about four months after what Joyce came to regard as his fateful first lunch with Henry, Charlie had his hair cut. Joyce returned to the boat one evening, having not seen him all day on campus, to find that her wild and hirsute young man now sported a short back and sides. With a parting too.

'Good God, this is a shock,' she had said, as mildly as she could manage. It wasn't the fact he'd cut his hair that bothered her; it was his failure to mention it beforehand.

'I don't see why,' Charlie replied curtly. 'You didn't think I was going to have hair down my back for the rest of my life, did you? One can't be a student for ever.'

'But you've over a year to go,' she reminded him.

'Maybe.' The response was short and sharp, and though further questions sprang to mind, Joyce dared not ask them.

A few days later she was emptying the bin from the galley when she noticed Charlie's Communist Party membership card amongst the rubbish. It was one of his most prized possessions, a kind of badge of honour. When over-excited or a bit drunk, he was inclined to brandish the card whilst berating those around him who did not share his beliefs, which if anything had become stronger as communism's influence waned.

Joyce fished the card out of the rubbish, scrubbed at a grease stain and presented it to Charlie.

'I've no idea how this got in the bin, but I rescued it for you,' she said. 'Do I get a big kiss and an even bigger thank you?'

A bright flush spread over Charlie's pale cheeks.

'Well, actually, I threw it away,' he said.

'You did what?' asked Joyce, staggered. 'Why?'

'I've resigned my membership,' Charlie responded. 'I don't believe in it any more.'

'But the Party is your religion. You're a damned missionary for it. I only joined because of you. You know that. Whatever brought this on, Charlie?'

'The small matter of the Berlin Wall falling might be a bit of a factor, eh?'

Ignoring the sarcasm in his voice, Joyce reminded him, 'You always said you weren't going to allow the fall of the Wall to affect your beliefs. You said the cause was the right one, and eventually the world would—'

'I know what I damn well said,' Charlie snapped. 'And you always argued I was wrong. Well, you've got your way now. It's over. So you've got what you wanted, haven't you?'

'Don't be ridiculous,' she said. 'C'mon, tell me the truth: what's really behind all this?'

'I'm growing up, I suppose,' he responded with a shrug. 'I've finally come to the conclusion that Marxism is nonsense, that's all.'

Joyce had been stunned. One of the things that had attracted her to Charlie had been his conviction and passionate advocacy for the ideals he held so dear. It hadn't mattered a jot that she had never really shared those ideals. That wasn't the point.

'Well, that's rich! You've resigned from the Communist Party without telling me and I'm still officially a member, even though I only ever joined because of you and your alleged principles,' she said, with more edge than she intended.

'I shouldn't worry about it. I doubt there will be a Communist Party of Great Britain for much longer,' said Charlie prophetically.

'So why the grand gesture?' asked Joyce.

Charlie made no reply. Instead he walked away from her – something he'd been doing more and more. Even in bed, although they were still at the stage where they made love almost every night, Joyce found him increasingly detached. But if she dared to mention it he would not be drawn, and when she persisted he bit her head off.

She consoled herself with the thought that at least Charlie's friendship with her father seemed to be going from strength to strength. There had been several more trips to London involving overnight stays at Henry's club. Henry also took Charlie to the races at Cheltenham and to watch Bath play rugby. Neither Joyce nor her mother were invited. Joyce was not used to it. She was used to being the apple of her father's eye, getting her own way with him. She was also used to going absolutely everywhere with Charlie.

'I thought you wanted me to get to know your young man. I thought you wanted us to be friends,' said her father when she remonstrated with him about excluding her from these invitations.

An expression of her paternal grandmother's came into her mind: 'Be careful what you wish for.'

What Joyce wished for right then was for things to go back to the way they had been. Her wish was to be emphatically denied.

At the end of a typical morning of domestic crisis aboard the *Shirley Anne* – the electric kettle had blown the entire system again, and then the bottled gas ran out as they tried to cook breakfast on the little two-burner gas hob – Charlie dropped the biggest bombshell yet.

'Well, at least we won't have to be putting up with this shit for much longer,' he announced. 'I've sold the *Shirley Anne*. Some twat of a first year has bought her. He's got absolutely no idea what he's taking on.'

'You've done what?' she asked. 'You can't mean it.'

'Yep, I can. And I have. I've had enough.'

'But she meant so much to you. And me, come to that.'

'Time to move on, Joycey.'

He didn't even sound like Charlie any more. 'Time to move on' indeed – the old Charlie would never have spoken to her in that patronizing way.

'I can't believe you'd do that, and without so much as a word to me!'

'Why would I need to discuss it with you?' Charlie asked curtly. 'She's my boat. And she was mine before I even met you. It was my decision to make.'

'But the *Shirley Anne* is part of our life together . . .' Fighting to hold back her tears, Joyce took a step away.

Seeing the hurt in her eyes, Charlie softened his tone. 'Look, I'm sorry, sweetheart. I thought it was my responsibility – I didn't want to burden you with it. You have to admit, it's time we moved on. We can get a little flat in town . . .'

He didn't want to burden her? For a moment Joyce was too stunned to speak; it was as if Charlie had suddenly morphed into her father.

'And you have the money for a flat, do you?' she snapped.

'Well no, not exactly,' Charlie continued, his tone patient and reasonable. 'But your father has offered to help.'

Joyce couldn't believe her ears.

'My father? Have you two been plotting this? The *Shirley Anne* is our home, yours and mine, Charlie. Did you connive with my father to get rid of our home?'

'No, of course not,' said Charlie, reaching out to her.

'And what about our gap-year odyssey?' Joyce demanded, brushing away his hand. 'What about sailing off into the ocean and letting the winds take us where they will? What about our dreams, Charlie?'

He shrugged. His face gave nothing away.

'Maybe I have different dreams, now, Joyce,' he said.

'Well, you know what, Charlie, when you told me that was what you wanted to do and that you wanted me to do it with you, to sail away with you aboard this wonderful old boat, I thought it was about the most romantic thing I had ever heard in the whole of my life.'

Charlie stepped towards her, wrapped his arms around her and pressed his lips on hers, thus making it impossible for her to say any more. At least he could still be unpredictable, it seemed.

He stroked her hair tenderly and stopped kissing her only in order to speak.

'I still have dreams, my darling,' he said. 'And I have one great big dream that only you can make come true. Will you marry me, Joyce Tanner?'

Joyce felt her jaw drop. She was taken totally by surprise. She had always assumed that she and Charlie would marry one day. They'd both been certain from the start that they wanted to be together for ever. But the last thing she expected that morning, after Charlie had so unceremoniously blurted out about the sale of the boat, was a formal proposal.

She stared at him in silence for a minute or so.

'Well?' he enquired, and flashed the old lopsided resist-me-if-you-can grin, which had become, she thought, a depressingly rare sight.

His hair had grown a bit, thankfully, the parting was crooked, and there was just a hint of the old tousled tangle she'd so adored.

She continued to stare at him.

'This isn't what I expected . . .' She struggled to find the words. 'To tell the truth, Charlie, I thought you'd gone off me.'

'Never.' He kissed her again on the lips, but lightly this time. 'I love you more than ever. Surely you realize that.'

She shook her head. 'Oh, Charlie,' she said. 'I love you so much. But you've changed lately. I mean, if you get married, does it mean you can't do daft things any more like bugger off in a boat and let the winds take you? 'Cos if it does, well, I don't know . . .'

He interrupted, raising one finger gently to her mouth and placing it there.

'Sweetheart, you didn't seriously think we could sail around the world on this old crate, did you?'

She thought for a second. The answer to that was yes. Yes, she had thought they could. He had made her believe that. And she told him so.

'I never had any doubts, Charlie,' she said. 'I thought we'd work on her until she was right, then take off. You and me and the ocean waves.'

'Joyce, I doubt we'd have got *Shirley Anne* out of the estuary, let alone on to the ocean waves. She's riddled with woodworm and rot!'

'But, Charlie,' she protested, 'I believed you. Absolutely. I thought we were going to do it – fulfil our dreams, find our Shangri-La.'

'We can still fulfil our dreams, my darling,' he said. 'But they'll be different ones, that's all. My dream is to marry you, for you to have my children, and to keep you and them safe and happy and well for the rest of our lives. Isn't that even more romantic?'

He stroked her face, his touch warm and suddenly every bit as exciting as it had been in the beginning. He kissed her cheek. His lips were soft, deliciously soft.

'Marry me, my darling,' he pleaded. 'Please, please, marry me. I cannot imagine that life could go on unless you say yes. Please, please, say yes. Say you'll marry me. Go on. Say it. Say it.'

He kissed her forehead, the tip of her nose, raised her hand and kissed her fingers, pressed his lips to her ears, the top of her head, her eyes, and oh so lightly, her mouth, again and again.

She found herself laughing uncontrollably through the kisses.

'Yes,' she cried out eventually, her words half smothered by his kisses. 'Yes, yes, yes, Charlie. Yes, I will marry you, my darling. Yes! Yes!'

He grabbed her by one arm and pulled her towards the bunk in the aft cabin. She noticed, and it made her laugh, that he was trying to get out of his trousers as they hurried to get there. He nearly tripped them both up. He tore at the buttons on her shirt, ripping one off, and tugged at her jeans whilst trying to get out of his own shirt at the same time.

The undressing was clumsy, terribly clumsy, but the love-making was fluent and seamless, as good as it had ever been, possibly better. Bold yet tender. Urgent yet without haste. Charlie was there. Right there. With her. On her. In her. No longer detached in any way. Instead, after so long, he was part of her again. At last.

And when it was over, for one crazy, wonderful, ecstatic moment, Joyce even thought they might be JC again.

She phoned her parents to tell them that she'd accepted Charlie's proposal, and to her amazement they both expressed delight. In spite of Henry's recent efforts to bond with Charlie, she'd expected him to urge caution, to point out that she was only twenty-two and Charlie twenty-one, too young to be taking such a step. Even though Henry and Felicity had been even younger when they'd married, Joyce had anticipated a long drawn-out argument before her father gave his blessing. His enthusiastic approval took her completely by surprise.

A date was set for the coming June, straight after Joyce's finals. The wedding reception would be held at the Tarrant Park tennis club, following a traditional ceremony at a nearby church. Henry took charge of everything. And he would be footing the bill, of course. Gladly he said, beaming at his daughter and her husband to be.

It did occur to Joyce that the next stage in her life appeared to be evolving without her having much of a say in it. But Charlie had been far more his old self since she had accepted his proposal, and she was far too excited to let herself dwell on anxieties she couldn't put a name to, let alone explain. Instead she gave herself up to the excitement and joy of becoming Mrs Joyce Mildmay.

Two

It was on their wedding night that Charlie dropped his next bombshell.

They were in their splendid garden suite at Gravetye Manor, chosen and paid for by Henry, who said it was one of the best hotels in the country, and close to Gatwick, the airport from which they would be flying off the following day for a honeymoon in the Maldives.

Joyce, exhausted after the excitement of the day and full of food and champagne, had collapsed on the four-poster bed. Charlie came and sat down next to her. He looked uneasy.

'There's something I've been meaning to tell you,' he said, taking her hand in his. 'I hope you'll be pleased. I'm quitting university. I'm going to work for your father.'

It was the last thing Joyce had expected. She was anything but pleased, and she was damned sure Charlie would have known that.

'Why on earth would you want to do that?' she asked, snatching her hand from his. 'At least you could stay on for your final year, complete your course, take your finals, and then work for Dad, if that's what you want.'

'No,' Charlie said. 'I'm done with studying politics. I've

totally lost interest, and I no longer want to be a politician so there's no point in my carrying on with it. I've had it with all that changing-the-world crap. I want to get real, earn some proper money, build a life for my wife.'

He tried the boyish grin. It didn't work. Undeterred, he leaned towards her, lips puckered, looking for a kiss.

Joyce brushed aside his attentions, impatient with his attempts to distract her from the matter in hand.

'For goodness' sake, Charlie, you don't have to be a politician,' she told him. 'A degree in politics could set you up for all sorts of things. You're a clever student. You like university life – you could be a full-time academic. Or a journalist. Maybe TV. You have a good speaking voice.'

'A journalist?' sniffed Charlie. 'What, and get myself locked up along with half of what still passes for Fleet Street? Do you want to get rid of me, Mrs Mildmay?' He tried the cheeky grin again.

'Be serious, Charlie,' she said. 'Apart from anything else this is the third major decision you've made in the last few months without consulting me or even letting me know what you had in mind.'

Charlie stopped grinning.

'OK,' he said. 'Perhaps I should have talked to you before selling the *Shirley Anne*. But I just knew I was acting for the best. And it's the same with this. I'm certain it's for the best. You father always says that where financial provisions for his family are concerned, a man has to make his own decisions.'

'I know what my father says, Charlie,' Joyce replied through gritted teeth. 'I didn't realize I'd married my bloody father.'

'Oh, come on, Joyce,' said Charlie. 'Let's not have an argument on our wedding night.'

He reached out his hand, searching for hers again. Angry as she was, she had to concede that Charlie was right. They couldn't quarrel on their wedding night. She let him take her hand.

'Shall we do room service?' he asked.

'I don't think I could eat anything. I'm upset, and I've eaten and drunk too much today already.'

'Something light,' he coaxed, picking up the menu. 'Look, they do plates of mixed hors d'oeuvres.'

She relented. Even forced a small smile.

'Sounds good. But don't think this is over. We should have our honeymoon and then discuss it when we get home. You haven't made any decision that is irrevocable, have you?'

Charlie looked sheepish.

'Have you, Charlie?' Joyce repeated.

'I've resigned from Exeter. I shan't be going back. I can't go back. It's done.'

Joyce removed her hand from his. She felt bereft. Whatever had happened to JC?

'Without telling me, let alone asking me?'

'Well, I'm telling you now and . . .'

Joyce could see Charlie searching for words.

'There's something else, isn't there?' she said. 'C'mon, Charlie, what is it?'

He reached in his pocket and produced a key with a golden ribbon attached. She took it from his outstretched hand and studied it for a moment, puzzled.

Then he dropped the biggest bombshell of all.

'It's the key to a house in Tarrant Park,' he said. 'Your father has given it us as a wedding present. He wanted me to be the one to tell you.'

I'll bet he did, thought Joyce. Henry Tanner knew all too

well what his only daughter wanted, what she had always wanted. And that was a life of her own, away from the confines of Tarrant Park.

'Charlie, how could you!' She leapt up from the bed and stood looking down at him. 'You fool, you bloody fool. Have you any idea what this will mean?'

'Yes, that we will start our married life in a dream home, a house most young couples could never hope to afford, where we can bring up our children and build our lives together. And I will have a dream job, doing interesting and well-paid work for a man I have come to both like and respect.'

'Really,' snapped Joyce. 'You sound as if you're reciting some sort of mantra, you pompous idiot. I thought your dream was to sail around the world aboard the *Shirley Anne*. And I loved you for that. It became my dream too. Not this. I've had a lifetime of Tarrant Park. You want to "get real"? Tarrant Park isn't real, Charlie, can't you see that?'

Charlie shook his head. 'Seems real enough to me,' he said.

'And what exactly is this "interesting well-paid work" that you're going to be doing for my father?'

'I'll be learning the ropes of the import-and-export trade. Your father is one of the leading brokers in the country. He's the master when it comes to cutting through red tape. He's done wonders for the UK economy over the years, like his father before him, and your Uncle Max. And I am going to be the newest junior partner at Tanner-Max.'

'Master at cutting through red tape, eh? Sounds bloody dodgy to me,' countered Joyce.

'Don't be ridiculous,' said Charlie. 'I have never met anyone more sound than your father. He would never be involved in anything he didn't believe to be morally right, let alone "dodgy". International commerce is rife with complicated rules and regulations. It takes someone with Henry's experience to deal with them – legally.'

'How come you're suddenly qualified to join the firm?' asked Joyce. 'Explain that to me.'

'Henry says my political knowledge will be a considerable help. Everything in life nowadays is politics, Henry says.'

'Henry says, Henry says,' growled Joyce. 'Don't you have a mind of your own any more, Charlie?'

'I thought you'd be pleased,' he replied plaintively.

'Did you?' snapped Joyce. 'Did you seriously think I would want to sit at home in some glorified luxury prison while you go off playing man games that you don't even tell me about, having to put up with the same thing my mother has put up with all her married life?'

'No, of course not. It won't—'

Joyce cut him off. 'If we set up home in Tarrant Park that is precisely how it will be. And you thought I'd be pleased, did you?'

Charlie shook his head sorrowfully. 'I don't understand,' he said. 'I've always thought your parents had a wonderful marriage. And that's all I want for us. Felicity has always seemed perfectly happy with her life. Isn't that the case?'

'Yes. She probably is happy,' Joyce sighed. 'But I am not my mother. I want more, can't you see that?'

'I will give you more, then. I promise you, Joyce, all I want is for you to be happy. Your father and I both thought this house would make you happy. What do you want me to do? Tell him we don't want it? Throw it back at him?'

'It wouldn't do any bloody good,' muttered Joyce.

'We can make this work, Joycey. I'll get another boat, one

that doesn't leak,' Charlie promised. 'We'll sail off into the sunset and let the winds take us where they will. We'll still find our Shangri-La. You'll see.'

'And did you and my father also happen to decide when we would be moving into this bloody house?'

'Well, when we get back from our honeymoon—'

Once more Joyce interrupted him. 'Have you forgotten that I'm still hoping to be accepted to do an MA at Exeter if my grades are good enough?'

'You could still do it,' said Charlie. 'I mean, it's just about commutable.'

'Commutable? It's an hour and a half's drive from Tarrant Park to Exeter. And that's on a good day. Besides, commuting isn't exactly what university life is about, is it? Be honest, Charlie. You assumed that if you quit university, I would too, didn't you?'

'No, of course not,' said Charlie. But he blushed deep crimson.

They continued to squabble for another hour or so, going over and over the same ground. In the end Charlie pleaded with her, 'Please, Joyce, can't we just put this on hold until after the honeymoon? This has been such a special day for me. Please don't let it be spoiled.'

There had been tears in his eyes, and the last thing Joyce wanted was to see her new husband cry on their wedding night. Grudgingly she agreed to let it drop, even though for her their special day had already been irrevocably spoiled. The obligatory nuptial lovemaking was perfunctory and un-imaginative. Joyce feigned orgasm, something she had never before done with Charlie, in order to be able to seek the release of sleep, then lay awake all night with her back to him.

She blamed her father, the master manipulator who knew her better than Charlie ever would, for the way she'd been set up. If she'd had the slightest inkling of Charlie's intention to join the family firm and start their marriage in Tarrant Park, one thing was certain: she would never have gone through with the wedding. As she set off on her honeymoon the following morning, she was still wondering whether to walk away from the marriage.

Her first sight of their idyllic Maldivian island, fringed with a ribbon of sand almost starling white against the turquoise sea, helped restore her spirits, and gradually, although a niggle remained at the back of her mind, the honeymoon became pretty much everything she had wished and hoped it would be. She acquiesced to Charlie's entreaty that they put all discussion about their shared future on hold until their return home, and allowed the Maldives to work its own special magic.

Their own piece of paradise was called Nakatchafushi. Back in 1991 Maldivian islands were strictly no shoes and no news. Joyce thought Nakatcha was perfect. Stylish but breathtakingly simple. They slept in a rondavel yards from the edge of the sea and ate at candlelit tables set out on the beach.

Mornings of swimming and sunbathing were followed by afternoons of lazy lovemaking, which returned almost to their usual standard, and evenings drinking cocktails as the sun went down and dining on local curries and fish.

Only very occasionally did that abiding little niggle force its way to the front of Joyce's mind. If she had known what Charlie and her father had planned, she almost certainly would not be on honeymoon.

*

On their return from the Maldives, Charlie was tactful and tentative in all matters concerning their future life together.

'Look, why don't we move into the house on a temporary basis?' he suggested. 'I'm not starting work with Henry for another couple of weeks. We have plenty of time to talk about everything. And, Joyce, I'm sorry I didn't involve you. It was supposed to be a surprise. I honestly thought you'd be pleased.'

No you didn't, you devious bastard, thought Joyce. But she didn't say so.

'Life on a leaky boat was all right for a few months, Joycey, but it couldn't have gone on, don't you see that? Your father calls you his princess, you've always been treated like a princess, you are my princess now, and I had no right to make you suffer for my crazy ideals.'

And he carried on in that vein, implying that he had sacrificed his own independence to show his love for her. How could she spurn such a gift? But the whole time Joyce had a nagging suspicion that he was spouting the lines he'd been told to deliver by her father.

She grudgingly agreed to move into the brand-new, five-bedroomed mock-Georgian house Henry had bought for them. A former show home, it had been partially furnished by the developer with state-of-the-art fixtures and fittings – none of them chosen by Joyce. It seemed to her that there was to be no aspect of her future life that bore any stamp of her personality. The thought of being sucked in, of slotting into this pre-programmed life and turning into her mother, appalled her. To Charlie's dismay, she informed him that she still wanted to go back to Exeter at the end of the summer to continue her studies. Despite his pleas to see reason, she remained adamant – until her results came through. She had obtained an acceptable history degree, but the grades were not high enough to qualify for an MA course.

Undeterred, she enquired about teaching courses and other academic options at Exeter and elsewhere. Anywhere, in fact, as long as it wasn't Bristol. She hid none of this from Charlie, but though unhappy he raised no objection. She suspected her father had told him not to. Henry Tanner always avoided confrontation with the women in his life.

Then, one morning, feeling nauseous, a devastating thought struck her. She had been so caught up with trying to escape that she hadn't paid her own body much attention. In that moment she knew: she was pregnant.

They had decided not to have children for at least a year or two. At least, she thought they had. She confronted Charlie as soon as he came home from work that evening.

'Have you been forgetting to use something in bed?' she asked.

'What do you mean?'

'You've always taken charge of the condoms. Maybe you haven't been putting them on right or something.'

He stared at her. Then he began to grin.

'Oh my God, Joycey, do you think you're pregnant? That's wonderful.'

She glowered at him. 'Oh yes, you would think that, wouldn't you? It would suit you down to the ground, wouldn't it? You and Dad. Well, I'm not sure, but I might be.'

The grin widened. 'That's the best news ever!'

'For you maybe. It pretty much puts an end to any plans I might have though, doesn't it? We'd agreed not to have a child yet, or at least I thought we had. Or maybe my opinion doesn't count for anything any more.'

'Of course it does, sweetheart. Don't be silly. And I know

what we agreed. But mistakes do happen. And this would be the happiest of mistakes, wouldn't it?'

'Thing is, I'm wondering if this was a deliberate mistake on your part, Charlie.'

'I wouldn't do that, Joycey, honestly I wouldn't. But if you are pregnant, well, I can't pretend to be anything other than deliriously happy.'

Once it was confirmed that Joyce was pregnant she was left with little choice but to put all thoughts of further education out of her mind. She was bitter about it at first, but her natural maternal instincts slipped into place more swiftly than she had expected.

She'd always wanted to have children. Just not yet. And neither had she intended to bring them up in the stifling atmosphere of Tarrant Park. However, she was aware that she was becoming seduced, in spite of herself, by her family, her parents, particularly her father, her husband, and, much to her annoyance, by the house. Perhaps in her heart of hearts she had known from the beginning that's what would happen – maybe that was why she had kicked so hard against it, and hit out at Charlie the way she had.

Her father, overjoyed at the news as was Joyce's mother, insisted that Charlie should take Joyce back to their Maldivian honeymoon island, which they had so fallen in love with, before she was too pregnant either to fly or to enjoy the trip.

'And before you've got a newborn screaming its head off,' said her mother. 'I only hope your baby sleeps better than you did,' Felicity added with a chuckle. 'You were a total nightmare, Joyce.'

Joyce smiled. And she went on the holiday. To her annoyance, she had a wonderful time. Charlie was proving the most attentive and loving of husbands. He never retaliated when she snapped at him, venting her frustration. Instead he coaxed and cajoled her, telling her how happy he was and how his one aim in life was to make her happy too. Nevertheless, Joyce couldn't shake off the feeling she was being manipulated, that her husband and father were trying to turn her into her mother.

Charlie had protested that, much as he adored Felicity, the last thing he wished for was for Joyce to be transformed into her mother.

Joyce flounced from the room, but returning a short time afterwards she overheard a snatch of phone conversation. Charlie, in the sitting room, was obviously talking to her father.

'It's all very well you telling me to walk away – you don't have to live with it, Henry.'

Then there was a pause.

'Well, yes, you're right. Things have improved. But it's still not how it should be.'

Another pause.

'OK, OK. I'll do as you say . . . Of course I knew what I was getting into, but . . . Yes, I'm sure everything will turn out fine – I don't have any bloody choice do I? Not any more.'

Then he said his goodbyes and ended the call. As he did so he glanced up and saw Joyce standing in the doorway.

'Talking about me, I presume?'

'What, dear?' he stammered. 'No, no. A work problem. A client who's being a pain in the arse.'

'You said, "*You don't have to live with it, Henry,*"' repeated Joyce coolly.

'Oh, just a turn of phrase,' said Charlie. 'I wouldn't talk about you like that, not to your father or anybody.'

'Not much,' muttered Joyce.

Charlie was obviously lying. But by then Joyce was eight months pregnant. She did not have the energy to pursue the matter. In any case Charlie continued to be the model husband. And she was aware that she had the kind of life most pregnant women would sell their souls for.

Mark was born exactly nine months to the day after their wedding night. It had been an easy pregnancy and his birth – at a private maternity clinic in Bristol – was a straightforward one. At the end of it, Joyce found herself with a healthy eight-pound bouncing boy in her arms. Indeed, Mark could have bounced for England. And yelled. And on top of that he hardly ever slept, or not at the right times anyway.

Joyce would have gone barking mad were it not for the unfailing support of her family.

Henry had given Charlie a month's paternity leave, saying: 'Well, it's the modern thing, isn't it?'

'Since when was there anything modern about you, Dad?' Joyce asked, realizing as she said it that it was the first affectionate banter between them since she'd moved into the house in Tarrant Park.

Charlie was besotted with his son, spending four nights a week in baby Mark's room so that Joyce could get the sleep she so needed. In spite of all the help from her husband and mother, she was frequently exhausted. But it was a happy time, for all that, and so busy that she had no opportunity for introspection. Soon she was totally immersed in her baby and her family life. As her mother had been before her.

Weeks turned into months. Charlie returned to work, though Henry insisted that he shorten his working day in order to continue helping Joyce with the baby.

Eventually Mark began to settle. By the time he was five

months old he was sleeping through the night, and gurgling through the days. He tuned out to be a happy and contented child. A joy to have around.

Joyce found herself in love with motherhood. She gave up all thoughts of further education and abandoned the notion of putting her degree to any practical use in the field of employment. Instead her days were spent looking after her son, or meeting up with female friends at the tennis or golf club, or joining them for the occasional lunch or shopping trip. She could do so whenever she wished because her mother was always on hand and eager to babysit.

She had a husband who loved and cherished her, an extended family who were wonderfully supportive, and a home that was the envy of her friends. Charlie, with the assistance of his father-in-law, had given her a BMW 325i estate car as a thank you for their son. Still a performance vehicle, but with plenty of room for a baby and all the resulting paraphernalia, said Charlie. Joyce had help with everything, including housework. If she didn't feel like cooking, the family's daily, Josie, whom she now shared with her parents, would prepare the evening meal. Sometimes Charlie cooked. And whenever she wished he would take her out for dinner.

It was true that her marriage had not turned out the way she'd expected or hoped. It lacked the passion and excitement of her early days with Charlie; JC had made way for a couple who were considerate of one another but distant. While Joyce was now preoccupied with motherhood, Charlie was embroiled, physically and mentally, in a world he made no attempt to share with her.

As the years passed, that distance grew. Charlie's business trips, with and without her father, became so frequent that Joyce wondered if he were having an affair. When she confronted him he would deny it, and, for a while, would be more like the man she had married again. Once she even plucked up the courage to ask Henry – who saw far more of her husband and seemed to be in his confidence in a way that Joyce was not – if there was another woman in Charlie's life. He had told her not to be a silly girl, leaving her cursing herself for having asked. Henry's stock response to matters of an emotional nature was to ignore them. Privileged and cosseted as she was, he expected her to know better than to delve into areas of her man's life it would be far better not to know about.

Even more disturbing than the spectre of infidelity were her husband's mood swings. He would sink into regular periods of depression, unable to sleep, unwilling to communicate, resisting all pleas to confide in her. He had turned into a man every bit as secretive as her father.

He did at least make an effort to hide his moods from the children, and she supported him in this. He would spend longer hours at the office, and his absences from home would increase during these periods. Sometimes, after the children had gone to bed, he would retreat to the garden shed, where, during the good times, and helped by Fred, he constructed model ships. It seemed to Joyce that he could not stand being within the same four walls as her. Once, when she woke in the wee small hours to find he was still out there in the shed, she had plucked up the courage to investigate. She found him smoking a joint; it was the first time she had seen him smoke marijuana since their student days. She had been surprised but not alarmed. If anything she'd hoped that the joint might help him attain the mellowness of the old Charlie, back in the days when they had smoked weed together. Trying to rekindle that old togetherness, she'd asked him to share the spliff with her, and he had done so, but only after protesting that she might find it too strong. The first couple of puffs had made her head swim, so much so that she'd had to hang on to Charlie as they walked back across the lawn to the house.

She'd had no idea whether Charlie was regularly smoking marijuana again, or if this was a one-off. Either way, it did nothing to mellow him.

Eventually she managed to persuade him to see the family doctor, Jim Grant. Grant was a GP of the old school; his solution to depression or mental problems was to write a prescription for Valium or Prozac and hope that would sort it out.

The cocktail of prescription drugs seemed to ease Charlie's mood swings for a while, but it wasn't long before he fell back into the same old pattern. That was how it remained throughout the rest of their marriage.

Concerned that the drugs were making matters worse, Joyce had broached the topic with Charlie.

'How dare you suggest such a thing?' he'd stormed at her. 'Who the hell do you think you are?'

His anger had taken her by surprise. She'd thought he was going to hit her. Although he didn't, she never dared mention his reliance on prescription drugs again.

Instead Joyce immersed herself in her children and in the gift-wrapped life she had never wanted. Charlie was not unkind or cruel. Or not deliberately so. As long as Joyce did not question or challenge him, he behaved reasonably most of the time. And he invariably made an effort when it came to special occasions. He saw to it that Christmas was always memorable for the children, and never forgot Joyce's birthday or their wedding anniversary.

His love of boats and the sea remained, and he continued

to sail throughout their married life, but, it seemed to Joyce, that was all that remained of the Charlie she had fallen in love with. At the time he disappeared from his latest boat – the pristine and plastic 28-foot sloop *Molly May*, named after their daughter – Charlie had been going through a particularly bad patch. Ironically Joyce had been glad when he'd told her he was planning a solo voyage. Time at sea calmed and restored Charlie in a way his wife could not. So she had encouraged him to go. And when she realized that he was not coming home, her genuine grief – because she did still love her troubled Charlie, in spite of everything – was intensified by her concerns over the way in which he had died.

Charlie was a capable and experienced sailor. He had set off on the fateful two-day voyage over the first weekend of November 2013, during an interlude of unseasonably good weather, saying it would be his last sail before winterizing the *Molly May*. It was believed that Charlie had fallen into the water whilst changing the rigging, and been swept out into the Atlantic. But Joyce found it hard to accept that he would have been foolhardy enough to sail alone without wearing a safety harness. Unless he had lost the desire to keep himself safe.

'Do you think it's possible Charlie might have taken his own life?' she had asked her father.

Henry's response had been predictable.

'Don't be ridiculous, darling,' he had said. 'Charlie had everything to live for. Why on earth would he do such a thing?'

'You must have noticed that he suffered from depression.'

'Joyce darling, I am sure Charlie would never have left you and the kids. Besides, people who commit suicide leave notes, don't they?'

'That's a myth,' she said. 'I looked it up online. The majority of suicide cases leave no note.'

'Oh, darling, don't torture yourself,' her father responded. 'Your husband loved you and the children to bits. Yes, he used to get a bit down sometimes, but not enough to think life wasn't worth living. And he would never have done anything to cause you and the kids such pain.'

Henry Tanner was at his most reassuring. But Joyce was sure she saw a flicker of doubt in his eyes.

She didn't pursue it though. Charlie's death had to have been an accident. She reminded herself how absent-minded and accident prone he had become in the months leading up to his death. There had been a succession of incidents, some of which seemed to be at least partly his own fault, and some not. He had sprained his wrist aboard the *Molly May* when he slipped on spilt oil – and Charlie would normally keep the deck spotless. He'd narrowly avoided being hit by falling roof slates while walking past a Bristol building site. And then the brakes nearly failed on his car due to leaking fluid.

Joyce had to believe that Charlie's death was down to carelessness or bad luck. The last thing she wanted was to further distress her children by suggesting he committed suicide. It had taken weeks before the younger two could bring themselves to accept that their father was dead. Fred and Molly had been oblivious to the stresses and strains that had dogged their parents' marriage. Joyce suspected that Mark knew things were not as they should be, but he never mentioned it – which was typical of the men in her family.

Charlie kept the *Molly May* at Instow in North Devon. Forty-eight hours after he steered her from the Torridge Estuary out into the Atlantic she was spotted drifting off

Hartland Point, driven there by the prevailing southwesterly. Appledore lifeboat was called and a rescue helicopter from Chivenor. The *Molly May*'s tender was still attached by a line and the yacht's inflatable life raft remained on board. There was no sign of Charlie. An intensive helicopter search resulted in the discovery of a life jacket, bright yellow in grey waters, which was identified by its markings as having belonged to Charlie and the *Molly May*.

A police investigation found no reason to suspect foul play. It was explained to Joyce by a helpful representative of the Maritime and Coastguard Agency that it was not uncommon for victims of accidents at sea to slip out of their life jackets when they hit water, particularly if they'd failed to fasten the strap which should be secured between their legs – a surprisingly frequent lapse in safety procedure. The absence of a body was not uncommon, she was told. The body of a drowned man would sink, rise after three to five days, sink again, then rise once more after eighteen to thirty days. If, however, the body was hit by a passing vessel or became entangled in an underwater obstruction, or if parts of it were eaten by sea creatures, the remains might never be recovered.

Joyce spared her children the gruesome details, but she felt she had to give them a diluted version of what had befallen their father.

Charlie was dead. How he had died would probably never be known. But there would be no miraculous rescue. And in the end even Molly and Fred came to acknowledge that.

There had been no funeral, because there was no body, but the family arranged a memorial service. They were still awaiting the inquest, which they were assured would declare him dead 'in absentia' and allow a death certificate to be issued. In the meantime Joyce had set about trying to rebuild their lives, taking things day by day. It struck her that, with or without Charlie, that was the way her life had always been, and it was how she expected it always to remain.

Until that letter from the dead had dropped through her letterbox.

The letter which would change everything.

Three

Joyce had no idea how long she had been sitting at the kitchen table staring unseeingly through the window at the far end of the room. Outside, it had finally stopped raining and the sun, peeping out from behind a large cloud, filled the kitchen with white light.

Her coffee had gone cold, like the previous cups. She poured it down the sink.

There were so many unanswered questions. Perhaps her earlier misgivings had been correct. Was the letter, which still lay on the table, some kind of bizarre suicide note? Or did it indicate that Charlie believed he might be in danger from others? Had the police investigation missed something? Was it possible that a third party had been involved, that Charlie had been murdered?

Joyce gave herself a mental shaking. She couldn't allow herself to be stampeded into some desperate course of action by a letter which might turn out to be the product of paranoia brought on by the cocktail of prescription meds Charlie had been taking.

Even if the danger to her children turned out to be genuine, there was no way she could do as Charlie had instructed. If would have been hard enough if they were babies, but it was inconceivable that she could persuade fifteen-year-old Molly and eleven-year-old Fred to leave behind their friends, their schools, their treasured possessions and run away with their mother – without a word to anyone. Just as it was inconceivable that she could ever abandon her first-born, no matter that he was now a young man of twenty-two.

Perhaps if she understood the nature of whatever threat was facing them she would feel differently, but the letter conveyed nothing beyond Charlie's anxiety and mistrust of her father. Too bad he hadn't seen fit to confide in her before he went and fell off his bloody boat. If there was a threat of such enormity that his family had no option but to take flight because of it, surely even a man as secretive and moody as Charlie would have thought to broach the subject with his wife?

His letter had done nothing but raise questions for which she had no answers. *He won't be interested in Molly* – what did that mean, for God's sake? Was he implying that Henry was some sort of paedophile?

An outsider who knew nothing of Henry Tanner might leap to that conclusion, but while Joyce was the first to admit that he was manipulative and devious, she had never known her father to behave in any way that was remotely inappropriate. Certainly she had never experienced anything untoward during her own childhood. But then again, Charlie had said that Molly was safe, so the inference was that Henry was only interested in boys, that he was in some way grooming Fred and already had Mark under his control.

The thought sent a cold clammy shiver down Joyce's spine. But she forced herself to consider the possibility. She had grown up with a brother two years older than her. Was it possible that Henry had been abusing William without her knowledge? Had there been anything, anything whatsoever, in her father's relationship with her brother that might, if only with hindsight, have been disturbing?

Joyce could think of nothing. William had been a happy, confident child. Henry frequently took him on golfing trips and other 'boys' adventures' as he called them, but far from being fearful at the prospect of spending time alone with his father, William had always been excited and enthusiastic, and on their return would talk endlessly about whatever they'd got up to.

Henry was a big man, and physically expansive. He was forever hugging his family, male and female. In her mind's eye, Joyce could see him standing by the fireplace with his arm around William's shoulders. The two had been very close, there was no doubt about that, but the idea of Henry having a sexual relationship with his son was preposterous. In fact the idea of Henry having a physical relationship with anyone of his own gender was inconceivable. He might proclaim himself liberal and non-judgemental when it came to homosexuality, but on the rare occasions she'd seen him in the company of gay men there had been an awkwardness and sometimes a distinct coolness in his manner. Try as she might to entertain the possibility that her father was a closet gay, Joyce could see no evidence of it.

And yet Charlie's letter had made it clear that Henry was the source of the danger. And that his concern was only for his sons, not his daughter . . .

Joyce felt as if she was going around in circles, getting nowhere. Part of her wanted to confront her father and demand to know what he had done that might cause Charlie to write such a letter. But she knew it was pointless. Henry would tell her not to torment herself, that there was absolutely nothing to worry about – all the usual platitudes. The one thing he would never do was treat her as an adult and an equal and divulge whatever he might know on the subject. If she wanted answers, she would have to come up with a more devious approach.

The silence was shattered by the sound of the front door opening and voices in the hall. Joyce glanced up at the clock on the wall: ten past four. Molly and Fred were home from school, delivered to the door by Henry's driver. Unlike other mothers, Joyce didn't have to worry about doing the school run; her father saw to it she was cosseted in that as in everything.

She sprang to her feet and hid Charlie's letter and the two envelopes under the bread bin, then made ready to greet her two younger children with the smiling hug they would expect.

As usual, Fred's first words as he bounded into the kitchen and flung himself at her were, 'What's for tea, Mum?'

Tall for his age with floppy dirty-blond hair like his dad's, Fred sniffed the air theatrically.

'I can't smell anything,' he said.

Joyce was a good cook and enjoyed cooking. On school days she always served the children's evening meal at five, but she'd been so preoccupied by the letter she had completely forgotten about food.

'I decided we'd treat ourselves and order in a pizza,' she said, thinking on her feet.

Fred's face split into a wide gap-toothed grin that was the image of his father's – except that his father hadn't had gaps in his teeth. Or not by the time Joyce met him, anyway.

'Wow! On a school night. Cool.' Then his expression turned thoughtful. 'It's not my birthday, and I haven't done anything good, I don't think. Well, not particularly good. Why the special treat? Has Molly done something good?'

His big sister nudged him. She took after her mother and was small, dark and pale skinned.

'What?' Fred demanded.

'Think before you speak, you little monster,' said Molly, nudging him again.

'What?' said Fred, frowning.

'You know Mum gets sad sometimes. She's missing Dad. She doesn't always want to cook like she used to.'

Fred stared at Joyce with big eyes full of remorse. 'Sorry, Mum.'

'Don't be silly,' said Joyce. 'You've nothing to be sorry for, sweetheart. Your mum's been lazy today, that's all.'

She wondered what she had done to be blessed with children so perceptive and sensitive to others' needs. Unlike his elder brother, who seemed to have inherited the Tanner gene for impenetrable inscrutability, Fred's every emotion was reflected in his face. There had been a time when Mark was open and unguarded too, and in light of Charlie's letter Joyce couldn't help wondering what manner of indoctrination into the Tanner way of life he'd been subjected to at the hands of his grandfather, particularly since Charlie's death. A frisson of panic ran through her again: perhaps Charlie had had a point. Perhaps something did need to be done to prevent her younger children falling under the spell of their grandfather.

Joyce realized Fred and Molly were studying her intently. They'd barely been in the house five minutes and already they were picking up on her anxiety. How would she get through the rest of the evening without alerting them to the fact that something was amiss?

It struck her then just how desperately she needed to

confide in someone, to vent her fears, and with luck find some answers – and she knew just the person to turn to. A pizza delivery would let her off parental duties for at least an hour, long enough to nip down the road to her mother and show her the letter, see whether she had any idea what could have prompted it. Henry's driver wouldn't have made it back to the office yet, so there was no way her father would be home before six. That left the coast clear for her to speak to Felicity alone.

Galvanized by the prospect that some answers might be within reach, Joyce reached out, wrapped an arm around each child and pulled them close to her.

'Thank you, my darlings,' she said. 'I'm not really sad. Well, no more than usual, anyway. It's just that I need to see your grandmother about something, and she was out when I called by earlier. I thought if we ordered pizza I could pop over now for an hour. You can order, if you like, Molly. Four seasons for me. Choose anything you want for yourselves – but easy on the garlic bread.'

'What time will you be back?' asked Molly.

'I shouldn't be long. Have them deliver at five thirty, if you can wait that long. And look after the monster for me, darling.'

'I'm not a monster,' said Fred.

'That's a matter of opinion,' said Joyce.

It took two minutes for Joyce to walk to her parents' house. Felicity was in the kitchen putting the finishing touches to a steak-and-kidney pie – Henry's favourite. She seemed surprised to see her daughter.

'Shouldn't you be getting the kids' tea?' she enquired.

'We're ordering in a pizza,' said Joyce. 'Molly's doing it.'

Felicity raised her eyebrows. 'On a school day?'

'Yes, on a school day,' replied Joyce tetchily and without offering any further explanation.

Was she really such a creature of habit that her entire family responded this way to the smallest change in the daily routine? She suspected that the answer was yes. Ever since she'd married Charlie and moved back to Tarrant Park, she'd clung to routine as a means of getting through each day, never deviating from her schedule during term time.

It was as if she'd turned into a sort of Stepford wife, a far cry from the girl she'd once been. Remembering the old Joyce, that determination to be independent, to follow her dreams, she felt the spirit that had been subdued for so long flare up inside her. It was that spirit that had carried her to her mother, with the intention of coming straight to the subject of the letter and quizzing her about what Henry could have done to warrant the accusation.

But the moment she was in Felicity's presence, her resolve evaporated. What could she possibly hope to glean from her mother? There was no question where her mother's loyalty lay: firmly with Henry. Felicity's first instinct would always be to consult her husband, and then defer to him in whatever course of action he saw fit to decide upon. Anything Joyce told her mother would immediately be disclosed in full to her father.

Since she had already eliminated the possibility of discussing the letter with Henry, Joyce was now at a loss how to proceed.

Perching on a kitchen stool, she tried for a breezy, casual tone: 'Hey, don't I get a cup of tea?'

'If you make it yourself,' responded her mother, lightening

her words with a warm smile. 'You can see I'm busy, can't you?'

Joyce stood up, filled the kettle from the sink and switched it on. Perhaps she could instigate a more subtle interrogation than she had originally planned. But the thought of deceiving her mother made her feel uncomfortable, and whenever Joyce felt uncomfortable she was inclined to blush. Already her cheeks were burning. Thankfully she had her back to her mother, and to keep it that way she took her time rummaging in the cupboard for the jar of teabags and selecting a mug.

'What time are you expecting Dad back?' she asked.

'Sixish – same time he always comes home,' responded her mother, puzzled.

'Yes. Sorry.' There was a long silence as Joyce searched for the right thing to say next. 'I wish I was expecting Charlie home.'

'Of course you do, sweetheart.' Her mother's voice softened. 'Has it been a bad day? Come and sit down.'

Hoping her hot cheeks had not turned too red, Joyce took the mug of tea to the table, and sat.

'I'm sorry if I wasn't as welcoming as I should have been,' said her mother. 'You know you can come around here and talk, or just be here, any time you like, don't you?'

Joyce sipped her tea and said nothing.

'I do understand how you're feeling,' Felicity continued. 'I don't think I'll ever get over losing your brother. Not completely. It's the little things, isn't it? You find yourself making sure you've got the breakfast cereal he likes, remembering how he likes his eggs, planning his favourite dinner. I do know, Joyce.'

Joyce could only stare at her. It was typical of Felicity to empathize, or try to. But losing Charlie was nothing like losing William. Felicity had no idea what a moody bastard Charlie had been at home. Or at least, Joyce assumed she hadn't.

She wondered again for a moment if she should summon up all her waning courage, plunge in and tell her mother about the letter and take it from there. Did it matter if Felicity told Henry? Presumably he would have to know sooner or later, if Joyce were ever to solve this mystery.

With one hand she felt the pocket of her cardigan. She had removed the letter from its hiding place beneath the bread bin and slipped it there before leaving The Firs.

Then Felicity spoke again:

'It's hard for your father too. After all, he worked with Charlie every day. He doesn't say much – you know what he's like. Nobody could ever replace William for your father. That's why he's shut the loss out. But I do think he'd come to regard your Charlie as a second son. And there's no doubt he misses him terribly.'

Joyce grasped the opportunity to steer the conversation toward the concerns raised by the letter, hoping she could find answers without mentioning the letter itself.

'Yes, they were close, weren't they,' she said. 'Not that Charlie ever talked about it much – or work, come to that. Is Dad still as tight-lipped as ever?'

'Well, you could put it like that,' said Felicity. 'It's the way your father is, that's all. He's the old-fashioned hunter-gatherer, bless him. He doesn't believe in bringing his work home. The way he sees it, a wife shouldn't have to worry about finances, work problems, or anything like that.'

'Wouldn't want you worrying your pretty little head, eh?' said Joyce mischievously, managing a grin in spite of the way she was feeling.

'Now, Joyce, you are terribly naughty,' scolded her mother, speaking to her the way she had when Joyce was a child. 'You know perfectly well that your father has never said such a thing to me in the fifty years we've been together.'

'So you say,' muttered Joyce.

'And I'm absolutely sure Charlie never said anything like that to you,' her mother continued, as if Joyce hadn't spoken. 'He wouldn't have dared.'

'Maybe not,' said Joyce. 'I sometimes thought he was on the verge of saying it, though. He would never tell me anything about anything. If I so much as asked him what sort of day he'd had, he'd go all secretive and change the subject.'

She paused, trying to get the right note of playfulness into her voice.

'Tell you what though, Mum, I bet you know everything about Tanner-Max. In fact, I bet you're the one who runs the place, only it's a deep dark secret. It's all a front, isn't it? Dad just won't let on how much he depends on you.'

Her mother leaned over the table and appeared to focus her attention on her pie-making as she answered: 'I can assure you, I know next to nothing about the business. Why would I want to?' she asked. 'That's your father's territory.'

Joyce sighed inwardly and changed tack.

'And he was always a good father, wasn't he?' she asked.

Her mother looked up from her pastry, eyes alert. 'What sort of question is that? You know he was a good father – and still is! What's got into you today, girl?'

'And a good father to William, too?' persisted Joyce, refusing to allow her mother to divert her from her purpose.

'Of course your father was good to your brother. They adored each other.' Her mother scrutinized her, puzzled.

'Yes, but did you ever think maybe they adored each other

too much, that they might have been too close?' Even as she blurted the question out, Joyce wondered whether she had gone too far. But if it occurred to her mother that Joyce might be implying something untoward in the relationship between father and son, Felicity Tanner gave no sign of it.

'I do know what you mean,' she replied, rather to Joyce's surprise. 'It was a bit like they were in their own private club. Nobody else could ever get a look in. But I was always glad that they got on so well. It's a shame more men don't get on that well with their sons.'

'True,' said Joyce. 'And it was much the same with Charlie, wasn't it? Being in their own private club, I mean, with their own private agenda. And we wives were kept right out of it.'

Felicity pushed aside the pie and put her hands on her hips. 'Joyce, you managed to make that sound quite sinister,' she said. 'Whatever has brought this on?'

'Brought what on?' Joyce responded, her blush deepening. 'I wonder about Charlie, that's all. I know he loved me, and I loved him. And he cared for me and was almost always kind. He did have some black moods, though. And there was definitely something missing in our marriage. I think it was honesty. I just wondered if you felt the same.'

'Joyce, just because a man likes to keep work and home apart, that doesn't mean he's hiding something,' said Felicity, wiping floury hands on her apron. 'It doesn't mean he has secrets. Well, not the sort of secrets a wife should worry about anyway.'

'And what does that mean?' asked Joyce sharply.

'Nothing, nothing at all.' It was Felicity's turn to blush. Her skin was even paler than her daughter's. Practically translucent. The flush started around her neck and spread instantly up over her cheeks. 'Only a figure of speech,' she said.

'You're blushing, Mum.'

'So are you,' countered Felicity.

'No, I'm hot, that's all,' lied Joyce.

'Well, if I am blushing it's because you're embarrassing me with all your questions,' said Felicity.

'It seems to me we don't ask enough questions in this family. I mean, Charlie died before his time – in a boating accident, even though he was such a good sailor – and we never did get to the bottom of William's death.'

'Don't be ridiculous, Joyce!' her mother snapped. 'You make it sound as if Charlie was doing nothing more danger-ous than messing about in a pedalo on the Serpentine. He was sailing in the Atlantic Ocean. On his own. In November. I know the weather was pretty good, and that it was what he liked to do, but the dangers were obvious, no matter how good a sailor he was. As for your brother: William was knocked down by a motorist who was probably drunk and therefore didn't stop. It was a tragic accident. They were both tragic accidents. Of course they were.'

'Maybe. But Charlie's body wasn't recovered, so there couldn't be a post mortem – which might have revealed exactly what did happen to him. And the motorist who killed William was never traced. Yet – and I suspect you remember me telling you at the time – the police manage to track down nine out of ten motorists who are involved in a fatal traffic incident and leave the scene.'

'Why are you bringing William's death up now?' asked Felicity, the pain clear in her voice. 'That was twenty-four years ago. What can you hope to gain by going over it again? It has nothing to do with Charlie's death.'

'Maybe not, but Charlie's only been dead six months and yet I know bugger all about the manner of his death. And it suddenly occurred to me today that I know bugger all about his life and his work. All I know about him is the bit he brought home at night, and I'm damned sure that was only the tip of the iceberg.' Seeing the concern in her mother's face she took a deep breath and tried to bring her emotions under control. 'I just thought, Mum, that you might be able to help me. I need to fill in the gaps. And I don't think I shall be able to move on until I do. Will you help me fill in the gaps, Mum?'

Well, it's worth a try, thought Joyce. Though she was aware that her softly-softly approach had gone out the kitchen window.

Felicity scrutinized her pie for a moment before answering. Then she looked up and directed a penetrating gaze at her daughter.

'Something's happened, Joyce, hasn't it?'

Damn it, thought Joyce. She had allowed herself to forget how astute her mother could be. Felicity Tanner might give the impression of being the meek little wife, content to live in her husband's shadow and acquiesce to his every whim, but she was a highly intelligent woman and not to be underestimated.

'No, of course not. I can't help fretting about things, that's all, and that's why I'm turning to you, to help me sort myself out,' responded Joyce, suspecting that she did not sound at all convincing.

'Joyce, I know you too well,' said her mother. 'Something's happened, I'm sure of it. Come on now, tell me what it is and then I can help you.'

Joyce could feel the outline of Charlie's letter in her cardigan pocket. If she was going to throw caution to the wind, confide in her mother and show her the letter, this was the moment to do it. And Joyce longed for Felicity to reassure her and put her mind at rest. If she was honest, that had been her real motive for coming here in the first place. Joyce didn't want to have to deal with the questions the letter had raised. Not on her own. And she certainly didn't want to uproot herself and her two younger children and take off for a new life. She simply wasn't capable of doing such a thing. It was perhaps indicative of Charlie's state of mind that he had overlooked that.

It felt as if the letter was smouldering away in her pocket. She almost expected her mother to drop her gaze to the pocket and demand to see what was in there. But Felicity was still looking her in the eye, a concerned expression on her face.

This was the mother Joyce loved, the mother who had always loved and cherished her. The woman who had been at her side constantly, through good times and bad times. The mother who had been the first person she'd turned to when the news came through that the *Molly May* had been found but Charlie was missing. The mother who had consoled her with all her heart, who had slept on the sofa in her bedroom for a month after Charlie had gone. If there was one person in all the world she could trust, even if she allowed herself to doubt her own father and the memory of her husband, it was surely Felicity Tanner.

Yet Joyce held back. She could not put her trust in Felicity because her mother had always put her trust in Henry – and always would. The letter must remain Joyce's secret. At least for the time being.

'Nothing's happened, Mum, I promise you,' she said.

She surprised herself with the ease the lie slipped from her lips. She didn't think she had ever lied to her mother before this day, not about anything important anyway. She had left an awful lot unsaid, particularly about her marriage and her concern over her husband's mental state. But that was the Tanner/Mildmay way.

'Joyce, I really think you should . . .' Felicity began.

Joyce stopped listening. She realized that her mother was telling her what she should do, but she wasn't interested. She'd had a lifetime of people telling her what she should do, and she'd gone along with it – until now. It was time she started making her own decisions, in her own best interests. And the first decision was that she would not allow herself to be deterred.

She would find out the truth, but she would do it alone. Much as she would have liked to share the burden, Joyce didn't have anyone she could turn to. She hadn't stayed in touch with old school chums and Charlie had been her closest friend and confidant at university. She had never worked so there were no workmates past or present. She didn't do the daily school run, so she'd never mingled with other parents at the school gates. Her golf and tennis partners were no more than that; they might have the occasional lunch at the club after a game, but they never socialized beyond that. Ever since she could remember, her family had been her entire world. So she had no choice but to keep her own counsel.

It was possible that Charlie's unnerving warning was the product of a disturbed mind. If that was the case and her father was blameless, to share the contents would only cause unnecessary distress to her parents. If, on the other hand, her children were genuinely at risk, she needed to identify the threat and act upon it – and she would have a better chance of success if no one knew what she was up to. Not even her mother.

'Sorry, Mum, but I must go,' she said lightly. 'I left Molly with my credit card so she could order the pizzas. She's probably bought herself the latest iPad by now!'

And then she was out the door without a backward glance, though she was conscious of her mother's eyes following her. She wondered what Felicity would say to Henry when he got home – it was inevitable that she would mention Joyce's visit, but would she mention the questions Joyce had asked about Charlie, about William, about Henry himself?

Despite her newfound sense of purpose, Joyce felt apprehensive and unsettled as she hurried home to her children.

Four

She made it just in time for the pizza delivery. She put on a bright smile and bustled about the kitchen, determined not to infect the children with her fears. They had enough to contend with, grieving for their father and adjusting to life without him.

The three of them sat up at the kitchen table, but they ate their pizzas with their fingers straight from the boxes, in big drooping slices. The proper way. That was part of the fun, particularly for Fred, who was delighted to be having junk food for supper rather than the healthy home-cooked fare Joyce usually prepared.

Not long after they'd finished the meal Joyce's mobile rang. She glanced at the screen – *missed call: Henry 18.33* – then switched it off. She'd been half expecting it. Felicity must have told him about her visit the moment he stepped through the front door. Even so, Joyce hadn't expected him to call so quickly.

A few minutes later, as Joyce was stacking the dishwasher, the house phone rang. Before Joyce could stop her, Molly picked up the nearest receiver from its bracket fixed to the kitchen wall.

'It's Granddad, for you, Mum,' said Molly.

Joyce kept her back to Molly and carried on filling the dishwasher. She daren't take his call now; he was bound to start interrogating her about her visit earlier and there was a danger she would blurt out more than she meant to. If she was going to succeed in fobbing him off, she needed time to come up with a strategy. Flustered at the thought of her daughter waiting expectantly for her to take the phone, she dropped a plate and cursed as it clattered noisily to the floor.

'Tell him I'm about to have a bath. I'll call him later,' said Joyce impatiently, focusing on picking up pieces of china rather than facing her daughter. She could sense Molly's puzzlement even without looking at her. It was unheard of for anyone to tell Henry Tanner he'd have to wait for them to call him back at their convenience.

'Go on,' instructed Joyce, waving both her hands at Molly. She reminded herself that she'd only been a couple of years older than Molly when she'd hatched her plan to break away from the family fold and attend the university of her choice. She'd outplayed her father on that occasion, achieving the result she'd set her heart on even though it went against his wishes. That all seemed a lifetime ago now, but for her children's sake Joyce knew she must dig deep and tap into that old Tanner guile. She just wasn't ready yet.

She heard Molly repeating her words down the phone. There followed a brief conversation, with Molly responding to questions about her day at school, and telling him what kind of pizza she'd had. The usual trivial family stuff. But Molly still looked puzzled when she replaced the phone in its wall bracket.

Joyce hated asking her daughter to lie for her. Even though it was only a little fib, it went against everything she'd tried to instil in her children about the need to be honest.

'I am going to have a bath in a minute, darling,' she said guiltily. 'And you know what your granddad's like. I could have been on the phone to him for hours. I'm a bit wiped out, to tell the truth. I'll perk up later.'

'Cool,' said Molly. 'You don't have to explain, Mum. I know what granddad's like.'

But the look she shot Joyce was a sharp one. A few minutes later Joyce felt obliged to retreat to the bathroom and run herself a bath, whether she wanted one or not.

When she emerged half an hour later, Fred asked her for help with his homework. Joyce was good at history, obviously, and not bad at English and geography. But she was hopeless at maths. That had been Charlie's department. Although he had chosen to read politics at university, he could have been a mathematician had he so desired. But maths had been too dry a choice for Charlie – the young Charlie at any rate.

Tonight was a maths night. Joyce could just about manage the maths curriculum of an eleven-year-old, and she was glad of the diversion. But she feared it wouldn't be long before she would be out of her depth with Fred's homework. Charlie's children were going to miss their father in so many ways.

Molly also had homework. Mercifully, she'd reached the stage where she knew better than to ask her mother about anything except history. Molly was astute for a fifteen-year-old. Too astute, Joyce sometimes thought.

Molly had earlier indicated that she had an essay to write, but claimed to have finished it within half an hour or so. Then she settled down in the sitting room to watch TV until bedtime – nine thirty for her on schooldays, and eight thirty for Fred.

Joyce remained in inner turmoil throughout. She couldn't wait until it was time for both children, after the usual protests and requests for ten minutes more, to retire to their bedrooms. She was not a big drinker, but the events of the day had left her desperate to open a bottle of wine. She and Charlie had frequently shared a bottle over dinner, when they were going through a good patch anyway. But Joyce felt there was something intrinsically sad and undesirable about drinking alone in front of her children, and since Charlie's death she had avoided doing so.

She shut up the house and took the bottle to bed with her. Her mobile was switched off and she intended to keep it that way until she'd sorted out what she was going to say to her father. The house phone rang once more, shortly after ten. She assumed it was Henry calling, though she made no attempt to check the display panel on the receiver, let alone answer the call. Neither of the children had extensions to the house phone in their rooms, and she only hoped they were both asleep and would not be woken by the ringing. It seemed that her hopes were realized. And the phone did not ring a second time.

More than anything Joyce wanted to go to sleep, then wake up in the morning and carry on as if today had never happened. Things had not been easy since Charlie's death, but Joyce had been coping. Before the letter arrived she had started to think about studying for a teaching diploma, or finding a way of attaining that MA at another university with different academic stipulations to Exeter, or even through the Open University. The years were flying by. She had to prepare for the day when her younger children would move on, even if it was only down the road to the flat above Henry's garage, as Mark had done . . .

Every train of thought seemed to bring her back to the letter. Mark, like her late brother William, had elected to stay in Tarrant Park and join the family firm. So there couldn't be anything seriously amiss, either with Henry or the business, could there?

Why then was Charlie so adamant there would be dire consequences if Fred were to do the same? Try as she might, Joyce could make no sense of it.

Eventually she fell into a fitful sleep. Her alarm went off at 7 a.m. to give her plenty of time to get the children ready for school. Twenty minutes later the house phone rang again. She answered, even though she knew, without checking caller display, that it would be Henry. She couldn't dodge him for ever.

'Your mother's worried about you, darling,' Henry began.

'Mum's always worried about me, Dad,' replied Joyce, reasonably.

'Oh, darling, she's convinced something has happened to upset you . . .'

'Yes, it has, Dad. My husband has died at the age of forty-three, leaving me with two young children to bring up. Something's happened to upset me, all right.'

Selective honesty, Joyce had decided, would be the best policy. She would stick to the truth with her father, but not the whole truth.

'Joyce, sweetheart, you know what I mean . . .'

'No, I don't. I'm trying to come to terms with Charlie's death and to rebuild my life and keep everything together for Molly and Fred. Some days I manage, and some days I struggle, that's all.'

'Well, if you want a break any time, you've only to say the word. Your mother would be straight over to take care of things. And it goes without saying that if you want to talk, we're both here, and you are always welcome—'

Joyce couldn't stop herself interrupting.

'Dad, we've never had those sorts of conversations, you will only talk about what suits you,' she said.

'I don't think that's quite fair, dear,' responded her father mildly.

'Look, it doesn't matter. I don't want to talk, anyway.'

Joyce did want to, but not to him. What would be the point? He was never going to let his guard down and talk openly with her. And thanks to the letter, she was now wary of talking openly with him, at least until she had established whether there was any substance to Charlie's warning.

'I just want to get on with things,' she said briskly. 'Now, I'm sorry, I have to go. I need to go up and drag Molly and Fred out of bed so they can get ready for school.'

'All right, darling. But maybe later your mother can pop over—'

'Dad, I can't stay on the phone a moment longer. I'm saying goodbye now.'

Joyce replaced the receiver. It had been a long time since she'd tried to fob off Henry, but it hadn't gone too badly. No doubt she'd get better at it with practice.

After Molly and Fred had departed with Geoff, Henry's driver, she cleared up the breakfast things and made the beds. She'd given up on trying to persuade them to make their own beds on school mornings; they were always racing against the clock and she had enough stress as it was without getting into a daily battle with the pair of them. Besides, it wasn't as if she had to make beds and do the housework every day. Ever since the start of her marriage she'd shared a daily with her parents. Until the beginning of last year it had been Josie, but when she retired they'd taken on an Albanian girl called Monika.

Thankfully, this was not one of Monika's days at The Firs. Not that Joyce didn't like the girl, although she did find her a bit hard going sometimes. Her English was excellent but Joyce's attempts to get to know her and learn about the life she'd left behind in Kosovo had met a stone wall. In the end she'd given up trying to cultivate the sort of chatty camaraderie she'd had with Josie and simply left Monika to get on with her chores. Today, however, she wanted the house to herself.

She'd woken up with the beginning of a plan forming in her mind. Still wondering how to execute it, she wandered around the house, picking up and putting away the odd pair of trainers, or even the odd trainer, straightening the cushions, adjusting the curtains and generally pottering until nine thirty.

Then she made a call to Stephen Hardcastle at the office of Tanner-Max.

She had first met the tall handsome old Etonian during her first term at university. Stephen, four years older at twenty-two, was in the final year of his law degree. To Joyce, young for her age and still a virgin, he seemed urbane, sophisticated, exotic – he'd told her his Zimbabwean father was a tribal prince – and wildly attractive. In short, everything she aspired to be. He'd asked her out for a drink, and after several glasses of Prosecco, tipsier than she'd ever been in her life, she had allowed herself to be seduced by him. The following morning she'd had no regrets whatsoever about losing her virginity. Stephen had proved an experienced and sensitive lover, and virginity always was and, Joyce suspected, would always remain, a heavy burden to carry around a university campus.

Nonetheless it had come as a shock to learn that she was merely the latest in a long line of conquests. Stephen, she discovered, was a serial seducer with a penchant for deflowering virgins. Joyce had been hurt, but she dealt with it in true Tanner fashion. She had no intention of allowing her much longed-for university life to be destroyed by one brief encounter. Even such a significant one. Neither would she allow herself to show her true feelings. She merely drew back from Stephen, with minimum fuss, vowing to be more careful in future.

He hadn't disappeared from her life though. After she took up with Charlie, Stephen had become a close friend of JC and had been best man at their wedding. Shortly before Mark was born he had joined Tanner-Max and his willingness to take on the extra workload had made it possible for Charlie to take extended paternity leave. Charlie had been blissfully unaware of their brief fling, and so far as Joyce was concerned it was ancient history. Until a week ago.

In the months since Charlie's death, Stephen had been attentive and solicitous of her welfare, calling to see whether she needed anything and inviting her for lunch whenever she was in town. It was after one of these lunches that history had repeated itself. She'd had too much to drink, so Stephen drove her home afterwards and in a moment of lonely, alcohol-fuelled weakness she'd invited him into her house and into her bed.

Far from rekindling an old flame, it had left her feeling embarrassed, she reflected as she waited for Stephen to pick up his phone.

'Joyce, how lovely to hear from you . . .' he began.

He must have known that she would have received the letter sent from his office, and that it had more than likely prompted her call, but he still contrived to sound flirtatious.

'This is business, strictly business, Stephen,' she interrupted, determined to nip that in the bud straight away.

'Of course,' he said, his tone suddenly formal.

'There are a number of things I need to speak to you about, as a matter of urgency,' Joyce continued.

'Ah, you got the letter?'

'Yes.'

'I'm sorry about the delay. Unforgivable. It must have arrived as things were beginning to get back to normal for you again.'

'Things are never going to get back to normal, Stephen,' she said with feeling.

'No, of course not,' responded Stephen. 'Damned silly thing to say. I'm sorry . . .'

'Stop apologizing, for goodness' sake, Stephen – I didn't call to remonstrate. I was hoping you might be able to drop by for an hour or so later so we can talk.'

'I'd be delighted.' He sounded rather too delighted in Joyce's opinion. Hopeful even.

'I need your professional advice,' she said.

'Ah,' said Stephen. 'Is it about the letter? I mean, I don't know what's in it, obviously, but—'

'I should hope you don't know what's in the letter,' said Joyce. 'We may have been friends for a long time but you're still the company secretary and the family solicitor. Ethics, and so on.'

She felt a little guilty, speaking to him in that way when it was quite possible that he'd done nothing to warrant her implied reprimand, but his response made light of it.

'Ethics?' he queried. 'County to the East of London, isn't it?'

'Oh very funny,' she said, her tone lighter now. 'As for the letter, you're right, it was a shock, but that's not what I wanted to talk to you about. I would like to go through Charlie's will again. And our financial arrangements. I owe it to the kids to make sure I know exactly what our position is.'

'Pretty rosy, I should say, Joyce. Financially, at least. But we can discuss it if that would put your mind at rest. Do you want me to bring Gordon along?'

Gordon Hawkins was the company accountant. Like Stephen he also dealt with personal matters for the Tanner family.

'No,' she said. 'I'd prefer to talk to you on your own first.'

They made an appointment for two o' clock that afternoon. Joyce supposed that she was taking a risk in inviting him to her home; even though she'd made it clear she was seeking his professional advice, Stephen might think it was a pretext and the real motive was her eagerness to repeat their sexual encounter. A lapse, as she now thought of it, that she had been regretting even before the arrival of that earth-shattering letter.

It had been all too easy to seek solace with Stephen. He remained a good-looking and charismatic man, she'd always suspected he still found her attractive, and they had a history. But much as she'd enjoyed the sex, she hadn't been ready to risk the kind of emotional entanglement she feared might follow. The last thing she wanted was to have to fend off an amorous Stephen, but she'd sooner that than run the risk of bumping into her father by going to the office. Not that her meeting with Stephen was likely to escape Henry's ultrasensitive radar for long; Henry's employees, like his family, had been trained to inform him of their every move.

Stephen arrived on the dot. Did he look anxious or was it her imagination?

He leaned towards her. They had always greeted each other with a kiss. She made sure it was a light one. On the cheek. Then she led him into the kitchen. He dumped his briefcase on the table and began to remove papers. Charlie's will, Joyce's will, the details of their various bank accounts and shareholdings, including Charlie's stake in Tanner-Max, which Joyce already knew had passed to Mark rather than to her – or would do, once a death certificate was issued. Henry was a firm believer in patrilineal inheritance – no female equality in the Tanner line of succession. Not that Joyce cared. She had never had the slightest desire to become involved in the family business.

Her request for an overview of her financial affairs was, in any case, merely a ruse. She'd decided that the best approach to adopt with Stephen would be to catch him off balance. If such a thing were possible.

She didn't offer him tea or coffee. Not at first. Instead she stood in silence, regarding him with a frosty stare as he emptied his bag on to the table. She waited until he sat down and began methodically arranging the papers in front of him before blurting out the real purpose of the meeting:

'Stephen, I know that something was worrying Charlie before he died, something to do with the business and my family. And I want you to tell me what it was.'

He looked up at her in alarm. 'I have no idea what you are talking about, Joyce.'

'I think you have, Stephen,' said Joyce, calling his bluff. 'You were Charlie's best and oldest friend. You worked together. In any case, Charlie made it clear in his letter that something was troubling him and that you knew all about it.'

She saw his eyes flicker, she was sure of it.

'Well, there you have the advantage of me, Joyce,' he said. 'I have no idea what was in Charlie's letter. And I find it hard to believe that he had any worries about the business. Charlie was a happy and successful man. He enjoyed his work. He had you and the kids. And he had all this.'

Stephen waved both arms as if trying to encompass the whole of Charlie Mildmay's world.

'You must have noticed his moods, for God's sake,' said Joyce.

'Well, yes, he had black days, but don't we all,' said Stephen. 'Pressure of work and all that.'

'You seriously expect me to believe it was nothing more than that?' asked Joyce.

Stephen shrugged. 'What else could there be? Charlie had everything. He loved his family. He had no financial worries. He had a great life.'

'Yes, and all of it provided by my father,' Joyce said bitterly. 'Perhaps it all came with a price tag, and the price was more than Charlie could stomach.'

Stephen looked even more alarmed.

'Joyce dear, it's understandable that you're upset. But I think you're imagining things.'

'Don't you dare patronize me!' Joyce snapped. 'I have a letter from my dead husband which makes it clear that I'm not imagining anything. It's more a case of my eyes having been closed until now, isn't it?'

'Joyce, I have no idea what you're talking about. Look, why don't you show me the letter? Then perhaps I can help. I'm totally in the dark here.'

'Are you sure you need to be shown the letter?' said Joyce. 'Are you sure you haven't read it already?'

'Joyce, what sort of a man do you think I am?' asked Stephen, aghast. 'Do you really think I would read a personal letter between a man – and not any man but, as you say, my best friend – and his wife? Do you think I would do that?'

'You were prepared to shag his wife though, weren't you?'

'His widow,' countered Stephen, his brows puckered into a hurt frown. 'I would never have acted upon my feelings for you while Charlie was alive, even though I never stopped wanting—'

'Shut up, Stephen!' Joyce was aware that she was being hard on him. It wasn't as if he'd forced himself on her. If anything, she'd been the one who made the first move. But she somehow couldn't stop herself venting her anger at him.

'I want to know about the letter,' she persisted. 'Why did it take six months to get to me. Why was that?'

'Oh, Joyce, it got misfiled, that's all. It should have been in with our copy of the will but it got put somewhere else. Janet's a first-rate PA, but even she makes mistakes sometimes. When she found the letter she sent it off straight away. It was human error.'

'Maybe.'

'Well, do I get to see it?'

She carried on staring at him, but Stephen had one of those faces that gave nothing away. Unless he wanted it to.

'The letter was personal,' she said coldly. 'I think I'll keep it to myself.'

'As you wish.'

'Oh, and I've changed my mind about all that financial stuff.' She waved a hand dismissively at the papers spread across the kitchen table. 'I mean, it's not as if it matters a damn whether I understand it or not, does it? No doubt you and my father will only ever show me what you want me to see. And you two will still control everything, whatever I think or do.'

'Joyce, it's not like that, I promise you,' said Stephen, looking even more hurt and misunderstood. 'Charlie has left you very well off. You will be a wealthy woman in your own right once all the legal stuff is settled and a death certificate issued. Nobody would want to stop you from looking after your own finances. It is what Charlie would have wanted, and it's what Henry wants too. And I can assure you that neither Henry nor I would ever interfere. Of course, if you were to require help, we would be only too happy to—'

'I'll bet you would!' retorted Joyce. 'I'm afraid I'm not too convinced by any of your assurances right now, Stephen. I think you'd better go, don't you?'

'But I've only just arrived.' He smiled seductively. 'And we were getting on so—'

'Oh, for goodness' sake,' she cut him off.

'No, I have very real feelings for you, Joyce. I always have. And I was hoping last week might be the beginning of something new for both of us. All I want is to take care of you, to make you happy again.'

'Please go, Stephen,' she told him.

There had been a moment earlier when she'd almost felt sorry for him, but now she was merely angry. He must have the skin of a rhinoceros, she thought, to make such a remark after the way she had treated him.

'Why does everybody want to take care of me?' she continued. 'It was one shag, Stephen. That's all we had. One shag after a quarter of a century. And you caught me at a weak moment. I am not ready for new beginnings. Not with you. Not with anyone.'

'Oh, Joyce, I would never rush you. But you have to know it wasn't just a sh-sh . . .'

He seemed to have difficulty even getting the word out.

'Not just a shag,' he managed eventually. 'Not for me, anyway.'

The sight of his stricken face only made Joyce even angrier.

'Go, Stephen. Please go!' She shouted the words at the top of her voice, surprising not only Stephen but herself as well.

Stephen re-packed his bag, doing so as carefully as he did everything, perhaps as a kind of protest against her behaviour, and perhaps in the vain hope that she might calm down and change her mind.

Joyce could not explain why she was in such a rage. And neither could she explain why she had vented at Stephen. She hadn't intended to. She had intended to be calm and cool and clever, yet somehow she'd failed dismally in all three respects.

As Stephen got back in his car and drove off, Joyce's rage began to re-focus. Now she was furious with herself. In allowing her temper to get the better of her she had not only revealed her hand, she had laid her cards out on the table. Worse, she had learned absolutely nothing in the process. And having alienated Stephen, it was unlikely that she ever would learn anything from him.

The plan she'd been so pleased with when she woke that morning had failed at the first hurdle, and there was no plan B.

Five

Stephen usually found the hum of his F-type Jaguar's motor and the comfort of its upholstered leather seats sufficient to soothe away most cares and worries. Not today though. He was too shaken by Joyce's outburst.

She should never have been allowed to see that letter. Her reaction was proof that Henry's policy of shielding women from the harsher realities was a sound one. Women – even educated women like Joyce – were loose cannons, incapable of conducting themselves rationally when their emotions were engaged – and that was the last thing you wanted in a business environment. Particularly a business like theirs.

Stephen knew what he should do next. He should call Henry straight away and tell him what had happened. But there were two reasons why he didn't want to do that. The first was that Joyce's anger would pale into insignificance compared to the rage Henry would fly into, and he would be on the receiving end. The second was that he had carried a flame for Joyce for twenty-odd years, and for Stephen, that over-shadowed his business obligations.

He found himself thinking, as he so often did, of the young undergraduate he'd seduced twenty-six years earlier. He had been a fool ever to let her get away, but he'd been just a kid himself, out to earn a reputation as a Lothario. Joyce had been particularly receptive, a warm and eager lover. But at the time she'd merely been one more . . . well, he'd never actually carved notches on his bedpost, but that pretty much summed up his attitude in those days.

He was sure Joyce had been upset when she found out about the other women, but whereas most of his conquests cried and pleaded with him, Joyce had responded with a cold and distant anger. She'd been strong too, telling him that she wouldn't stand for it, and that their relationship, such as it was, was over. At first he hadn't cared a jot. It was only when Joyce and Charlie became an item that he began to have regrets, to wonder whether Joyce had meant more to him than he'd realized. He'd hoped that he might get a second chance, so he could prove that, beneath his devil-may-care facade, he really cared for her. Indeed he found himself hoping that the relationship between Joyce and Charlie wouldn't last.

In spite of that, he set out to make friends with Charlie. He reckoned that if he was close to Charlie, he would be well placed to keep an eye on the state of their relationship and step in if it began to wane. Joyce accepted him as a friend far more readily than he would have expected. Whatever grudge she might have borne against him was forgotten the moment Charlie came on the scene.

It soon became evident that what Joyce had with Charlie was no fling. The pair were convinced that they would be together for ever – an opinion shared by anyone who came in contact with them. So there would be no second chance for Stephen. The best he could hope for was a platonic friendship with both halves of the couple who were soon to be known as JC.

The three of them remained firm friends even after Stephen graduated, a year ahead of Joyce. Having also completed his Legal Practice Course, he immediately joined a local firm of solicitors on a training contract.

But the more Stephen saw of Joyce, the more he wanted her. The attraction fascinated him. He knew the sensible thing would be to distance himself from her, that there was nothing to be gained by maintaining contact when he daren't make any sort of move on her, but it was almost as if he relished the torment of being around her. Charlie, of course, was oblivious. He even asked Stephen to be best man at their wedding. And when a vacancy came up at Tanner-Max due to the retirement of Paul Gould, who'd been company secretary since Edward Tanner and Maxim Schmidt founded the firm, it was Charlie who recommended his newly qualified friend Stephen for the job.

Henry Tanner liked to say that he ran a tight ship. Tanner-Max was a close-knit affair and Paul Gould was not only a valued family friend but also something of an elder statesman in the company. Henry wasn't comfortable with bringing in an outsider. The fact that Charlie could vouch for Stephen was as important a factor in landing the job as the professional qualifications Stephen had worked so hard to achieve.

Within months of his joining Tanner-Max, Charlie went off on extended paternity leave. That was when Stephen cemented his place at the family firm. He discovered there were intriguing and challenging aspects to the job, which he had not expected but which he found himself embracing willingly. Moreover the financial rewards were substantial, providing him with an enviable lifestyle. He bought himself an apartment in the regenerated dock area of Bristol, treated himself to long weekends in New York, and holidayed at the exclusive Coral Reef Club in Barbados, sometimes alone and sometimes with one of the never-ending string of young women he still seemed to be able to attract easily enough when he put his mind to it.

A few years ago he had re-established contact with the father his mother had left behind in Zimbabwe when he was only a boy. Stephen now made regular trips to Africa to visit his father and was building a relationship with his two half-brothers. They were the only family he had. Though Stephen was never short of female company, he'd not found anyone that he wanted to devote himself to and spend the rest of his life with. Invariably he'd find himself comparing the women in his life to Joyce and finding them wanting.

Charlie's accident had opened the door for him to hope that he might yet be able to get close to Joyce in the way he so longed to. He had waited months, hovering in attendance, biding his time for the right moment to make his move. And it had gone so well too: in the event, she'd been the one who had suggested adjourning to the bedroom. Stephen had always been adept at subtly manipulating women so that they thought they were taking the initiative. He'd been convinced that their afternoon tryst would be the first of many. But perhaps he'd misjudged her and moved in too soon. Or maybe it was just the lousy timing of that damned letter turning up. Either way, there seemed little chance of a repeat performance now. He wondered how much of a setback this latest turn of events would prove to be. How long would it be before he'd be given another chance?

He tried to tell himself that Joyce's anger towards him was a sign that she cared. Hopefully, now she'd got it out of her system, it would all blow over quickly so that they could carry on where they'd left off the previous week. But he wasn't convinced.

Joyce clearly suspected him of having opened the letter, of having deliberately delayed forwarding it to her. She also seemed sure that he knew all about what had been troubling Charlie.

She was at least half right. Stephen hadn't intended to open the letter. Not to begin with. He still considered himself to be an honourable man, although he followed his own particular code, which did not stretch to his relationships with women. Charlie had entrusted him with the letter, and believed it safe to do so, to be passed on to Joyce only in the event of his death. Charlie had been a young and healthy man. To some, writing that letter may have seemed a morbid thing to do. Stephen had understood, though. He knew that Charlie was a troubled soul, and he knew much of what had made him so, though not everything. And Stephen wanted to honour his friend's wishes, he really did. But Stephen also had his own agenda in his abiding desire for Joyce. He also continued to harbour certain ambitions. He needed to protect himself. And he was not, of course, entirely his own man. Just as Charlie had not been entirely his own man. Indeed, nobody who came into close contact with Henry Tanner ever remained totally in charge of their own destiny.

Henry had always been alert to the slightest telltale sign that someone was keeping a secret from him, whether it be a family member, an employee or a business associate. That uncanny sixth sense had gone into overdrive in the period leading up to Charlie's accident, and with his son-in-law's demise Henry had turned his attention to Stephen. He knew the two men had been good friends, and he was convinced that Stephen had information that he was keeping to himself.

Stephen had caved in and given Henry the letter – after steaming it open and taking a quick peek first. When dealing with Henry it was advisable to at least keep up with the game, even if you couldn't get ahead of it.

Horrified by what he read, Henry had ordered Stephen to destroy the letter immediately and say nothing to Joyce of its existence.

Joyce was wrong in her assumption that Stephen had informed Henry of their meeting. He hadn't, any more than he had confessed to Henry that the letter still existed. Let alone that it had reached Joyce.

Having reached a stretch of dual carriageway, Stephen hit the accelerator. A whoosh of G force pressed him back into his seat as the high-powered coupe surged forward, passing a family saloon travelling at the regulation 70 mph as if it were stationary.

Stephen couldn't explain even to himself why he had kept the letter. Partly, he supposed, it was his legal training kicking in: it went against the grain to destroy a document that had been entrusted to him. And he supposed he had thought it might be useful one day. That if anything came to light to corroborate what Charlie was alleging, it might be needed as evidence in any legal proceedings. But the last thing he had wanted was for Joyce to read it.

There were speed cameras along that stretch of road. Stephen had no idea whether or not they were operating and didn't care. The speedometer needle shot past 100 and was still rising as the dual carriageway ended and a sharp bend came into view. Only then did he come off the accelerator and step on the brake. The back end slewed as the Jag slowed and Stephen found himself propelled against his seat belt, though he barely noticed the discomfort, his mind was preoccupied with the inevitable fallout once Henry learned that the letter had reached Joyce.

Chances were, Henry already knew. The mood Joyce was in, she'd probably called her father to hurl accusations at him. Even if she hadn't, Felicity might have spotted Stephen's Jag entering or leaving Tarrant Park and mentioned it to her husband. As he pulled into the Tanner-Max car park, Stephen tried to steel himself for the interrogation that would doubtless ensue.

Sure enough, when he arrived at his third-floor office he found Henry waiting for him.

'Why didn't you tell me you were going to see Joyce?' he demanded.

As a child, taken from his homeland and brought up by a stepfather in the UK, Stephen had learned the art of concealing his true emotions. Fear only incited bullies to escalate their taunts, so he'd become adept at masking his unease and maintaining a calm, untroubled demeanour. Henry Tanner, however, was in a different league to the public-school bullies of his childhood.

'I didn't have a chance,' he responded as casually as he could manage. 'And, anyway, I didn't think it was important.'

'I understand she asked to see you?'

Stephen nodded. So it was Janet who'd told him. Their joint PA, allegedly, though there had never been any doubt where her loyalties lay. She'd played a big part in creating this mess. But bloody Henry would never see that.

'What did she want?'

'Oh, to go through the will, review her financial situation.'

'Don't lie to me, Stephen. Don't ever lie to me.'

'That's what she said when she phoned. That's what she told me she wanted.'

'She came over to the house to see her mother yesterday,' Henry said, his eyes boring into Stephen. 'She was asking some odd questions and she seemed on edge. Her mother's been doing her best to console her ever since Charlie died, but she said this wasn't the usual outburst of grief, it was something else, something bothering her. Can you throw any light on that?'

Stephen shrugged in what he hoped was a noncommittal way.

'You're dissembling, Stephen. I can see it written all over your face.'

Stephen was known for being inscrutable. Yet somehow Henry Tanner, and only Henry Tanner, could penetrate the facade. Still Stephen said nothing, determined not to crack under that steely gaze.

'It's the letter, isn't it,' said Henry, making Stephen wonder not for the first time if Henry Tanner could read his mind. It was a statement, not a question. 'You didn't destroy it, did you?' Henry persisted. 'You didn't destroy that bloody letter, did you?'

'Well, not exactly—' began Stephen.

'You bloody fool!' barked Henry. 'You didn't destroy that letter and now Joyce has seen it, hasn't she?'

Stephen nodded. That wasn't enough for Henry.

'Hasn't she?' he yelled, rising from Stephen's chair and leaning forward across Stephen's desk.

'Yes,' Stephen agreed, giving in. 'She has.'

'Right,' said Henry, sitting back down again. 'Now we've got that over with you're going to tell me why you disobeyed my instructions, how this debacle came about, how it got to my daughter – and then we're going to work out what we have to do to get ourselves out of this mess.'

Six

Joyce's anger had quickly turned to regret at having lashed out at Stephen in that manner. She knew it had been unfair of her. The truth was that she wouldn't have done so, not to that extent anyway, if it hadn't been for her embarrassment over their recent sexual encounter. She had over-reacted. And that had set her wondering again: was she over-reacting to Charlie's letter?

She told herself she should get a grip, not allow her mind to run away with itself, conjuring threats to her family purely on the basis of a rambling letter from her late husband. She'd loved Charlie and would miss him terribly, but the last few years he'd fallen prey to those black moods of his more and more often. If he had raised those fears with her in person instead of in a letter, she would probably have told herself it was all in his mind, that it was down to the medication – so why give any credence to it now?

Tired of going over and over it in her mind, she decided to make a supreme effort that evening to put it all to one side and focus on Fred and Molly.

She cooked her children their favourite tea in order to make up for what she saw as her shortcomings of the previous evening. Home-made burgers and chunky chips served with her own special tomato relish, and accompanied by a salad as a gesture towards healthy living.

Then, when the homework was out of the way, the three of them played table tennis in the area above the big connecting garage, which had been turned into a games room.

Since Charlie could only be relied upon as a fourth for doubles when he was in one of his 'up' moods and felt like participating in family tournaments, Joyce and the children had long since devised a complicated points system that enabled them to stage competitions that were not too swiftly completed. And Fred was helped by a handicap he no longer seemed to need. While all three were good at ball games, Fred was showing signs of a real talent for sport.

That night he was again the winner.

'I think that handicap may have to go,' threatened his mother as she prepared to dispatch him to bed.

'I'll still beat the pair of you,' Fred boasted, chest puffed with victory.

'Right, that's it young man,' proclaimed Joyce. 'You're going to have to live up to that. No more handicap for you. We're all on equal terms from now on.'

''Bout time too,' muttered Molly, slumping in front of the TV to make the most of the extra hour before her bedtime. She was completely addicted to *Big Brother*, but in its absence she would settle for any reality show. That night it was a repeat of a particularly banal episode of *Come Dine with Me*.

'That programme is going to numb your brain,' warned her mother.

'If she had a brain,' Fred called down the stairs.

'Oh, Einstein, if only I was as clever as you,' Molly shouted back. 'The boy who told me only this morning that the VW Polo was named after Polo mints.'

'Was too. At least I'm not soppy over a moron like Wally Johnson. Yuk!'

'Shut up, you horror, or I'll drown your iPhone!'

'That's enough, the pair of you,' hollered Joyce, walking out into the hall. 'Into bed now, Fred!' she shouted up the stairs. 'As for you, Molly, if you don't pipe down you'll be going up to bed too.'

Joyce listened for a moment to make sure Fred was obeying orders, then returned to the living room. 'Who's Wally Johnson?'

Molly flushed. 'Nobody. Just a boy at school, that's all.'

A voice came from upstairs: 'Yeah, but you're soppy over him. Soppy soppy soppy. And he's really stupid stupid stupid.'

Molly jumped up from the sofa and set off in the direction of the stairs.

'Fred, I'm going kill you, you little bastard,' she shouted.

Joyce ordered her to sit down again.

'And watch your language, too,' she told her daughter. Then she turned her attention to the owner of the voice from above.

'Fred, you have thirty seconds to get into bed or I'll help your sister drown your iPhone,' she called.

From upstairs she heard a chuckle, followed by silence.

The relentless clamour of *Come Dine with Me* filled the sitting room. Why did everybody have to scream all the time in these shows? Joyce wondered. Her daughter had nothing more to say to her. Her attention was riveted on the screen.

It had been a normal family night. Perhaps the most normal since Charlie's death. Joyce had enjoyed it more than she would have thought possible after the day she'd had. She'd even enjoyed her children's noisy banter. Molly and Fred's incessant barbed teasing of each other had helped banish all thought of the letter, if only for a few hours.

She pottered around the kitchen until Molly had gone to bed, then decided to have an early night herself, once again armed with a bottle of wine.

There was a Joan Hickson *Miss Marple* on ITV 3 which she didn't think she'd seen. And as she settled into the pillows, with a glass of red at her side, to watch the definitive portrayal of Agatha Christie's unique detective, Joyce realized she felt surprisingly content.

The letter continued to hover at the back of her mind, coming to the fore during commercial breaks. But she dealt with it by reminding herself how erratic Charlie's moods had become under the influence of the various drugs he was taking. He could have been in the grip of drug-induced paranoia when he wrote the letter. Perhaps it was as simple as that, and there was absolutely no substance to his allegations about her father and the family business.

Maybe the best course of action would be for her to forget about the letter and focus on trying to rebuild her life, and bringing up Molly and Fred alone as best she could. Realistically, what else could she do? She was no Miss Marple; if Henry and Stephen couldn't be persuaded to divulge the secret workings of Tanner-Max to her, it wasn't as if she could come by the information by any other means. And even if she could, did she really want to risk finding out something she'd be better off not knowing?

That damned letter had not only made her fearful for the future, it had made her dangerously nostalgic for her past. Particularly the one truly carefree and happy time of her life, when she'd been a young student, madly in love with Charlie.

It had also brought back memories of her early feelings for Stephen, which he'd treated so carelessly. She'd been a bit hard on Stephen that afternoon, she decided. But she'd let him stew a bit before relenting and telling him all was forgiven, she resolved before drifting off to sleep.

Joyce woke a few minutes before her 7 a.m. alarm after the best night's sleep she'd had since Charlie's death. While not exactly bursting with cheerfulness and the joy of being alive – she wondered if she'd ever feel that way again – she felt well rested and more positive about the future than she had in a long time.

The sun was shining, filling her bedroom with mellow morning light. Even the weather was showing signs of improvement. When the alarm sounded, she quickly got dressed and went downstairs to begin preparing breakfast for Molly and Fred. Half an hour later, she shouted up the stairs for them to rise and shine.

'Or at least make the best impersonation you can of shining at seven thirty in the morning,' she called, chuckling at her own wit.

Molly made it downstairs at twenty to eight, which was good by her standards. She lowered herself, yawning, into a chair at the kitchen table and started to pick disinterestedly at the bowl of fruit and cereal her mother had prepared for her.

Joyce removed four golden slices from the toaster and put them on the table along with assorted condiments. Peanut butter and honey for Fred. Low-fat spread and sugarless strawberry jam for Molly, who was starting to fret, unnecessarily in her mother's opinion, about her weight.

This was one of Monika's days. She arrived on the dot of

eight and immediately began tidying up the kitchen around Joyce and Molly. One of her more irritating habits, but Joyce didn't mind. Her taciturn presence was somehow reassuring, and she couldn't imagine how she'd have coped these last few months without Monika.

Joyce gave it a few more minutes before poking her head through the kitchen door and shouting up the stairs, 'Come on, Fred, or you won't have time for breakfast. It's five past eight – Geoff will be here in fifteen minutes.'

Five minutes later there was still no sign of him.

'Right, that's it,' muttered Joyce, heading for the stairs. And as she climbed, she shouted a warning:

'I'm coming to get you, my lad. And if I find you still in bed, I swear I'll pull you out by your hair and drag you to the car!'

That should do it, she thought. Even though her son would know full well that she was joking. Perhaps it was time for her to surprise him with a little parental brute force.

Smiling in spite of her irritation, she opened the door to her son's bedroom.

There was no sign of Fred, although his bed had clearly been slept in. She made her way to the family bathroom. He wasn't there either.

'Where are you hiding, Fred?' she called, anxiety rising within her. 'Come out this minute – this isn't funny.'

She raced through the first floor, checking each of the five bedrooms and three bathrooms. There was no sign of Fred.

Heart pounding, her legs turning to jelly beneath her, she practically fell down the stairs in the rush to enlist the help of Molly and Monika. The three of them searched the entire house and garden.

Fred was nowhere to be seen.

Joyce kept shouting out his name until she was hoarse, yet already she knew it would do no good. Her son was mischievous at times, like any eleven-year-old, but there was no way he would torture her like this. The moment he heard the panic in her voice, he'd have emerged from his hiding place, full of apologies for having frightened her.

And she was frightened. Terrified.

Someone had come into the house in the night and taken her child.

Seven

The Major Crime Investigation Team were alerted to the disappearance of young Fred Mildmay at 10.05 a.m., an hour after his mother had dialled 999 to report her son missing, the first responding officers having conducted a preliminary search of the house and the gated community in which it was located and found no trace of the boy.

Detective Inspector David Vogel, a recent transfer from the Metropolitan Police Force, was unfamiliar with the area where the supposed abduction had taken place. His first action was to type the postcode into his computer and study satellite imagery of Tarrant Park. Then he began a meticulous study of the report submitted by constables Yardley and Bolton, the two uniformed officers who had been dispatched to the Mildmay home to carry out the initial search.

According to Mrs Joyce Mildmay, she had last seen her eleven-year-old son the previous evening, when he went to bed at his usual time, just after 8.30 p.m. She did not realize he'd gone missing until breakfast time the following morning.

Yardley and Bolton reported that the boy's bed appeared to have been slept in, and his pyjamas were lying on top of the covers, as if tossed aside. They could find no signs of forced entry and the burglar alarm had not gone off. Neither the boy's mother or sister had heard anything suspicious during the night.

The officers had then asked Mrs Mildmay to check whether any clothes or other possessions were missing. She reported that the clothes he had been wearing the previous evening – black jeans, blue T-shirt and grey sweatshirt – were not on the bedroom chair where he usually left them. His favourite trainers and a much-prized All Saints leather bomber jacket were also missing. So, it appeared, was his iPhone.

Mrs Mildmay didn't know how much money her son had left of his weekly pocket money, but she was certain it couldn't be more than a few pounds at most. Not enough to get him far, and in any case she was adamant that her son would never run away from home – it was completely out of character.

Years of experience as a police officer had taught Vogel that parents were rarely willing to believe that their child had left home voluntarily. The fact that there were no signs of an intruder and the boy appeared to have left the house fully clothed and carrying his precious phone would, ordinarily, lead him to conclude that the mother was deluding herself. But as he monitored the reports coming in from officers responding to the missing person alert, he couldn't help feeling uneasy.

His senior officer, DCI Reg Hemmings, was of the same opinion. Within the hour a full-scale MCIT investigation was under way with Hemmings at the helm as Senior Investigating Officer, and Vogel working alongside DI Margo Hartley as joint deputy SIOs. Hartley, who was renowned for her organizational skills, was designated operations manager, overseeing the mechanics of the investigation from a dedicated incident room at MCIT headquarters in Kenneth Steele House. This left Vogel free to play a more flexible role.

In order to create an account on HOLMES, the Home Office Large Major Enquiry System, a case name had to be assigned. For the sake of confidentiality, the names of victims or suspects are never used; and ever since the infamous and unfortunately named Operation Swamp in the 1980s, which involved swamping inner-city and predominantly black communities with a zero-tolerance police presence, the names chosen have been as neutral as possible, and unconnected with the case. In the Met, these names are chosen from an approved list that has been decided in advance. Within the Avon and Somerset Constabulary, however, it fell to the senior officer working the case to come up with a name, the only criteria being that it must begin with the initial of the appropriate constabulary district – E for Bath, J for Weston-Super-Mare, F for Yeovil, and B for Bristol. It was Vogel, a devotee of backgammon, who came up with Operation Binache a backgammon redoubling convention – for the case of missing Fred Mildmay.

Like most forces, Avon and Somerset had a specialist kidnap and abduction unit. However, it was decided that until conclusive evidence emerged that Fred Mildmay had been taken by persons unknown, the operation would remain in the domain of the MCIT.

Vogel's first step was to do a preliminary Internet search on the Mildmays. Which was how he learned of the death of Charlie Mildmay. The yachting accident which claimed his life six months earlier had received considerable local media attention. Such a traumatic loss might well have left the boy upset and disturbed, and therefore liable to do something as drastic as running away from home.

Then Vogel looked deeper, investigating the family in the way that he did best, through the numerous records now stored online and readily accessible to those who knew their way around the Internet, whether or not they were a police officer. Records of business activities, financial status, property ownership and so on. For Vogel, accessing such records – and more – was child's play.

By noon he had assembled quite a dossier on young Fred Mildmay's family. And the more he learned, the stronger became his gut feeling that all was not as it should be.

As yet, Vogel still had no idea why or how Fred had gone missing, or whether foul play was involved. But that familiar sensation in his gut was telling him that this case was neither a straightforward domestic crime, nor – as part of him continued to hope, regardless of his misgivings – a small boy running away because he had fallen out with his mother or a sibling, or couldn't face going to school that day.

At 12.40 p.m. DCI Hemmings, frustrated at the inability of officers attending the scene to come up with a single sighting or clue to the boy's disappearance, told Vogel he wanted him to re-interview the family in person. Though they hadn't been working together long, Hemmings had faith in Vogel's ability to see things others didn't. And given Henry Tanner's status in the community and his influential connections, the DCI was determined there must be no slip-ups in their handling of the case.

Vogel was happy to comply. He preferred to take a hands-on approach. In fact his biggest flaw as a police officer was that he wasn't good at delegation. Aside from his old boss, DCI Nobby Clarke, whom he'd left behind at the Met when he'd secured his transfer to Avon and Somerset, there was only one person whose abilities Vogel had complete faith in and that was himself.

'I've requested a family liaison officer, too,' said Hemmings. 'We've no one available here, so Division are sending a uniform over: PC Dawn Saslow. She's just completed the FLO course. Oh, and she can drive. She'll be picking you up in a few minutes.'

Vogel was pleased that he would be accompanied by a woman. There was an old-fashioned side to him. He still reckoned, whether an FLO was assigned or not, that it was best to have a woman present when investigating a delicate family matter, particularly when it was something as serious as a missing child.

He ignored his senior officer's heavy-handed reference to PC Saslow's ability to drive. Vogel, having lived in London all his life, had never learned to drive. Previously stationed in the heart of the West End, he had relied on public transport and the occasional nerve-shattering ride in a squad car driven by some young constable desperate to show off their all-too-often dubiously acquired advanced driver's skills. This was not an option in the vast rural area covered by the Avon and Somerset Constabulary, and so it had been a condition of Vogel's transfer that he take driving lessons.

Thus far, Vogel had managed to complete only three lessons, which had been enough to convince him that it was unlikely he would ever pass his test. He had not, however, confided this in his superiors. Thus he was more than content to be PC Dawn Saslow's passenger as she navigated Bristol's nightmare traffic system.

By the time Saslow arrived in a squad car, squealing to a halt by the front doors to Kenneth Steele House, the early morning sunshine, which Joyce Mildmay had so fleetingly relished, was long gone. Aside from a brief respite during March and early April, it had rained incessantly since Vogel's arrival in the West Country. And it was pouring down now as he hurried to the waiting car, shoulders hunched and the collar of his inadequate corduroy jacket turned up against the elements.

If he'd realized how exceptionally wet it was in the West of England, Vogel told himself, he might not have allowed his wife to persuade him to move there. He'd never paid much attention to the weather in London, where tall buildings gave considerable protection. But he'd become obsessed with checking the forecasts since his transfer to the back of beyond. He was aware that most Bristolians would be horrified to hear their thriving and much-regenerated city referred to in such terms, but Vogel had lived and worked in the heart of the capital, and by his criteria Bristol barely qualified as urban. Green dripping stuff everywhere. And no backgammon scene worth mentioning. Or if there was, he had yet to discover it.

But the move hadn't been for his benefit, or even his wife's. They had uprooted themselves from London for their beloved daughter's sake. And as far as Vogel was concerned, when it came to Rosamund no sacrifice was too great.

The truth was that he would do anything for his daughter.

As he folded his long frame into the passenger seat of the standard-issue Ford hatchback, Dawn Saslow flashed a smile in his direction. She was small and dark with big eyes and seemed to be bursting with energy and enthusiasm. Just looking at her made Vogel feel old and weary. She was also impatient to be on her way; before he'd had time to introduce himself the squad car took off with another squeal of tyres and shot into a momentary gap in the city-centre traffic.

A local girl, Saslow knew her way round all the back-doubles, but even so it wasn't long before they found themselves caught in a crawling snake of vehicles inching along the Bath Road.

Saslow glanced at Vogel questioningly.

'Go on then,' murmured the DI with a distinct lack of enthusiasm.

Saslow grinned as she switched on the squad car's system of flashing lights and engaged the siren.

The procession of vehicles ahead veered to the left, as did the oncoming stream of traffic. Saslow guided the squad car at speed right down the middle.

'Like the parting of the Red Sea,' said Vogel, hunkering down in his seat.

'Me Moses!' said Saslow, flooring the accelerator.

She kept the lights flashing and the siren wailing for the rest of the journey and they seemed to reach Tarrant Park in no time.

Thanks to his morning's research, Vogel knew that Tarrant Park was the brainchild of a Bristol-based architect who had wanted to recreate the rarefied atmosphere of the famous St George's Hill development in Weybridge, where wealthy residents were closeted within a 900-acre estate with its own tennis club and golf course. The name, Tarrant Park, was a tribute to the man who created St George's Hill in the early twentieth century: Surrey builder Walter George Tarrant. Mansions were built in painstaking parody of the past – mock-Tudor, Georgian, art deco, arts and crafts – each in a minimum of an acre of land, and loosely grouped together, according to their style, along leafy lanes, drawing their names from their periods of architectural inspiration. And so the Mildmay home, The Firs, stood in Palladian Close, whilst

the faux-Tudor home of Henry and Felicity Tanner domi-
nated the corner of Drake Road and Raleigh Way. The prices
might be a fraction of its Thames Valley counterpart, where
properties frequently changed hands for sums in excess of ten
million pounds, but Tarrant Park had become the natural
habitat of the Somerset nouveau riche, who believed that just
living there gave them kudos.

Vogel, who had once attended the wedding reception of
an old chum of his wife's at St Georges Hill, knew what to
expect.

He checked his watch: 1.06 p.m. Fred Mildmay had been
reported missing four hours and one minute earlier. But
despite continuing house-to-house enquiries, the investigation
was no further forward. No one had seen Fred since he
climbed the stairs to bed at eight thirty the previous evening.

A uniformed security guard opened the electronic security
gates to let them in. Vogel wondered whether PCs Yardley
and Bolton had managed to track down the guard who'd
been on duty last night. Apparently he'd gone fishing straight
after his shift. CCTV coverage of the gate area was also
already being studied by the specialist unit back at Kenneth
Steele House. In the meantime Vogel had little interest in the
guard on duty that morning, who it seemed had little interest
in Vogel. He didn't bother to approach the vehicle, let alone
check their identities. The rain, which was still falling heavily, may have been responsible for his reluctance to leave the
shelter of the gatehouse. Vogel supposed it was fair enough
that he would merely wave them through, but all the same he
couldn't help wondering about the diligence of the estate's
security operatives. Tarrant Park was a relatively trouble-free
place. Professional burglars were inclined to pick easier tar-
gets, and the gated community would not be remotely on the

radar of casual thieves or vandals. It was possible that the security guards who worked there were not as alert as they should be. They might also have been distracted by the big wedding reception which had been held at the tennis club the previous evening, resulting in a considerable number of strangers entering and leaving Tarrant Park throughout the day and evening.

PC Saslow motored slowly through the gates and Vogel began to look around him. Even though he thought he had known what to expect, he found his jaw dropping.

This was another world, an unreal world displaying little semblance to any sort of reality. Or to any sort of reality that Vogel had ever encountered. The houses were massive and imposing, each one set within a considerable expanse of land; some were not even visible from the leafy lanes which ran through the estate. Vogel felt no envy. Indeed, the thought of trying to make a home in such a closeted place filled him with horror.

'Did you ever see that movie *Stepford Wives*?' he enquired of PC Saslow, unknowingly echoing Joyce Mildmay's opinion of the place.

'No, sir,' replied the PC.

'No. Of course not. You're too young.'

'I like old movies, sir.'

'Ummm, you should watch out for it on TV then.'

'What's it about, sir?'

'It's about a place where all the women are programmed to do as they're told without question and to feel no emotion,' said Vogel.

PC Saslow considered this for a moment.

'Bit like your average police station, then,' she said, flashing him a toothy grin.

Vogel was busy peering morosely through the rain at the street and house names. He wondered how Saslow could see to drive in the torrential downpour. The windscreen wipers could barely cope, and even though the air-conditioning was going full blast the windows were misting over.

He was just making a mental note to check whether it had been raining heavily all night, which would make it less likely that young Fred Mildmay would have run away from home voluntarily, when he spotted the sign.

'There it is,' he said, pointing back at the turning they had just driven past. 'Palladian Close.'

Saslow reversed. Far too quickly, Vogel thought. Visibility was even worse through the rear window. He had become far more aware of the difficulties driving presented since he'd started taking lessons, and more and more convinced that every journey he took was likely to end in disaster. And that he would never learn to drive.

The Firs was the second property on the right. Later, when the media got wind of the boy's disappearance, there would no doubt be crowds of reporters standing around in the rain, brandishing notebooks, microphones and cameras. For now though there was no one in sight.

The wrought-iron gates – which in Vogel's estimation rivalled the Queen Mother memorial gates at the Park Lane entrance to Hyde Park both in size and vulgarity – opened as if by magic as they approached. The missing boy's mother had known Vogel was on his way. She or someone in the house must have been looking out for his arrival.

The paved drive was fifty metres long and lined on either side by narrow flower beds planted with daffodils, now in the process of dying down at the end of their season. Each plant had been neatly tied. Vogel suspected that everything about this property, and more than likely the lifestyle of its occupants, would be similarly ordered. At the top of the drive was a circular turning area, mainly gravelled, with a shrub-surrounded ornamental fountain in the middle. To the left, just off the drive before the circular area was reached, was a covered parking area in which several cars were already parked. Saslow slowed down, but Vogel gestured for her to carry on and park in front of the porticoed mock-Georgian front entrance. As they climbed out of the car Vogel noticed that the door already stood open.

A tall, good-looking black man in a well-tailored grey business suit stepped through the doorway. Ignoring the rain, he loped down the wide marble-tiled steps towards them, confidently offering an outstretched right hand to Vogel. The detective inspector, suddenly aware that his elderly corduroy jacket was so damp that it was sticking to his shoulders, shook the hand and introduced himself and PC Saslow.

'I'm Stephen Hardcastle,' said the man. 'I'm the family's solicitor.'

Vogel shot Hardcastle an enquiring glance. 'They thought they needed a solicitor?'

Hardcastle looked momentarily startled but recovered quickly. He would, thought Vogel. 'Of course not,' he said. 'I'm also an old family friend. I was at university with Joyce, Fred's mother, and her late husband Charlie. We've always been extremely close. And I'm godfather to their eldest son, Mark.' His accent was upper-class English. His manners and easy style had clearly been public-school honed.

'I see,' said Vogel, who was wondering why Hardcastle felt the need to explain himself in so much detail.

'We are all so pleased to see you, Detective Inspector,' said Hardcastle. 'It's imperative that we find Fred quickly. His mother is near breaking point, I fear. Please, come on in, come on in.'

The three of them hurried up the steps together. Vogel's feet, clad in unfamiliar leather-soled shoes because he had yet to replace his recently deceased Hush Puppies, slipped on wet marble as he glanced up at the burglar alarm just below the eaves. More security which would have to have been evaded, had the Mildmay boy indeed been abducted.

At the top of the steps Stephen Hardcastle stepped aside and ushered Vogel and Saslow through the door into a large hallway, then down a black-and-white tiled corridor towards a door at the far end, which was standing ajar. Vogel paused when he reached it and glanced enquiringly at the solicitor.

'Everybody's in there, in the kitchen,' said Hardcastle. He pushed the door open and waved Vogel in.

'Major Crime Investigation Team,' he announced. 'Perhaps something will bloody well happen now.' Then he glanced guiltily at Vogel and muttered an apology: 'It's the waiting, Detective Inspector, it's been terribly stressful for all of us.'

Vogel inclined his head in acknowledgement. He understood. Waiting for news of a lost loved one was torment of the worst kind. Even the dreadful confirmation that there was no longer hope, the knowledge of death and the closure of learning the manner of it, could be less painful.

But it was far too early to be harbouring thoughts of that nature. Step by step, that was Vogel's mantra. No matter how impatient, how wealthy, how influential the next of kin, he would take each step at his own pace.

Eight

Vogel strode purposefully into the kitchen. At least he hoped he looked purposeful. And authoritative. Although he never thought he did authoritative terribly well.

He again introduced himself, and PC Saslow, explaining that she was a family liaison officer who had been assigned to assist the anxious family in any way she could.

Everybody was gathered in the kitchen. It was a big room, but appeared to be full of people. And they were all staring at Vogel.

Vogel found his own eyes drawn to a woman in her early forties who was sitting at the table with her arm round a teenage girl. Both had obviously been crying and looked as if they might start again at any moment.

It was obvious that this must be the mother and sister of the missing boy.

'Mrs Joyce Mildmay?' enquired Vogel.

The woman nodded, wiping her eyes with one hand and struggling to pull herself together.

Vogel shifted his questioning gaze to the girl.

'M-my daughter, Molly, Fred's sister,' Joyce said, confirming Vogel's assumption.

Merely giving voice to Fred's name caused her eyes to fill up again.

'Good afternoon, Mrs Mildmay,' said Vogel. 'I want you to know that my team and I have one aim, and that is to do everything we can to bring your son safely home to you. In order to do so, I'm afraid I need to ask you some more questions. I know you have already given a statement to the police officers who responded to your 999 call, but I need to make sure we haven't overlooked anything – even the smallest detail could turn out to be significant.'

Joyce Mildmay nodded. 'Of course,' she said in a weak, shaky voice. Her daughter stifled a sob.

'Firstly, could you tell me the names of everyone in this room, please,' Vogel continued, still looking at Joyce Mildmay.

Joyce tried to speak but her voice failed her. She took a moment to compose herself, then waved a hand towards the tall man leaning against the Aga at the far side of the room.

'Th-that's m-my father, Henry Tanner.'

Vogel studied Tanner with interest. This was some man, he thought. Thanks to his online research he knew that Henry Tanner was the undisputed patriarch of a prominent family, and chief executive of an intriguing and possibly questionable company, Tanner-Max – the family firm in which Fred Mildmay's father Charlie had been a partner until his premature death.

In addition to its high annual turnover, Tanner-Max owned a considerable amount of valuable property in the area. As did individuals within the family; primarily Henry Tanner, but there were also properties in the names of Felicity Tanner and Joyce Mildmay.

Furthermore, from the Avon and Somerset Constabulary's

own records, Vogel had discovered that over the years no less than three investigations had been launched into the activities of Tanner-Max. No specific reasons had been given, other than that the company's financial records did not appear to match the level of business. All three investigations had been abandoned at an early stage, and there was no trace of the more detailed records which Vogel would have expected to find in the archive.

He had fired off an internal email or two enquiring about this, but had yet to learn anything of consequence.

Henry stepped towards Vogel, gesturing to his daughter that he would take charge. Vogel had expected no less.

'Good afternoon, Detective Inspector,' he said. 'Please, let me assist.'

He pointed first to a lanky young man with a shock of unruly hair, standing awkwardly by the window. He bore a striking resemblance to the photos Vogel had found online of a young Charlie Mildmay, though the hair was not quite as long.

'That's Mark, my grandson, Joyce's eldest boy,' said Henry. 'Stephen you've already met. Next to him is my wife, Felicity, Fred's gran. At the table, opposite Joyce and Molly, that's Janet, our PA at Tanner's, who damn near runs the place for us.'

Henry stretched his lips into a thin, forced smile as he gestured towards a tall young woman who was washing up cups and mugs at the sink.

'That's Monika. She helps Joyce out, and Felicity too. Don't know what we'd do without her.'

Monika turned from the sink and contrived a nervous stretch of the lips that didn't quite pass for a smile. She too looked as if she had been crying.

Henry waved one hand at a tall portly man in his sixties, who was sitting in the room's one armchair but in a rather upright, uncomfortable manner.

'And that's Jim Grant,' said Henry. 'Dr Jim Grant, our GP and a family friend. He's been looking after us for years. I thought it might be a good idea to get him over in case any-one needed medical assistance. The women, you know . . .'

His voice trailed off. Vogel knew what Henry Tanner meant all right. Women were obviously the weaker sex in Henry's eyes. To be diligently cared for, to be nurtured, but almost certainly never to be treated as equals. Vogel had learned enough about Henry from his morning's research to have assumed that. The older man's words merely reinforced his assumption.

Henry then pointed towards a small woman with a dis-proportionately large bust who was hovering around the room, even now there was a police presence, unable it seemed to settle anywhere. She was no chicken, as Vogel's mother would have said, and was wearing far too much make-up for a woman of her years. Her top was too tight over her strain-ing bosoms. Her hair was peroxide white. She looked com-pletely out of place.

'And this is Miriam Fox, our neighbour—' said Henry.

Before he could elaborate, the woman leapt in: 'Yes, I'm right next door. Came as soon as I heard. Dreadful thing. Poor little lad. Only yesterday I watched him playing in the garden. Such a sweet little boy. I had to come round, but if you don't want me, well, I'd better be getting back. My Joe's due home early today and I haven't started on his dinner yet and . . .'

Miriam Fox spoke estuary English with more than a hint

of Essex. And she was gabbling. It was Vogel's turn to interrupt.

'Yes, yes, Mrs Fox. As you're only next door you can leave. It's the family I need to speak to first. But we will need to talk to you again later. Perhaps you would be kind enough to give your details to PC Saslow here?'

Miriam Fox said of course she would.

Vogel turned his attention to Joyce Mildmay.

'Right, Mrs Mildmay, perhaps we could have our chat straight away?' he asked. 'Is there somewhere private we could go?'

'Yes, we can go into the sitting room,' said Joyce, standing up.

'Thank you,' responded Vogel, turning to address the others. 'And, please, would everyone else stay here. You may already have given interviews, but I'm afraid we do need to speak to you all again.'

The two police officers followed Joyce out of the room. In the sitting room she sank into one of the two big brocade sofas on either side of what Vogel assumed, somewhat uncharitably, to be a reproduction Adam fireplace. Well everything else about the house was fake. His wife would never have anything reproduction in their home. Antiques were Mary's passion. She couldn't afford to pay a lot, but she was an expert bargain hunter interested only in the genuine article.

Vogel sat on an upright chair, with Saslow on another alongside, looking slightly down at Joyce.

'So, Mrs Mildmay, would you please take me through the chain of events which led to you discovering that your son was missing?' he asked.

Joyce did so, in as much detail as Vogel could have hoped for in the circumstances. Once or twice, she seemed about to burst into tears again, but she managed to hold herself together reasonably well.

'So after you went up to Fred's bedroom and discovered that he wasn't there, after you, Molly, and Monika had been right through the house and made certain that Fred was no longer inside, what did you do then?' he asked.

'We checked the garden. And the shed down the bottom where Charlie used to mess about with bits of carpentry and stuff. He was always good at that sort of thing. He was restoring an old wooden sailing boat when we met . . .'

Joyce paused for a moment, disappearing into a long-ago world.

'Fred seemed to take after him in that,' she continued. 'They were building a model boat, the pair of them. They used to spend hours down there. When Charlie could spare the time, of course. He was always so busy . . .'

Joyce swallowed hard. Vogel wondered what she was thinking.

'We didn't expect Fred to be there, though. Not at that hour in the morning. Likes his bed too much, Fred. And in any case I don't think he's spent any time in the shed since his father died. He misses his dad terribly. Anyway, we looked there, just in case. Then I rang Mum and she came over, and we phoned round anyone we could think of who Fred might have gone to. We didn't really believe he would have done that, gone to any of the people we called, but we made ourselves go through the motions, tried not to panic too much, tried to think clearly. Molly joined in. She and Fred are at the same school, so she knows a lot of Fred's classmates. She went on to directory enquiries and got the home numbers of anyone she could.'

'And nobody had seen or heard anything of Fred?'

'No. As soon as it was nine o'clock we called the school, just in case. But he wasn't wearing his school uniform. Fred was never early, and even if he had taken off on his own he wouldn't have gone to his school. I was pretty sure of that.'

'Was that when you called us?'

Joyce nodded. 'Yes. Mum, Molly and I were all positive Fred wouldn't have taken off on his own. I think all three of us wanted to call the police earlier, but we were kidding ourselves that it was going to be all right, that it was maybe some silly prank. Somehow dialling 999 made it real. Brought home what we were all thinking. What we were afraid of. That somebody had taken Fred.'

Vogel nodded encouragingly.

'We'd already called Dad. He, Mark and Stephen came straight back from the office, with Janet. They took Molly and Monika and some of the neighbours we'd contacted and set off to look for Fred. I don't suppose any of us thought they were going to find him wandering around the estate, or nearby, but it was better than doing nothing. Mum and I stayed here, with Miriam from next door, in case he came back. Although by that time I'd stopped thinking he was going to. Not of his own accord . . .'

Joyce's voice tailed off again.

'Mrs Mildmay, I noticed on the way in that you have a burglar alarm,' said Vogel. 'Do you normally switch it on at night, and was it switched on last night?'

'Yes,' she said. 'There's an exclusion setting so that it operates only downstairs. I'm sure it was on. I switch it on every night. Dad had the alarm installed. He's very keen on security. I didn't think about it before.' She paused. 'It didn't go off, obviously . . .'

She let the words drift.

'I'll get it checked out, but these systems are not easy to tamper with,' said Vogel. 'So the likelihood is that if you switched it on, somebody must have switched it off in order for Fred to leave the house without activating the alarm.'

'Oh my God,' said Joyce.

She shook her head. 'I can't explain it, Mr Vogel.'

'Did Fred know how to operate the alarm?'

'Well, yes. We each have our own remote control, so we can switch it on and off.'

'Do you remember if the alarm was on when you got up this morning?'

'Yes . . .' She looked uncertain. 'That is, I think so. I may not have noticed. I always push the button on the remote before I go downstairs. It could already have been off, I suppose.'

'Or switched on again, having been switched off. This suggests that either Fred left of his own free will and deactivated the alarm in order to do so, or whoever took him was able to deactivate the alarm. Does anyone else apart from you and your children know the passcode or have a remote control?'

'Mum and Dad . . . I can't think of anyone else.'

Joyce had been looking down. She raised her gaze to meet Vogel's. He could see the panic in her eyes.

'Look, Detective Inspector, I can't explain about the alarm. I really can't. But Fred would never leave the house in the middle of the night of his own free will. Someone's taken my boy, I'm sure of it.'

There was no doubt in Vogel's mind that Joyce Mildmay's distress was genuine. The woman was in pain. From the look in her eyes, the mental anguish she was suffering went far beyond anything she had ever experienced. There was also bewilderment there, and something else, something Vogel could not quite put his finger on. Fear, perhaps, but not just the fear of a mother who dreads that she might have lost her son.

'We don't know that, Mrs Mildmay,' he said, still trying to evaluate the woman's response, and also trying to sound more reassuring than he actually felt. 'We have to keep an open mind while we continue with our enquiries. Meanwhile, I know it's difficult for people to think straight when something like this happens, but I want you to try to stay calm and think as hard as you can. To begin with, are you absolutely positive there is nowhere else Fred would have gone?'

Joyce shook her head.

'Think, Mrs Mildmay,' Vogel persisted.

'I am thinking,' responded Joyce sharply. 'In any case, you don't understand. Molly spent the morning going through every number on Fred's phone. She called everyone on it – his school friends, his football team-mates and the coach, his cricket mates. Even people who live miles away. There is no one and nowhere else. There really isn't.'

Vogel was blinking furiously behind his horn-rimmed spectacles.

'Mrs Mildmay, you told the officers who came here earlier that Fred's phone was missing, that he must have taken it with him. Indeed, you said that he never went anywhere without it. And you mentioned that Molly had to get on to directory enquiries to get numbers for his classmates. But now you're saying that Molly went through every number on Fred's phone.'

Joyce nodded. 'We didn't have Fred's phone when Molly first tried to call his schoolmates. Nor when the two policemen came. But eventually we found the phone in the bathroom, in the pocket of his dressing gown. That was typical Fred. He's so attached to that phone, he would take it with him to the bathroom rather than leave it in the bedroom for a few minutes. But he's also absent-minded. So he must have forgotten about the phone and gone to bed. We're always finding it in odd places.'

'But what if he planned to leave the house – he would look for his phone then, presumably. And he'd be reluctant to leave the house without it, wouldn't that be the case?' asked Vogel.

Joyce nodded. She was having real trouble holding back the tears now. Vogel gave her a moment to compose her-self. The business of the alarm had led him to believe that, although allegedly so out of character, young Fred Mildmay must have taken himself off somewhere in the middle of the night. The fact that he'd left his phone behind was a totally contradictory piece of evidence.

'You do realize the significance of this, don't you, Mrs Mildmay?'

Joyce sniffed, swallowed and nodded again, almost imper-ceptibly.

'Mrs Mildmay, I'm sorry to have to tell you this but I sus-pect this new information makes it far more likely that your son has been removed from this house by a third party, and possibly against his will,' said Vogel.

'I know,' said Joyce, in a voice that was little more than a whisper. 'Oh my God, I know. I realized it as soon as we found the damned phone.'

Vogel continued to stare at her. There was something about her that wasn't right. Police officers are trained not to exclude the parents of a missing child as suspects. It is a statistical fact that in the majority of cases either the parents or somebody close to them, more often than not another family member, is responsible for that child being missing. Vogel's initial gut reaction had been that Joyce would not have harmed her son. He saw nothing in her behaviour to suggest that; her demeanour was unmistakably that of a caring, shocked and distraught mother. However, something was troubling him about Joyce Mildmay.

He cast his mind back over the case notes, including the first interviews conducted by PCs Yardley and Bolton.

'You didn't report it, did you, when you found the phone?' he continued. 'You must have realized how important it was. Why didn't you call the police again straight away?'

Joyce looked puzzled. 'We didn't think,' she muttered. 'We were too busy hoping that now we had his phone we had a better chance of finding Fred. Molly just pounced on it. Later we knew you were coming, and obviously we would tell you . . .' She stopped speaking. Then began again after a brief pause. 'I guess we didn't want to dwell too much on what finding that phone might mean.'

Vogel changed tack. 'Mrs Mildmay, do you know of anyone who might have wanted to take your son from you?'

Joyce appeared startled, as if she hadn't expected that question. But again there was something else there. Vogel thought she was trying to avoid meeting his eye. She shook her head, leaning forward slightly at the same time.

Vogel decided to go for it.

'Mrs Mildmay, is there something you are not telling me?' he asked.

Joyce shook her head again.

'Mrs Mildmay, have you heard of the golden hour period?' Vogel enquired, and continued to speak without giving her time to respond. 'It's the twenty-four hours or so after a crime has been committed. That's the period when we are most likely to find a person who has been abducted. If you know anything that might help us take full advantage of the golden hour, you should tell me now. You seem certain that your son has been taken. If there is even the slightest chance that you know something that might lead to whoever could have taken Fred, then every minute you hold that information back you lessen the chances of his being returned to you safely.'

Joyce did not respond for several seconds. Then she raised her head and looked Vogel straight in the eye for the first time since the interview had begun.

With his floppy brown hair, greying at the edges, and those horn-rimmed glasses, he was more like a university lecturer than a copper. He appeared to be clever. She so hoped he was. She decided she had to trust him. Up to a point, anyway.

Wordlessly she reached into the pocket of her cardigan and handed Vogel the letter from her dead husband which she had received two days earlier.

Nine

Vogel read the letter carefully. Joyce sat in silence whilst he did so. When he'd finished he stood up and turned to Dawn Saslow.

'Please stay with Mrs Mildmay, PC Saslow,' he said. 'I need to make an urgent phone call.'

He left the room, and once outside used his mobile to call his senior officer, DCI Hemmings.

'There's been a development, guv,' he said. 'I don't reckon this is a kidnap. More likely somebody in this family knows darned well what's happened to Fred Mildmay. I'll explain later. I'm calling now because I need back-up soonest. If we put some pressure on this lot I reckon we could get an early result. And I could well be bringing at least two of 'em in for formal questioning.'

Hemmings agreed to do what he could as soon as he could. Vogel returned to the sitting room. He again sat down opposite Joyce Mildmay, and next to Dawn Saslow.

Joyce Mildmay looked absolutely drained. Vogel didn't care. He had far from finished with her.

'Who else knows about this?' he demanded, holding up the letter in one hand.

'Well, Charlie left it with Stephen Hardcastle to be

delivered to me only after his death, and Janet must have known about it too,' Joyce replied. 'But Stephen claimed neither he nor anyone else knew the contents. The letter came in a sealed envelope. And I certainly haven't told anyone what it said.'

She explained how Charlie's letter hadn't arrived until two days previously, more than six months after her husband had died, something explained away by Stephen as a clerical error.

'Do you accept that explanation?' asked Vogel.

'I don't know, I suppose so,' muttered Joyce. 'It was only, well, when Stephen came round and I confronted him about it I had this feeling he was hiding something. He didn't seem quite himself. He's such a po-faced bloke. It's hard to know what he's really feeling or what's going on inside his head . . .'

Joyce looked down at her hands. Vogel wondered what she was thinking about. She had just told him that she felt Stephen Hardcastle was hiding something. He felt pretty sure she was also still hiding something.

'But this time, well, he seemed uncomfortable, and didn't seem able to hide it,' Joyce continued. 'The whole thing didn't feel right somehow. He was definitely on edge.'

'So you thought Stephen had read the letter, that he knew what it said, did you?' asked Vogel.

'I wasn't sure,' Joyce replied again. 'But I did have the feeling that he might have done.'

'Do you have the envelope?'

'There were two, the one with Charlie's handwriting on it containing his letter, and then the bigger Tanner-Max envelope that Janet had put it in when she sent the letter on to me.'

Joyce delved into her pocket again and handed the detective the two envelopes. He examined the one carrying Charlie's handwriting, reading the inscription on the front first: *For my darling Joyce, to be opened only in the event of my death*. Then he held the envelope up to the light so that he could study its seal.

The envelope had clearly been ripped open. Vogel glanced enquiringly at Joyce. She appeared to understand at once what he meant.

'I was so shocked I just tore at it,' she said.

Vogel nodded. It was more or less impossible for him to ascertain whether or not the envelope had been opened before its delivery to Joyce. But he was pretty sure forensics would be able to tell him.

'Have you any idea what your husband meant by any of this?' he asked.

Joyce shook her head.

'No, I haven't.'

She explained how neither her father nor her husband ever talked about their work, and were both inclined to be secretive about their lives away from the family.

'Or protective, Dad would say, if pressed,' she said.

She also told Vogel how her father had always been such a good grandfather, and had been a good father both to her and her dead brother.

'So was there never anything . . .' Vogel paused, searching for the right words. 'Never anything inappropriate concerning your father when you were growing up?'

Joyce uttered a mirthless laugh.

'You mean, did he grope us? Is he a closet paedophile?'

Vogel inclined his head. He supposed that was exactly

what he did mean. He didn't speak, waiting for Joyce to continue, which she eventually did.

'No, Mr Vogel. I will admit it did cross my mind that was what Charlie meant in the letter. Particularly when he said I should protect Fred, but Dad wouldn't be interested in Molly. Then I thought about it, remembering my own childhood. That was one thing I would have had to have known about Dad, surely, if there was any truth in it. I thought about Dad's behaviour with William. They always appeared to have a pretty wonderful relationship, and Dad was devastated when William died. They were extremely close, but I can't believe there was ever anything creepy about it. I would have noticed, wouldn't I?'

'And yet your husband specifically warned you that you needed to protect Fred. And now your son is missing.'

Joyce stared at him blankly.

'Mrs Mildmay, I do wish you had told us about this letter earlier,' Vogel continued. 'It does throw a rather different light on things and could be hugely significant. May I ask you why you didn't show it at once to the officers who answered your 999 call this morning?'

Joyce took several seconds to answer.

'I think there may be a culture of secrecy in this family,' she said eventually, an answer that took Vogel by surprise. 'I've been brought up that way. I knew the letter could have all sorts of unpleasant implications. I thought about giving it to the officers, but then, I didn't. I somehow couldn't . . .'

'Mrs Mildmay, you had just discovered that your son was missing. You'd called the emergency services. Isn't it surprising, and reprehensible, that you didn't do and say everything in your power to help the officers who responded to that call?'

Vogel knew he was probably being overly tough on the woman. It was deliberate. He wanted to make sure she wasn't concealing any more vital evidence, keeping any more secrets.

'I suppose it is, yes,' admitted Joyce, stifling a sob. 'But you have to understand I was still thinking Fred might turn up at any moment. Making myself believe that. Hoping it, anyway. A part of me couldn't accept that something serious was happening. And I didn't let myself link it with the letter. Not at first. It was when we found the phone, well Molly found it, she kept going round and round the house looking for anything that might help, it was then that I started to get really frantic. And now, well half a day has passed and nobody has any idea where Fred is. Please find him, Mr Vogel. Please find my son.'

Vogel blinked at her through those thick spectacles as she broke down in floods of tears. He was never comfortable with displays of emotion. For him that was one of the most difficult aspects of cases like this. There was nothing he could do or say that would comfort the woman – and the more he learned about the machinations of this family, the less inclined he felt to offer them comfort. His priority was the welfare of young Fred, the innocent victim in all this.

'I will do everything in my power to find your son, Mrs Mildmay,' he said. 'But if I am to do that I will need to confront both Stephen Hardcastle and your father with the contents of this letter. You have already told me that you suspect Stephen of having read the letter. Do you think your father may have read it too?'

Joyce wiped away her tears. Vogel detected an edge of bitterness in her voice as she told him, 'If Stephen read the letter then he would definitely have shown it to Dad. Nobody around here does anything without consulting my father.'

'And you believe that they deliberately withheld the letter from you, is that so?'

'Well, yes. My father wouldn't have wanted me to see the things Charlie said about him and the business. I mean, I know it doesn't make sense – why keep it from me for six months and then send it? I'd have expected them to destroy it. I had no idea it existed, so I'd have been none the wiser.'

'That's a question I also would like the answer to, Mrs Mildmay,' said Vogel. 'Now, I must ask you again: are you sure you didn't tell anyone about the letter, even if you didn't reveal the contents?'

'No, I was too shocked by it,' Joyce replied. 'I decided I would try to find out what lay behind it in a subtle way. That was the idea, anyway. I began by asking Mum. I tried to be casual, but I failed dismally. Mum cottoned on at once that I had an ulterior motive. I denied it. But she knew I wasn't being straight with her. She kept telling me that she knew something must have happened and demanding I tell her what it was.'

'But you didn't?'

'No. Half an hour later I had Dad on the phone; Mum had told him as soon as he got home from work.'

'And yet you didn't challenge your father about the letter, not even after Fred's disappearance. Why is that, Mrs Mildmay?'

'I don't know. I was in shock, I suppose. And denial – I kept telling myself that there had to be some simple explanation and clinging to the hope that Fred would walk through the door any minute. That's how it is in this family: we don't do confrontation, not with Dad. I just couldn't. Not then . . .'

'I see.'

In truth, Vogel did not begin to see. But then a thought occurred to him. If he hadn't been so caught up with the implications of Charlie Mildmay's message from the dead, he would have thought of it earlier.

'Mrs Mildmay, was there an accompanying letter from Stephen Hardcastle, along with the one left for you by your husband?'

Joyce nodded. She glanced at the crumpled handful of papers Vogel was holding.

'Isn't it there?' she asked.

Vogel shook his head.

Joyce delved again in her pocket and came up with a folded sheet of A4 paper, which she held out to him.

Printed on Tanner-Max headed stationery, it read:

Dear Mrs Mildmay,

We would like to apologize for failing to forward the enclosed letter from Mr Mildmay until now, due to an error in filing. If there is anything else we can do to assist you, please do not hesitate to contact this office.

It ended in the way solicitors and other businesses frequently sign off their correspondence, without reference to a specific individual: *Yours sincerely, Tanner-Max.*

Vogel was puzzled.

'Bit formal, isn't it, considering that it came from a man who is one of your oldest friends?' he enquired.

'Is it?' responded Joyce. 'I barely looked at it. I saw Charlie's handwriting on the enclosed envelope and that was all I was interested in.'

There was a scratchy signature after the typed sign-off, or

was it initials? Vogel couldn't make it out. He passed the letter back to Joyce.

'Is that Stephen Hardcastle's signature?' he asked.

Joyce glanced down. 'Oh. No. I don't think it is. I didn't notice. It's Janet's.'

'Janet, the PA?'

'Yes.'

'I can see you're surprised,' Vogel commented. 'I find that surprising too.'

'Well, not exactly,' responded Joyce. 'More surprised that I hadn't noticed. Janet does sometimes address the family as Mr and Mrs. She's quite formal in written correspondence. And she often signs letters on behalf of Stephen, my father, and Charlie too, when he was alive.'

'Routine correspondence, yes, but surely not something as sensitive as this?'

'I don't know. Maybe Stephen was embarrassed about the delay. Maybe that's why he asked Janet to send the letter on. How do I know what his reasons were? Is it important?'

'It could be, Mrs Mildmay, it could be very important,' replied Vogel thoughtfully. 'I will certainly be taking it up with Stephen Hardcastle and with your father. In the meantime, you can go back to the kitchen and join the others, but I must ask you not to mention anything that we have discussed, particularly the letter. Do you understand?'

'Oh yes,' said Joyce. 'I wouldn't dream of it.'

Vogel was just emerging from the kitchen, having escorted Joyce back to her family and discreetly instructed PC Saslow to make sure no details of the interview were shared with the family, when the doorbell rang. It was PCs Yardley and Bolton, returning from conducting house-to-house enquiries.

Vogel rapidly brought them up to date on the latest developments:

'We need information fast, so provided they cooperate I'm hoping it won't be necessary to caution and formally interview everyone in the house. But there are two people I may need you to transport to the video suite at Lockleaze so that their interviews can be recorded. First let's see how the preliminary interviews go, then we can take it from there.'

He led the two constables to the kitchen, where PC Saslow was standing by the door like a sentry. Under the circumstances, Vogel rather approved of that.

Joyce Mildmay had returned to the same chair at the kitchen table where she'd been sitting when Vogel had arrived.

'PC Bolton, please accompany Mr Tanner and Mr Hardcastle into the sitting room, and I'll join you in a moment,' the DI instructed.

Vogel wanted them separated from the rest – even though he had PC Saslow on sentry duty and intended to keep her there.

Stephen Hardcastle made his way to the door without demur, but Henry Tanner looked as if he was about to protest. Then he thought better of it and fell in behind Hardcastle as Bolton ushered them both from the room.

Vogel wanted to let them stew for a bit while he gleaned what he could from the others, particularly the PA, Janet. But even though she was the most promising subject, he intended to delay talking to her. He had a feeling he might learn something from the others which would prove useful in persuading her to cooperate.

'I need to talk to each of you individually,' Vogel announced.

He glanced towards Joyce. 'Is there another downstairs room I could use?'

She nodded listlessly. 'The dining room,' she said.

He thanked her, then asked Monika to join him.

'You too, Yardley,' he instructed, leading the way out of the kitchen.

In addition to the kitchen and the sitting room there were two other doors leading off the hallway. Vogel glanced enquiringly at Monika, who gestured to the one which was nearest.

Vogel pushed the door open to reveal a room furnished with a big Georgian dining table, chairs and sideboard – all of it, like the Adam fireplace in the sitting room, reproduction.

He pulled two of the chairs away from the table and gestured for Monika to sit. Yardley was still standing. Vogel invited him to sit too. He wanted these preliminary interviews to be as informal as possible.

The young woman confirmed that she had arrived at the house at eight that morning.

'During term time I help with the children's breakfast and getting them ready for school, then when they go I load the dishwasher with the breakfast things, I tidy the kitchen, and I help Mrs Mildmay clear up after them,' explained Monika.

Vogel, as ever, had done his homework. He knew that she was twenty-four years old and came from Kosovo, Albania. Her English was good, if a tad stilted, with only the occasional grammatical error. Her pronunciation was excellent.

'They are lovely children, but perhaps not the most tidy,' said Monika with a half smile.

She was a pretty girl, tall and slim with cropped dark

brown hair and pale skin. But Vogel noticed that the smile did not reach her eyes. There remained an emptiness in them.

'When did you come to the UK, Monika?' he asked, opening with an easy, unthreatening question to put her at ease.

'In 1999,' she replied. 'At the end of the war. My father, he fight in the Kosovo Liberation Army. We do not know what happened to him . . .'

Her voice tailed off. She glanced down at her hands, lying on the table before her.

Vogel was aware that the Serbian military had decimated the KLA, amidst widespread allegations of atrocities. So Monika had arrived in the UK as a nine-year-old refugee. The poignant emptiness in her eyes was disturbing; it made Vogel wonder what horrors Monika and her family had experienced.

'I see,' said Vogel inadequately. 'I'm sorry. I interrupted you. You were taking me through your morning here.'

'Yes. Usually I stay until midday. I clean all the house. I have a routine. A rota. This morning I was to clean bedrooms . . .'

Monika paused, frowning. Remembering what had happened, Vogel thought.

'Go on, Monika,' he prompted.

'But soon after I arrive today, Mrs Mildmay went upstairs to hurry up Fred and discovered he was not in his room,' she said, corroborating the account Vogel had been given by Joyce Mildmay.

'At once we began to look everywhere for him, the three of us: Molly, Mrs Mildmay and I. We couldn't find him. Not anywhere. Mrs Mildmay called her mother. We all kept looking, and Molly began phoning people. Then Mrs Mildmay called the police. I do not believe this has happened. I just do not believe it. The family, they are like my own family, already they are . . .'

Now that she'd started, Monika couldn't seem to stop talking. Maybe it was a kind of nervous reaction, Vogel thought. He let her ramble on for a while, but eventually he ended the interview, thanked Monika, and asked PC Yardley to escort her back to the kitchen.

Next to be interviewed was Dr Grant. The GP confirmed that he had been called by Henry Tanner some hours after Fred's disappearance, and had not seen the boy, his mother or his siblings for at least a month previously. Jim Grant seemed to have no information that might assist the investigation, so Vogel quickly moved on to his next subject: Mark Mildmay, whom Vogel felt to be far more likely to be of interest. The DI already knew that Fred's older brother worked with his grandfather in the family business, and the letter had implied that he was already embroiled in whatever it was Charlie Mildmay had tried to warn his wife about. Vogel did not propose to question him in that regard, yet. For the time being, he did not wish to reveal the existence of Charlie's letter, let alone its contents, to anyone who was not already aware of it. Instead he set about trying to ascertain the kind of man Mark was, and to study his reactions to the disturbing events of the day.

Mark Mildmay's whole body seemed to be trembling when Yardley led him into the dining room and indicated that he should sit down at the table opposite Vogel. His face was ashen beneath his shock of dark-blond hair. He was a thin young man, but his distress made him look even thinner, emphasizing the hollows beneath his cheekbones.

He also looked frightened. Could it be that Mark Mildmay was afraid of something beyond the prospect of losing his younger brother?

Mark relaxed a little as Vogel began to take him step by step through his movements that morning. He had left his flat above the garage at his grandparents' well before eight, driving off not long after his grandfather, he said. They were both in the habit of starting work early.

'Grandma called about ten past nine on Granddad's mobile,' he said. 'We share an office. I knew straight away that something was wrong. Granddad went white. He told Grandma we'd be straight over, then he put the phone down, looked across at me and said: "Fred's gone." I couldn't believe it.

'We were both shocked, naturally, but at the time . . . well, I suppose we thought Fred would soon turn up. He's been very upset since Dad died. Not hysterical or anything like that, just that he wasn't always himself. He did funny things. We were hoping it was another one of those funny things, I suppose.'

Vogel studied the young man carefully. Everything he said had a ring of truth, but there was something behind his eyes that Vogel couldn't quite make out. Just as there had been something about Joyce that hadn't felt right. And in her case it had turned out that, for reasons she'd failed to explain to Vogel's satisfaction, she had been hiding something important. Was it possible that Mark Mildmay was also hiding something?

'So you drove over here straight away, did you?' Vogel asked, studying every flicker in Mark's eyes, every facial twitch, every bit of his uneasy body language.

The young man nodded.

'Yes. And Granddad came with me in my car. Geoff had taken the Bentley in for a service.'

'What about Stephen Hardcastle? Doesn't he work in the same building? Wasn't he there? Didn't he come with you?'

Mark nodded.

'He'd arrived at the office a few minutes before Mum called, and he came to the house straight away – he's like family, Steve. But he drove here in his own car. Mine's a two-seater.'

Vogel had noticed the metallic grey Porsche parked outside and had taken an educated guess that it would be Mark Mildmay's two-seater. This family had money and clearly liked their trophy homes and their toys for grown-ups. There was something about these people that Vogel didn't quite approve of. And it went beyond the suspicions aroused in him by those unfinished police enquiries into Tanner-Max which he had learned about that morning, or even Charlie Mildmay's letter alluding to questionable goings on. For Vogel was a bit of a Puritan at heart. He wasn't comfortable with excess. And everything about Tarrant Park and the Tanner–Mildmay clan seemed excessive to Vogel.

He was, however, an old hand at not letting his innermost thoughts and suspicions show.

Vogel ended the interview and thanked the young man, informing him that though he had no further questions for the time being, he would be in touch should anything arise. Mark looked even shakier after the interview than he had before, which Vogel considered to be a perfectly satisfactory result.

Felicity Tanner was ushered in next. At first glance she seemed composed, but Vogel could see that she was struggling to control her emotions.

'Mrs Tanner, perhaps you could confirm for me what time you came to the house this morning?' he began.

Felicity nodded. 'Yes. I got here about twenty to nine, I think. Joyce called me as soon as she and Molly were certain Fred wasn't in the house. We were still hoping he was somewhere close by. Silly, I know, but we kept on looking and looking.' She paused, screwing up her face in pain. 'We haven't stopped all day – we can't help it. Everyone's been checking the same places over and over again.'

Vogel felt for her. Felicity Tanner was a good-looking woman for her age, which Vogel assumed to be mid sixties. Her grey bobbed hair was streaked with blonde, probably by a hairdresser rather than nature, Vogel thought, but it looked natural and suited her skin tone. Beneath the grief and the pain, Felicity had intelligent eyes. There was also an air of vulnerability about her.

Felicity went on to substantiate the arrival times of her husband and of Stephen Hardcastle, and everything that Joyce had told Vogel concerning the sequence of events that morning.

Vogel then asked to see Molly. He rose as Yardley brought the teenager into the dining room, then sat down next to her at the table, not opposite as he had so far positioned himself with the adults.

'I'm sorry I have to speak to you now, sweetheart,' he said quietly. 'But I know you want to help find your brother, don't you?'

Molly was sitting with her head down, fighting back the tears. She glanced up at him and nodded.

It was obvious she had been weeping. Her pretty face was streaked with tears. Her eyes were badly swollen. Surely this was one family member even he could not suspect of any wrongdoing. Everything about Molly radiated her honest distress. Unlike the rest of the family, she seemed quite transparent and unguarded.

Molly scrubbed her eyes with both hands and gulped a couple of times.

'I need all the help I can get if we're going to find Fred quickly,' Vogel continued.

Molly nodded again, biting her lip.

'So will you please take me through exactly what happened this morning?' Vogel asked. 'Perhaps you could start by telling me when you and your mother first realized Fred was missing, and so on.'

Molly's story was the same as her mother's, barely differing in even the slightest detail. If people are not telling the truth, there are almost always discrepancies, unless they have concocted a story, in which case it would often be repeated word for word, the phrasing suspiciously similar. Neither seemed to be the case in this instance. Molly told her story in her own words and in her own way.

'Good, now perhaps you could tell me about the last time you saw your bother,' Vogel encouraged. 'Can you tell me when that was?'

'Yes, last night,' answered Molly.

'And do you remember the time?'

'It was eight thirty. That is, it should have been eight thirty because that's Fred's bedtime on school nights. But I think it was a bit later. We'd been playing around . . . fighting a bit . . . it was only fun, but . . .'

Molly's face clouded over again. Vogel feared her tears had not departed for long.

'But what, Molly?' he enquired gently.

'It's only that, well, he was being the little horror that he can be. He was teasing me rotten. So I said, "I'm going to kill you, you monster."' Molly stared at Vogel, her eyes wide open, her lips trembling. 'That's what I said, Mr Vogel. I told my little brother I was going to kill him. That was the last thing I said to him before he went to bed. And this morning he wasn't there, he was gone. He's still gone. And that was the last thing I said to him . . .'

Her words were overtaken by sobs.

'But you didn't mean that, did you, Molly?' Vogel's question was rhetorical, and he murmured it softly.

Molly shook her head.

'No. And your brother knew that, didn't he?'

Molly nodded again, more of a half nod this time. 'I suppose so,' she managed.

Vogel leaned towards Molly, careful not to touch her or to do anything that might intimidate her, but leaning so that his face was quite close to hers.

'You love your little brother very much, don't you, Molly?' he said.

She nodded weakly.

'And you know that he knows that, too, don't you?'

She nodded again.

Vogel dropped his voice even lower.

'So don't you worry,' he said. 'I'm going to bring him back for you, darling, I promise you.'

Molly looked at him with hope in her eyes.

'Th-thank you,' she said.

Then she started to cry again. It could have been Vogel's kindness that had sparked her off once more, or it could have been that she simply couldn't stop. He straightened up, mentally kicking himself. He knew better than to make promises like that, didn't he? Particularly to a child, because children took promises at face value. As a rule, they didn't understand about saying things just to make someone feel better. As a rule, children were more honest than adults. Sometimes brutally so.

But Vogel hadn't been able to help himself. He had a daughter at home who was only a little younger than Molly. Rosamund Vogel was a sensitive, caring girl. She didn't have a brother to worry about, but if she had and she feared that anything might have happened to him, she would be distraught. She could never be what Molly Mildmay was. Rosamund Vogel had her own problems, but like Molly, she was still at that stage where she loved her family unconditionally.

Vogel found it difficult to watch Molly's distress. Whenever possible he tried to keep his questioning methodical and nonconfrontational in style, cool, controlled, dealing with facts not emotions. He had tried so hard not to add to her misery, to try to come up with some words of encouragement to lift her spirits.

Vogel sighed inwardly. Would he never learn? He only hoped he could keep his promise in this instance and bring Molly Mildmay's little brother home.

At least they were still within the golden twenty-four hours, he reminded himself. He just had to get on with things. As ever.

'Yardley, take Molly back to her mother will you, and bring Janet Porter in,' he commanded.

The PA had short wavy hair dyed an unnatural dark brown and cut in a severe bob. She was wearing a striped business suit and at a glance looked every inch the competent, dedicated aide. In sharp contrast to young Molly and Joyce Mildmay, she had not been crying. But then, she was no relation to the missing boy, Vogel reminded himself. Her surprisingly bright blue eyes did, however, betray a hint of alarm.

'Nothing to worry about,' Vogel said briskly. 'I only need a moment of your time, Miss Porter.'

Janet said nothing. She clasped her hands together and placed them on the table. Vogel couldn't help wondering why everyone seemed to do that during police interviews. Most people, innocent or guilty, were nervous when interviewed by the police, particularly as part of an investigation into something as serious as the possible abduction of a child.

Janet told Vogel that she had arrived at the house at around 10 a.m., not long after Mark Mildmay, Henry Tanner and Stephen Hardcastle. They had all left the office as quickly as they could when Joyce had called them with the shocking news. Janet had remained a little longer than the men in order to lock the place up.

She seemed to have nothing more to offer concerning the immediate circumstances of Fred Mildmay's disappearance, but there remained the matter of the delayed letter.

Vogel cut to the chase.

'Miss Porter, something has come to my attention which I hope you may be able to throw some light on,' he began. 'I don't want to alarm anyone unnecessarily at this stage, nor cause further distress to Mrs Mildmay, so I would appreciate it if you would not discuss with anyone else the matter I now wish to ask you about. Is that clear?'

Janet cleared her throat and looked even more nervous.

'Uh, yes, of course,' she said.

'Good,' said Vogel. 'I understand that Mr Charles Mildmay left a letter to be given to his wife and read only in the event of his death. And I think you know about that letter, is that correct?'

'Well, yes . . .' began Janet hesitantly.

'I also understand that it was you who forwarded the letter to Mrs Mildmay, along with an accompanying letter which I believe bears your signature,' Vogel continued. 'Can you confirm that?'

'Yes,' said Janet.

'And when did you post it to Mrs Mildmay?'

'On Monday. I'm certain of that, because Mr Tanner and Stephen were away from the office.'

'This letter, bearing a clear instruction that it be passed to Mr Mildmay's wife in the event of his death, had presumably been in your office since before he died. Given that he lost his life last November, can you explain why the letter was not sent then?'

Janet hesitated.

'Well, I sort of can. It had been wrongly filed. It wasn't in Charlie's file, you see, along with his will and other papers.'

'So how did it finally materialize? And who instructed you to send it on to Mrs Mildmay?'

'Nobody did,' Joyce replied quickly.

'What do you mean?' asked Vogel.

'Nobody told me to send it on. I found the letter myself, misfiled. Stephen had asked me to deal with something concerning his own affairs – he's trying to buy a new property and the mortgage company wanted to know about his life insurance – and when I went to his file to look for the policy I found Charlie's letter there. I realized it must have got in the wrong place.'

Janet paused as if an unwelcome thought had occurred to her.

'It wasn't my mistake, Mr Vogel, I can assure you of that,' she continued, suddenly going off at a tangent. 'I had never even seen the letter before. I don't know how it came to be in the wrong place, but I certainly didn't put it there.'

'I'm sure you didn't, Miss Porter,' murmured Vogel, stifling a smile.

Janet Porter clearly had considerable professional pride, and was not prepared to allow her competence to be questioned.

'Please go on, Miss Porter,' said Vogel.

'When I saw what was written on the envelope – that it should be given to Joyce Mildmay in the event of Charlie's death – well, I was horrified to think that it had been sitting there in our office all that time,' Janet continued. 'I thought it should be sent to Mrs Mildmay straight away.'

'So you posted it on yourself, without checking with Mr Hardcastle, or Mr Tanner?'

'Well, not exactly. As I told you, Stephen and Mr Tanner were out of the office. They were in London that day, you see. They had an important business meeting in the morning, then lunch at Mr Tanner's club. It was about lunchtime when I found the letter. I called and left a message on Stephen's voicemail telling him about it and asking if he wanted me to pop it in the post with a covering note, but he never got back to me, not all afternoon. I wasn't surprised. Mr Tanner's club lunches are legendary. Anyway, both Stephen and Mr Tanner trust me to use my own initiative – indeed, they encourage me to. So when it came to five o'clock I phoned Stephen again and left a message saying I would put the letter in the post unless I heard from him to the contrary. I didn't hear from him, so on my way home I dropped it in the post box opposite the office. It seemed the right thing to do. And I was afraid that if Mr Tanner found out about the letter being in Stephen's file, he might be angry with Stephen. He has rather a temper on him, you see. Also, I didn't want to keep the letter from Joyce any longer . . .' She looked at him quizzically.

'Shouldn't I have done that, Mr Vogel?'

'You were doing what you thought was the right thing, Miss Porter,' said Vogel, his tone noncommittal. 'Did you not get any response whatsoever to your phone messages?'

'Oh yes, eventually,' replied Janet. 'Stephen called me at home a bit later on. His voice was a little slurred – those London lunches are inclined to be rather liquid. Mr Tanner never gets the worse for wear, but his guests always do.'

'What did Mr Hardcastle say when he called you?'

'He asked if I'd already posted the letter. I told him I had.'

'And what did he say to that?'

'He didn't say anything much that I remember. Just "right", or "OK", or something. Then he said he'd see me in the morning. And goodnight, I suppose. Nothing much. Why?'

Vogel ignored the question.

'Did you not think it strange that he called you at home to ask if you had posted the letter?'

Janet looked surprised.

'No,' she said. 'I assumed he was making sure that I had. After all, it was embarrassing that we'd kept it all that time, in the wrong file, without anyone knowing it was there.'

Without *you* knowing it was there, thought Vogel.

Aloud he asked: 'Were you aware of the contents of the letter, Miss Porter?'

Not for the first time during the interview, Janet looked shocked.

'Of course not! It was a sealed letter from a dead man to his widow. How on earth would I know what was in it?'

'Indeed,' murmured Vogel ambiguously. 'What about Mr Tanner and Mr Hardcastle? Do you think they knew anything of the contents of the letter?'

'I have no idea,' said Janet, but Vogel could almost see the wheels turning as she considered this. Then her expression hardened.

'If you are suggesting that either of them would have opened a letter of that nature and then resealed it, I can assure you that you are totally wrong, Detective Inspector. Neither Mr Tanner nor Stephen would ever do such a thing. In any case, I'm not sure Mr Tanner knew of the existence of the letter. Stephen was Charlie's personal solicitor as well as representing the company. Presumably Charlie gave the letter to him. And Stephen always does things by the book. He would regard that as confidential, I'm sure.'

'No doubt you are right,' replied Vogel, who thought just the opposite.

So that was it then. The letter had been sent on to Joyce without the prior knowledge of either Tanner or Hardcastle. And Vogel was pretty sure that both men were aware not only of the existence of the letter but of its contents, and that they had deliberately refrained from sending it on to Joyce. But why had they kept it, albeit filed in a place they thought was safe? Why hadn't they destroyed it? And if they had destroyed it, would young Fred Mildmay still be safe at home?

He thanked Janet Porter, reminding her that she should not discuss the letter or anything pertaining to it with anyone else, then told her she could go back and join the others, or was free to leave the house if she wished.

As Janet headed back to the kitchen, Vogel made his way to the sitting room, where he found Tanner and Hardcastle sitting at either end of one of the two big settees. PC Bolton was standing by the door, and Vogel hoped that this uniformed presence might have given the two men cause to feel a little less self-assured than they had been earlier.

Tanner and Hardcastle stood up almost in unison as soon as Vogel entered, and looked at him expectantly. The DI kept his expression stern and tried to sound as officious as he hoped he looked.

'Gentlemen, I am afraid I need to interview you both on record,' he announced. 'I must ask you to accompany me now to Lockleaze police station.'

Tanner's face was expressionless. This was a big-game player, thought Vogel. No doubt about that.

Hardcastle, the lawyer, was the first to speak: 'Mr Vogel, are you arresting us?' he asked.

'No, sir, merely asking for your cooperation. I am sure you are both as eager as I am to find young Fred, and as I believe you have information which could be extremely helpful, I feel it would be beneficial to all concerned to conduct our interviews in a more formal situation where everything that you tell us will be digitally recorded and can therefore be properly assimilated.'

Vogel was replying to Stephen Hardcastle's question. But he stared straight at Tanner. The older man returned the stare without so much as a flicker.

Hardcastle began to speak again. 'Well, I'm not sure about that, Detective Inspector,' he said. 'As I told you, I am the family solicitor, as well as an old friend, and as such I feel I should advise my client that neither of us are under any legal obligation at this stage to—'

Tanner held up one hand, effectively silencing Hardcastle. 'It's OK, Stephen,' he said, still staring unblinkingly at Vogel. 'You are absolutely right, Detective Inspector. I am more than willing, indeed I am eager, to cooperate in any way that might bring about the speedy return of my grandson. And I am sure that Stephen, whilst correct as my lawyer to point out our rights, feels the same way. So if you believe that it would help to interview us at a police station, then I am happy to accompany you there. As Stephen will be.'

The last sentence was not even an instruction, more a statement of fact.

Stephen Hardcastle merely nodded his agreement.

'Thank you,' said Vogel. Then he turned to Bolton: 'I want you to drive us, Constable Bolton,' he said. 'PC Saslow has been appointed FLO, so she will stay here and continue with her duties. PC Yardley, I'd like you to stay here with her, please.'

Turning his back on Hardcastle and Tanner, he leaned towards Yardley and added in a whisper, 'You're both on a watching brief, OK?'

Yardley nodded.

Vogel led the way out of the house, with Hardcastle and Tanner immediately behind him and PC Bolton bringing up the rear, and all four men climbed into the squad car parked outside.

No one spoke during the journey. There was considerable tension within the small Ford. And that suited Vogel perfectly. The more unnerved these two men were, the better his chances of getting answers.

Ten

Felicity Tanner heard an engine start and the sound of a vehicle pulling away. Neither the paved drive nor the gravelled area at the front of the house could be seen from the kitchen window. She glanced enquiringly at her daughter, who stared blankly back at her.

Joyce was not her normal self at the moment. Felicity realized that you could not expect a mother whose child had gone missing to behave in a manner that could, by any standards, be described as normal. However, something had been bothering Joyce even before Fred's disappearance. And when she'd told Henry, he'd been concerned enough to immediately get on the phone to her. But he hadn't been surprised. In fact Felicity could have sworn he'd been half expecting it.

'Joyce?' she asked. 'Who was that just leaving? Has the Detective Inspector interviewed your father and Stephen yet? What's going on?'

Joyce shrugged her shoulders and said nothing. Felicity Tanner was about to question her further when PC Bolton entered the kitchen. Instead she turned her attention to him.

'I heard a car leave,' she began.

'Yes, DI Vogel asked your husband and Mr Hardcastle to

152

accompany him to a police station for a video interview,' explained PC Bolton.

Felicity looked alarmed.

'Have they been arrested?' she asked, her eyes wide with shock.

'No, they are helping us with our enquiries, that's all,' responded Bolton.

'Please don't worry,' interjected PC Saslow. 'This is routine procedure. As your FLO, I will remain with the family and talk you through anything that is worrying you.'

Joyce looked up. 'My son is missing, that's what's worrying me,' she snapped.

Dawn Saslow flushed and mumbled an apology.

Felicity felt sorry for the young PC, but even more concerned about her daughter. She tried to put an arm around her. Joyce pulled away.

When Charlie died, Felicity had been the person Joyce turned to for comfort. She wished she could do the same now, and just couldn't understand why Joyce had been so prickly of late, and why, even now, she was rejecting her parents instead of welcoming their support.

Felicity was also well aware, in spite of PC Saslow's bland reassurances, of the significance of asking someone to attend a police station instead of interviewing them at home. She read crime novels and watched detective series on TV. They were her diversion from real life, particularly on the days when Henry's perpetual lack of communication got her down. Which it frequently did, though she was careful never to let on.

She had taken Henry aside that morning, when he'd arrived at their daughter's house after being told that Fred had disappeared.

'I know something's going on,' she'd told him. 'Both you and Joyce have been behaving peculiarly the last few days. What is it, Henry? What's happened?'

Henry had given his standard blandly reassuring and yet non-communicative response: 'Nothing's happened, Felicity. You're imagining things. Please, don't upset yourself.'

Undeterred, Felicity tried a different tack: 'Henry, I want you to promise that you know of nothing that could have led to Fred going missing,' she said. 'Will you do that? Can you promise me that?'

'Felicity, have you taken leave of your senses?' Henry countered. 'What sort of question is that?'

'Promise me,' Felicity persisted.

'I promise you,' replied Henry, a note of irritation apparent in his normally implacable manner. 'I'm hurt that I should need to, but I promise you. How could you possibly believe such a thing? If I were in possession of information that might help us to find Fred, I would tell you. And the police. Straight away.'

He had taken hold of her then, gently but firmly, and looked straight into her eyes. His were the clearest blue eyes she had ever known. And whenever he looked at his wife they were invariably full of love. Today was no exception.

Felicity had found herself apologizing. Apologizing for allowing herself to question his devotion to his family.

'I'm just so desperately worried,' she said, by way of explanation. 'I don't know what I'm saying.'

Henry had pulled her close to him. 'It's all right, my darling,' he whispered into her ear. 'It's going to be all right. We will find our boy. Soon. I will make sure of that. Don't I always look after my family?'

Felicity had merely nodded. It was true: Henry Tanner always looked after his family.

But as the hours passed with no news of her youngest grandchild, Felicity's anxiety grew. Henry liked to promote an image of himself as all-powerful, but much as he might try to look after his family he hadn't been able to prevent the loss of their only son, William. Only last year their son-in-law had drowned in a sailing accident. And now Fred . . .

It was as if her family was cursed. But the thought had also occurred to Felicity that it might not have been fate singling them out for tragedy. The driver who ran William down had never been identified. Charlie had been an experienced sailor who never went without a safety harness. What if their deaths were not random? What if Fred's disappearance was the latest in a series of cruel acts targeting her family?

And if that was the case, Henry must have some idea who was responsible or at least why they were being targeted.

For the first time in her long marriage, Felicity was beginning to doubt her husband. The total and unshakeable faith in Henry that had carried her through the loss of her son had been shattered.

Eleven

At Lockleaze, Vogel was joined by DC Angela Lowe, a bright young officer trained in the techniques of audio-video interviewing. Vogel himself had undergone similar training when he'd been a detective sergeant in the Met.

Henry Tanner and Stephen Hardcastle were to be interviewed separately. They would speak to Tanner first, leaving the lawyer, who'd struck Vogel as overly protective of his employer and client, until later.

The video room at Lockleaze took most interviewees by surprise. Instead of upright chairs separated by a table, there were armchairs arranged in an apparently casual fashion. The set-up had been designed to give an impression of informality, the intention being to lull interviewees into a false sense of security.

Henry Tanner, however, was unlikely to be tempted to let down his guard. This was a strong and powerful man, accustomed to being in control. Although concerned about the welfare of his grandson and professing himself willing to cooperate, Henry showed no sign of being prepared to relinquish command.

Vogel began by covering the obvious details, such as when did Henry last see his grandson, which had apparently been the previous Sunday. The day before that fateful letter had been posted.

'He was playing cricket,' said Henry. 'Local youth team. Useful little batsman he's going to be, too, our Fred. I took him. Windy old day, and rain stopped play a couple of times. But I do that stuff for Fred because he's not got a dad any more. I'm the one who takes him to sports things now. So I stayed to watch, and afterwards I took him back to our house for a bite to eat. Felicity's an excellent cook and she loves to spoil him. She'd laid on lots of his favourite things. We kept him until it was almost his bedtime to give his mother a bit of a break. She needs that occasionally, has done ever since Charlie died.'

Vogel then asked about the sequence of events that morning: when Henry had heard about Fred being missing, the details of the call from his daughter, his arrival at the house, and so on.

Henry had answered readily and in detail. It was only when Vogel strayed into other areas that he began to clam up. Particularly when it came to Charlie Mildmay's letter to his wife.

When asked if he knew about the letter, Henry paused before replying. His words were cautious, measured.

'I do, yes,' he said. 'But I only learned of its existence yesterday.'

'I see, and how did you learn of it? Did your daughter tell you?'

Henry shook his head. 'No. Stephen told me. He wanted me to know what had happened. You see the letter should have gone to Joyce right after Charlie died. That was Charlie's wish. But it was delayed – a clerical error, Stephen said. Very embarrassing for him. For any lawyer. But all the more so

157

because Stephen and Charlie had been best friends. Stephen was mortified. And the whole thing was extremely distressing for Joyce.'

'You had no idea the letter existed before then?'

'No. Why would I? It was a personal letter from my son-in-law to his wife, to be delivered to her in the event of his death. And to be opened only by her. Charlie had entrusted it to Stephen in his capacity as the family's lawyer. There was no reason for either of them to confide in me.'

Vogel studied the older man carefully.

'Mr Tanner, I am under the impression that nothing, nothing whatsoever, occurs within your company or concerning your family without your being informed about it. I therefore find it surprising that you would be unaware of the letter's existence.'

Tanner's eyes narrowed. Vogel could see he was struggling to contain his anger, but when he spoke his tone betrayed no sign of it.

'Well, I was unaware of it. Stephen didn't inform me until he felt he had to. Not until Joyce confronted him about the letter, and it became clear how upset she was. Even then he did so reluctantly, because it meant betraying the trust of his client, technically anyway.'

Vogel knew he was blinking rapidly behind his horn-rimmed spectacles. It was a nervous tic that he'd tried without success to master, all too aware that, when interviewing suspects, it could be interpreted as a sign of weakness, a chink in his armour. He took his spectacles off and turned away from Henry Tanner, wiping the back of one hand across his eyes.

Tanner had a script, the detective reckoned, a script he had prepared and would not stray from, despite the fact that the purpose of this interview was to find his missing grandson. Nevertheless, Vogel persisted.

'So did Mr Hardcastle confide in you the content of Mr Mildmay's letter?' Vogel enquired, barely in hope let alone expectation.

Tanner's blue eyes opened disingenuously wide. 'Stephen doesn't know what was in the letter. Joyce decided to keep it to herself. Surely you can understand that? A letter from a deceased spouse is a very personal thing. She didn't even tell me or her mother that she'd received it, let alone the content, and I thought it best not to mention to her that I knew about it.'

Vogel managed to stop blinking and replaced his spectacles.

'So neither you nor Mr Hardcastle opened the letter before it was sent to Joyce?'

'Mr Vogel, I take considerable exception to that question. I am Joyce's father and Stephen is her solicitor. I regarded Charlie as my second son and he was Stephen's closest friend. Neither of us would dream of doing such a thing. In any case, I believe I have already told you more than once that I didn't know that the letter existed until yesterday.'

'Mr Tanner, there is no need for you to take exception to anything,' interjected Angela Lowe in a neutral tone of voice. 'The purpose of this interview is merely to clarify every detail and put that clarification on record.'

Vogel understood exactly what the bright young DC was doing, but he carried on with his questioning as if she had not spoken.

'So, Mr Tanner, you continue to maintain that you have no idea of the letter's contents?'

'What do you mean, "continue to maintain"? I find your

insinuations insulting, and what's more I cannot see what you hope to achieve by this line of questioning. What possible connection can there be between Charlie's letter and Fred's disappearance?'

Vogel let the question hang in the air for several seconds before replying: 'I am afraid I am not at liberty to discuss that with you, sir.'

Tanner leaned back in his chair, spread his arms wide, his body language speaking volumes. 'So what do you want from me?' he asked.

'The truth, Mr Tanner,' replied Vogel.

'I assure you, Detective Inspector, that I have told you the truth, the whole truth, and nothing but the truth.'

Tanner half smiled. Then he shifted in his chair so that his upper body leaned closer to Vogel. His manner was both resigned and conciliatory.

'I want to help, Mr Vogel,' he said. 'How could you doubt that? My grandson is missing. I would never do or say anything that might hinder your investigation – never.'

Vogel, while keeping his eyes on Tanner, opened a folder on his desk and removed a handwritten letter. He could tell from the flicker in Tanner's eyes that the older man recognized it for what it was. Then again, the topic of conversation would inevitably have led Henry Tanner to conclude that this was Charlie's letter, whether he had seen it before or not.

'I'm going to read you part of this letter, Mr Tanner,' Vogel said, adding with as much sarcasm as he dared: 'Since you are unaware of its content, perhaps I should make you so.'

Tanner shrugged and waited.

Vogel then began to read:

'*My biggest mistake was to allow myself to become*

immersed in your father's world. I couldn't bring myself to destroy your illusions, so I kept things from you, thinking I was sheltering you, but I see now that what I was really doing was living in denial, dodging my responsibility to protect my family. Now that I am gone, I'm afraid that responsibility falls to you.

'It is probably already too late for Mark. But you must protect Fred. Whatever you do, please don't let your father get his hands on Fred . . .'

Vogel broke off and glanced enquiringly at Tanner. 'So what do you think your son-in-law meant by that?'

If Tanner did have previous knowledge of the contents of the letter, as Vogel suspected, then his performance was impressive. But then, Vogel reckoned the older man was quite a player in his field, whatever that field might be.

'I have no idea,' said Tanner. 'I am shocked. Shocked to the core. I love my grandchildren, all my family. I would never do anything to hurt Fred. And I can't believe that Charlie would suggest that I might.'

Vogel adjusted his spectacles and looked down again at the letter.

'It is probably already too late for Mark. But you must protect Fred. Whatever you do, please don't let your father get his hands on Fred,' he repeated. 'Come on, Mr Tanner, you must have some idea what Charlie was getting at.'

Tanner shook his head again. 'No, absolutely not . . . Unless he wanted Fred to break free, to do something other than come into the business like all the rest of the men in our family. Maybe that's what he meant. But he'd only have had to tell me that. I would never force Fred to do anything he didn't want to.'

Vogel thought that was probably true. But he had met

powerful, dominant men like Tanner before. They weren't necessarily bad people, but they were people who had to be in control. Tanner struck him as an expert in manipulation. No doubt he was adept at persuading his family and those who came under his influence to believe that they were following their own destinies, as opposed to one laid down for them by Tanner.

Vogel decided against reading out the remainder of the letter. In light of Fred's disappearance, it could be of considerable significance that Charlie Mildmay had urged his wife to run away with her two youngest children to prevent Henry Tanner '*getting his hands on Fred*'. Had Tanner snatched the boy to pre-empt that possibility?

'Your son-in-law also indicated to your wife that she needn't worry about Molly, you wouldn't be interested in Molly, it would only be Fred you were interested in. Have you any idea what Charlie may have meant by that, Mr Tanner?'

Tanner went pale. His lips were a tight line. He clenched his fists. Then he asked: 'I hope you're not insinuating what I think you may be, Detective Inspector?'

'I am not insinuating anything,' replied Vogel, deadpan. 'I asked you a question, Mr Tanner, and I would be most grateful if you would answer it. Have you any idea what Charlie meant by this comment?'

There was fury in Tanner's eyes, but he replied in the same steady tone of voice: 'I have absolutely no idea what Charlie might have meant by that, Detective Inspector.'

'Are you sure?'

'I am sure,' Tanner replied, fighting to control his anger.

'I see.'

Vogel stared at Henry Tanner long and hard, wishing he

could read the other man's mind. He was beginning to fear he might end up giving away more information than he was getting from this man.

'Right, Mr Tanner,' he said eventually, his manner brisk. 'Thank you for your cooperation. I have no further questions – for the moment. You may leave.'

Tanner didn't move.

'Look, if there is any way I can help you, Mr Vogel, please tell me,' he said. 'My grandson is missing. If it will help you find him, you can ask any questions you like. I want you to. Please. Even if I find it offensive, I will try to answer. Anything to get Fred back.'

The man was a picture of honest perplexity, a worried grandfather in great distress but still eager to assist.

Vogel was unimpressed. 'You may leave, Mr Tanner,' he repeated coldly.

'We will let you know if and when we need to speak to you again, sir,' added DC Lowe.

Henry shot her a derisory glance. Then, without another word, he rose from his armchair and left the room.

Vogel asked for Hardcastle to be brought to the video room immediately, before he and Tanner had time to exchange notes.

Hardcastle entered the room without speaking. Vogel gestured for him to sit on the armchair Henry Tanner had vacated. The DI allowed DC Lowe to declare who was present, the time and so on, for the benefit of the recording equipment.

He then began the interview much as he had with Tanner, asking Hardcastle for an outline of that morning's events.

When he approached the topic of the letter, it was as if a shutter came down. Neither Tanner nor Hardcastle could have known before their respective interviews that Joyce had informed the police about the letter. Vogel wondered if they had speculated about that before leaving their office, if they had guessed that she would, and if they had in any way colluded in their stories. Or indeed, if they needed to do so. It was possible that Henry Tanner had been telling the truth. Vogel didn't like the man, but that was no reason to assume that he was guilty of involvement in the disappearance of his own grandson.

Asked when he first learned of the existence of the letter, Hardcastle responded cockily, 'When Charlie gave it to me, of course. His instruction that it was to be opened by Joyce in the event of his death was written on the envelope.'

'I see. And when was that?'

'I'm not sure exactly,' said Hardcastle. 'Though I probably have a record of it somewhere. It was about two or three months before his death.'

'Did Mr Mildmay indicate why he felt it necessary to write such a letter?'

'No.'

'Was he ill, or did he suspect that he might have some condition that would shorten his life?' interjected DI Lowe.

'No. Charlie was in robust good health, as far as I knew anyway. Liked his sport, and his sailing in particular. Didn't smoke or drink to excess – well, not often.' Hardcastle smiled.

'And he was only forty-three,' commented Vogel. 'Didn't it strike you as rather morbid for a fit and relatively young man to write a letter with such an instruction?'

'Well, actually, no,' replied Hardcastle. 'It's not as unusual as you might think. A lot of people do it when they write their wills, just in case, as it were. Come to think of it, Charlie and I had been clarifying one or two minor points in his will, and he wrote the letter at around the same time. So it seemed natural enough to me, and certainly not morbid. Like an insurance policy.'

'What points were you clarifying in Mr Mildmay's will?' asked Vogel.

'I'm not at liberty to discuss that with you Detective Inspector,' said Hardcastle. 'I have to respect client confidentiality.'

'Mr Hardcastle, your client is dead, and his son has disappeared. I think there are more important matters to consider here than your concept of ethics within the legal profession, don't you?'

Hardcastle was silent for a few seconds, as if considering what Vogel had said. Finally he appeared to relent.

'It wasn't anything major. His financial situation had changed in that Henry was in the process of handing over far more of the running of the company to Charlie, and his income and stake in the company had increased as a result. The majority of Charlie's estate was always to pass to Joyce, and that is tax exempt, but there were certain bequests to his children that we needed to review for tax purposes. Mark was to inherit his father's share of the business and Charlie wanted assurance that the inheritance process would run smoothly.'

Vogel felt his antennae waggle. He thought about the nervous young man he had met earlier. The young man his instincts had told him could be afraid of something more than the possibility that his little brother might have gone for good.

'Mark inherited that?' Vogel enquired. 'Not Joyce?'

'Yes, Mark,' agreed Hardcastle. 'Or he will, once Charlie has been officially declared dead and a death certificate issued. But that's only a formality. And there's no surprise there: father to son has been the tradition with Tanner-Max since the outset.'

'I see,' said Vogel. 'And your instruction was to forward that letter to Joyce immediately in the event of his death, was it not?'

'Well, yes.' Stephen Hardcastle sounded less sure of himself now.

'Well, yes,' Vogel repeated. 'But in fact the letter was not forwarded to Mrs Mildmay until earlier this week. Can you tell me why that was?'

'It was filed in the wrong place,' replied Hardcastle. 'In my personal file, in fact.'

'And you weren't aware of that?'

'No, of course not. Not until a few days ago when Janet told me she'd found it there.'

'You didn't notice that the letter was missing at the time of Charlie's death, Mr Hardcastle?' asked DI Lowe.

'No, I didn't, and I can't explain that except to say I was in a state of total shock,' replied Hardcastle.

'So you didn't notice that it wasn't in Charlie's file along with his will, and you didn't think to look for it?' persisted Angela Lowe.

'No, I didn't. You have to understand, it was a dreadful time for everyone connected with Charlie. There were all sorts of papers concerning the business that had to be sent to Joyce for her to sign – Joyce had power of attorney for Charlie, thank God. And Janet dealt with the mechanics of most of that. I suppose I assumed that Janet would have sent the letter to Joyce along with everything else. To tell the truth, I don't remember much about that period immediately after Charlie's death. He was my closest friend. It was all I could do to function. I did my best to fulfil my professional obliga-tions, but I know full well I wasn't up to speed. So it's hardly surprising I didn't give the letter a second thought until Janet told me she'd found it.'

'And when was that, Mr Hardcastle?' asked Vogel.

'Don't you know, Mr Vogel?' snapped Hardcastle. 'On Monday of this week. Janet left messages on my phone when I was in London with Henry. I was busy and didn't get back to her. Quite correctly, she acted on her own initiative and posted the letter without further delay.'

'Who would have been responsible for wrongly filing that letter, Mr Hardcastle?' asked Vogel. 'Who put it in your per-sonal file rather than Mr Mildmay's?'

'Well, I don't know for certain, but presumably Janet. She does most of the filing. I rather assumed that was why she was so keen to get the letter off to Joyce when she did find it.'

'Janet says she didn't place the letter in your personal file either by intention or otherwise, nor in any other file.' Vogel paused to let his words sink in. 'She is adamant that she had never seen the letter before finding it in your file earlier this week.'

Hardcastle shrugged. 'Janet is one of our most trusted employees. But none of us like to admit our mistakes, do we?'

'I see. Are you absolutely sure, then, that you didn't file that letter yourself, Mr Hardcastle? In your own personal file, either by mistake or deliberately.'

'Of course I'm sure. Why on earth would I have misfiled it deliberately?'

'And what about Mr Tanner?' Vogel asked. 'Did he know about the letter?'

'I shouldn't think so,' replied Hardcastle, guarded now.

'This is what I really need to know, Mr Hardcastle. Did you tell your employer about Charlie Mildmay's letter, and if so when did you tell him?'

Vogel could almost see the wheels turning inside Hardcastle's head as he tried to second-guess what Henry Tanner may or may not have told Vogel. He allowed the silence to drag on for an uncomfortably long time before chivvying him for an answer.

'Come on, Mr Hardcastle, it's a simple enough question. Did you tell Henry Tanner about the letter, and if so when did you tell him?'

Hardcastle shifted in his seat and was finally opening his mouth to reply when the door to the video room opened. Hardcastle closed his mouth again.

Vogel swivelled in his armchair to see a young uniformed constable standing in the doorway looking embarrassed. As well he might, thought Vogel irritably. Hardcastle's next words could have been crucial. Thanks to the interruption, he'd now been given extra thinking time.

'What is it?' the DI barked.

'Your boss wants to talk to you right away, sir,' said the constable, colouring slightly. 'He's on the phone in our super's office.'

'Can't you see I'm conducting an interview?' snapped Vogel. 'Tell your super I'll be there as soon as I've finished.'

The constable stood his ground. 'I'm sorry, sir. I was told to tell you straight away, and that you were to stop whatever you were doing and go to the super's office at once.'

Vogel turned back to Hardcastle. Was it his imagination or was the man smirking? There was a sinking feeling in his stomach. He had an inkling it was no accident that this interview had been interrupted.

'Wait here,' said Vogel. It was all he could do to restrain himself from pointing an admonishing finger at Stephen Hardcastle. Turning to DC Lowe, he added: 'And you stay with him.'

Hardcastle shrugged, then leaned back in his chair and stretched out his long legs to make himself more comfortable. Complacent bastard, thought Vogel as, with rising misgivings, he allowed himself to be led to the office of Lockleaze police station's chief officer. The superintendent was on the phone to Reg Hemmings; with only the briefest of preliminaries he handed the phone to Vogel and left the room.

Hemmings came straight to the point: 'I am afraid I have to ask you to cease questioning Henry Tanner and Stephen Hardcastle, at least for the time being,' said the DCI.

Vogel was stunned. Reg Hemmings was a senior officer he had come to respect, even to like. He had a feeling this telephone conversation might change that. Although he'd realized something serious was afoot the moment the young copper interrupted the video interview, he hadn't been expecting anything like this. It was, in Vogel's experience, unprecedented.

'Can I ask why, boss?' he asked, fighting to keep his voice level.

'You can ask, but I can't tell you,' replied Hemmings. 'This is an order from on high. Even I don't know what's going on. Neither of us have the clearance, old boy.'

'Boss, a child is missing,' persisted Vogel. 'You're the SIO and I'm your deputy. Your hands-on man. I must have the freedom to pursue my enquiries as I see fit.'

'Under normal circumstances that would be absolutely the case,' responded Hemmings. 'But these, apparently, are not normal circumstances. We are wallowing in murky waters, I was told, whatever the heck that means.'

'So I can't speak to either of these two men in the pursuance of my enquiries into an extremely serious and possibly life-threatening incident involving an eleven-year-old child,' Vogel continued. 'Is that what you're telling me, boss?'

'I'm afraid I am, Vogel. For now, anyway.'

'But that's outrageous, sir. The child's life may be at a stake—'

'Hold on, Vogel, hold on,' Hemmings interrupted. 'The brass are aware of that. They're sending somebody from London who does have the necessary "clearance" to deal with these people.'

'Well, isn't that good of them!'

'Sarcasm is not going to help, Vogel,' said Hemmings.

Vogel ignored that. 'So are you still SIO on the case?'

'Only until the brass from London arrives.'

'And what about me? Am I no longer deputy SIO?'

'That depends on London,' responded Hemmings. 'I'm surprised at you, Vogel. I didn't have you down as the type to be paranoid about his own rank and standing.'

Vogel glowered at the telephone receiver in his hand.

'I do need to know where I stand, sir,' he said. 'I mean, am I still on the case? Or isn't there any case any more? Are we backing off and leaving this little lad to his fate, whatever that is, because we don't have the "clearance" to find him?'

'Don't be ridiculous, Vogel,' said Hemmings. 'This force will continue to make every effort possible to find the missing boy and bring to justice whoever might be responsible for his disappearance. We will both continue to work the case until London arrives. We just have to lay off Tanner, that's all. What's more you will work with whoever arrives from London in whatever capacity is required. Is that clear, Detective Inspector Vogel?'

Hemmings didn't often raise his voice. Vogel was therefore taken aback when his superior officer bellowed the last sentence down the phone. Involuntarily moving the telephone an inch or two from his ear, he replied, 'Yes, sir, absolutely clear, sir.'

Then he left the superintendent's office, inwardly seething but trying desperately to maintain the appearance of being unperturbed.

Twelve

The moment his video interview was over, Henry Tanner had left the police station and ducked into the limited privacy offered by a doorway down the road to make a series of calls on his mobile. One was to his personal driver, Geoff Brooking, asking him to bring the Bentley as fast as he could.

The nature of the other calls was such that Henry did not anticipate having to wait long for Stephen Hardcastle to join him. So when Geoff arrived he ordered him to park illegally across the road from the station. Sure enough, Hardcastle emerged moments later.

'In the nick of time,' he said, as he climbed into the back seat alongside Henry. 'If you'll excuse the pun.'

Henry Tanner ignored the remark, regarding Stephen with neither interest nor enthusiasm. 'Detective Inspector David Vogel was always going to be the least of our problems,' he said. 'The man's a minnow.'

'You saw him off, anyway, Henry,' said Stephen.

Tanner fixed him with a stare. 'I hardly think this is a moment for us to feel pleased with ourselves, Stephen,' he said coldly. 'My younger grandson is still missing. My wife and daughter are distraught. My granddaughter is in pieces and my elder grandson is barely holding himself together.

172

This is the biggest crisis ever to face this family. Have you forgotten that, Stephen?'

'No, no, of course not, Henry,' said Stephen, mortified. He was used to being put in his place by Henry. That didn't necessarily make the experience any less unpleasant. But he had to acknowledge that on this occasion he deserved the reprimand. 'I'm sorry, I wasn't thinking straight. I'm not used to being questioned by the police.'

Henry made no further comment. He had no intention of discussing confidential matters in the presence of his driver, who had started the engine but was awaiting instructions.

'Come on, Geoff,' he said. 'Back to Joyce's place as quick as you can.'

The driver nodded and took off in the direction of Tarrant Park.

Henry Tanner hunkered down in the back seat, his body language sending a warning to Stephen of the inadvisability of further attempts at conversation. The chief would have to discuss the matter with him sometime soon, surely, Stephen thought. After all, he needed to get his story straight should the police question him again, which he suspected they would. Stephen hadn't known what to say when the detective asked if Henry knew about the letter. And he still didn't know what Henry had told Vogel.

He wiped the sweat from his brow. He could have landed them all in it if he'd been forced to answer Vogel's last question. He reckoned he'd had a narrow escape from disaster. And he also reckoned that far worse lay ahead.

Meanwhile, back at The Firs, Joyce felt utterly alone, even though the kitchen was still full of people. Nobody had left the house, in spite of most of them having been told they were free to do so.

Joyce was sitting next to Molly by the window in the kitchen, holding her daughter's hand. She'd taken over from Felicity in trying to comfort the girl. Felicity was at the table with Janet and Mark, who was pale and drawn but trying to hold it all together. Monika continued to busy herself about the place, and Dr Grey was leaning against the worktop, looking as if he wished he were somewhere else.

Joyce could derive no comfort from their presence. Worse, she no longer knew whether she could trust any of them.

Janet had signed the note that had accompanied Charlie's letter. Felicity, she was certain, knew more than she was telling. Even Mark seemed to have inherited, or been well schooled in, the family art of keeping secrets. He had never, in all the time he had been working with Henry, talked to Joyce about what that work involved. The same had been true of all the men in her life: her grandfather, father, husband – even her late brother.

Joyce had no idea whether any of the secrets that were being kept from her had any bearing on Fred's disappearance. It could be that all this secretive behaviour was merely an ingrained family habit. But it left her feeling that there was nobody she could turn to. Charlie's letter had started a ripple effect; she had begun by questioning everything she knew of her father, then moved on to questioning what she knew of Charlie, and now she was wondering whether she even knew her own son. And all the while her youngest son was missing.

She wished now that she'd done as Charlie told her and taken Fred and Molly away. Now it was too late.

She wondered if the letter might have sparked something off. Like Vogel, she had a nasty feeling that both Henry and

Stephen Hardcastle had seen and read the letter before it passed into her hands. She'd wondered from the beginning why it had taken six months to reach her. Her experience of the meticulous Janet Porter could only ever lead her to believe that the woman didn't make clerical errors. And it was Janet who did the filing.

If Henry had seen the letter, once he knew that it had reached Joyce he might fear that Joyce would obey her husband's instructions.

But that begged the question: why would her powerful and all-controlling father have allowed her to see the letter in the first place?

Joyce squeezed Molly's hand tightly, more tightly than she had realized.

Molly gave a little yelp. 'Mum, you're hurting me!'

'I'm sorry.' Joyce slackened her grip, and with her free hand gently touched Molly's tear-stained cheek.

Her attention was distracted by the sound of a vehicle pulling to a halt by the front door. Joyce knew that it couldn't be the police again, or any other outsiders, because the gates would have had to be opened from inside The Firs. Someone in the vehicle obviously had a remote control to operate the gates, which meant it had to be either her father or Stephen Hardcastle.

Everyone in the kitchen heard the arrival, but nobody moved. They just waited. There followed the sound of the front door opening, then slamming shut.

Henry Tanner walked into the kitchen first, followed closely by Stephen. At first glance Henry looked his usual self, confident and assertive, but Joyce could see the strain in her father's eyes. That was both unusual and disconcerting. He was a past master at concealing stress from his family, so for him to betray even the slightest sign of concern brought home the magnitude of the situation they were facing.

Monika was once again making tea nobody wanted. She stopped and, like everyone else, turned to look at Henry.

'How did you get on?' Felicity asked, moving towards her husband. 'What did they want? Why did they take you and Stephen to a police station?'

Henry reached out and touched her lightly on one shoulder.

'It was fine, my dear. They asked a lot of questions, that's all. Stephen and I gave them as much assistance as we could. All we can hope is that we helped them in some way. I must admit, I can't see how we did, but I do know now that there is a huge operation underway to find Fred, and we just have to hope that he is found soon.'

It was practically a speech. And Henry had somehow turned his visit to Lockleaze police station around, as if he had gone there to ensure that the investigation met with his approval. He'd also managed to sound reassuring. Until you analysed what he had said, and realized it amounted to nothing.

'Oh come on, Dad,' Joyce remonstrated, standing up and walking towards her father as her mother had done, only her body language indicated anger rather than concern. 'Why don't you tell us what the police wanted, why they took you and Stephen in for a formal interview. Go on, tell us. My son is missing. Will you stop playing your bloody stupid games and talk to us for once?'

Henry didn't flinch. 'I really don't know what you mean, dear,' he murmured, giving her his kindest, most fatherly smile.

He glanced towards Janet and Monika, then at Dr Grey.

Even if Henry Tanner were suddenly to become forthcoming, he would never say anything of consequence in front of outsiders.

Joyce wasn't about to be pushed aside. She could feel the anger tying itself into a nasty knot somewhere in the region of her upper abdomen. Trying not to let it show, she looked her father in the eye. 'I want you to tell us exactly what the police said to you and exactly what you said to them.'

'Not now, Joyce,' replied her father, still in a kindly manner but more firmly than before.

And just as patronizing, in Joyce's opinion.

'You've got enough to worry about, dear. Let Stephen and I deal with the police. It was a routine interview, that's all. And as I have said, we gave DI Vogel all the help we could.'

'Did you?' Joyce barked the words at her father.

Finally realizing that he was not going to subdue his daughter with platitudes, and that she was intent on berating him in public, Henry tried to usher her towards the door.

'Look, darling, why don't you come into the sitting room with me. We clearly do need to have a proper chat. No need to upset everybody else.'

Joyce had no desire for a cosy private chat. She wanted to tell her father that she was no longer prepared to tolerate his culture of secrecy. And that she didn't give a damn if there were people in the kitchen Henry Tanner regarded as outsiders, people to whom, even in these dreadful circumstances, he was desperate to present a united family front.

But she couldn't help glancing back at her daughter. Molly's tear-filled eyes were wide open in disbelief. She now looked confused as well as upset.

Henry had already turned and begun to walk through the door. Typical, thought Joyce. He expected obedience, or at least compliance, whatever the circumstances. Joyce followed him. That glimpse of her daughter's face had left her with little choice.

Once in the sitting room, Henry turned to face his daughter.

'Joyce darling, you must try to keep calm,' he began. 'We're all on the same side here, and you know you can trust me to do everything in my power to get our boy safely back—'

'Shut the fuck up, Dad,' yelled Joyce.

Her father physically recoiled. Joyce did not think she had ever used the f-word in his presence, let alone directed it at him.

'Just shut the fuck up,' she repeated, quietly this time. 'And listen for once.'

Her father sat down, with a bit of a bump, on the nearest of the room's two sofas. It was as if Joyce had pushed him, causing him to lose his balance. Which, in a way, she had done. Verbally, at any rate.

'Right now, I have no idea whether or not I can trust you, Dad,' she began. 'My husband sent me a very clear message telling me not to trust you.'

'I don't know what you—'

'Oh, for God's sake, Dad,' interrupted Joyce. 'If you didn't know about the letter Charlie left me before you were escorted to the police station, you damned well do now. I am well aware of the reason DI Vogel wanted to speak to you and Stephen at the station. He wanted to question you about Charlie's letter, didn't he? He made it pretty clear to me that he believes the content of that letter makes you a suspect.'

Henry narrowed his eyes. 'Well, I don't know about that, darling. But, yes, Mr Vogel did tell me about the letter.'

'Did he show it to you?'

'No,' replied Henry Tanner truthfully. 'But he read me bits of it.'

'Did he read you the bit where Charlie warned me off letting the children, particularly Fred, have anything to do with you?'

'Yes, he did,' said Henry. 'But I have no idea what Charlie might have meant by—'

'What about the bit where he told me to take the children and run? What about that?'

'Take the children and run?' Henry said, aghast. 'I have no idea why Charlie should have told you to run, Joyce. Honestly, darling—'

'Don't you "honestly" me,' interrupted Joyce, raising her voice again. 'I doubt you've been honest with me in your entire life. "*Get Fred away from your father. He won't be interested in Molly*" – that's what Charlie said. You must know what he meant by that, Dad.'

'I really don't know, I promise you,' said Henry, fixing wide-open blue eyes on his daughter's face.

Joyce stood silent. Waiting.

'You're not suggesting . . . s-suggesting that . . . that you think Charlie was implying I might, uh, interfere with Fred,' he finished lamely.

Joyce could not hold back a twisted smile.

'Interfere with Fred?' she repeated, making it a question. 'What a quaint old-fashioned way of putting things. If you are asking me do I think Charlie was suggesting you're some sort of filthy paedophile, the truth is I don't bloody know. I don't bloody know what to think any more about anything.'

'I can't believe you can even say such a thing, Joyce,' Henry spluttered.

'Oh, that's the tip of the iceberg, Dad, I can assure you.' She carried on staring him down, arms folded across her chest, defiant. 'So, am I supposed to believe that you knew nothing of this letter from Charlie until DI Vogel mentioned it, is that what you are saying?'

'Not exactly,' admitted her father. 'Stephen told me on Wednesday when you called him over. He said you'd been upset by the letter, and explained how it should have been delivered after Charlie's death but had been delayed because of a filing mix-up. Stephen was concerned for you, and he thought that I, as your father, should know what had happened to distress you. But he didn't tell me what was in the letter, obviously, because he didn't know. Stephen would never have betrayed Charlie's confidence by reading the letter, and he told me that you had refused to share the letter with him. Which is understandable, given what I now know of the contents, or at least the part that Vogel chose to tell me. But I didn't know any of it until today, if that's what you're asking.'

'That's what I'm asking, all right,' said Joyce. 'Because if you're lying, the implications are pretty damned obvious. Aren't they?'

'Are they?' Her father's face was expressionless now.

'Oh yes, Dad. Because if you already knew what was in that letter, if you knew that Charlie had urged me to take my children away from you and to disappear, to never come back, if you knew that, and if you believed that I might do it, then you might well have decided to take action to stop me doing so.'

Henry's face was a picture of hurt bewilderment.

'I don't know what you mean,' he said.

'I think you do. Come on, tell me: did you take Fred? Have you abducted my son, removed him from this house in the night so that you can keep him under your control, the way you've always controlled everybody in this family? Have you taken Fred to stop me taking him away from you? This house is burglar-alarmed. Whoever took Fred must have had a remote control or known the code to disarm the alarm. The alarm was set that night, I'm sure of it, but it didn't go off. And Fred didn't make a sound either, so he must have co-operated with whoever came for him in the middle of the night. I think that person was you, Dad. You have the code for the alarm, and Fred would do anything you told him to. Like all the bloody rest of us.

'I think you're the one who abducted my son.'

Thirteen

Vogel was on auto pilot after leaving the Lockleaze super's office. He made himself pick up a cup of coffee from a vending machine. He made himself breathe deeply. Neither helped.

Vogel liked Hemmings and knew his senior officer was merely the messenger boy in this instance. He also knew that Hemmings would have been left with no choice but to comply with his instructions from London.

None of this prevented him from wanting to race back to Kenneth Steele House and slap the man.

Vogel didn't like being angry. He considered any police officer who allowed emotion to engulf him to be immediately a lesser officer. In any case, it wouldn't alter the fact he was no longer free to continue with this investigation in whatever way he felt best. And neither was Hemmings. Most unusually for Vogel he was beginning to wonder why he bothered. Even to question whether he wished to continue to be a police officer.

He checked his watch. It was coming up to 6 p.m.

Normally when there was a major investigation on the go, particularly when it involved a child whose life might be in danger, Vogel would stay on duty until he was close to collapse from exhaustion. That was the kind of man he was. Sometimes he even stayed in his office overnight, sleeping

182

on a roll of foam he kept in a cupboard specially for that purpose.

This was not going to be one of those nights, Vogel decided. No. He wasn't heading back to Kenneth Steele House to vent his anger on Reg Hemmings. He was going home to see his wife and daughter. He had phoned Mary earlier and warned her to expect him when she saw him. Not that she needed warning; she knew him too well. He only hoped the shock of his early arrival wouldn't prove too much for her.

Thinking of his family cheered him as he set off for Temple Meads railway station, from where there were frequent trains to the suburb of Sea Mills. After all, it had stopped raining. And he was going to be home early.

By the time his train trundled into the little station the rain had begun again. Vogel hunched his shoulders against it as he hurried along the street. He really had no idea why he had yet to grasp that a raincoat, and a heavy-duty one at that, was necessary attire almost every day in his new location. In London, hopping on and off buses and in and out of squad cars, in the middle of a city which itself provided considerable protection from the elements, Vogel had rarely bothered with a coat even in the middle of winter.

Vogel's corduroy jacket, one of a small selection which formed his invariable working attire, was about to go the same way as his beloved old Hush Puppies. He very much feared he could smell it. Either that or he had mistakenly wrapped himself in a horse blanket. Even he was beginning to realize that almost all of his four or five corduroy jackets, in varying shades of murky brown and green with one dark grey one for formal occasions, had now reached a state which would soon demand replacement. What seemed to him to be a more or less daily drenching was not helping at all.

He turned up the collar. Just like earlier in the day, it didn't help much. He reached the gate to his bungalow, hurried up the brickwork path which cut through the gravelled front garden with a circular rose bed in the middle, unlocked the front door and stepped into the small carpeted hallway.

Tim, the family dog Vogel regarded as more his than anybody else's, threw himself at his master. Vogel rubbed the old border collie's head fondly and called out for his wife and daughter. There was no reply. He knew exactly where they would be.

He made his way into the kitchen and then headed for the narrow door that led into what had once been the connecting garage, generously large for a small two-bedroomed bungalow. The previous owner had converted the garage into a mini health spa, with a seventeen-foot endless pool and a sauna in one corner.

And that, although Vogel still couldn't get his head around it, was the reason he and his little family had uprooted themselves from their rented flat in a Pimlico mansion block and moved to the West.

Vogel's daughter, Rosamund, suffered from cerebral palsy. Although confined to a wheelchair, she could manage to walk a few steps with aids. She had quite good movement in her arms, and reasonable control, although she was liable to knock things over if she reached across a table for the salt and pepper. From the earliest age swimming therapy had helped her a great deal. More than that, she seemed happiest when in the water, and showed considerable aptitude for swimming.

Rosamund's mind was entirely unaffected by her condition and she was a bright child, although her speech was slightly hesitant and slurred. Sometimes Vogel wondered if her intelligence made her condition harder for his daughter to bear. He so hoped that it didn't.

Rosamund's great hero was the Welsh swimmer David Roberts, winner of eleven Paralympic gold medals and arguably Britain's greatest ever Paralympian. Roberts also suffered from cerebral palsy, albeit a milder form of the disorder than Rosamund's.

When they had lived in London Mary had taken Rosamund every Monday night to the Pimlico Puffins, a swimming club for people with disabilities. An hour once a week wasn't nearly enough for her. Mary, and Vogel when his work commitments allowed, had tried to take her swimming at other times. But it wasn't easy in a busy London pool with power swimmers thundering past, often with no consideration for other pool-users, disabled or otherwise.

They'd often thought how wonderful it would be to have their own pool where Rosamund could swim as often as she liked, but it had been one of those 'if we won the lottery' dreams. It hadn't seemed possible that a home with a swimming pool would be within their reach on Vogel's salary, even since his promotion to DI.

Then Mary had spotted an ad in *Somerset Life*, which she had picked up at the dentist, for this property in Sea Mills, conveniently adjacent to Bristol city centre. The bungalow was modest enough to fit their budget, even with the extraordinary addition of a small but ultra-modern pool equipped with a system of air jets for Rosamund to swim against. Because it was so small, only just over a metre deep, and well insulated, even the cost of heating the pool was affordable. Much as he hated leaving the rent-controlled apartment in the heart of London, Vogel hadn't hesitated. Nothing mattered more to him than the happiness of his wife and their only daughter.

The Vogels were not extravagant. They had saved enough over the years to be able to buy the Sea Mills bungalow with the help of only a modest mortgage.

Vogel opened the connecting door. The garage had been partially tiled in mock marble and decorated in the style of a Roman bath. Trompe-l'oeil pillars and urns entwined with vines adorned the walls. It never failed to surprise him every time he stepped inside.

Mary, wearing a big fluffy turquoise dressing gown that matched the colour of the water, was sitting at the edge of the pool, watching her daughter. It took her a moment to realize he was there. She turned, opened her eyes wide in surprise, then smiled.

Vogel raised one finger to his lips and mouthed, 'Shhhh.'

He wanted to watch Rosamund for a bit whilst she was still unaware of his presence. It was wonderful to see her, arms flailing, legs kicking as best she could, throwing all her energies into trying to combat the force of the endless pool's jet. She was so at home in the water that, at a glance, her disability, although severe, was not apparent.

After a minute or so Rosamund sensed her father's presence. She paused and turned to look at him. Her hair was wet and tousled. Her cheeks were flushed from her exertions. She beamed at Vogel. And, even to he who knew better, she looked not only blissfully happy but also a picture of health.

At moments like this, he thought, the move to Bristol was absolutely worthwhile. And even the prospect of having to deal with some up-himself Whitehall upstart in the morning seemed inconsequential.

'My goodness,' said Mary. 'I wasn't expecting to see you this early. To what do we owe the pleasure?'

'Don't ask,' said Vogel. 'All I want to do this evening is to enjoy being here with you and Rosamund.'

Next morning Vogel left for the station an hour later than usual – an unheard-of occurrence. Unable to totally disassociate himself from an investigation into a child's disappearance, he had phoned Margo Hartley at 7 a.m. for a progress report.

Only one new lead had come to light. CCTV analysis had revealed a blue Honda Accord arriving and leaving the development on the night Fred Mildmay disappeared. The owner of the vehicle, who had been away in London overnight, had reported it stolen when he arrived at Bristol Parkway the following morning to find it missing from the car park. The footage did not provide a clear view of the car's occupants, but it was possible to see that in addition to the driver there was a passenger who appeared to be of small stature. A suspect vehicle alert had been put out to police forces nationwide, and the Honda's details registered on ANPR (Automatic Number Plate Recognition) cameras throughout the country.

Once he was content that Margo had everything in hand, Vogel sat down for breakfast with his family, again surprising both his wife and daughter.

He wasn't behaving in this out-of-character manner because he was sulking. It was simply that he didn't see how he could function under the restrictions now imposed upon him. While he wasn't ready to conclude that Henry Tanner had abducted his grandchild, he was convinced that the man was withholding vital information. To be forbidden to contact

Tanner was not only infuriating, it was potentially cata-strophic. The fact that Tanner had friends in high places should never have been allowed to take precedence over the welfare of his grandson.

He arrived at his desk at Kenneth Steele House shortly before 9 a.m., still early enough for most men and women beginning a long working day, but a positively leisurely hour for Vogel, carrying, as was his habit, a cup of black coffee acquired from the vending machine in the corridor.

He switched on his computer, and sat for a moment star-ing at his screen saver, which featured his wife and daughter on a day trip to Torquay. Then he gave himself a bit of a mental shake. A child was missing. He must do what he could until the cavalry arrived. The unwelcome cavalry, in Vogel's opinion.

He resumed his covert checks on the Tanner family, focus-ing on the three aborted investigations into Tanner-Max. The first had taken place in the 1970s, when Edward Tanner had been running the company. There had been a second in the early 1990s, by which time Henry was chief executive. The third and most recent investigation had got underway in 2001. Vogel assumed there would be a box-file in the archives filled with papers detailing the findings of the first investiga-tion. The latter two investigations were on the computer database, but there was a suspicious lack of detail. And each investigation had been closed with no reason given. There were no further references to Tanner-Max on file after the aborted 2001 investigation.

Vogel decided to instigate checks on every officer whose name featured in connection with the investigations. He had always preferred assimilating data to talking to people, and the events of the previous afternoon had only confirmed to him that his preference was the right one.

They, that anonymous 'they' responsible for giving him orders he considered to be often incomprehensible and occasionally reprehensible, couldn't stop him using his brain, he thought. Not yet anyway.

After an hour of searching he had found no links between any of the officers, no common thread connecting the investigations, nor even any clear indication as to what had triggered these three investigations into the affairs of Tanner-Max.

He was debating his next line of enquiry when there was a knock on his office door. Without waiting for an invitation to enter, in walked a tall blonde woman wearing a sharply tailored black trouser suit. Vogel's jaw dropped. Literally. He had to make a concerted physical effort to close it.

Detective Chief Inspector Nobby Clarke looked at him with amused eyes.

Vogel struggled to his feet, almost knocking over his chair in the process. It was DCI Clarke who had headhunted Vogel, then a humble Met sergeant stationed at Charing Cross, to her Central London Murder and Serious Incident Team.

He still remembered with embarrassment his gauche behaviour when he had discovered that Nobby Clarke was not some wizened old male detective but an attractive woman. It was the name which had thrown him, of course. Nobody in the Met had ever managed to discover her real first name – assuming that she hadn't been christened Nobby. Even the DCI's driving licence, temporarily removed from her handbag one day by a pair of determined and devious detectives, gave her name as Nobby Clarke.

Vogel and Clarke liked and respected each other. Indeed Clarke had not been best pleased when Vogel requested a transfer to the Avon and Somerset Constabulary so soon after she had secured his MIT appointment, but he knew that she understood his reasons.

He was aware that Clarke too had a new job. He'd heard through the grapevine only a couple of weeks previously that she had been appointed to the recently reformed National Crime Squad, operating out of Scotland Yard, and primarily dealing with matters of importance to the state, and acts of terrorism. It hadn't occurred to him that she might be the London 'brass' sent to take over his operation. Why would it? How could the disappearance of an eleven-year-old child in Bristol merit the attention of the National Crime Squad? All the same, he was inordinately pleased to see Nobby Clarke.

'Bloody hell, boss,' he said. 'I wasn't expecting you.'

'All right, Vogel, take it easy. Am I that great a shock?'

Vogel smiled. 'Yep, but you've no idea how glad I am to see you, boss. I hadn't a clue who was going to be sent here, and nobody's told me what's going on. I've been trying to run an investigation with both hands cuffed behind my back and a blindfold on.'

Clarke raised one eyebrow. Vogel had never been able to do that.

'Run an investigation?' she queried. 'I thought DCI Hemmings was SIO?'

'Yeah, well, you know what I mean.'

'I sure do, Vogel.'

'I just need to know what's going on, so that I can do my job, that's all.'

'Don't expect me to be able to tell you much – not yet,

anyway,' said the DCI, sitting down in the chair opposite Vogel's desk. 'In the meantime, we have a child to find. So let's get on with it, shall we?'

'Right boss,' said Vogel, his spirits rising even though he was still none the wiser as to why Henry Tanner's family should command special treatment.

Fourteen

Henry Tanner felt lower than ever. He was the strongest of men. His complex way of life, his predilection for keeping so much of himself and his activities secret from most of his family and those around him, or at the very least compartmentalized, had made him so. But any sort of rejection from his family, not to mention an accusation as terrible as the one his daughter had made against him, was more than he could bear.

Also he had spent the night alone in his bed, because Felicity had decided to stay over at The Firs with her daughter. Henry was used to travelling alone; Felicity never accompanied him to London or on his occasional working trips abroad. He did not believe in mixing his family life and business. So throughout his marriage he had, sometimes for a night or two, sometimes a week or more, been accustomed to sleeping alone. Because Henry never shared his bed with anyone else. He was the most faithful of husbands.

But at his family home, the Corner House, he had never spent a single night without Felicity by his side. Until now.

It felt strange. Very strange indeed.

His alarm clock went off as usual at 6.30 a.m. It didn't wake him. He was already awake. He had hardly slept all night. As soon as the alarm bleeped, he rose, went down-stairs, put the kettle on and picked up the kitchen phone to call his wife on her mobile. Even at that hour he was sure everyone at The Firs would be up and about. In fact he doubted any of them would have had much more sleep than he'd managed. But he had no intention of calling the house phone at The Firs. He didn't know what he would say if Joyce answered the phone. And on present form he feared she could even hang up on him.

When his daughter had launched her attack on him the previous evening Henry had felt his legs buckle. His head went cold, as if his life's blood were draining from him. He suspected he'd turned quite grey. He'd been so shocked by Joyce's tirade that he hadn't even tried to defend himself when she had accused him of abducting Fred.

Afterwards he'd gone to the kitchen to join the rest of his family, along with Stephen, Janet, Monika, and Jim Grant.

Felicity had told him that Stephen had left in a taxi. Henry suspected he'd left because he was embarrassed. Henry was embarrassed too. He hated the thought of anyone seeing signs of weakness in him, so he asked Geoff to drive him home to the Corner House. He could have walked the hundred metres that separated the two houses, but he was afraid there might be reporters hovering at the end of the drive, and he didn't want to have to walk past them. On the way in he'd noticed a dark Mercedes estate car with tinted windows parked opposite the gates to The Firs. As Geoff had used his remote to open the gates and begun to steer the Bentley through, a young woman had leapt out of the estate car. Henry was sure he had guessed correctly, that this was a lurking news team, and that a photographer was hiding behind those tinted windows with camera focused on the entrance to The Firs. He'd wondered how they had got into Tarrant Park, and made a mental note to call security, give them a bollocking and tell them to sort out the press presence. But he just didn't have the energy.

He had felt numb. He still felt numb.

Felicity answered on the third ring.

'How are things, my dear? Any news?' he asked. He had no intention of letting his wife know that he, too, was suffering. Henry equated distress with weakness, and it would never do for him to admit to such a thing.

'No news,' she said, then added: 'Look, Henry, I've talked to Joyce. Is it true what she's saying? Did you know about this letter from Charlie before Joyce did, and did you know what it contained?'

'No, of course I didn't. I had no idea that the letter existed until Stephen told me. You must believe me.'

'I always believe you, Henry.'

For a moment it seemed to Henry there was an inflection in his wife's voice that he didn't recognize. Then he told himself he was imagining things.

'Good,' he said.

'Look, we can't have this going on between you and Joyce,' Felicity continued. 'We need all our strength. Perhaps you should pop round before you go to work . . . I assume you are going to work?'

Henry grunted.

'Thought so,' said Felicity. 'Right. Hang on a minute and I'll check with Joyce. Then I'll call you back.'

Henry had little choice but to agree, but he felt hard done by. Didn't anyone realize that he was upset too? He had enough self-knowledge to realize that was a damn silly question, given the effort he'd always put into concealing the fact he was capable of being upset. He was, however, annoyed. And he reckoned he had a right to be. His daughter owed it to him to trust him no matter what anybody said. Including his son-in-law.

All right, so he'd known about the letter. But he had his reasons for not wanting Joyce so see it. Reasons that had nothing to do with Charlie's diatribe against him.

Henry had been looking out for his family, like he always did.

He made himself tea, strong and sweet, dropping two Miles English Breakfast bags into a big china mug, adding boiling water, three sugars and a splash of milk. Then he paced up and down the kitchen, taking hurried sips of the hot liquid while waiting for his wife to call back.

He had to wait just over ten minutes. It seemed longer to Henry.

'Joyce says it's OK for you to call round,' said Felicity.

Her voice sounded flat. Henry was disappointed with the tone of the message. It was OK for him to call around – what was he, a passing insurance rep? He was even more disappointed that his daughter hadn't called herself. He assumed that meant she was still angry with him, still questioning his integrity.

He also found himself thinking how big it was of Joyce to allow her father to visit the house he had bought and presented to her as a gift.

Nonetheless he abandoned his up-market builder's tea, pulled on an old sweatshirt and a pair of jeans, somehow in too much of a hurry to get dressed for work before joining his family again, and hurried down the road.

He had totally forgotten the news team waiting outside The Firs, and had failed to call security as he'd intended.

There'd been other things on his mind. The press were still there. He cursed silently. He didn't know whether the same team had waited all night. There were two more of them now, four altogether, and a second car he didn't recognize was parked a little further down Palladian Road. Two reporters and two photographers, it seemed. Henry had instructed Geoff the previous evening that he wanted to be picked up at 7.30 a.m. as usual to be driven to work. He wished he'd waited for his driver to arrive so that he could have dropped him at The Firs. It would have been so much easier to pass the gathered press in a vehicle than to walk through them. But that was what he had to do. Either that or turn back, which he had no intention of doing. In any case they would probably follow him.

Even though he was unshaven and out of sorts, Henry marched through the vultures with his customary composure, remaining expressionless, saying nothing except to ask them coldly if they realized they were on private property.

As he walked up the drive he used his mobile to call the head of security and deliver the bollocking he had planned the previous night. The man promised to sort the matter straight away. He sounded nervous. Well, so he should. Not only had two carloads of press managed to blag their way into the allegedly protected gated development, but security had also allowed Fred to slip through their extremely suspect net. It now seemed impossible that the boy remained anywhere within Tarrant Park.

Inside the house Joyce was polite, but cool. Henry greeted his daughter warmly, attempting to behave as if nothing untoward had occurred between them. Which, of course, was the Henry Tanner way. He stepped towards Joyce, arms outstretched. She dodged his embrace and merely murmured a good morning.

Confrontation was not Henry's way. Neither was he any good at talking things through. He only hoped his daughter would come round. People did, in his experience. If you left them alone. And that suited him. It was his natural inclination.

He made a huge fuss of his granddaughter, who, unlike her mother, fell into his arms, seeking the reassurance he invariably gave, but on this occasion could not. Although he did his best.

Henry held Molly close so that she could not see his face and muttered platitudes which sounded, even to him, to be just that.

'It will be all right, sweetheart. The police will find Fred very soon now. Granddad will see to that. Granddad will look after you.'

And so on.

Felicity, he pecked on the cheek. As always. And she gave him a peck back. As always.

Monika had left the previous night to sleep in her own home, a one-bedroomed council flat on the old sixties tower-block development near the airport. But, to the surprise of the appreciative family, she had already returned. At least Monika had good wheels. Because Tarrant Park was not served by public transport, Henry had decreed that Mark's old Mini, which was no longer needed now that he'd been presented with a Porsche to mark his induction into the family business, should be put at her disposal. And Monika had seemed to accept that there was no such thing as a free lunch, let alone a rather good motorcar. She was invariably available when needed, and not only in a time of crisis such as that currently engulfing the family. Not that there had ever been anything like that before.

Monika offered Henry coffee and toast. Realizing suddenly that he had eaten nothing the evening before and little the previous day, Henry accepted gratefully.

The family sat around the kitchen table together. They were all out of bed and up and about, as he had expected. Assuming any of them had been to bed. Felicity, Joyce, Mark, and Molly. Henry's entire remaining family. But they were only physically together, Henry thought. Mentally each was in his or her own world.

And he could feel the distrust and suspicion still emanating from the daughter he so loved.

However, being Henry, he didn't push the point.

Instead, just before nine, after he had been at The Firs for almost two hours, every minute of which had felt like a day, Henry could stand it no longer. He knew that Geoff was waiting outside in the Bentley. Henry had redirected him when his driver had phoned after arriving at the Corner House at the appointed hour to discover his boss was not at home. Henry had no intention of running the press gauntlet for a second time that morning.

'Right,' Henry said, addressing the entire family. 'I'm off home to grab a quick shower and get ready for work.'

Felicity merely stared at him. She didn't protest. Neither did she look surprised. Merely resigned. She had already made it clear that she assumed he planned to go to work. She had also somehow made it clear that she disapproved. But this had done nothing to change Henry's mind.

Joyce was less subtle. She went for her father's jugular again, her voice trembling with rage.

'I can't believe you're going to bloody work, Dad,' she

snapped. 'But then, as it's you, I suppose I can bloody believe it.'

Henry made himself appear to be as calm as ever, although he felt a rare burst of emotion bubbling up inside him.

'You don't want me here, Joyce, I know that,' he said quietly. 'I can feel it. I think it's better that I go to the office. You know where I am if anything, uh, changes.'

'Glad you can feel something, Dad,' snapped Joyce.

Henry winced. 'If only you knew, darling,' he muttered.

He checked his phone again. He was still waiting for a call he had been half hoping for and half dreading. Perhaps he had missed it? Of course he hadn't. His phone had been glued to him all morning. He'd held it in his hand for most of the time and was still clutching it as he left the house and climbed into the back of the Bentley. Perhaps there was never going to be any such phone call.

He told Geoff to run him back to the Corner House. There were still press outside The Firs, but two uniformed security guards were at last in attendance and were remonstrating with them. That gave Henry some satisfaction. His bidding had been reasonably swiftly done. He still couldn't understand how the reporters and cameramen had been allowed into Tarrant Park in the first place.

It took Henry less than half an hour to shower, shave, dress in a business suit, and also to make a quick call to Stephen on his mobile to tell him he was on his way. Stephen sounded surprised.

'Uh, I didn't think you'd be in today, Henry,' he said.

'And why not?' enquired Henry crustily.

'Well, I thought you'd be with the family.'

Henry grunted. He had no intention of commenting on this.

'And where are you?' he asked.

'Um, I'm at home. Wasn't sure what to do . . . or where I'd be most needed.'

Stephen stumbled over his words. He sounded unsure of himself, Henry thought. After all, the younger man knew all about Henry Tanner's work ethic. Had it honestly not occurred to Stephen Hardcastle that he would be expected to go into the office as usual that day, and that Henry would be sure to do the same?

'Where you're always most needed, old boy,' said Henry sharply. 'In the office. Where I pay you to be.'

'Sure,' Stephen replied easily enough. 'I'll get myself there straight away. But . . . are you all right, Henry?' Stephen continued. 'I mean, it's so terrible about Fred. Awful for the whole family. You're the one everyone always relies on, though. How are you?'

'When I want you to know how I am, old boy, I'll tell you,' said Henry.

It was vintage Tanner. The kind of put-down that rolled automatically off Henry's tongue.

'I'll see you at the office,' he continued. 'I'm about to leave home.'

Henry almost managed a smile then. His intention to carry on with business as usual had surprised Stephen. And Henry liked to surprise people, keep them on their toes, even people who had worked with him for many years, people such as Stephen whom he regarded as a friend as well as a member of his staff in spite of being aware that he seldom treated Stephen that way.

All he had to do now was to find a way to surprise the mystery caller whose number was withheld and who had so far only left a text message on the pay-as-you-go mobile very few people knew that Henry had. Henry had a fair idea who the texter was, or at least who he represented. As soon as he'd been told that Fred was missing Henry had sent an email. An innocuous enough email, he hoped. And he was pretty sure it was the email recipient who had texted him. If he could wrong-foot the bastard then maybe he could sort this mess out. The police were no help; that DI Vogel probably thought he was a clever bugger, but he wasn't nearly clever enough to sort out this situation. There was only one person with a hope in hell of doing that, and that was Henry Tanner himself.

Yet, for once in his life, Henry had no idea how he was going to do that.

However, when he left the Corner House, Henry would have appeared to any observer to be setting off for a normal day at work with nothing more pressing on his mind than dealing with a spreadsheet or two before breaking for a spot of lunch. Which was Henry's intention. He always behaved as if he were being watched. And quite often, not merely at this moment of crisis, he suspected that he *was* being watched. He was dressed in one of his immaculately tailored suits, his silk tie carefully knotted, his handmade shoes gleaming.

And so, as he climbed into the Bentley, also gleaming in the morning sun, Henry looked the same as he always did. Nobody watching him would have guessed his inner turmoil. Something Henry had made absolutely sure of.

Henry always had to be the man in charge. He felt that he had no choice. There had never been anyone else, not since his father, and sometimes Henry thought there never would be. But that morning he was battling terrible uncertainties. Henry so wished he had someone to turn to, someone to confide in. Someone who might help him. But that was not the way he had structured his life. He never cried for help. And he wouldn't now. Not least because there was no one to answer his cry.

Geoff drove through Tarrant Park and along the leafy country lanes in an almost leisurely fashion. Henry didn't hurry his driver. The truth was that Henry was only going to the office out of habit and because he had nowhere else to go. Nor, until the next call came, anything better to do. It was an attempt to numb the pain, and to keep himself occupied until he did have something constructive to do. His house was empty and would be no kind of home for as long as Felicity was staying at The Firs with her daughter. And he was clearly not welcome there.

Tanner-Max had its own parking area in Traders' Court, a cobbled courtyard at the rear of the building. The name dated back to the murky heyday of the port of Bristol when the old courtyard had been used by traders bartering slaves shipped in from Africa and the West Indies. Henry always used the rear entrance; he was a creature of habit. As Geoff turned into Traders' Court, Henry's mind was all over the place. He was barely aware that they had arrived at their destination.

Absent-mindedly, out of habit again, Henry checked his watch. It was five minutes past ten. Two hours later than he usually started work. Even Henry had to admit that this was not a usual day.

Geoff pulled to a halt and climbed out of the vehicle to open the rear door for his employer. Only then did Henry hoist himself off the back seat and out of the car in a manner he had perfected that did not, he hoped, draw attention to his creaking joints in general and his stiff right knee in particular. He stood up straight as quickly as he could, using one hand pressed against the roof of the car to give himself extra support.

He muttered a thank you to Geoff and took a step away from the Bentley.

Then, suddenly the world went mad. There was a single loud crack.

Henry fell to the ground as if he had been shot. He *had* been shot. But as he lapsed into unconsciousness he was not even aware of what had happened. He neither heard the gun being fired nor felt the bullet which entered his body. He just went down. Like a felled animal.

The shot had come from above. There had only been the one. So far.

Geoff was slow to register what had happened, but when he did he sprang into action. It could have been instinctive, but was actually something he had been trained to do long ago yet had almost forgotten about. He threw his body forward and flung himself on top of Henry Tanner, completely covering the fallen man and protecting him from any further gunfire. But Geoff Brooking was already too late. There was no need for any further gunfire. Henry Tanner was down.

On the rooftop of the building next to Tanner-Max a black-clad hooded figure carrying a sniper's rifle melted away into the murky skies of yet another damp Bristol morning. He had not attempted to fire a second time. One shot was all that had been required.

Fifteen

Vogel was first to hear the news. Dispatch alerted him at 10.15 a.m., saying there had been a 999 report of a shooting in Traders' Court. They didn't have the identity of the victim, but given the proximity to the Tanner-Max premises and the disappearance of Henry Tanner's grandson, the young PC on duty thought Vogel would want to be informed.

The DI half ran to Nobby Clarke's office, a cubicle off the Operation Binache incident room. Hemmings was in there with her.

'There's been a shooting,' he blurted out. 'Behind the offices of Tanner-Max.'

'Fuck,' said DCI Clarke.

'Get down there, both of you,' instructed Hemmings.

He wasn't actually in a position to order Nobby Clarke about, but such was the habit of senior station officers.

Clarke and Vogel took off at speed down the corridor. When they reached the stairs, Clarke paused and put a hand on Vogel's arm.

'I don't suppose you've done anything useful like learn to drive in the time you've been here?' she enquired.

Vogel shook his head.

'And I came on the bloody train,' muttered Clarke.

Both officers looked around desperately for someone to commandeer to drive them.

On cue, Constable Bolton appeared, carrying a packet of sandwiches and a cardboard beaker.

'Forget breakfast, you're needed,' barked Vogel.

'But I only came here to drop in some stuff for the tech boys,' protested Bolton. 'I'm supposed to get my arse straight back to Lockleaze.'

Neither Clarke nor Vogel had any jurisdiction over Bolton, but Vogel didn't care.

'I don't give a damn about that,' he snapped. 'This is an emergency. I'll square it with your sergeant. Come on, there's been a shooting and we need you to get us there fast. You in a squad car?'

Bolton nodded. Vogel saw the expression in the young man's eyes change. A shooting. That was something far removed from routine police work. PC Bolton abandoned his breakfast, turned on his heel and set off at a run, leading Vogel and Clark to a squad car at the far side of the car park. Bolton zapped the vehicle open as he ran. He climbed quickly behind the wheel. Vogel and Clarke got in the back. So that they could talk, Vogel hoped.

Vogel's mobile rang: Dispatch. Vogel put his phone on speaker so that Clarke could also hear.

'There's an officer on the scene now, guv. He's reported that the victim of the shooting is Henry Tanner.'

'How bad is it?' asked Vogel.

'PC Tompkins doesn't know, guv. Blood everywhere, though, and Tanner is unconscious.'

'Shit,' said Vogel, ending the call. 'C'mon, Bolton, step on it!'

'Yessir!'

Bolton stepped on it all right, swinging the little Ford around a passing pantechnicon with a screech of rubber, then in and out of lanes and dodging oncoming traffic, siren wailing, lights flashing and blazing.

Unusually, Vogel was oblivious to the wild driving. He had other things on his mind. Clarke didn't speak, but Vogel could see that whatever intrigue had brought her to Bristol, she hadn't been expecting this any more than he had.

Vogel had only even been involved in a shooting once in his life, a little over a year ago in London, and his stomach still churned at the thought of it. David Vogel had behaved in a rather out of character way on that occasion. He'd been positively cavalier in fact. And he had ended up in hospital. He didn't share DC Bolton's excitement at the thought of approaching the scene of a shooting. Indeed, he sincerely hoped the shooting would be over by the time they got to Traders' Court.

'So what do you think, boss?' he asked, turning to the DCI. 'Henry Tanner has copped one. Could be dead. Where does that leave us?'

'I have no idea,' she replied.

'Oh come on, boss, the grandfather of our missing child has been shot. Please will you tell me what's going on?' he demanded.

'Not now, Vogel,' said the DCI, glancing pointedly at PC Bolton.

Vogel didn't think Bolton was aware of anything much except the road ahead. But he refrained from saying more.

It was Janet who broke the news of Henry's shooting to the family. She had been in the office when the Tanner Bentley arrived in Traders' Court. Unlike Stephen Hardcastle she'd had no doubt that was where her boss would want her to be. As usual. Even on such a highly unusual day.

She heard the noise of the shot whilst sitting at her desk. She told herself it was a car back-firing, but somehow she immediately knew better. And she'd had a pretty clear idea of the direction from which that noise had come. She hurried to the toilet at the back of the building, the only place from which there was a window overlooking the courtyard.

From that window she had seen Henry lying motionless on the ground, eyes closed, with Geoff Brooking lying half on top of him.

It took a second or two for Janet to take in what had happened. The bang, the loud crack she had heard, had been a shot. Henry Tanner had been shot. Geoff Brooking must be trying to protect him from any further fire.

Janet withdrew from her vantage point and dialled 999. She was about to run downstairs and see if she could help, when her natural survival instincts kicked in. Whoever had shot Henry might still be out there. Janet was afraid. She decided to stay exactly where she was. But there was something she could do. The family had to be told, and it would be far better coming from her than some anonymous police officer. She debated with herself how best to tell them. It would be another tremendous shock to people already dealing with the turmoil and heartache of a missing child.

She decided to call Mark Mildmay. He would almost certainly be at The Firs with the rest of the family. Even Henry Tanner would not expect his grandson to be at the office that day.

Mark answered at the second ring. Hesitant. Nervous. Yet his voice was also expectant, hopeful even. She imagined all the family were in a similar state, hoping each phone call would bring good news, and fearing that it might bring bad.

She had bad news all right. But not the bad news they would all be dreading.

'It's your grandfather, Mark,' she told him bluntly, unable to think of a gentle way. 'I'm so sorry. He's been shot.'

She could hear Mark Mildmay's sharp intake of breath. It seemed a long time before he spoke.

'Dear God,' he said.

In the background she could hear female voices, Joyce, Felicity and maybe Molly. She couldn't make them out individually. It was obvious though that they had been listening, anxious yet half hopeful, and were reacting to Mark's response. She heard them asking Mark what was wrong, what had happened.

'Is he d-dead?' asked Mark.

In the background there was a stifled scream, a woman's cry so shrill that it rose above the chorus of voices.

Then Mark's voice, distant, not directed at the receiver: 'No, no. It's not Fred. Everyone, it's not Fred. Wait a minute . . .'

'Mark, are you still there?'

'Yes, Janet.' Mark's voice was louder. He was speaking into the receiver again.

'I don't know,' said Janet. 'I don't know how your grandfather is. He was shot in the car park. I've called for the police and an ambulance. He's on the ground. Just lying there. Geoff seems to be trying to protect him. In case there are any more shots, I think . . . Oh Mark . . .'

Janet began to cry. She couldn't help it. She supposed she was in shock too. She'd done what she knew she must: she'd called the emergency services and then the family. Like the good PA she was. But now the reality of it all was beginning to hit her. She could no longer hold herself together.

'I'm on my way,' said Mark.

Throughout the call Joyce had been at her son's side, trying to hear what Janet was saying. She had grasped enough to have the gist of it. But she stepped back and allowed Mark to break the news as gently as he could to Felicity and Molly.

Felicity already seemed to know. It was she who had screamed. Not Joyce.

Molly wasn't taking anything in. Felicity had turned a ghostly white and collapsed into a chair with her hand over her mouth.

'It'll be all right, Mum,' Joyce said, running to her side and putting an arm around her. 'Dad is tough as old boots, he'll be all right. He has to be. What would any of us do without him . . .'

She realized she was babbling. She couldn't stop herself.

'But who would shoot Granddad?' asked Molly, her face full of bewilderment.

'I don't know, darling,' said her mother.

'First Fred disappears and then Granddad is shot.' Molly was frowning now, trying to make sense of it. 'There must be a connection, mustn't there? I mean, things like this don't happen. Now we have Fred missing and Grandpa shot. Is that a coincidence? I mean, it can't be, can it?'

'I don't know, darling,' said Joyce again.

She too was beginning to think. Her last words to her father had been to tell him to fuck off. The family seemed to specialize in making unpleasant remarks to each other, only for something terrible to happen to the family member they'd made the remark to. Molly had told her brother she was going to kill him. And that was the last time any of them had seen him. Molly might have been joking, but that hadn't stopped her from feeling dreadful about what she had said, and it had made her brother's disappearance even worse for her.

Joyce had not been joking. She had meant every word that she'd said to her father over the last day or two. And she had told him to fuck off because she held him responsible for Fred's disappearance. Charlie's letter had led her down that path. She had built up a dossier of doubts about her father inside her head and thrown them at him. Culminating in telling him he was no longer welcome in her home and that he could fuck off.

Now she was in turmoil.

Her father had been shot. She only hoped the words she'd said to her mother would turn out to be true, that he'd pull through, that he wasn't at this moment lying dead in Traders' Court. The fact that he had been shot surely meant that he was innocent of any involvement in Fred's disappearance. Most likely he'd been shot by whoever abducted Fred. Because Joyce now had no doubt that Fred had been abducted. As Molly had said, it would be too much of a coincidence to think that Henry had been shot and Fred taken by anyone other than the same perpetrator.

'I'm going down there,' said Mark, interrupting her train of thought. 'One of us should be there. One of us should be with Granddad.'

'I'll come with you,' said Joyce.

'No, Mum, you stay here,' said Mark. 'We don't know what's going on yet, it could still be dangerous, and you have to stay here in case there's any news of Fred.'

Joyce found herself nodding her agreement. She was used

to deferring to the men in her life. But she had never heard her eldest son assert himself like this. It was as if the Tanner gene was kicking in and he was instinctively stepping in as head of the family. It occurred to her that he might well be the last man standing. Her brother William was dead, her husband was dead, her father might be dead ... and Fred, not yet a man, might never have the chance to grow into one.

It was a terrifying scenario. Joyce felt the tears rising. She hadn't thought she could be any more shocked, but every day seemed to bring some new horror. Molly was right: coincidence was out of the question. Joyce supposed she had always suspected there was some form of conspiracy surrounding her family. Now it seemed to her that they were under attack. And she wanted to know why. If Henry survived, nobody would keep her from his side. She was going to make him tell her what he knew, she was damned sure of that. But for the moment there was little she could do except wait.

Beside her, Felicity had rallied and was rising unsteadily to her feet.

'You're right about your mother staying here, Mark,' said Felicity. 'But I am coming with you and please don't try to stop me. Henry is my husband and my place is by his side.'

Mark did not try to stop her. Instead, her son, her suddenly strong son, put his arm around his grandmother and walked with her to the door, where he turned to speak to his mother.

'I'll call you as soon as I know anything,' he said. 'I promise.'

Joyce nodded. As the door closed behind him, she wrapped an arm around her daughter and pulled her close. Neither of them could stop the tears.

*

An ambulance, it transpired, had arrived moments before Vogel, Clarke and Bolton. Paramedics were attending to the fallen man, who lay in a pool of blood. A second man, his clothes also covered in blood, was standing alongside.

Clarke led the way across the car park to join them.

'How bad is it?' she asked one of the paramedics.

'He should live,' the man replied. 'It's a shoulder wound. Right shoulder, well away from the vital organs. But the bones are shattered.'

Henry lay prone on the ground, unconscious. There was no sign of movement.

'Would a shoulder wound cause him to lose consciousness?' Clarke asked. 'The pain must be excruciating, I suppose.'

'Doubt he's felt any yet,' said the paramedic. 'He will when he comes round though . . . assuming he comes round.'

'So what are his chances?'

'He must have fallen heavily when the shot hit him. See that patch of matted blood in his hair? Cracked his head when he hit the ground – that's what knocked him out. And you never know with head wounds.'

Clarke turned her attention to the uniformed police officers on the scene. One was PC Tompkins, the officer who had called in the shooting. The other two, an older man who had introduced himself as PC Hawkins, and his younger female partner, PC Phillips, had got to Traders' Court soon after Tompkins.

'Have you checked the place out?' Clarke asked. 'Any sign of our gunman?'

Constable Phillips answered: 'Checked it best we can, ma'am. There was no one suspicious about the place when we arrived. Just one shot fired, and it seemed to come from above.' She waved a hand towards the rooftops. 'We haven't been able to get up there yet, but we've been keeping an eye, and we've had a team checking out the surrounding streets. I reckon the bastard took off straight away, ma'am.'

Clarke nodded. She thought that probably nobody should be in Traders' Court. Neither she nor the rest of the police officers or the paramedics. But it was too late to worry about that. They were there. And as there had been no further shots, PC Phillips was probably right in her assessment of the situation.

The DCI looked enquiringly at the man with the blood-stained clothes.

'I'm Geoff Brooking, Henry Tanner's driver,' he told her.

'Are you hurt?' asked Clarke, indicating the blood on his jacket.

Geoff Brooking shook his head. 'It's Mr Tanner's blood.'

'And how did you get it all over you?' the DCI asked.

'I was trying to protect him, ma'am,' said Brooking. 'Only I was too slow.'

Clarke registered his reaction to the shooting and the way he had immediately begun to address her as ma'am.

'Are you ex-job?' she asked.

Brooking nodded. 'Sort of.'

'What did you do, throw yourself across Mr Tanner?' Clarke enquired.

Geoff Brooking nodded again. He didn't appear to want to say any more.

'Are you Mr Tanner's bodyguard then, as well as a driver?' Clarke persisted.

'No, ma'am. Not really. Just trying to help.'

'Right, and what does "sort of" ex-job mean, exactly?'

'I was a civil servant, that's all.'

Brooking sounded as if he'd been programmed to with-hold information.

'Protection work?' queried Clarke. It was an educated guess.

'Well, you know the sort of thing, ma'am,' said Brooking.

Clarke continued to look at him enquiringly, but the driver-cum-bodyguard seemed to have clammed up. The DCI decided to leave it for now. She had a shrewd idea what his background might be.

She looked around the cobbled courtyard surrounded by high- and middle-rise office blocks. At that moment a red Jaguar came through the alleyway leading into the courtyard, tyres screeching noisily as it jerked to a halt at the police cordon. The driver jumped out, ducked under the ribbon, and started to run towards the prone man, shouting: 'Oh my God, is that Henry? Oh my God, what's happened?'

Hawkins and Phillips swiftly grabbed an arm each and restrained him. Then they led him back towards his vehicle, all three of them ducking under the cordon ribbon.

Clarke glanced enquiringly at Vogel, who was standing by her side. He told her the driver of the Jaguar was Stephen Hardcastle.

Clarke approached Hardcastle and introduced herself.

The lawyer was sweating. His eyes were wide open with shock. He was displaying none of his usual cool, but his voice was calmer and at a more normal level when he next spoke.

'Is that Henry?' he asked, gesturing towards the prone man on the floor, partly concealed from view by the para-medics.

Clarke affirmed that it was. 'I am afraid Mr Tanner has been shot.'

'Oh my God,' said Hardcastle for the third time. 'I mean, how? Who? Why?'

'That's a lot of questions, Mr Hardcastle,' said Clarke. 'At this stage in our enquiries I'm afraid we don't have the answers – but I do have some questions for you. Let's start with when you last saw Mr Tanner?'

'Yesterday evening,' Hardcastle replied, a slight tremor in his voice. 'We were all gathered at his daughter's house. Henry's grandson is missing – but you know about that, don't you?'

Clarke affirmed that she did.

Hardcastle seemed to notice Vogel for the first time.

'Yes, DI Vogel took Henry and me to be interviewed at Lockleaze police station. Henry's driver, Geoff, drove us back to The Firs afterwards. I, uh, thought I would leave the family to it. They needed to be alone.'

Hardcastle then noticed Geoff, standing there in his bloodstained clothes. He gulped, propping himself against the bonnet of his Jag, as if he needed support.

'The boy, the boy being missing, you don't think that's connected, do you – to Henry being shot?' he asked.

'At this point I cannot comment, Mr Hardcastle,' replied Clarke. 'Can you tell me your movements since yesterday evening when you left the Mildmay home.'

'I went straight back to my place. Got there about six, I think. Oh, I stopped at the Waitrose up the road. I suddenly realized I hadn't eaten all day and I was starving. Then I went home. I microwaved a ready meal and ate it watching TV. Anything to take my mind off what had happened. And this morning I was at home until Henry called me. He told me to get my arse into the office.'

Hardcastle's features stretched into a forced grin. 'Typical

215

Henry, that. It hadn't occurred to me that he'd want me at work today, let alone that he would come in himself. Not with young Fred still missing. I might have known it though. He gave me a bit of a bollocking.'

'What time did he call you?' Vogel asked.

'It was about half past nine, I think,' said Hardcastle. 'I was just wondering whether to call the family. I didn't want to disturb or bother them, but I wanted them to know I was there for them.'

'And where do you live?' Vogel asked.

'Down by the Floating Harbour,' replied Hardcastle. 'Conqueror House, one of the new apartment blocks.'

'So you could drive here in ten minutes?'

'Well yes, thereabouts,' Hardcastle stumbled.

Vogel checked his watch. It was ten forty-five.

'Then what took you so long?'

'Well, I was in total shock last night. I took a bottle of whisky to bed with me – something I don't normally do. I'd only been awake for a minute or two when Henry called, and I had a fearful hangover. I'm not used to booze. I shaved and showered and was about to leave when I began to feel sick. Before I could make it to the bathroom, I threw up down the front of my shirt. So I had to change, then I drank some water and lay down on the bed until my stomach settled.'

Vogel and Clarke both stared at him hard. They were a good double act. They were weighing up whether to believe Hardcastle or not, and somehow made that quite obvious.

'So you would have been pretty sure that Henry Tanner would get here before you?' asked Vogel.

'Well, yes.'

'And wouldn't it annoy him that you had taken so long to follow his instruction?'

'Not as much as it would have annoyed him if I'd thrown up over his desk,' muttered Hardcastle.

Vogel did not look amused.

'Is there anyone who can confirm what you have told us, sir?' he asked. 'Or were you alone at home?'

'I was alone.' Hardcastle wiped the back of one hand across his forehead. He was sweating. 'If I need an alibi, I'm afraid I don't have one. But I wouldn't know how to do something like this even if I wanted to.'

'And might you want to?' Vogel asked.

'Are you out of your mind!' snapped Hardcastle, finding some spirit. Then he glanced nervously up at the silhouettes of rooftops surrounding the courtyard. 'How do we know the bastard who did this isn't still up on a roof somewhere? How do we know it was only Henry he was after?'

Clarke studied him carefully. Hardcastle had echoed her own worst-case scenario thoughts. Nonetheless there was something about the man's responses that didn't feel right to her, though she couldn't grasp what it was. Then again, people's responses were often difficult to fathom in traumatic circumstances, and the shooting of one's employer certainly qualified on that score. Nevertheless Clarke remained uneasy.

'We don't, sir,' she said. 'But I'm puzzled by your last remark. Have you some idea who might have been "after" Henry Tanner?'

Clarke knew far more about Henry Tanner than Vogel did. She'd read the confidential files and acquainted herself with his history before leaving London. But she was beginning to wonder if she knew the whole story, or even anything approaching it.

Hardcastle shot a nervous glance up at the skyline again. But his shock and confusion were beginning to lift. He sounded wary when he spoke again.

'I have no idea who might be behind this shooting,' he said. 'I'm in a state, that's all. I suddenly thought I might be next.'

'For any particular reason?' asked Clarke.

'No, of course not. But no one knows yet why Henry was shot, do they? He was gunned down by a sniper outside his own office. I'm his closest associate, now that his son and son-in-law are both dead. Wouldn't anybody in that situation think they might be next? Or even that they could have been supposed to be first. I could have arrived here at any time, maybe even before Henry.'

He had a point, thought Clarke.

'Or it could have been one of those random shootings, like Hungerford and that lunatic in Cumbria. I'm a bit shaky, that's all.'

'We believe only one shot was fired,' said Clarke. 'It seems our gunman made himself scarce once he'd shot Mr Tanner. Nothing random about that, is there?'

'I didn't know that, did I?' responded Hardcastle. 'You didn't tell me how many shots had been fired.'

You couldn't argue with that either, thought the DCI.

'All right, Mr Hardcastle. You look a bit shaky, so I'm going to ask the paramedics to have a look at you, and then you can go. But we'll need to interview you fully later on, all right?'

The man nodded.

Clarke walked away, turning to Vogel, who was still at her side. She thought he was probably keeping close in the hope of learning something. Vogel was neither a man to give up nor one who took kindly to being kept in the dark. She decided he needed something to do, a task that would take his mind off matters that she wasn't in a position to share with him.

'Vogel, get a search team down here, would you,' she ordered. 'Oh, and check where the fuck CSI are.'

Clarke shook her head wryly. The familiar SOCOs, Scenes Of Crime Officers, had a year or two previously been 'rebranded' by most police forces as Crime Scene Investigators. They weren't even police officers nowadays, but civilian staff who wore dark-blue uniforms bearing the CSI logo. Clarke thought it had given them an exaggerated sense of their own importance. That and the American TV series some of them seemed to think they were part of.

'The paramedics are trampling all over the scene,' she observed. 'Let's hope it's worth it and they can keep Tanner alive.'

Vogel nodded, took his phone from his pocket, and started to move away from his senior officer. He hadn't spoken a word to her since their arrival at the car park, except when she had directly addressed him.

'Oh, and Vogel, stop fucking sulking,' she called after him.

'Don't know what you mean, boss,' replied Vogel, deadpan.

'All right, I give in – we'll have a chat at the end of the day,' Clarke promised, rather against her better judgement.

Vogel smiled. Almost. It was more a stretching exercise with his lips, thought Clarke.

Sixteen

Henry Tanner showed signs of beginning to recover consciousness as he was being loaded into the ambulance which would take him to Southmead, the newly renovated and extended hospital complex that housed Bristol's premier accident and emergency department.

His eyes flickered open then shut again. He raised one hand a few inches then let it drop. He moaned two or three times, and even seemed to be attempting to speak.

But Henry had received a nasty bang on the head and been shot. He was not a young man. None of those gathered in Traders' Court, not even the paramedics, were in a position to speculate on Henry's chances of recovery, even though the signs were encouraging.

DCI Clarke climbed into the ambulance alongside the injured man. Vogel made a move to follow.

'No,' commanded Nobby Clarke. 'This won't take the two of us. You go tell the family what's happened. I'll see what our Henry has to say when he's a bit more lucid.'

I'll bet you will, thought Vogel. And you don't want me to know what that might be, either, I'm pretty damned sure of that.

'I'd rather come with you, boss,' he protested. 'I feel I need to know more . . .'

'Just get on with it, Vogel,' instructed the DCI. 'I want this area properly checked out – have someone pull up all the CCTV in the vicinity. And ANPR too – let's get the registration of every vehicle arriving and leaving the area around the time of the incident. You never know . . .'

You certainly didn't, thought Vogel. The Avon and Somerset Constabulary, in common with other police forces, was not even privy to where ANPR cameras were positioned. There was, however, a specialist team of civilian investigators trained to study and evaluate CCTV and ANPR footage.

'Yes, boss,' he muttered resignedly.

Clarke gestured for the paramedic nearest the open ambulance doors to shut them in the DI's face.

Vogel stood back and watched as the ambulance trundled off. He doubted he was going to learn much more from Nobby Clarke. Not for the time being anyway. Even if she did fulfil her promise to brief him later, he had a feeling she might still be economical with the truth.

Clarke had always been open with information in the past. Whatever lay behind this curious business, it had to be something at government level; that was the world Nobby Clarke moved in nowadays. Vogel was beginning to suspect a cover-up, the sort of thing that allowed criminals to get away with their crimes. He had no time for that sort of thing. He was a copper, not some latter-day George Smiley.

But despite his reservations he did what he always did and got on with his job. As Nobby Clarke had told him to.

When he'd finished coordinating the search and forensic teams who would investigate the shooting, Vogel asked PC Bolton to drive him to Tarrant Park. He didn't know for certain that the family would be there, but he deemed it unlikely they would leave The Firs empty whilst young Fred Mildmay was still missing. On the way he called PC Saslow to tell her he was en route. She told him the family had not wanted her to stay the night, even though she had offered to do so, but that she was heading back there now.

'I'm only about five minutes away, boss,' she said. 'Do you have some news.'

'Not about the boy,' Vogel replied. He told her about the shooting.

'Shit,' said Saslow.

'Exactly,' said Vogel.

He asked her not to say anything about the incident to Joyce Mildmay or anybody else until he got there.

It was midday by the time he arrived at Tarrant Park. Vogel had had only limited experience of missing persons cases, but he knew that no matter how remote the possibility, families continued to cling to the hope that their loved one might walk in unharmed at any second.

He was not to be disappointed. Joyce Mildmay's first words when she opened the door were: 'Have you got news of Fred?'

Vogel thought that was normal enough behaviour for a woman in her situation. Even though it quickly became apparent that she already knew her father had been shot.

Once she had ascertained that the DI's visit was not directly linked to Fred's disappearance, she told Vogel that her elder son and her mother had gone to the scene of the shooting, arriving soon after the ambulance conveying Henry Tanner to A & E had left, and presumably not long after Vogel had departed.

'Mum called a few minutes ago,' Joyce explained. 'They've gone on to the hospital.'

She went on to say that her mother had been told by one of the police constables on duty at the scene that Henry had been unconscious but had appeared to be coming round when he was being loaded into the ambulance. Vogel made a mental note to find out which officer and give him a bollocking. It wasn't a policeman's place to give medical reports.

Joyce then led Vogel into the sitting room instead of the kitchen, where he assumed Molly and PC Saslow were.

'I'd like to speak to you alone first, Mr Vogel,' she said, closing the door firmly behind them.

He nodded, waiting for her to continue.

'When Dad comes to, I bloody well want him to tell us why all this has happened. Because one thing's certain, Mr Vogel: my father knows the answer. He has the answer to everything that happens in this bloody family.'

Joyce spat the words out. She seemed more angry than anything else. Vogel didn't blame her. He too was angry at being kept in the dark; as deputy SIO he felt he had a right to know what was going on. And like Joyce, he suspected that Henry Tanner knew what had triggered the sequence of events culminating in his shooting.

Before he could compose a response to Joyce's outburst, she spoke again.

'They decided I should be the one to wait here, just in case there was news of Fred. But I must admit I'm beginning to question everything now. Maybe the real reason they don't want me to go to the hospital is because they don't want me near my father.'

'Who do you mean by "they" Mrs Mildmay?' asked Vogel.

Joyce Mildmay looked startled. 'I don't know, I don't know what I'm saying. Ever since Fred disappeared I've been thinking Charlie was right, that there's some sort of conspiracy. And I don't know who's behind it, do I? It's got to the point where I don't know if I can trust my own mother. Or my son – my lovely son Mark, who took charge of everything this morning. And then there's my father. I'm damned sure I can't trust my father. Charlie was obviously right about him. I mean, he's got to have been mixed up in something, else he wouldn't have been shot.' The desperation was evident in her voice as she added, 'I want to know what he has to say for himself.'

And that makes two of us, thought Vogel. Only he had been effectively banned from Henry Tanner's bedside. Perhaps Joyce Mildmay was right, and they were both being prevented from hearing what Henry had to say.

'I understand how you feel,' he said.

'I am going to see Dad, Mr Vogel,' Joyce continued. 'Whether the rest of them like it or not.'

'Maybe we can talk again after you have done so,' responded Vogel, a tad lamely, he thought. What he wanted to do was to go with her. But that wasn't in his brief.

If Joyce heard what he said she showed no sign of it. She seemed to have her own agenda now.

'I'm not waiting here any longer,' she said. 'If Fred comes back, he isn't going to disappear again because I'm not here. I'm going to the hospital, and I'm taking Molly with me. I'm not letting my daughter out of my sight.'

Vogel was on the brink of offering to take her there, but even he drew the line at so blatantly disobeying the direct order of a senior officer.

Joyce stormed out of the sitting room and headed for the

kitchen. Vogel followed her. Molly and PC Saslow were sitting at the table. Vogel had an idea.

'Saslow could go with you to the hospital – you shouldn't be on your own,' he told Joyce.

He was thinking that, even if he were not allowed near Henry Tanner, it might be possible that he could glean something second-hand from PC Saslow. Nobby Clarke might be less guarded with the young PC than she was with an experienced DI with legendary antennae.

Joyce glowered at him. 'I don't want or need a bloody nursemaid in blue. And I won't be alone. I shall have my daughter with me.'

Vogel was in no position to insist. No family member had been accused of any crime. And that included Henry Tanner. He could only watch as Joyce led a distraught Molly out of the house and installed her in the passenger seat of the family Range Rover before climbing behind the wheel.

Meanwhile, Henry Tanner was lying in a private room in the spanking new Brunel building at Southmead Hospital. It even had a balcony. He'd been moved there from A & E as soon as the bullet lodged in his shoulder had been removed. He would require further surgery on his shattered bones, but had been told that was unlikely to be thought advisable until at least the following day.

Henry hadn't had the strength to arrange the move himself, and he doubted that any of his family would have had the presence of mind to do so at such a time. The innovative design of the new Brunel building, and a budget unusually high for the NHS in the current climate, meant that the majority of patients at Southmead would soon be given private rooms with en suite facilities. And Henry was merely one of a number already installed in such rooms. But he didn't know that. He was convinced that he was being given privileged treatment because of who he was. And he was also convinced that he knew who had arranged it. There were people in high places whom he believed would not want him to remain in A & E in a state of delirium any longer than necessary, nor to be placed in a ward alongside other patients.

For the first time in his life, Henry was afraid, truly afraid, as he lay there, wondering who in the world he could trust, and how he was going to get the remains of his family out of this mess.

There was one person, he supposed. There always had been. He'd alerted Mr Smith as soon as Fred disappeared, and then again when he and Stephen Hardcastle had been taken to Lockleaze police station. And Mr Smith, whose weighty presence from afar had been part of his life for so long that Henry could barely remember a time without it, had delivered. Stephen's interview had been brought to a close in the nick of time and the hounds, in the form of the Avon and Somerset Constabulary, had been called off. Mr Smith had not, however, been able to throw any light on the matter of Fred's disappearance. Neither, Henry feared, would Mr Smith be of much assistance in apprehending the sniper who had shot Henry that morning.

Henry suspected that the person responsible was not someone he had come into contact with due to his dealings with Mr Smith. It remained a possibility that the Mr Smith connection was at the root of it all, of course. But Henry didn't think so.

Felicity and Mark were at Henry's bedside. Though he had a terrible headache and his right shoulder was in agony, Henry was fully conscious. But he chose to continue to keep his eyes shut most of the time, and to feign confusion when he did open them, because it suited him. Henry Tanner always did what suited him. Being shot wasn't about to change that.

He wasn't ready to answer questions from his wife or any of his family, come to that. And he certainly wasn't ready to answer questions from the police.

Henry had taken over every aspect of Tanner-Max from his father, and had long ago come to the conclusion that only he could keep all aspects of the company's activities operational. Charlie had turned out to be a grave disappointment; he was every bit as weak as he had described himself in that damned letter. And Henry despised weak men. Weak men had their uses, but they were dangerous. It was thanks to Charlie that cracks had begun to appear within the Tanner business and family, cracks that over the last few days had split into huge chasms. It was thanks to Charlie that Henry had been shot. And it was probably thanks to Charlie that young Fred had disappeared.

Henry had suspected from the start that Charlie had taken his own life. He'd been an experienced sailor, and the weather conditions when he'd disappeared had been favourable for the time of year.

Then there was the letter. That letter. Stephen Hardcastle had assured Henry it was not an uncommon occurrence for someone to write a letter to their nearest and dearest to be opened only after their death, even when the writer was a healthy and relatively young man. Henry was not so sure.

He had kept his suspicions to himself, but he knew things about Charlie, things of which nobody else in the family was aware. Least of all Joyce.

The pain emanating from Henry's shoulder and coursing

through the entire right side of his body was excruciating. He had been injected with morphine earlier. The effects seemed to be wearing off with a vengeance. Henry Tanner had always been both physically and mentally an extremely strong man. However, he was almost seventy and he knew that this injury was sapping his strength. Not only physically. He didn't have his usual mental strength either.

He opened one eye a crack. There was a third person in the room. A tall, striking woman, well dressed, confident. He had been aware of her presence in the ambulance too. Probably some sort of plainclothes police officer. Henry needed to know exactly what sort before he said anything. He needed help. But it had to be specialist help. And he thought this woman might be the person to give him that help. She wasn't just some local plod, that much he was certain of.

Felicity and Mark were talking non-stop. He wondered if they'd been told that was what they should do to keep him alert.

Felicity was chatting away in a falsely cheerful voice about nothing of consequence. Mark was holding his phone in his hand and had an earpiece in one ear. He was listening to the *News Quiz* and giving his grandfather a running commentary, explaining the questions and repeating the jokes.

Their babbling was getting on his nerves and Henry desperately wanted Felicity and Mark to shut up. In the end he decided that the only way to achieve that would be to respond. So he opened his eyes fully and spoke.

'It's all right, I'm all right,' he said. 'I'm fine. But I need some peace.'

Felicity reached out to touch his face, her eyes full of joy and hope, in spite of everything.

'Oh, Henry, you've come back to us,' she murmured.

'Yes, yes,' he snapped, pulling away from her touch. 'But everything hurts. I'm in the most awful pain. Will you please go away and give me some peace.'

Felicity looked offended. Hurt even. Henry was sorry about that, but he didn't know how else to play this. Mark merely looked puzzled. Until recent events, even before Charlie's death, Henry had been hoping that his grandson might be the person to eventually take over Tanner-Max, to handle all aspects of the business, including the undisclosed side involving Mr Smith. Henry had been quite sure that Charlie would never be able to do so. Stephen Hardcastle could not even be considered: he wasn't family. Tanner-Max was a family business, always had been and, Henry still hoped, always would be.

But Mark was young and new to the business. There could be no question of him taking over the reins for several years at least. Right now Mark knew no more than his grandmother about Tanner-Max. Indeed, Henry suspected that Mark knew a great deal less than his grandmother. Like Henry, Felicity was prone to keep her thoughts to herself, but there had been times he could have sworn she knew exactly what was going on in his mind.

Henry reached out with his good arm and took his wife's hand. He saw her face light up. He knew that she loved him, regardless of the secrets and lack of communication. It warmed him to see her react in that way.

'Listen, darling, I need a bit of time, that's all,' he said, managing a strained smile. 'Why don't you and Mark leave me to sleep for a couple of hours. I'll be stronger then.'

'But we want to know what happened, Granddad,' began Mark. 'I mean, who would want to shoot you? And why? What's going on, Granddad?'

Henry didn't look at Mark. He continued to stare at his wife.

Felicity was well aware what was expected of her. She and Henry had been sweethearts since they were teenagers. She knew that her husband required her to do his bidding, as she had done for the last fifty years. In return he'd given her an enviable lifestyle and a wonderful family. True, that family was now a shadow of its former self. Their only son was dead. Their son-in-law was dead. Their grandson was missing. Their daughter was in a state of anguish. And now Henry had been shot.

Nonetheless, Felicity knew what was required of her, and that Henry was confident she would comply with his wishes, as always.

She did, too.

'C'mon, Mark,' she instructed. 'Let's leave your granddad alone. Let's do what he wants. We need him well again. All of us.'

Mark began to protest, but Felicity got to her feet and put a hand on her grandson's shoulder, soothing, quietening.

Henry's attention had already left his wife and grandson. They had been dealt with. His gaze was fixed on the woman sitting by the door.

DCI Nobby Clarke stood up, stepped forward, and introduced herself.

'I'm from the National Serious Crime Squad,' she said.

Henry nodded.

'I hope you feel well enough to give me a few minutes,' Clarke continued.

'If granddad isn't well enough to talk to his family then he isn't well enough to talk to the police,' Mark protested.

Henry raised one hand, effectively silencing him.

'It's all right, Mark,' he said. 'I can do a few minutes. Fred is still missing. I must help if I can.'

Mark looked ready to protest further, but his grandmother ushered him out of the room.

'We'll be back in a couple of hours,' she said.

Henry waited until she and Mark had closed the door behind them.

'Tell me who's sent you,' Henry commanded.

'Um, uh, Mr Smith,' Nobby replied, her voice little more than a murmur.

She looked and sounded somewhat self-conscious. But her answer was the one Henry had hoped for.

'Thank God,' he said. 'I need your help, DCI Clarke. It's possible that Mr Smith will be able to ascertain why this has happened to my family, and who is responsible. Then again, it may not be possible, because these events may be unconnected to my work for Mr Smith.'

'That sounds like a riddle,' responded Nobby Clarke. 'And I can't help unless you are honest with me, Mr Tanner. I reckon I only know half the story.'

Henry nodded. 'I understand,' he said. 'I will tell you everything. Everything I know, anyway. I don't have any alternative.'

Clarke moved closer to the bed.

With some difficulty because of the pain he was in, Henry hoisted himself up into a sitting position. He had no intention of embarking on any sort of serious conversation whilst lying flat on his back.

But the movement dislodged a splinter of shattered bone in his injured shoulder. He was later to be told that this did no serious damage. However, the excruciating agony which seemed to be attacking his every nerve end was such that

Henry fell back on to his pillow with a blood-curdling scream.

A nurse arrived in the room at once. The Brunel wing at Southmead was that sort of medical establishment. Or, at least, it was in May 2014, with as yet only 150 patients installed, way below its projected capacity of 800.

Henry was gasping for breath. He seemed incapable of further speech. In any case Nobby Clarke was asked to leave the room at once.

Cursing under her breath, she did as she was told.

Seventeen

Joyce and Molly were a mile from Southmead when Molly's phone bleeped to signal an incoming text message.

She opened the message, gasped, then emitted a little cry, which caused Joyce to take her eyes from the road and glance anxiously at her daughter.

Molly was staring at her phone, in shock.

'What is it?' asked Joyce.

'It-it's Fred,' stumbled Molly. 'I have a message from Fred.'

'What?'

Her mother almost forgot to steer and the car lurched across the road. Joyce recovered just in time to avoid a head-on collision with an oncoming vehicle.

Molly was so preoccupied by the message on her phone that she seemed not even to notice.

Spotting a lay-by ahead, Joyce pulled over. When she turned to her daughter, Molly was still staring at the screen of her smart phone, frozen in a kind of limbo of disbelief.

'What?' Joyce enquired again, hardly believing her ears.

'It's Fred, it has to be Fred,' Molly repeated. 'This message can only be from Fred.'

Joyce immediately snatched the phone from her daughter and looked at the screen, her heart racing.

The message was brief and to the point.

I need to see you and mum alone. Get mum to take you to where we saw the big buck. Don't tell her where you are heading until you're on your way. And don't tell anyone else anything. I'm all right. But I need you both. Fred.

'Do you recognize the number?' Joyce asked, studying the screen carefully.

'No, no, I don't,' replied Molly. 'It's not Fred's number. But we know that. It couldn't be, could it? Fred left his phone behind.'

'If it is Fred, then he must be using somebody else's phone,' said Joyce.

'Or he could have got hold of a pay-as-you-go,' Molly suggested.

'But he didn't have enough money with him,' said Joyce. 'And he couldn't be doing this on his own. He's only eleven.'

Joyce gulped as she thought about the vulnerability of her young son.

'What makes you so sure the text is from Fred? It could be a hoax. A cruel one, I know, but I've heard that this sort of thing does happen when somebody disapp—'

'It's him, I know it is,' Molly interrupted.

'How?'

'He wants to meet us where we saw the big buck. Only Fred would know to say that. Remember when you and Gran went shopping in London, and Dad took us to Exmoor, where Granny and Gramps Mildmay used to take him when he was a boy? We saw this huge stag at this place we'd walked to from the car park by Landacre Bridge. Dad made a big thing about it and said we must protect it by not ever telling anyone about it. Fred loved the idea that it would be our secret for ever. It was he who called it the big buck.'

'And you can remember the place?'

'Oh yes, I'll never forget it.' She put a hand to her mouth. 'Fred said not to tell you until we were on our way,' she said. 'But I already have.'

'And we're already on our way. More or less. In any case he just didn't want anyone else to know where we were going. Not that I could imagine anyone would be able to find where you saw the big buck without your help.'

Molly smiled wanly.

'Look, before we do anything or go anywhere, let's call that number, see if we can speak to Fred. You do it, Molly. It's you he's tried to contact.'

Molly did so. The phone rang for a minute and then cut out. No reply, and no message service.

'Try again,' urged Joyce.

Molly did so, with the same result.

'All right, text him,' instructed her mother. 'Tell him you understand the message. Ask him when he wants to meet.'

Molly began tapping her phone. Joyce leaned across the car, watching her daughter's screen as she composed her text:

Fred, we have all been so worried. It is you, isn't it? I understand your message. I know where you mean. When do you want to meet us there?

The reply came straight away.

It's me, all right, Muggins. I want to meet soon as you can. When can you be there?

Molly looked at her mother. Joyce thought for a second.

'It'll take us the best part of two and a half hours from here,' she said, checking her watch. 'Tell him we'll be there between two and two thirty.'

Molly did so. Again the reply came straight away.

See you then. Remember, don't tell anyone, and don't answer your phones, or you could put us all in danger.

Molly looked at her mother, aghast. 'What does he mean by that?'

'I've no idea,' replied Joyce. 'But tell me something, do these messages sound like your brother to you?'

'I don't know,' Molly said hesitantly. 'It's kind of like Fred. But it's a bit grown-up, isn't it? Like someone's telling him what to say.'

'That's what I think too,' replied Joyce, her voice shaking. At last she had been given hope that Fred was safe and well, yet she was full of fear. 'The language doesn't sound right to me. God, bloody texts – we've no way of telling whether it's genuine or not.'

'Only Fred would know about the big buck,' repeated Molly.

'Maybe.' Joyce wasn't convinced. 'How about you text him a question, something else only he would know about. C'mon, Molly, you're good at this sort of thing. What can we ask?'

Molly thought for a moment, then began tapping out a new message. Joyce continued to read over her daughter's shoulder.

What did you discover last week that I made you swear on your iPhone not to tell Mum?

The reply came quick as a flash.

That you and Janie Mitchell had both had butterfly tattoos done, like Harry Styles.

Despite the strain she was under, Joyce couldn't help her initial response.

'Oh, you haven't, Molly? Where?'

'On my left shoulder. Why do you think I've been keeping myself covered up in front of you?' She looked back at the screen, grinning triumphantly. 'That's it, Mum. It's Fred. It has to be!'

Joyce found herself smiling too. Molly was right: it had to be Fred. She remained anxious and fearful, but at least he was alive.

'Tell him we're on our way,' she instructed her daughter, at the same time restarting the Range Rover and swinging it around in a reckless pavement-mounting U-turn. Then she turned back on to the main drag, heading towards the M5 west and a hidden glen in the Exmoor Hills where, and she could still hardly dare to believe it, her younger son would hopefully be waiting for her and his big sister.

Still smiling, Joyce glanced sideways at her daughter.

'We'll discuss that tattoo later,' she said.

Molly didn't look like she gave a damn. And neither, in fact, did Joyce.

They stopped for petrol before turning off the M5 at the Tiverton junction to join the A38 heading for North Devon and Exmoor. Joyce didn't want to. She was fired up with impatience. But she had no choice, not if she wanted to reach their destination in the heart of the moors.

Both her and Molly's phones had been ringing repeatedly. Felicity was the persistent caller. Mother and daughter both ignored the calls. They agreed that they would continue to abide by Fred's wishes. What choice did they have? In any case what could they say to Felicity?

The sky was ominously grey as they began to climb to the higher altitudes of moorland, but no rain fell. Not at first. It was two thirty by the time they arrived at Landacre, where a medieval bridge spans the River Barle. Joyce parked the Range Rover and locked it.

It was cold and the air felt damp, but to Joyce's surprise the rain held off. A strong easterly wind was beginning to blow, though.

Molly led the way along a series of paths, some little more than sheep tracks, which ran through thick undergrowth. Joyce was wearing unsuitably light leather-soled shoes. At least Molly was wearing trainers. After twenty minutes they came to a clearing where the river formed a deep and still pond.

'This is it, Mum,' said Molly, gesturing with one hand. 'Dad spotted the stag over there, by the blackthorn bush at the water's edge. He signalled for us to be quiet and we crouched here in the bracken and watched. He had huge antlers. He was having a drink, so it took him a while to notice us. Then he suddenly raised his head, looked all around him sniffing the air, waded off through the river and trotted up the hill over there.'

She waved a hand again.

'We saw him silhouetted against the sky up at the top. It was wonderful.'

'And you didn't even tell me. Did you not tell anyone?'

Molly shook her head. 'It was our secret.'

Secrets again, thought Joyce. This may have been a magical secret, but it was somehow typical of her family that even special moments were cloaked in secrecy.

Joyce told herself off for being small-minded. She led the way out into the clearing. Molly followed. There was nobody else about, no one visible. Certainly no Fred.

'He's not here, Mum,' said Molly, stating the obvious. 'Not yet, anyway.'

Her mother took her hand. 'Perhaps he's making sure we are alone, that we haven't brought the police or anyone else with us.

'Or somebody is,' she muttered, adding the remark under her breath.

But Molly heard her.

'What do you mean by that, Mum?'

Joyce squeezed the hand she was holding.

'Darling, Fred can't be on his own,' she told her daughter. 'There's no way he could have got hold of a phone, let alone come all the way out here by himself. And we still don't know where he's been since Wednesday night.'

'So who's been helping him? And why?'

'I don't know, darling.'

Joyce looked up at the sky for the umpteenth time. The cloud formations overhead had become blacker and lower. Denser too, she thought. She shivered. The weather had turned even colder, but it wasn't only the chill in the air that made her shiver; it was a sudden sense of dread. Throughout the long drive she'd been wondering whether she was doing the right thing, bringing her daughter to this remote place, putting her in danger. But then, what choice did she have? She could never have found the place on her own.

She pulled Molly close. 'Look, I'm not sure it was a good idea for us to come out here like this, without telling anyone,' she said. 'Perhaps we should go back to the car.'

'We've only just got here,' said Molly. 'We have to wait. At least for a bit.'

'Look, Molly, there's a possibility that someone has been keeping Fred against his will. So it is also possible that this is some kind of trap.'

'But why? Why would anyone want to do that to us?'

'I don't know,' said Joyce.

It was on the tip of her tongue to say that she suspected Molly's grandfather might have a pretty good idea, but she stopped herself. She didn't want to cause her daughter further distress.

'Please, Molly, let's go. I was as excited as you to think we had a message from Fred, but it doesn't make sense that he would ask us to come all the way out here alone. I think we should go back to the car, sweetheart.'

Molly shook her head determinedly.

'The message has to be from Fred – no one else knows about this place. And no one else knows about the tattoo. Only Janie Mitchell, and those messages definitely weren't from her. We can't go yet, Mum.'

Joyce sighed. 'All right. Why don't you try to call that number again, or at least send another text.'

Molly attempted to do both, with equal lack of success.

'I can't get a signal,' she said.

'Then perhaps we should go somewhere where we can.'

'If Fred's anywhere around here, he won't be able to get a

signal either,' said Molly stubbornly. 'We have to wait.'

Joyce marvelled that her daughter was so strong-willed. More like a Tanner man than a Tanner woman. Before this awful string of events had engulfed the family, Joyce had sometimes amused herself by wondering how much control anyone, even her powerful grandfather, would have over a grown-up Molly.

Mother and daughter waited, half sitting, half leaning against a sandstone boulder on the riverbank. Joyce kept checking her watch. Molly barely moved a muscle, just stared into the middle distance, perhaps watching for movement in the undergrowth, or anything that might indicate the presence of her brother.

The rain that had threatened ever since they arrived finally began to fall. Neither mother nor daughter were dressed for a wet day on the moors.

'We've been here nearly an hour,' said Joyce.

Molly remained silent.

'C'mon, darling,' urged Joyce. 'We can't stay out here. We're both getting wet through and there's no one in sight. Let's go back to the car, drive somewhere where we can get a signal and try the phone again.'

'No,' said Molly. 'No. We have to wait. We must. I know Fred's here somewhere.'

Joyce put an arm around her daughter's damp shoulders.

'Sweetheart, you have to accept that this whole thing might be a cruel hoax. We both have to.'

Molly shook her head vehemently. 'Only Fred knew about the stag. Only Fred knew about the tattoo.'

'You can't be sure,' said her mother gently. 'Not absolutely sure, anyway. Fred could have told a friend at school, more than one. They could have told their parents—'

'No,' Molly interrupted. 'Fred wouldn't have.'

Joyce conceded defeat and they waited another half hour. With no protection against the wind and rain, both mother and daughter were wet through and chilled to the bone. Molly's teeth were chattering; neither her face nor lips had any colour left in them, except around her eyes, which were rimmed with red.

'That's it,' said Joyce. 'We're leaving. We're going back to the car park even if I have to carry you there.'

This time Molly didn't protest. Joyce wasn't surprised. If her daughter felt anything like the way she looked then she would not have the strength to protest.

The rain was even heavier now, driven horizontal by the wind.

Mother and daughter clung to each other, half holding each other up as they hurried to the car.

Joyce unlocked it with her bleeper and helped Molly into the passenger seat before scurrying around the vehicle to climb in behind the wheel.

She switched on the engine and simultaneously turned the heater on full.

'I think there's a rug on the back seat. Why don't you reach over and get it,' Joyce suggested as she switched on the engine.

'Don't turn round,' commanded a muffled male voice from the back.

Molly did so at once, of course, but could see only a huddled grey form crouched down behind the driver's seat.

'Keep facing the front,' said the voice again. 'Someone could be watching.'

'Do as he says, Molly,' said Joyce.

Her heart had sunk to the soles of her inadequate shoes.

For once, and to her mother's relief, Molly did as she was told.

'Pass me your phones,' instructed the man.

Both mother and daughter did so immediately. Even Molly knew better than to argue.

There were some small scraping noises from the back seat, metal rubbing against metal. Then the sound of one of the rear windows being opened.

'Right, let's go,' said the voice. 'Turn left when you get on the road, over the bridge. I'm taking you to Fred.'

Joyce, too, did as she was told. Although she had no idea whether or not this man was really taking her to her son. What choice did she have? She was not only frightened by what was happening, she was also bewildered. She had left the car locked, hadn't she? She always locked her car. It was like a reflex action. She'd unlocked it with the remote before getting in, and there hadn't been any sign that the Range Rover had been tampered with, yet there was someone crouched in the back.

She could only think of one explanation. But it couldn't be, it wasn't possible. She felt a knot form in her stomach. It felt as if she might be sick. But from the moment the man in the back of her car had first spoken, she'd known.

She glanced at her daughter. Molly was staring at her, jaw slack. Joyce felt sure that Molly was thinking the same thing. Even so, Joyce was not yet ready to put it into words. She reached out with her left hand to enclose her daughter's freezing cold right hand. Molly just looked at her, eyes wide with amazement. Joyce shook her head, almost imperceptibly.

She couldn't be sure who was in the back of the car. Not entirely, could she?

As she steered the big four-wheel drive over Landacre

Bridge, through the corner of her eye she spotted two tiny objects flying through the air towards the river below: the SIM cards from her and Molly's phones. Mobile phones could be tracked nowadays, even when you weren't using them – except when the SIM cards were removed.

The voice began to give her directions, speaking only in monosyllables. It sounded familiar, even though muffled and distorted, as if their unwanted passenger was speaking through a wad of material, maybe a scarf. Joyce continued on the main road towards Exford until she was told to turn off and then directed along a succession of tracks, which the heavy rain had already made impassable for anything other than a powerful four-wheel drive.

Finally they came to a derelict stone-built barn in a patch of dense woodland. It looked like there might once have been a crofter's cottage next to it, but the foundations were all that remained of it now.

Joyce was told to drive around to the far side of the barn and pull up in front of a set of double doors. She registered that these looked to be in comparatively good order.

The grey-clad figure climbed swiftly out of the Range Rover, hooded head down, keeping his back to the vehicle.

He removed an iron bar, which formed a kind of improvised bolting device across the barn doors, then beckoned Joyce to drive in.

She hesitated, uncertain what was waiting inside. Wondering whether she should swing the car around and take off at speed with her daughter. At least that way she could convey one of her children to safety.

She glanced at Molly again. Her daughter was still shivering.

'Drive in, Mum. Do it,' ordered Molly, her voice shaky and high-pitched.

Joyce opened her mouth to explain her fears. But Fred might be in that barn. He might still be in danger. Considerable danger. She couldn't drive away, abandon him there.

And the hooded creature now standing alongside the car, head bowed and shoulders hunched, had obviously known that full well.

Slowly Joyce drove forward through the big wooden doors, which were immediately closed behind her, then switched off the engine.

She glanced quickly around her, taking Molly's hand in hers and squeezing it tightly. It was light inside the barn. Most of the roof was missing and the rain was falling as heavily within its crumbling walls as without. The barn offered little protection from the elements, but it did, of course, effectively conceal those inside its walls, which were almost entirely still standing. Just about.

There was another vehicle parked to one side. An old blue Honda Accord. Several large Calor gas canisters were lined up along one wall, next to a tarpaulin-covered lump. She looked at it in alarm, then became aware of the large military-style tent which had been erected in another corner.

The middle panel was being unzipped.

A familiar small figure in unfamiliar clothes – military-style heavy-duty wear, too big for him – stepped through the gap. Joyce involuntarily let go of Molly's hand.

It was Fred.

'Mum! Molly!' he cried, his face lighting up with joy.

Oblivious to anything except the appearance of their

beloved Fred, mother and daughter both opened their car doors and jumped out to greet the boy.

Fred ran towards them. Joyce reached out and grabbed him. Then she wrapped both her children in her arms.

Eighteen

Vogel was in his office, reflecting on another disturbing day in the Tanner/Mildmay case. By the time Joyce Mildmay was being reunited with her younger son, he had known for four hours that Joyce and her daughter Molly were missing. Or, at least, their whereabouts was unknown.

Joyce's mother, Felicity, had called the DI when Joyce and Molly had failed to turn up at the hospital. Felicity had, it seemed, plumbed the policeman's mobile number into her phone when he'd given her his card on the day that Fred had been reported missing.

'I'm calling you direct, Mr Vogel, because I know you will understand my concern,' she told him. 'They should have been here an hour ago. Joyce called to tell me she was coming to see her father, and that she was bringing Molly with her. She was determined. Aggressive, even. And I've been trying to call them ever since. Neither of them are answering their phones.'

'An hour isn't long, Mrs Tanner,' Vogel had said, trying to sound reassuring.

He doubted he was convincing. Under the circumstances, he was inclined to agree that the woman was right to be alarmed.

'It doesn't necessarily mean anything ominous. Perhaps they've stopped off to do some shopping, or they could have had a puncture.'

As he spoke he realized he had made a pretty stupid remark. Felicity picked him up on it straight away.

'Mr Vogel, my grandson is missing and my husband has been shot. Do you seriously think my daughter would stop off to do some shopping on her way to the hospital?' Felicity responded sharply. 'And if they'd had a puncture or been delayed, Joyce or Molly would have called or texted. Or at least answered their phones when I called them. No. Something is wrong. Something has happened to them.'

Vogel gave up trying to allay her fears. Clearly he wasn't making a very good job of it.

All he said was: 'I'll check out what you've told me and get back to you.'

Nobby Clarke had returned to Kenneth Steele House as soon as it became clear that Henry Tanner would not be able to speak to her. Vogel found her in the incident room and informed her that they could now have two more missing people on their hands.

The DCI was edgier than Vogel had ever known her to be, but still reluctant to launch another missing persons enquiry.

'Joyce Mildmay is an adult and her daughter is fifteen,' she said. 'They could have gone anywhere.'

'True,' Vogel had muttered.

But that exchange had been nearly four hours ago. During that time Vogel had organized routine checks of road traffic and emergency call data. There had been no reported incidents that might relate to Joyce and Molly or their vehicle.

Vogel had also asked for CCTV coverage of the route Joyce Mildmay would most likely have taken to Southmead to be checked. Starting with the CCTV at Tarrant Park itself. This was not a task which could be swiftly completed, and Vogel had yet to be made aware of any significant footage.

He'd also organized checks of both Molly and Joyce's mobile phone accounts, and had already been told that neither mother nor daughter had made or received a call since five hours earlier when Molly had unsuccessfully tried to call an unidentified pay-as-you-go phone. She had successfully sent and picked up texts to that number, the content of which was as yet unknown. Molly had been in the Bristol area at the time. The location of the pay-as-you-go phone had yet to be ascertained. Neither had it yet proved possible for the tech boys to track the present whereabouts of either that phone or those belonging to Molly and her mother. The techies reported that it was probable the SIM cards had been removed from all three phones. Which was clearly disturbing.

Because of the unique circumstances, a full-scale missing persons investigation was launched far earlier than would usually be the case. Vogel felt sure that the unexplained disappearance of Joyce and Molly had to be linked to Fred Mildmay going missing, and he knew that Nobby Clarke must feel the same. Even though she was still not really sharing her opinions or much else with him.

By 6 p.m. that investigation had stalled and Vogel had had enough of waiting around. And of not being kept informed. He stormed into Nobby Clarke's temporary office and told her so.

'Boss, I don't care what you say,' he announced, 'I'm off to the hospital. We now have three missing people. And I reckon if there's one man who can tell us what's going on, it's Henry Tanner. You know damned well he holds the key to all of this. A woman and two children—'

'One of those children is with her mother, Vogel, and she is fifteen. Let's not over-react,' said the DCI reasonably.

'But what if Joyce Mildmay received a ransom demand of some sort and decided not to tell us? That fifteen-year-old and her mother could be off somewhere trying to deal with the kidnappers,' persisted Vogel. 'Imagine the danger that would put them in. That's not over-reaction.'

'Neither is it a theory we have any evidence to support,' responded Clarke. 'Vogel, this is a complex case. Anything could have happened.'

'That's what I am afraid of. And I am far more afraid than I might otherwise be because I am being kept in the dark about what's going on.'

'You know all you need to, Vogel.'

'I don't accept that, boss, and I'm going to the hospital to see Henry Tanner whether you like it or not. The old bastard must have come around again by now.'

DCI Clarke sighed wearily.

'All right, Vogel,' she said. 'I give in. We'll both go to the hospital. Though who knows whether or not Tanner will be in any condition to talk to us. And if you are good, on the way I'll tell you what I know. Or most of it, anyway . . .'

Nineteen

Joyce felt the wet warmth of tears running down her face as she held her son close. But this time they were tears of joy.

Fred was alive, and apparently well. And he was in her arms. She vowed never to let her son out of her sight again. She knew it was stupid, and totally impractical, but at that moment of enormous relief that was how she felt.

She closed her eyes, savouring the moment.

By the time she opened them again the man who had climbed into the back of her car had removed his hoody and was standing before her bare-headed, his white-blond hair glistening in the rain. Like Fred he was wearing camouflage gear. From the apparel of both man and boy, and the khaki tent, it looked like they were playing one of those character-testing war games.

The hair was unnaturally blond, fashionably bleached and cropped. The eyes were dark brown instead of the familiar pale grey flecked with hazel. Both hair and eyes were the wrong colour, and the man was far too thin. Much thinner than before.

But it was him, all right. She had known it must be from the moment she'd become aware of his presence in the car. The voice had been familiar, even though muffled and distorted. And who else would have been able to so easily gain entry to her locked and alarmed vehicle? Who else would have a key?

Yet throughout the drive from Landacre to the barn hidden away in Exmoor woodland, there had been a niggle at the back of her mind telling her it couldn't be him. He was dead. True, his body had never been found, but the police and coastguard authorities who'd recovered his abandoned boat had concluded that he was dead.

'Hello, Joycey,' he said softly.

His voice was no longer muffled. It was unmistakable.

She stared at him over her son's head. Then she stepped back from Fred and rushed towards him.

She could hear herself screaming. She hadn't intended to scream. She barely knew she was doing it. It was an involuntary reaction to what was happening.

His arms were outstretched, held akimbo as if he expected her to run into them. And she did run to him. But when she reached him she pushed his arms further apart with her own, then clenched her fists and began to pummel him as hard as she could on his chest.

'You bastard!' she shouted. 'You utter bastard! I thought you were dead. Your children thought you were dead!'

Charlie Mildmay stood there and took it. He was a tall, once fit man. If Joyce had been able to grasp anything beyond the fact that he was there, that he was alive, she would have noticed how grey and drawn Charlie was. Along with the pounds he'd shed, he seemed to have lost much of his physical strength. The blows she was raining on him caused him to flinch and gasp for breath.

'Don't, Mum, don't!' Fred cried out.

Joyce carried on as if she hadn't heard him.

Eventually Charlie took hold of her wrists and gently pushed them away. She let him do so. She did not struggle. Perhaps she began to remember the presence of her children. Children who must both be as frightened and bewildered as she was.

Her frenzied attack ended as abruptly as it had begun.

She shook off her husband's hands from around her wrists and stepped back.

'You let us all think you were dead, Charlie,' she said, speaking more quietly. 'That was evil. Wicked. How could you?'

Charlie bowed his head.

'You let us think you were dead,' Joyce repeated. 'I wept over your loss. Your children wept over your loss. How could you do that to us?'

'I'm sorry,' Charlie said, his head bowed.

'You're fucking sorry?' Joyce stormed, raising her voice.

Then she again remembered the presence of her children. She didn't know how to deal with what was happening. She had no idea how to deal with it. But screaming at her children's father while they stood and watched was not going to help.

She knew she should wait until they were alone before questioning Charlie, but she couldn't stop herself. In any case, it seemed unlikely that there was anywhere to go where they could be alone, unless they were going to go off for a tramp through the wet and dripping woodland.

'Why, Charlie?' she asked, her voice as quiet as she could make it. 'Why did you do it?'

Charlie looked up, and met her eyes for the first time.

'I had no choice,' he said. 'You have to believe me, Joyce, I had no choice.'

253

His gaze shifted. He was looking over Joyce's left shoulder at Molly, who, eyes wide, lips trembling, was still standing with one arm around Fred.

'Baby?' he said, his voice full of uncertainty, wondering how receptive his daughter was likely to be.

'D-dad?' Molly's uncertainty was even greater. After all, she had never expected to see her father again.

'Baby,' Charlie repeated. This time he grinned. That old disarming grin. A tad forced, perhaps, but there all the same. A grin that split his overly thin face, a grin that lit up those erroneous eyes; eyes which were the wrong colour. Contact lenses, Joyce assumed.

Molly removed her arm from around Fred's shoulders and ran to him, as her mother had done. But unlike her mother she did not beat his chest with her fists. Her face displayed no anger. It was as if the grief and torment of the previous six months had been washed from her very being by that one word from her beloved father:

'Baby.'

Molly threw her arms around Charlie. He drew her to him and lifted her a few inches from the ground, as he had done since she was a toddler.

'My darling girl,' he murmured into her hair.

Joyce could cheerfully have throttled him. She had so wanted Charlie to be alive when they told her he had disappeared at sea. Now she was outraged. How dare he come back into their lives and behave, with Molly anyway, just the way he had before.

'I want to know why, Charlie,' she said.

She felt near-physical pain. There was so much anguish, and it seemed Charlie was responsible for all of it – deliberately so.

He looked up at her over Molly's head.

'I don't know where to begin,' he said.

'I don't suppose you do,' Joyce responded. 'Not only did you let us think you were dead, you took Fred from me. I thought that he might be dead too. Now you've more or less kidnapped me and Molly.'

She was struggling to maintain control. Her voice was growing louder and sharper.

'Have you gone mad?' she asked.

It wasn't a figure of speech. She was absolutely serious. Perhaps that was it. Perhaps Charlie had lost his mind.

He shook his head.

'I had to do it,' he said. 'Look, I want to tell you everything. All three of you.'

'I think you and I should speak alone,' said Joyce quickly.

Charlie shook his head. 'No, the children have to know this too. It's important for all of us. They have to know why I have done what I have done. Why I disappeared and why I have come back. If we are going to survive as a family, then they have to know.'

'Survive as a family?' Joyce let out a hysterical laugh. 'After all that you have done to us? No, Charlie, you must have gone mad.'

Fred ran to her side, and pressed his small body into hers. 'Please, Mum, listen to him,' he said. 'He can explain everything, really he can.'

Joyce glanced down at him, then looked enquiringly at her husband.

'I had to tell Fred what's been going on,' he said.

So far as Joyce was concerned, that only made things worse. It went against her instinct to protect her son.

'Does that include why you wrote me that letter and why you took our son from his bed and brought him out here, why you abducted him?' she enquired coolly.

Charlie lowered his head. 'Well, not absolutely everything, obviously.'

'I can't believe what you've done, what you are doing.'

'Please, Mum,' said Fred again.

'It's all right, Fred,' said Joyce, though it most certainly wasn't. Absolutely nothing was all right.

She turned to her husband again. 'And what about today's pantomime? What was that all about? Molly and I spent more than an hour freezing to death, waiting and hoping for Fred to turn up while you lurked in the back of our car – then you kidnapped us too.'

'I had to do it that way,' said Charlie. 'I am in danger. We all could be in danger. I was terrified of anyone seeing me, recognizing me. You could have been followed. Your phones could have been tracked. I couldn't meet you any-where public, not even in the middle of the moors. You don't understand. We're safe here. Hidden away. For the time being, anyway. That's why I had to get rid of your SIM cards. And you can't even get a signal here, so we can't be tracked directly to this place. I drove over the moors almost to Barnstaple this morning so that Fred could text you. Risked being spotted, of course, but on the roads there was less of a risk of using the phone than there was using it near to where we were hiding out.'

Joyce could only stare at him. Charlie's eyes were unnaturally bright. Was he on drugs? For years she'd worried about his reliance on prescription medication. Had it pushed him over the edge? Had his state of mind been so adversely affected by his excesses?

'You are mad, aren't you,' she said.

It wasn't a question.

'I'm not mad,' said Charlie quietly. 'But I may have been before I staged my own death.'

Then, whilst Joyce was still trying to work out what he meant by that, he spoke again.

'Won't you please come into the tent,' he said. 'It's dry and warm in there. We can talk properly.'

'I don't remember us ever talking properly, Charlie,' said Joyce. 'Maybe that's the problem.'

'Please,' said Charlie.

'All right, I will listen to your story. But unless you have something amazing to say to make me change my mind, I shall be driving our children home. Without you. And meanwhile, Fred, Molly, I'm sorry, but whatever your father thinks, I do need to speak to him alone.'

Charlie looked as if he were about to protest. She silenced him with an impatient flick of the wrist. 'I mean it, Charlie. Alone or not at all.'

She looked around the ruined barn, trying to work out a way of organizing some privacy.

'OK,' she said, addressing her children. 'You two go into the tent and try to keep warm. Charlie, we can sit in the Range Rover. Now, nobody argue. Please. That's my condition for listening to you, Charlie. Else I shall take off now and go straight to the police.'

She paused, wondering if that would even be possible, or if Charlie would attempt to stop her. She decided to challenge Charlie while the thought was in her mind.

'Assuming you don't intend trying to prevent me or our children leaving,' she said. 'You wouldn't do that, would you Charlie?'

257

Charlie looked at his feet. Clad in the kind of cheap army boots you can buy on the net. Boots no real soldier would ever consider going for a yomp in.

At least he seemed to realize he would not be able to persuade Joyce to listen to his story as long as their children were in earshot. He remained silent.

Fred looked at Molly.

'Come on, you,' said Molly. 'Let's do what Mum says. You know she means it.'

Joyce did mean it too. Her children had picked up on that straight away, and so it seemed had her husband. Even if he had avoided her question about whether or not she and the children would be free to leave.

Charlie said nothing but stepped towards the Range Rover and climbed in behind the wheel. Joyce watched Molly and Fred disappear into the tent and zip up the flap, then she climbed into the passenger seat beside her husband.

Twenty

Henry Tanner was beginning to come round from the dose of morphine the nurse had administered a few hours earlier. He was still in extreme discomfort, but he could cope with that. And he knew that he always healed well. Age had yet to change that.

It was the awful stress of what was happening to his family that was so hard for him to cope with.

Felicity had told him about Joyce and Molly. Indeed, she had been sitting at his bedside when she'd called Vogel. But Henry had been semi-conscious at the time, and had barely taken it in. He had a vague recollection that she'd asked if he knew where they might have gone. Henry had no idea whatsoever, and for once in his life he didn't know what to do or say.

The suspicion that had been lurking in the back of his mind ever since Fred had gone missing no longer seemed fanciful. Ever since he could remember, he'd lived with the possibility that he might one day be a target. His dealings with Mr Smith and others of that ilk had made it a real possibility.

But the threat had never materialized, until now. Or had it? Henry thought back to the death of his only son, mown down by a hit-and-run driver. Apparently an accident, though Henry had always had his doubts about that, doubts he had kept from his family and most particularly from Joyce. Mr Smith had assured him that an extensive investigation at the highest level had concluded William's death had been a tragic accident. And Henry had chosen to accept that. And to ensure that his entire family did likewise.

This time, Henry didn't know what to think. His instincts told him that the crisis engulfing his family was unrelated to the work he had undertaken for Mr Smith. No, it was down to Charlie. Charlie's bloody nervous breakdown, or whatever it was that had led him to go so spectacularly off the rails. Charlie's meddling in matters that were way out of his league. Charlie had brought Armageddon upon the family. And Henry wasn't sure that even Mr Smith could save them now.

He was so desperate, he'd been prepared to tell DCI Clarke the whole story. But something was still holding him back. It went against every fibre of Henry's being to reveal the rot which had taken hold of all that he held dear. He had thought that, with the help of Mr Smith, he would be able to put everything right, he would be able to get Fred back, to restore normality. He and he alone. Like always. But this was not proving to be so. Instead, one catastrophic event seemed to be following another.

For the first time ever Henry Tanner wished he were someone else. He wished his life's work had been something else. The morphine had worn off to the point that his brain was once more fully functional, but he was torn between wishing he could think with even more clarity, and wishing he could slump into semi-consciousness again.

He cursed Charlie. And he cursed his father and his

father's partner for luring him into a world which, one way or another, was now threatening to destroy him.

Being Henry, he did not consider that the real reason they had landed in this terrible and dangerous mess was because he, like his father before him, had inveigled other members of his family to join him in the precarious world he had inhabited for so long.

A world that he feared was about to crash irrevocably.

Nobby Clarke commandeered an unmarked CID car to take her and Vogel to Southmead. And she elected to drive it herself.

Vogel assumed she did not want another pair of ears listening in on the information she was finally going to share with him. Or at least that he hoped she was going to share with him.

She started the car, activated the sat-nav, and began to accelerate away before Vogel had got himself fully into the passenger seat. He had no idea whether or not she'd ever undertaken one of those police advanced driving courses everybody else seemed to be so damned proud of, but he did know the woman did everything at speed.

He sat silently alongside the DCI, waiting for her to speak. After ten minutes of this, Vogel reckoned he'd waited long enough.

'C'mon then, boss,' he said. 'Are you going to tell me what is going on or are you going to leave me floundering around in the dark like a . . . like a blind duck.'

'Interesting analogy,' said Clarke, with a tight smile.

Traffic lights at a major road junction changed as they approached. Clarke put her foot down, and swung the CID car past the three or four vehicles ahead of them which had already halted at the lights. She accelerated hard through the dangerously narrow gap between a bus coming from the left and a truck from the right.

Vogel shut his eyes. When he opened them again Clarke was glancing sideways at him, the same tight smile lurking on her lips.

'All right, Vogel,' she said. 'You win. Henry Tanner is not entirely what he seems.'

'I'm kinda aware of that,' Vogel snapped.

'As long as you're prepared,' said Nobby. 'Knowing you, you're not going to like what I'm about tell you.'

And then, finally, she began.

Twenty-one

Meanwhile, in a muddy Range Rover parked in a derelict barn in the heart of Exmoor, Charlie Mildmay, who was supposed to be a dead man, began to tell his wife his version of the same story. But his was not a recital of facts gleaned from government files. His was the story of a family caught up in a world the existence of which most of its members were unaware. And a man driven, partly by his own weakness, to extremes of behaviour beyond his own conception.

As soon as he and Joyce were settled into the car, sitting side by side in the front seats, Charlie reached out to take Joyce's hand.

'I don't know how you've got the bloody nerve,' she snapped, jerking her hand away.

'Look, I'm ready to explain.'

Joyce thought Charlie's voice was unpleasantly wheedling.

'I can explain, you know.'

Joyce said nothing. She was still in shock. But she reminded herself that at least her two younger children were now with her. Fred had been found. He was not only unharmed but seemed, at first glance, to be remarkably unaffected by his experience. But then, he had been with his father. The father he idolized. Joyce wondered what story Charlie had told Fred. And she wondered what on earth Charlie was going to tell her. Would it be the same story?

'You remember your Uncle Max?' Charlie began. 'It all started with him. You know all about how he saved your granddad's life during the war, the bond it created between them, and how they always kept in touch after that?'

He seemed to be waiting for a response. Joyce nodded wearily. She had heard that story often enough.

'Well, Max had been sent to the UK in 1939 from Germany, where his entire family lived. He got out aboard one of the kinder trains. In 1941, right after his sixteenth birthday, he lied about his age, said he was seventeen, and joined the Royal Artillery. The military weren't too fussy about checking out ages by then – they were too desperate for manpower. Most of Max's family, including his parents, his elder sister and her husband, and a baby brother whom he never saw, died in the camps. But some of his cousins survived, and after the war they became involved in the struggle to build Israel.

'As soon as the state was established in 1948, Max travelled to Israel to offer his services, but he was told that he could be of more use back in the UK. The newly formed Israeli government needed him to be a kind of international broker for them. There were contacts in government in Britain and America who would help. Pro Israeli contacts. And Max was put in touch with them.

'Max approached your granddad with a proposal to form a specialist import-and-export agency, one of the first in the UK. He needed a partner, someone intrinsically English. Your grandfather was working in Covent Garden market at the time, as a porter. He didn't want to spend the rest of his life humping crates of fruit and veg around—'

'How about you tell me something I don't know!' Joyce

interrupted. 'This is my family history, remember. I've heard all about how Granddad and Uncle Max set up their company and called it Tanner-Max because Tanner-Schmidt would have sounded too Germanic and too Jewish. And they relocated from London to Bristol because it was a thriving port in those days, with a couple of airports within easy reach, making it perfect for their purposes. I know all that. What I want to know—'

'What you don't know is that the import and export activities of Tanner-Max International, although lucrative, were from the beginning merely a cover for what both men regarded as their real work.'

'Which was?' Joyce barked. If he didn't get to the point soon she thought she would hit him.

'Their real work was to broker arms to Israel,' Charlie continued. 'They started doing this when the Israeli state was still in its infancy. In 1957 they arranged for twenty tons of heavy water to be transported from Britain to Israel. It was picked up from a British port – no prizes for guessing which one, although that isn't a matter of record. Officially the stuff was sold to a Norwegian company called Noratum. But Noratum was a front. The company took commission on the transaction and made sure the paperwork looked in order, but the heavy water was shipped directly to Israel. And your granddad and your Uncle Max were the men who made it happen.'

Joyce was totally bewildered.

'Charlie, I don't even know what heavy water is,' she said.

'Ah,' Charlie turned to face her. 'Heavy water is a key substance in the development and manufacture of nuclear weapons. Without it, no atom bomb can be produced. Tanner-Max went on to facilitate dozens of secret shipments of restricted materials to Israel throughout the fifties and sixties, including specialist chemicals like uranium. Thanks to your granddad and Uncle Max, Israel was able to embark on a full-scale nuclear weapons programme. This has grown from strength to strength over the years. It is believed Israel currently has more than a hundred atom bombs at its disposal. Even though that is not officially admitted.

'Your granddad and your Uncle Max were masters of subterfuge. They knew how to put up a smokescreen and keep it there. I don't think that will surprise you, given the way your father is. Henry is his father's son, through and through. And I was Henry's protégé. He needed someone to take your brother's place. No one could, of course, but Henry regarded me as the next best thing, or the best he could come up with. Because of you. Or he used to, anyway. Now it's Mark.'

Charlie sounded bitter. Joyce said nothing. She was lost for words.

'Anyway, the British government has continued to use Tanner-Max on a regular basis when they need defence materials moved around,' Charlie continued. 'And not only the British government but other governments too. Tanner-Max are involved in putting armaments into what the UK and its allies consider to be the right hands across the world. Afghanistan. The Gulf. Syria. The current hotspot is Ukraine, obviously.

'The business keeps coming our way because your father knows better than anyone, certainly anyone in the UK, how to move sensitive material around the world without it becoming known where it originated or where it's ultimately going to. By the time it reaches its destination the place of origin can no longer be traced.'

Joyce stared at him, speechless.

'Well, he knows more than anyone except me, that is,' Charlie muttered.

'You?' Joyce found her voice. 'You have been involved in the arms business all these years, surreptitiously sending defence materials to war zones? You of all people?'

Charlie nodded.

'So, those lunches and boys' days out with my father when you were at Exeter, was that when it all began?' Joyce continued. 'Were you so seduced by the glamour of it that you changed from the committed communist I knew, the wild young man of principals, into, into . . . my father's poodle? Or was it the money? Were the pickings Dad offered rich enough to corrupt you?'

'It wasn't like that,' protested Charlie.

'So it wasn't the money, is that what you're telling me? The glamour, then? Excitement? Did you fancy yourself as some sort of James Bond?'

Charlie shook his head.

'It wasn't the money. Certainly not at first. Though that did come later, I suppose. And no, I didn't see myself as a James Bond figure. As for my communist leanings, that was nostalgia more than anything. The Karl Marx dream was already dead, and far more people were suffering because of communism than benefiting from it. Your father said I was old-fashioned and out of touch. If I wanted to change the world then I should consider entering his world. He didn't say so straight away, not in so many words. But that was what it amounted to. And he was so persuasive.

'He told me stuff back then that nearly blew my mind. Tanner-Max had been involved in almost all the anti-communist uprisings: Poland . . . Hungary . . . Those were popular uprisings, he said. He told me that his father and your Uncle Max had been every bit as idealistic as I was, and they had gained the power to change things. He swore they only ever became involved in arms deals for causes they thought were just.

'I was bowled over, Joyce. And I believed your father absolutely. You know how plausible he is. It was a long time before I realized he had only one motive . . .'

Charlie paused for dramatic effect.

'Money,' he said, spitting out the word. 'Money. That's all your bloody father has believed in for a long time. Probably all he has ever believed in. Your grandfather may have been different. Your Uncle Max almost certainly was. He had real ideals. And a cause: Israel. But your father? Nothing but a mercenary.'

'Yet you carried on working with him, and not once did you voice any doubts or fears, not a word of any of this to me,' said Joyce. 'To your poor bloody ignorant wife.'

She spoke quietly, thinking aloud.

'I was sucked in.' Charlie sounded desperate for her to accept his version of events. 'Please, try to understand,' he pleaded. 'You're his daughter. Once we had the house, and then the children came, what else could I do? Plus I knew everything. I knew it all by then. Henry wouldn't have let me go, even if I'd tried . . .'

'What do you think he would have done, for God's sake, taken out a contract on you? Had you shot?'

As she spoke, the grim reality of that day, the memory of the hospital visit she and her daughter had been about to make when they'd received Fred's message, hit her. So much else had happened, she'd half forgotten. Crazy as it sounded, maybe there was some truth in what Charlie was saying.

'As a matter of fact, I thought that was exactly what was going on,' she heard Charlie say.

His voice was so strained. For a moment she wanted to reach out to him. Then she remembered what he had done.

She put her head in her hands. 'Charlie, you don't know, do you?'

'Know what?'

'Dad has been shot. He's going to be all right. But he's in hospital.'

'Oh my God,' said Charlie.

The remaining colour left his face. He didn't ask any more questions. She had a nasty feeling he already had the answers.

'Charlie, what changed for you?' Joyce asked. 'What made you decide you couldn't take it any more? Tell me honestly, what made you stage your own death? What happened? What changed? And why that? Why do that?'

'Well, I became more and more disillusioned, and more and more afraid for our children.' Charlie gulped in a big breath of air, then continued: 'I found out Henry was dealing in chemical weapons. Or at least, we were shipping out the chemicals used for making those weapons. To Iran, and worst of all to Syria. It's more than likely our chemicals have been used in the barrel bombs Assad has been using. Chlorine to make chlorine gas. It's reckoned twenty thousand Syrians may have died from attacks with chemical-laden barrel bombs since the conflict began there in 2011. That was too much for me to take in.

'Chemical warfare is banned by international law, so I threatened to go to the authorities. But ultimately I let Henry talk me round. Like always. You see, Henry Tanner reckons he is above the law. And maybe he is.'

Joyce was horrified. 'I don't believe my father would do

that. I don't believe he would be involved in something so terrible. In any case, why? How?'

'I've told you why,' snapped Charlie. 'Money. And power. As for how, well, the Tanner-Max set-up is geared to transport illicit material around the world, and the pathways are smoothed by those in high places who pull Henry's strings.'

'Who are these people?'

Charlie shrugged. 'I don't know. Only Henry had direct contact. Secret Services, the Foreign Office? Bit of both, probably.'

'I don't believe it,' said Joyce. 'I can't believe it. It's all too far-fetched.'

'That's as maybe,' said Charlie. 'Believe what you like. But that's the business your father has been in for all of his working life, and me too. I couldn't stand it any longer. And I couldn't bear to watch Mark being sucked in. My life – and you might well be right, my entire bloody sanity – has been blighted by the sheer crazy awfulness of what our company, our own family company, does. What it is. I can't believe I allowed myself to get involved in the first place. If it hadn't been for how much I loved you, well . . .'

'Are you daring to blame me? It's my fault, is it?'

'I didn't mean it like that. But I couldn't watch history repeating itself with Mark, I couldn't do it any longer. And as for Fred . . .'

'How much does Mark know?'

'I'm not sure. Maybe not much. He is aware that the company is involved in some security activities overseas. Not the exact nature. Not yet. He only deals with paperwork, and everything is camouflaged. That's the name of the game. What we are all such experts at. But I could see Mark's future looming, his grandfather talking him into believing he was doing something worthwhile. Working towards world peace, probably. The way he convinced me. Except now I knew what Mark's life would be like: shrouded in mystery, fear of some kind or other always lurking. I should have done something to stop it, but now I'm afraid it's already too late for Mark. He is so much in the clutches of his grandfather. I couldn't watch any longer. I really couldn't.

'But I could still save Fred, provided I could get him away from your father. Away from all of it. That's why I wrote you that letter. I waited and waited, but you made no move to get away. That's when I decided I'd have to do something . . .'

Joyce thought he sounded lame, pathetic. She also felt, deep inside, that he still wasn't telling her the truth. Not the whole truth anyway. That there was something else. And how had he known that she'd made no move to get away? Had he been watching the house? After dark, perhaps. She said nothing. She didn't want to do or say anything that might stop him talking.

'So I thought, well, if I took Fred, I stood a chance of getting all my family together again,' Charlie continued.

'You thought that removing our son from his home in the middle of the night was a way of getting your family together?' Joyce stared at him in disbelief.

'Well, yes, you s-see—'

'You really are mad,' she said again.

Charlie shrugged. 'I had to do something.'

'Well, you've done something all right.'

Joyce was incandescent with rage. She was also frightened.

'First you staged your own death, then you abducted your son, and now you seem to have abducted your wife and daughter.'

271

'No, it's not like that—'

'Isn't it? In that case I'm going to ask you again, am I free to go? Free to take our children away from their crazy, deluded father, to the place that used to be our home? Where I will tell the police about everything you have done. And about everything that you have told me today. They can look into your claims. They can sort it out. All I want is for my children to be safe at home again. I'm free to do that, to take my children home, am I, Charlie? You wouldn't try to stop me.'

Charlie shrugged.

'I'll take that as a yes,' said Joyce. 'I'm going to get the kids. Then I'm leaving with them.'

She reached for the door handle, pulled it, pushed the door open, and began to climb out.

'No,' he said. 'I can't let you.' Charlie made a move to grab her arm.

'Don't you touch me,' Joyce snapped, shrugging him off.

But Charlie was quicker than her. He jumped out of his side of the car and ran around it so that he was blocking Joyce's way before she even had time to stand up straight.

'I can't let you go,' Charlie repeated.

'Can't you?' Joyce remarked levelly, slamming the car door shut behind her. 'Then you have abducted us. You are keeping me and my children here against our will. You must be out of your mind, Charlie.'

'Joyce, you simply don't understand,' said Charlie. 'I have to do this. Like I had to leave.'

He ran the fingers of one hand through his cropped hair and stared at her, his unfamiliar eyes beseeching her.

'Listen, Joyce, I never wanted to hurt you, honestly,' he pleaded. 'Just listen. When I decided to stage my own death,

I did it to protect you. There was no other way. You see, I found out something, something far worse and far more dangerous than anything I already knew about your father.'

He paused again. But he still did not attempt to move out of Joyce's way.

'Stop being so bloody melodramatic, Charlie, and get to the point.'

'Your father has got greedy. Or should I say, even greedier. He's been doing a bit of moonlighting, siphoning off some of the arms whenever we do an international deal. Only a few at a time. And then he's been selling them to an organized crime syndicate here in the UK. That's what he is, Joyce, not only an international supplier of ingredients for chemical warfare but an underworld arms dealer.'

'Oh, don't be ridiculous, Charlie!' she said. 'Dad would never get involved with criminals. Why on earth would he? He's a wealthy man. And what other reason could there be, apart from money?'

'Joyce, you don't know your father. You really don't. Trust me on that. There isn't enough money in the world for Henry Tanner. Nor power. He lusts after power. I found out what he was doing by accident. I'd challenged him big time on the chemical warfare issue, and Henry doesn't like being challenged. I was planning to go to the police without telling him. I think he would have known he couldn't talk me out of it, not when he was involving the company and all of us in serious criminal activity. But he was a step ahead of me. As usual. I'd been cross-checking all the company records. I'd been using my laptop so my footprints wouldn't show on the office system, because on that you can see straight away who has signed in and out and what they've been working on. But

I think Henry had someone hack into my laptop. He knew what I was planning, and he knew he had to stop me.

'I discovered that he was trying to take out a contract on me, like you said. He wanted me killed, and he knew the people to do it—'

'Charlie, if there is any truth in what you say, how come it's my father who got shot?'

'I don't know,' said Charlie. 'He was playing with fire and I guess he got burned. He was dealing with dangerous people. Gangsters. People who kill for a daily rate, for God's sake. Maybe he couldn't give them what they wanted. Maybe they thought he'd reneged on a deal. I don't know.'

'I'm sorry, Charlie, I can't believe—'

'Joyce, sweetheart, I know this is hard for you, but I honestly believe that if he'd had the contacts he has now back when you and I first met, I wouldn't have lived to cause Henry any bother. I've always known he didn't like me, he never rated me, never wanted me in his business or in his life. He thought I was weak. And he was right. He never wanted me to be part of his family. It was all a pretence. He only took me on because he feared that otherwise he would lose you. He could see how close we were. And then, after William died, he needed someone, some puppet he could mould. My weakness became attractive to him then. He thought he could turn me into whatever he wished. And for years I let him.

'You must have known that I was the last man on earth he would have wanted you to marry, me with my left-wing ideals. Mind you, nobody would have been right for you, Joycey, not in Henry's eyes. But did you never wonder why he changed his mind about me? What led him not only to welcome me as his son-in-law, but to take me into his precious business?'

Joyce said nothing. Of course she had wondered that, many many times. Her head was buzzing.

'Only I turned on him in the end, and then he decided it was time to be rid of me.'

'What on earth are you saying? You're not making any sense, Charlie.'

'Aren't I? Don't you remember all those accidents I had last year? Like the brakes failing on the car, slates falling off a roof right by me, oil on the deck of the boat causing me to slip. Did you think it was all just bad luck?'

Joyce supposed she had, at the time. And carelessness.

'Well, I'd come to think those incidents may not have been accidental. I reckoned I was living on borrowed time.'

'So you staged your own death, gave me – and your children – months of grief and despair, and left us, if you are to be believed, which is highly fucking debatable, in the clutches of a man you say is so dangerous. Not only an arms dealer but a criminal. Is that what you are saying? You put your own safety ahead of that of your wife and children. And that is probably the least of your sins.'

Charlie shook his head.

'No, you and the kids never were and never would be in any danger from Henry,' he said. 'You and Mark and Molly and Fred are his blood. That's the most important thing in the world to Henry: family. His bloodline. More important to him than making money. That is how he justifies all that he does. He's like a fucking Mafia godfather! I reckon that's how the deluded old fool sees himself too.'

Charlie's voice was harsh as he went on: 'I am not Henry's blood. He never gave a shit about me. I was always going to be dispensable in the end. When I was his pet poodle, as you put it so accurately, my darling, he put up with me. Once I

275

started to nip at his heels, he turned against me as I suppose I always knew he would. Which is why I had to act.'

'Act?' snapped Joyce. 'Is that what you call leaving your wife and children in such a cowardly way?'

'I left you the letter. I thought you'd understand. I thought you would act on it. At least take it seriously. That's why I put in the letter about us wanting to find our Shangri-La, and how it was still possible.'

'What?'

'I was hoping you'd guess from that that I was still alive. I couldn't be too explicit in case your father got his hands on the letter. Not that I didn't trust Stephen, but I couldn't take the chance, knowing how devious your father is. I had to phrase it in such a way only you would understand.'

'Charlie, were you that caught up in your stupid spy-master world? Did you think I was some sort of code-breaker? How was I supposed—'

'I was watching you. All of you. I wanted you to make a move. I was going to find you, once you'd got away, so that we could plan our next move.'

Charlie's eyes were unnaturally bright. Everything about him, from what he was saying to the way he looked, was unnerving.

'I didn't get the letter until this week, Charlie. A clerical error, Stephen said.'

'That explains a lot. No doubt your father was behind that too, for some twisted reason,' Charlie continued. 'Maybe you would have done something about it if you'd got the letter when you should have.'

'I'm not sure that I would,' said Joyce. 'I don't think I could ever have taken the kids, walked out on my life. Not without a much better reason than some cryptic letter. That must have occurred to you, surely. So was this some mad contingency plan of yours, taking Fred?'

'Well, I knew you wouldn't rest till you found him. I thought if I had Fred then I could let you find me, when the time was right, and we could all be together again, somewhere away from your father's clutches.'

'So what changed your mind about that? You didn't wait. You've snatched Molly and me too.'

'It's not like that, really it's not like that. Fred wouldn't come with me. He wouldn't go anywhere without you two. Mark as well, Fred said at first, but I think I've talked him out of that.'

'You've talked him out of that?' Joyce queried, incredulous. 'He's an eleven-year-old boy – what did you think you were doing, putting him in a position where he was having to make such monumental decisions about his own future? Was he going to run away with Daddy or was he going to stay with Mummy? For God's sake, Charlie, how could you?'

'Look, I've told you everything. You know the truth about your father now. You know how he seduced me, and corrupted me—'

'Don't you take responsibility for anything, ever?'

'I'm trying to,' said Charlie.

He stepped back from her at last, everything about his body language unthreatening. She still felt threatened. She made no attempt to move away either from him or the car.

'I came to my senses in the end. It took a long time, but I did it. That's what this is all about. So now can we talk about the future? Our future. I want us to be together, away from all of this. That's all. That's all I have ever wanted. Now we can do it, get away from your father and everything that is

Tanner-Max for ever. He doesn't even know I'm alive. We can do it, Joyce, you and me and the kids . . .'

Charlie carried on talking, but Joyce stopped listening. She slumped against the side of her car. He had to be mad; it was the only possible explanation. She felt numb. She didn't know what to believe.

She waited until the drone of his voice finally stopped.

'Did you shoot Dad, Charlie?' she asked.

Charlie looked aghast. 'Don't be ridiculous. Apart from the fact that I don't have a gun and wouldn't know how to begin, I've been here, two and a half hours from Bristol, all day. Apart from driving over the moors to send those texts. Still miles from Bristol. And with Fred, the whole time. Ask him.'

'I have no intention of asking our son anything. If you didn't do it yourself, are you sure you weren't involved in some way? Are you sure you don't know who shot Dad?'

'Of course not.'

Joyce thought Charlie didn't look too certain, but he gave her no time to question him further.

'I just want to look to our future. I want to take you and our children away. I want us to start a new life. That's all I have ever wanted.'

Joyce was wondering how to end the conversation and get away from this place when a voice from somewhere behind her cut in.

'Is it? Well then, what a fool I have been.'

It was the voice of a young woman, instantly familiar. But so out of context Joyce couldn't place it at first.

She was still struggling with her memory when a female figure dropped athletically into the barn from the top of the broken wall upon which she had apparently been perched, listening to everything that had been said.

It was a young woman wearing grey jeans, grey jacket, and a grey woolly hat.

Monika.

Charlie took a single step towards her.

'What the hell are you doing here?' he asked. 'I told you to stay in the flat.'

'And you think always I am going to do what you say, eh?' responded Monika.

She seemed to be seething with anger. Her English was not nearly as good as usual.

Charlie turned to face Joyce again. Joyce just stared at Monika.

'What is the matter, Joycey, you never look at me before, is that it?' Monika enquired, using Charlie's name for Joyce, and loading it with sarcasm.

'That is possible, no? After all, Mrs Mildmay, I am a servant only.'

Joyce stepped back and, out of habit, looked towards Charlie, seeking reassurance, or at least an explanation.

He seemed to be rooted to the spot. His mouth had fallen open. He said nothing.

Joyce turned towards Monika again. Her being there was so absurd, so ridiculously out of context that Joyce couldn't make sense of it. Why would Monika be doing this? Speaking to her as if she had a nasty taste in her mouth. As if she hated Joyce. Monika, who came into her home and looked after her children and managed her affairs. But this was a different Monika. An arrogant, angry Monika. The look in her eyes was chilling.

Monika turned on Charlie then. 'You bastard liar,' she

yelled, so angry she was trembling with rage. 'I hear every word you say to your . . . your wife. Think what I do for you. The risks I take. I help you steal car. Because I believe you. I believe it is all for us. For you and me. The only way, you say. Now I know truth. You use me to get you out of fucking mess. That is what you do.'

'No,' said Charlie. He turned to Joyce. 'You have to believe me, darling. I have no idea what she's talking about.'

Monika narrowed her eyes and took a step towards Charlie.

Joyce wouldn't have thought it was possible for him to look any more grey. But he did. He was standing quite still. She saw his Adam's apple move, as if he was trying to swallow, but without much success.

Her own mouth was dry. No doubt his was too.

What had he done? What had Charlie got himself into? And how had she remained so totally unaware of it? Or was she kidding herself? There had been times over the years when she'd suspected that he was seeing someone else. Times when he'd disappear in the early hours or come home way after midnight without explanation. But she had not suspected anything like this. How could she? Never in a million years had she suspected that her husband might be engaged in a relationship with Monika. Neither had she suspected that Monika could be so full of hatred.

Suddenly she could contain herself no longer.

'So this is the truth, then, Charlie,' she said. 'Nothing to do with your stupid conscience or my father's alleged greed. You staged your own death to be with a girl young enough to be your daughter, a girl about the same age as your eldest son. Someone I trusted in my home. Now I understand.'

'No, you don't understand anything,' said Charlie. 'I never

wanted to be with Monika. But I had to escape. I thought your father would find me wherever I went and whatever I did. Unless he thought I was dead. I couldn't do it alone. I couldn't. I used Monika – she's right about that. I didn't do it to be with her. I had no intention of being with her. It was you I wanted, Joyce. You and our children. I thought the letter would alert you. I suppose I put too much store on it . . .'

'You say you had no intention of being with me?' Monika stepped forward. 'You use me? Now you tell me, yes, that is so?'

'Shut up!' commanded Charlie.

He didn't even look at her. His eyes remained fixed on Joyce. Pleading eyes.

'You betray me,' said Monika. 'I believed in you.'

'I told you to shut up,' Charlie shouted, still not looking at her.

'Then that is it,' Monika said. Her voice suddenly confident. 'I go to the police. I will tell them everything I know. You will go to prison, Charlie. You commit many crimes. There is abduction, I think you embezzle money from your company. And, what is the charge? You pervert the course of justice. I think also there is more I do not know about. You will go to prison for long time, Charlie. And I will be glad.' She gave a short bitter laugh. 'I go to the police. I shall tell everything.'

'No, you mustn't do that,' said Charlie, his voice calm.

'Yes, I must,' she said. 'Because I do not let you get away with this. I who have done everything you ask me. I get you your drugs. I even go to doctor and I lie. I get you everything you need. I smuggle you into my home. I know I break law. I keep you in flat for months. While you stay all day in my bed and smoke your stink—'

281

'Skunk,' Charlie corrected her.

For Joyce this was yet another shock. Skunk, which hadn't been around in her long-ago smoking days, was by far the most potent and dangerous strain of marijuana ever to have been developed. Of course. It must have been skunk Charlie had been smoking that night she interrupted him in the garden shed. That was why the effect on her had been so powerful. Skunk is known to cause psychosis. According to Monika, Charlie had been smoking the stuff day in and day out for months. If that was the case, what mental state might he be in, and what might he be capable of?

Monika had begun to speak again. 'Skunk. You call it how you like. It stink anyway. I look after you, Charlie. I keep you safe. Until we are able to go away together, you say. I continue work for your family, because you say if I leave it will be suspect. I spy for you. I even do what you want when you tell me you cannot go away without your son. I go along with your crazy plan to take him from the house in the night and bring him out here where you can hide. Away from everything and everyone, you say. You will tell him then about me, about us, you say. He will be fine with it. What was I doing, believing you? I am idiot. Now I will make you suffer for what you do. I report you for all of it.'

Everything was beginning to fall horribly into place now for Joyce. Monika said she had spied for Charlie. No wonder he seemed to know so much about what she and the children had and hadn't been doing.

Charlie was still staring at her. She hated him now for what he had done. She hoped he could not read her mind. Finally he removed his gaze from Joyce and looked at Monika directly. It was a chilling look.

'I can't let you do that,' he said, his voice still disturbingly calm.

'You cannot stop me,' said Monika. 'I have car parked on the road. I go now. And I go straight to police.'

Joyce saw the expression on Charlie's face change. Something came over him. There was a glint in his eye she had never seen before. She hadn't imagined, for all the ups and downs of their marriage, that she could ever be afraid of Charlie. Afraid of what he might do.

Suddenly she was very afraid.

Twenty-two

Charlie moved quickly. In three strides he was across the barn and had reached Monika. In one fluid movement he lashed out with his clenched right fist, smashing it straight into her face. There was a crunching sound. Joyce thought the girl's nose must have been broken. Blood spouted everywhere. All over Monika and all over Charlie.

Monika did not utter a sound. Joyce saw her knees buckle. It looked as if that one punch had knocked her out cold. But Charlie did not stop.

He swayed back on his heels, crouching as he formed a fist with his other hand, and aimed a vicious left hook into the young woman's belly, right below her ribcage. There was the sort of noise you get when air is ejected from a rubber cushion. Monika folded like a concertina and fell motionless to the floor. Joyce had never before witnessed an act of such violent brutality. And this from her husband. A man she had always considered to be so gentle. Only now did it occur to her that he had probably never been that, merely weak. And weak men can often be the most vicious of all. And the most dangerous.

Joyce was horrified. She heard herself screaming. She hadn't meant to scream because of her children. Molly and

Fred were still zipped in the tent at one end of the barn. Whatever they may or may not have heard before, they must have heard their mother scream. The tent opened and they both came rushing out.

They stopped in their tracks when they saw the scene before them. Their father was standing, legs akimbo, blood on his hands, over the prone body of Monika.

Their mother had managed to stop screaming but was looking on in horror.

'Dad,' shouted Molly, taking in the dreadful scene. 'What's Monika doing here? She's hurt. Did you hurt her? What's going on? What have you done?'

'Nothing, I haven't done anything,' said Charlie. 'This isn't what it seems, sweetheart, honestly it's not.'

It was, of course, exactly what it seemed. Charlie was behaving like the weak man Joyce already knew him to be, although she had not imagined for one moment that he could ever be capable of anything like the display of violence she had just witnessed.

He was desperate, obviously. Desperate and weak. What a combination.

Charlie turned to face Fred directly and opened his arms, inviting the boy to run into them the way he always had done. After all, whatever else may have been going on in their marriage, Charlie had always been a good father. Or at least, that's what Joyce had thought until now.

'It's all right Fred, honestly,' said Charlie.

Fred started to move towards him again. Then he stopped. 'No, no, Dad. It's not. You've got blood on your hands.'

Charlie looked down at his hands, surprised. He rubbed them hastily on the back of his trousers.

'Look, you can trust me, Fred,' he said. 'You know that,

285

don't you?' Charlie's glance took in his wife and his daughter too. 'You can all trust me,' he said.

Joyce at that moment thought her husband was the last man in the world she would ever trust. She heard Monika moan. At least the girl was alive. The way she'd gone down, Joyce had feared Charlie may have killed her.

It was clear that Charlie had told Monika he was running away with her. He must have sworn his love for her so that she would help him stage his disappearance. He couldn't have done it alone. His dinghy had been left on the boat; his life jacket had been found. He had to have had an accomplice who had rendezvoused with him at sea. Was Monika his accomplice in that too? She must be a reasonably competent sailor then. Joyce wondered if Charlie had coached her, and how often she'd accompanied him on those 'solo' trips aboard the boat named after his daughter. This young woman who, as she said, had risked everything for him. Yet as soon as Monika presented a threat to him, Charlie had viciously attacked her. And without a moment's hesitation. What would he do to his wife, or even to his children, if any of them presented a threat? Joyce wondered. He said he had done everything for them to be together. But that didn't make any sense. They had been together before. Before Charlie had decided he wanted his new life!

Aloud she said in the kindest most reassuring voice she could manage: 'I want to trust you, Charlie. We do all need you, I know.'

It was as if by sounding understanding she had flicked a switch in Charlie. By giving him even the merest flicker of hope she had cut through the charade of his being in control of himself or the situation.

He sank to his knees on the wet and muddy floor of the barn, alongside Monika, and began to blub like a baby.

Joyce knew she must seize the moment. Trade on her husband's inherent weakness. Take the initiative while there was a chance that he might allow her to do so.

She walked across to him and rested a hand on his shoulder.

'Come on, Charlie, remember JC. Let's do this together, like we used to do everything,' she coaxed. 'We need to get out of here. Please listen to me. We need to get our children to safety, and we need to get Monika to hospital.'

Charlie shook his head and did not move.

'You're not a murderer, are you?' asked Joyce. 'Whatever else you might be, you don't want to be that, do you?'

Charlie looked up at her through his tears.

'I don't know what I am any more,' he said.

'You are my husband,' responded Joyce, although the words nearly stuck in her throat. 'I want you to be the man I married again. Can you do that Charlie? For me.'

Charlie stopped crying. He seemed to be totally broken, thought Joyce. And totally pathetic. She had no sympathy for him. She had no feelings for him whatsoever. All she wanted was to be safe again, and for her children to be safe again. Particularly the two who were standing in stunned silence watching all this.

'I w-will try,' he said.

Joyce took one of his hands in hers and half pulled him to his feet.

'Come on,' she instructed with as much authority as she could muster. 'Let's go home. We'll go home and then we can decide what to do next.'

'I can't go to jail, Joyce,' said Charlie.

'I'll make sure you don't,' said Joyce, who at that moment didn't care if her husband spent the rest of his life in jail, and in fact rather hoped that he would. 'Fred went with you of his own free will, didn't you, honey?'

She glanced towards Fred, who nodded uncertainly.

'See – no abduction, Charlie. Molly and I came here of our own free will too. We'll get Monika to hospital, make sure she's all right, say she was attacked in the street, we found her the way she is. Then we'll sort out everything else. Dad won't pursue anything. He will have to do exactly what I say or he'll be the one going to jail. C'mon, Charlie, let's all go home, shall we?'

Charlie did not move. He was staring at the prone Monika. Joyce was still holding his hand. He hadn't done a very good job of wiping it clean. She noticed that she now had blood on her own hand. It took an effort not to snatch it away from his grasp.

Joyce wondered how convincing she was being. It was hard to tell whether she was getting through to him. He must be seriously mentally ill, and probably had been for a long time. She tried a new tack.

'If you don't want to come, then at least let me take the children,' said Joyce. 'You don't want them seeing you like this, do you? You're in no state to look after them, that's for sure. And you don't want then to, uh, misunderstand about Monika. They can't stay here with you, you must see that.'

Charlie shrugged.

Trying not to make any sudden movement, Joyce eventually removed her hand from Charlie's. He allowed her to do so without protest. She turned away from him and slowly returned to the car. She opened the tailgate of the Range

288

Rover then looked towards her children, who were still clutching each other.

'Fred, get in,' she instructed.

Molly was looking her mother straight in the eye, seeking reassurance. With a nod and a little smile Joyce tried to give it.

Molly gave her brother a small push. 'Do as Mum says,' she told him.

Fred obediently climbed into the rear compartment behind the doggy gate that no one had got around to removing after the family dog had died the previous spring. Fred had ridden in the back many times before when the car was full. Sometimes along with the dog. That in itself was not a problem for him.

Joyce continued to give instructions. Charlie remained where he was. Then she saw his shoulders heave. He seemed to be starting to sob again. For the moment Joyce ignored him.

'Molly, we can't leave Monika here,' she said. 'We have to take her to hospital. Help me get her into the car. She can lie across the back seat.'

Molly nodded her agreement. Mother and daughter lifted Monika and half carried, half dragged her towards the car. Molly hesitated only briefly when Monika's head rolled limply to one side, as she and her mother were manoeuvring the young woman into the back of the Range Rover.

Joyce proceeded to climb into the driver's seat and gestured to Molly to get in alongside her. It was then that Charlie finally moved.

'No,' he said. 'Wherever we go from now on, whatever happens, I want us to be a whole family.'

He walked towards the car. Joyce reached out to turn the

ignition. She didn't want this man with her and her children. She was afraid of him. She wanted to leave him behind. And that was exactly what she intended to do. She would start the engine and drive away. He couldn't stop her. If necessary, she would run him over. She didn't want her children to see that. But she would do it. If necessary, she would damned well do it.

She groped for the key with extended fingers. It wasn't there. She realized at once that Charlie must have taken it. She hadn't noticed, but she supposed he must have done so while they were having their not-so-cosy chat earlier.

'Give me the key, Charlie,' she demanded. 'Give it me now.'

Charlie was standing by the car. He shook his head and reached for the door handle. Joyce reached for the lock. Again Charlie was too fast for her. He jerked open the driver's door.

'No,' he said. 'You don't go anywhere without me. None of you do. I never want us to be apart again. I'm not going to let that happen.'

His eyes were wild. He was sweating. He must have rubbed his hands over his face, because it was now streaked with blood as well as tears. He was a terrifying sight. Joyce was now convinced that he was in the grip of a serious nervous breakdown. God knows what regular use of skunk might have done to his brain. She suspected he'd been hanging on to the vestiges of sanity during this six-month period he'd pretended to be dead, hiding in his girlfriend's flat, smoking a hazardous mind-altering narcotic, watching and waiting, to see if Joyce would do as he had told her in his letter, and plotting his next catastrophic move when she did not.

The scene with Monika in the barn must have pushed him right over the edge. Certainly it had driven him to a shocking level of violence. And in front of his children.

Charlie caught hold of her arm and pulled.

'Get out,' he said. 'I will let you leave. But anywhere you go, I go. From now on we go as a family. I'll drive.'

'All right, all right.' Joyce wrenched her arm free. 'We will all go together. We will do what you want. But please, let me drive. You are in no state to drive your children. Look at yourself. You're wet with sweat, even though it's so damn cold, and you're covered in blood.'

Charlie looked down at himself, raised a hand to his sweating forehead, then looked at the blood on his fingers. Again he seemed surprised. His shoulders slumped. But he was not prepared to give in.

'I'm fine,' he said.

He took a dirty tissue from the pocket of his combat jacket and rubbed at his face in a desultory manner. There wasn't much improvement.

'There,' he said. 'That's the best I can do for the moment. I'm perfectly able to drive. So move over to the passenger seat, Joyce. Molly, get out, and climb in the back.'

'Charlie, no,' said Joyce. 'Please. I will do whatever you tell me. But please, let me drive.'

'No,' insisted Charlie, his voice unnaturally high. 'I am not letting you drive me anywhere, Joyce. If you want to get out of here, if you want to go home, for us to take our children home and work everything out, like you said, you will have to let me drive.'

'Oh no, Charlie—' Joyce began.

Charlie put a hand over the pocket in which Joyce

presumed he'd put the car keys. 'Otherwise we stay here,' he said. 'All of us, together.'

Joyce stared at him. At this man she barely recognized. It seemed that she had no choice. She would have to take the risk. To hope that he really did intend to take her and the children home, and not to some other crazy hiding place.

'All right,' she said resignedly. She turned to her daughter: 'I'm moving over, sweetheart. Your dad's going to drive.'

Molly looked as afraid as Joyce felt.

'Where am I going to sit?' she asked in a small voice.

'Out you get, Molly,' instructed her father sharply. 'You must ride in the back with . . . with . . .' Charlie hesitated as if he could no longer bring himself to speak the name of the young woman to whom he had promised so much. 'W-with Monika,' he finished with an effort.

'Oh no, oh, Mum, don't let him make me do that,' Molly began pleadingly, and she started to cry. 'It's too scary.'

Joyce made one last attempt to avoid what seemed to be becoming inevitable.

'Why don't you follow us in your car, Charlie? Then Molly wouldn't have to move.'

She gestured towards the Honda.

Charlie shook his head. 'The police are sure to be looking for it by now, and after all this rain I don't even think it would make the track. Anyway, I've told you: we're sticking together from now on.'

Joyce thought the police might be looking for her Range Rover by now too. She hoped so. But that didn't seem to have occurred to Charlie.

Mollie was sobbing quietly. Much as Joyce felt for her daughter, she knew that none of them had any choice. She could only do what she believed was for the best.

'Molly, do as your father says, please,' said Joyce. 'We need to get away from here. It will be all right, I promise.'

Molly began to cry more loudly. But she obediently got out of the front of the car and climbed into the back. She chose to sit at the end where Monika's feet were, making herself small in the corner, so that Monika could remain lying along the seat.

'Good girl,' murmured Joyce encouragingly as she man-oeuvred herself across the front of the Range Rover and into the passenger seat. 'We'll be home in no time, you'll see.'

Charlie climbed in behind the wheel, produced the key and switched on the ignition.

Without another word he started the engine, reversed out of the ruined barn, along the rough track now swimming with mud, and on to the Landacre–Exford road, turning in the direction of the A38 and the M5.

A two hour journey to Tarrant Park – assuming that was where Charlie was planning to take his family – lay ahead. Joyce was dreading every long minute of it.

Twenty-three

Meanwhile, Vogel and DCI Clarke had arrived at Southmead Hospital. Clarke was still talking as she pulled into the car park. Vogel had expected the DCI, who operated on a need-to-know basis, to restrict her briefing on Henry Tanner and his family firm to the bare minimum. What he hadn't appreciated until now was just how little she herself knew.

Nobby Clarke had only a sketchy idea of what Tanner-Max's defence brokerage actually involved. She didn't know the details of the many countries they had dealt with over the years, or of the conflicts they had influenced and perhaps even indirectly instigated. She did not know the company history. She knew nothing of their initial dealings with Israel, including the heavy water transaction, which had so impressed Charlie Mildmay when Henry had revealed it to him all those years ago. She knew nothing of involvement in shipping chemical substances to be used in warfare contrary to international law. She knew of no dealings with criminal elements, as Charlie was at that moment alleging to Joyce. All she knew about Henry Tanner had been passed on to her by the government of the United Kingdom. By people who themselves may or may not have known all that they should about Tanner and Tanner-Max.

'I've been told by the Foreign Office that Henry Tanner is a man of considerable importance to this country, and indeed to half the Western world,' she informed Vogel.

And she went on to tell him, albeit only in the broadest of terms, without nearly as much detail, and without many of the salient points, much the same story as Charlie Mildmay's.

'Henry Tanner is an internationally known arms broker,' Clarke related. 'His front is his own legitimate import-and-export agency. He brokers arms deals with countries and organizations in the world where it is in the interest of the UK and her allies to place consignments of what are called defence materials. Some of these are manufactured in the UK, and it's big business. There are 130-odd British arms manu-facturers, who between them generate in excess of forty million quid a year for the exchequer. And I am sure you know that the West Country is where the majority of Brit-ain's arms-producing factories are located, and that is why the company was originally set up here. The majority of Tanner-Max's undisclosed cargoes are, however, merely chan-nelled from their countries of origin through our ports and air corridors, primarily here in Bristol where Tanner has a network of warehouses and loading bays at what remains of the docks and at the airport. It's all highly political, obvi-ously, and top secret. Tanner-Max is a family business and its cover is impeccable. Since the Second World War the com-pany has been looking after British interests in parts of the world where we cannot be officially seen to have any kind of presence.'

Vogel was poleaxed. He had not expected anything like this, even when his hands had been tied behind his back by Reg Hemmings.

'Think of it as a kind of money laundering,' the DCI

continued as she switched off the engine of the CID car. 'Tanner makes sure vast quantities of arms and other defence products end up where our government wants them, without anybody knowing they came from us. And that, Vogel, is why we have to look after him. And why, if anything untoward happens to him or any of his family, it has to be investigated at a level above country plod.'

Clarke smiled then. A crooked challenging smile.

Vogel didn't rise to the bait. He knew he was about as far removed from country plod as it was possible for a copper to be. And that DCI Nobby Clarke was more aware than most of that fact.

He was quiet as Clarke led the way to Henry Tanner's private room. Vogel didn't like this sort of thing. It got in the way of proper policing. He didn't like the idea of a British citizen being given protection that might prevent them being bought to justice for their involvement in criminal activity. He didn't like it one bit.

He looked at Henry Tanner with distaste, expecting him to try to take charge as on previous encounters. Tanner, however, was displaying none of his usual bravado. He seemed reasonably alert, but the bullet wound was obviously causing him pain. His wife looked worried sick.

When Clarke asked him if he now felt well enough to talk, Henry commanded his wife to leave the room so that he could speak to the police alone. Vogel was surprised any woman would tolerate such behaviour in this day and age.

To Henry's obvious astonishment, it seemed Felicity had come round to Vogel's way of thinking.

'Those days are over, Henry,' she said in a tone of voice that brooked no argument. 'I'm staying. I want to know exactly what is going on.'

Henry sighed but did not demur.

Felicity sat close to him by the bed. Clarke sat down next to her on the only other chair in the room. Vogel stood at the foot of the bed. He would have chosen to do so in any case; from his chosen position he could look down at Henry and straight at him.

'Right, Mr Tanner, this case is growing more serious by the minute,' began Clarke. 'Obviously I know the, uh, job you and your company do, and I know how sensitive that is. Under normal circumstances I would not ask you to jeopardize the . . . uh, confidentiality of your work. But something is wrong here, dangerously wrong. If you have any information whatsoever that could even remotely pertain to the events of the last couple of days, the time has come for you to confide in us. In particular, if you have any idea where, or with whom, your daughter and grandchildren may be, you should tell us. If you don't . . . I hate to say this, but you could come to regret not doing so.'

Tanner shrugged. It was ill advised. He winced as the pain from his injured shoulder coursed through his central nervous system.

'I've told you all I know, Detective Chief Inspector,' he said. 'You know who I am and what I do. Does Mr Vogel also know?'

Vogel confirmed that he did, adding: 'That does not in any way put you above or beyond the law, Mr Tanner. I hope you are aware of that. If you have broken the law in any regard you will be dealt with exactly like anyone else. And that includes withholding information.'

Clarke frowned at Vogel as if she thought it unnecessary for him to have made that point in the way that he did. He didn't care.

Henry Tanner seemed oblivious to the undercurrents between the two detectives.

'You must appreciate, Mr Vogel, that there are people in the world who might like to harm me,' he said. 'People who blame me for certain events. People who could seek revenge.'

Vogel had no idea what he meant. It was Clarke who responded.

'Neither DI Vogel nor I know nearly enough about your activities, business or personal, to be able to pass comment on that, Mr Tanner,' she said. 'I was sent here from London simply to lead the investigation into your grandson's disappearance, whilst at the same time dealing sensitively with you and your family because of the work that you do. Since then there have been further disturbing developments: you have been shot, and two other members of your family are unaccounted for. I believe it is likely that you have information that would be of assistance to us in locating your missing grandchildren and their mother, and apprehending those responsible.'

Henry Tanner stared hard at Clarke through bloodshot eyes, but remained silent.

'For God's sake, Henry!' interjected Felicity. 'For years I've put up with your silly bloody games. You and your father, thinking you're some sort of master spies. Now is the time to stop. Joyce and the children could be in terrible danger. Somebody took a shot at you and tried to kill you. Are these secrets you're guarding worth losing your life over? Your daughter and your grandchildren's lives? Please, tell the truth. Before something worse happens.'

Henry lifted himself up on his pillows, wincing with pain. He looked directly at his wife.

'I know, darling, I do understand. I realize it may be time to put an end to all the secrecy . . .' he began.

It seemed he had finally given in.

Then the door opened and in walked Stephen Hardcastle.

'Henry,' he exclaimed. 'Felicity. I wanted to come before but the hospital wouldn't let me. How are you, Henry? I've been so worried . . .'

He stopped, apparently noticing Vogel and Clarke for the first time.

'Oh, I'm sorry, am I interrupting something?' he asked.

'Yes,' said Vogel.

'No,' said Henry Tanner.

'Mr Hardcastle, it may be better if you come back later,' DCI Clarke told him.

'Oh yes, of course.'

But Hardcastle looked uncertain. Perhaps out of habit, he immediately deferred to the man in the bed.

'Henry?'

'Makes no difference. I have nothing more to tell these officers. I am unable to give them any help.'

If Henry had been about to reveal all, the arrival of his visitor had caused him to change his mind. Or perhaps merely given him the time to do so.

'Please leave us, Mr Hardcastle,' DCI Clarke repeated.

'Right,' said Stephen. He turned and headed for the door, where he paused.

'I'll be outside if you need me, Henry,' he said.

Clarke returned her attention to the man in the bed.

'Mr Tanner, I have full clearance at the highest possible government level to deal with your family. I do not understand your reticence.'

She remonstrated with him in exactly the same way that

Vogel had earlier remonstrated with her. Repeating her earlier warnings.

'Your daughter and two of your grandchildren could be in grave danger,' she said.

Henry tightened his lips. His one good arm lay at his side, fist tightly clenched.

'I do not feel that I am at liberty to help you any further, DCI Clarke,' he said stubbornly. 'And I am no longer sure that you are the person to help me, to help any of us.'

Felicity sighed in exasperation. 'What does that mean, Henry?

'It means what it says. I need to make phone calls. I'm still waiting for a phone call . . .'

'Mr Tanner, I understand that you may wish to make certain phone calls, but I would suggest you do so immediately. For the sake of your family. You could all be in great danger.'

Henry seemed to think again.

'All right,' he said. 'I can make no promises, but I will call Mr Smith. I can be guided only by Mr Smith.'

He reached for his phone on the bedside table.

In doing so he seemed to cause himself considerable pain again. He fell back against the pillows, dropping the phone on the bed. Then he started to shake. The blood had drained from his face. He was fighting to breathe. Just like before.

His wife made no move to help him. She didn't seem to care.

'Get a nurse,' said Clarke to Vogel.

He did so. Even though he had a strong suspicion that Henry Tanner could be faking the whole thing. And that maybe he had done so the first time too.

Twenty-four

Joyce reckoned the journey from Landacre was going to seem much longer than the couple of hours it would actually take. Assuming Charlie was taking them home. At least he seemed to be heading in the right direction. He had turned on to the M5 and was driving steadily northwards, keeping to the speed limit – which was a relief; she'd been afraid he might drive faster. Then again, the last thing he'd have wanted was to attract attention by driving erratically.

Fred was, for him, strangely silent in the rear compartment of the vehicle. Then again, there was nothing strange about being silent in the face of such a terrible experience. Molly, too, was so traumatized she couldn't speak; she huddled next to Monika, sobbing non-stop.

Joyce was exhausted. It had been a long day and she'd driven for several hours. The husband she had believed to be dead had suddenly turned up alive, albeit half out of his mind. His account of the events that had led to his staged death had been shocking and at the same time ludicrous. On top of that, she'd witnessed a brutal attack on a young woman who, it seemed, had been having an affair with her not-so-dead husband.

At least she had Fred back, that was the main thing. All

she needed to do now was to get her children away from her husband. And then find a way to deliver him into the hands of the police. She had no doubt that was where he belonged.

As to how she was supposed to achieve her two aims, she hadn't a clue.

Charlie had indicated that he was prepared to take Monika to hospital. It seemed Joyce had got through to him: rather than risk being accused of murder, he'd see to it the girl got the medical treatment she needed.

In addition to helping Monika, Joyce hoped that a stop at A & E would give her a better chance of freeing herself and her children from Charlie's clutches than if they went straight home. At the hospital there would be people – doctors, security guards, people in authority. The Firs would most likely be empty; with the family absent, any police presence would surely have been withdrawn.

She noticed that they were approaching the Exeter turn-off.

'Why don't we come off the motorway here, Charlie, and take Monika to A & E at the Devon and Exeter,' she suggested, more in hope than expectation. 'The quicker she gets medical attention, the better for all of us.'

Charlie made no reply.

Right on cue, Monika, who'd been drifting in and out of consciousness, let out a horrible, incoherent cry.

Molly gasped through her sobs. Joyce rested her right hand lightly on her husband's forearm.

'We could just drop her off at A & E. We don't even need to get out of the car,' she said tentatively.

'No!' Charlie screamed at her. 'I'm taking us home. Like you said.'

And he accelerated sharply so that they hurtled past the Exeter junction.

Joyce daren't say more for fear of provoking him further. She was even more afraid now. All she could hope for was that he would have calmed down by the time they neared Bristol.

Eventually Charlie spoke again, reasonably calmly this time.

'We're going home, Joyce,' he said. 'That's what you wanted, isn't it? You said let's all go home and we can sort everything out there. Well, I'm doing what you wanted.'

'Yes, but Monika does need to go to hospital, and soon,' Joyce ventured.

Molly joined in from the back: 'Monika seems worse, Mum,' she said through her sobs. 'She's unconscious again. Her breathing's shallow. I'm frightened, Mum.'

So am I, thought Joyce, but I mustn't show it.

'Can't you hear your daughter, Charlie – your daughter who loves you so much,' Joyce coaxed. 'She's frightened. Monika might be dying back there. And it was you who attacked her. She has to go to hospital. For your sake as much as hers.'

Charlie said nothing, just carried on driving as if he hadn't heard. Joyce lapsed into silence, fearful of antagonizing him. They continued, no one saying a word, until they came to junction 22, the turn-off for Burnham-on-Sea, Weston-super-Mare, Bristol Airport and the A38 leading to Tarrant Park.

Charlie drove straight past it.

'You've missed the turning, Charlie,' Joyce said, hugely alarmed but trying to hide it.

He glanced at her sideways, then returned his eyes to the road.

'You wanted us to take Monika straight to hospital, didn't you?'

'Well, yes,' agreed Joyce.

'And that's what I'm going to do,' said Charlie. 'I know you're right. I don't want to be a murderer. We have to get Monika to hospital. Quickly. And I have to give myself up to the police. Then hope they will deal with me, with all of us, the way you seem to think they will.'

He touched her hand. Barely a touch. More of a brushing of flesh. But it seemed like a gesture both of affection and apology.

Relief washed over Joyce. Charlie appeared to be having a change of heart. Could it be that he was coming round to her way of thinking? She still felt uneasy, but she told herself that this was a good sign. He'd expressed some regret over what he had done. He retained at least some of the human decency she'd thought to be an integral part of him.

'I'm so glad, Charlie,' she told him. 'I know you're doing the right thing. The only thing.'

He smiled at her. Well nearly. It was more of a grimace.

At junction 18, the main Bristol turn-off, Charlie swung the Range Rover into the exit lane and on to the Portway towards the city centre.

So far so good.

Then, after a couple of miles, he drove straight past the turning for Southmead, the hospital Joyce had assumed he was heading for.

'W-where are we going?' she asked.

'Bristol Royal Infirmary,' he replied. 'Why? Where did you think I was taking you?'

'Southmead,' she said. 'The main A & E department is there now. It's just moved from Frenchay.'

'I didn't know that,' said Charlie. 'I knew the move was about to happen, but I wasn't sure which of those hospitals was operational. So I thought it safest to go to the Royal Infirmary.'

'Right,' said Joyce.

'It won't take long,' Charlie reassured her.

He sounded so reasonable. As if he wanted to end this thing as much as she did.

She stole a quick look at him. His expression gave nothing away. And what he'd said did make sense. You had to drive pretty much through the city centre to get to the Royal Infirmary, but it was nearly nine thirty at night. The traffic shouldn't be too bad. She hoped not, anyway.

'Thank you, Charlie,' she said.

'Good,' he said. 'We have a plan then. We will take Monika to A & E at the Bristol Infirmary and leave her there. We don't have to go in. Nobody need see me. Then we'll go home. To Tarrant Park. We'll all be together. Like before. If I can't have you and the kids with me in a new life, then I'll settle for the old. Like you said, we can fix it. As long as I have you on my side, everything will be all right . . .'

Charlie had suddenly gone from morose silence to incessant talking. He was manic. Joyce felt she had no choice but to go along with him.

'Yes, we'll go home and be together, then we'll be able to work things out,' she said, praying she sounded more convincing than she felt.

Again Charlie lapsed into silence. He appeared to be deep in thought, as if weighing up his options.

To Joyce's disappointment, even though it was late in the evening, there were still queues of traffic along the A4 Portway heading into the city centre. Possibly because of the terrible weather. She kept stealing glances at Charlie, who was sitting stiffly upright, grasping the steering wheel tightly, peering with considerable concentration through the windscreen in between the incessant swishing of the wipers.

By the time they reached the Floating Harbour, the city's old dockland area, which in Victorian times had been formed by impounding 80 acres of the tidal River Avon so that visiting ships could remain afloat at all times, much of the traffic ahead had mysteriously cleared. Had it not been late on a wet and windy night, they might have had a view of the old wooden sailing vessel moored alongside Mardyke Wharf. But visibility was terrible in spite of the street lights, and in any case Joyce was too preoccupied with the nasty little drama which was taking place inside her own vehicle to enjoy the view.

She did notice that there were suddenly only a few vehicles ahead and that the traffic was now running smoothly. Charlie began to accelerate. Joyce was not unhappy about that. She wanted to get to the Royal Infirmary as quickly as possible. She still wasn't sure exactly how she was going to make things pan out the way she wanted when they did get there. All she knew was that she had to get this nightmare to end. And the faster Charlie got them to the hospital, the faster that might be achieved.

She could see beads of sweat standing out on his forehead, even though the car's climate control was working perfectly and the air con control panel monitor showed that the temperature inside the vehicle was a comfortable 20 degrees.

Charlie leaned forward in his seat, then looked across the road towards the harbour.

There was a gap ahead in the ornate iron railings along

the roadside, one of several left to allow access to the quay by maintenance and port authority vehicles.

Charlie suddenly swung the steering wheel to the right and slammed his foot hard on to the accelerator.

The Range Rover was an automatic, requiring no gear change. The car hurtled towards the harbour, and shot through the gap.

A metre to either side and the railings might have halted or at least slowed the vehicle, which also only narrowly avoided collision with an oncoming taxi. There would still have been a crash, but nothing like what lay in store.

With a terrible lucid clarity, Joyce grasped at once what was happening: Charlie intended to drive them all straight into the harbour. He had spotted that gap and deliberately aimed at it. But she had no time to do anything to prevent the inevitable. There was a second set of railings at the water-side, which she hoped might provide a preventive barrier. However, the new Range Rover Sport boasts a 0 to 60 acceleration speed of under seven seconds. Charlie had been driving at around 35 miles per hour along the Hotwell Road when he'd suddenly accelerated. It took only three or four seconds for the vehicle to reach those railings, but by the time it did so the speed of the Range Rover had increased to over 60 mph.

Joyce heard Molly screaming and thought she probably was too. Charlie didn't utter a sound. His body was rigid, his eyes focused straight ahead. If they were actually focused on anything.

The Range Rover crashed into the waterside iron railings, which only partly gave way on impact. The front of the vehicle caved in, but the impetus carried it forward, sending it somersaulting over the railings until it met the murky waters of the Floating Harbour nose first. It was almost instantly submerged.

The glass in the window next to Joyce shattered. So did the windscreen. The driver's door burst open. The car was totally wrecked. Water flooded inside, causing the vehicle to become more quickly submerged than had it remained intact and any kind of significant air pocket formed. The Range Rover weighed more than 240 kilos. It sank to the bottom like a bloody great stone.

The Mardyke Wharf section of the harbour had a depth of only around four metres. There was therefore only two and a half metres of water above the sunken car. But under such circumstances that was potentially as lethal as ten times the depth.

Joyce was covered in broken glass. She had no idea whether or not she had suffered any cuts. Both the front safety bags had inflated. Joyce was half trapped by hers, and her safety belt still held her firmly in her seat. It was pitch-black in the car, although some light from the street lamps above permeated the gloom. She could not see Charlie, but she was aware that he was totally still. She didn't know if he had been seriously injured or if perhaps he was dead. He certainly was not fighting for his life as she was trying to fight for hers. Presumably he had wanted to die, along with most of his family, and he seemed to have achieved his intention.

The big vehicle had landed upright underwater, with all its four wheels on the harbour bottom. A small air bubble had formed at the top of the car, above the line of the doors, but the water had already reached Joyce's neck. She knew she had little time to free herself and her children. She fumbled for the catch of her seat belt. Mercifully she was able to release it at once. She leaned over the back of her seat, reaching for Molly. Only then did she realize that her daughter, not wearing a seat belt in the back, had been thrown forward, her upper body smashing into the head rest of the front passenger seat. Molly remained in that position, her head forced backwards at an impossible angle.

Joyce's brain was barely functioning, yet somehow she registered that Molly's neck was broken. For a second she hesitated, her hands reaching out towards her daughter's poor twisted body.

She knew there was nothing she could do for Molly. But there had to be something she could do for Fred. He remained in the rear compartment, trapped by the doggy gate dividing that area from the rest of the vehicle. A doggy gate she had never managed to insert or remove unaided, a task she couldn't even consider underwater in such conditions. If only she'd removed it after the dog had died. If only the bloody thing had never been fitted in the first place.

She hadn't heard a sound from Fred. And the whole car was now virtually full of water. As the water rose to cover her nose and mouth, Joyce turned away from Molly. She knew she had to leave her daughter. It was just possible she could squeeze her way out through the broken window of the front passenger door. Joyce had always been athletic. Desperation gave her greater strength and agility than ever before. Somehow she managed to force herself out of the vehicle, even though several of her ribs were broken. The pain from where her seat belt had bitten in was extreme. She ignored it.

She was never to know how, nor to care how, she got out. And although sporty on dry land, she was only an average swimmer. She used the sides of the stricken vehicle, the back-door handle, the roof-rack rails, to haul herself around to the tailgate. Then she reached out for its handle, which, to her relief, turned with surprising ease. Momentarily encouraged, she pulled at the tailgate with all her remaining strength. It wouldn't budge. Water pressure kept the rear door firmly closed. She wished then that she had at least attempted to remove the doggy gate from inside. It couldn't have been more hopeless than this. But she hadn't. Now her lungs were bursting. She had no chance whatsoever of re-entering the car to try to save Fred that way.

She didn't even know if her son was still alive. She pressed her face against the rear door's unbroken glass panel, desperate for a glimpse of Fred. She opened her eyes as wide as she could in order to see through the murky water, barely even aware of how much that stung. It didn't help. She could hardly see a thing.

Then in a shaft of pale light from above, directly before her, right on the other side of the glass, she saw Fred's face, a couple of inches from hers. His poor, drowning face. Fred's eyes and mouth were wide open. Was he screaming or was he already dead?

Joyce clawed at the glass and pulled again, with renewed strength, at the rear-door handle. The terrible shock of suddenly seeing Fred like that had caused a physical spasm within her which had made it impossible for Joyce to fight any longer to keep air in her lungs. She began to breathe in water. She too was drowning. But she could not leave her son. Nor her daughter, even though she knew for certain that Molly was already dead. She would die there in the harbour alongside her children. It was all that was left for her.

But Joyce Mildmay did leave her children. She did not die

with them beneath the murky waters of Bristol's Floating Harbour.

Ultimately the human body's desperate and undeniable animal desire for survival overwhelmed her whole being. She was unable to stop herself rising up from the harbour depths even though she had no conscious wish to do so.

Nature and gravity lifted her to the surface where, coughing and spluttering, she took big gulps of air, every breath causing pain to her ribs, but nothing like the terrible terrible pain of grief and despair, which was a much more excruciating agony. A quite unbearable agony.

Twenty-five

Alvin Nightingale was a twenty-one-year-old civilian investigator of West Indian descent employed by the Avon and Somerset Constabulary at Kenneth Steele House. He was intelligent, alert and ambitious. And he was not satisfied with his work. He was currently engaged in studying CCTV and other camera footage and had earlier that day been trying to follow the route of Joyce Mildmay's Range Rover, with limited success. It was work he was good at, because Alvin was a meticulous young man, but he found it tedious beyond belief.

Alvin wanted to be a police officer. He had always wanted to be a police officer. Unfortunately he had so far been prevented from following his dream by a sight defect which meant that his long sight fell below required standards and was likely to further deteriorate. Corrective lenses and spectacles alone could not improve Alvin's sight to the required level. Alvin had, however, managed to get himself on an NHS waiting list for an operation about which he was fiercely optimistic, even though the success rate was only 30 or 40 per cent. But he knew he could be in for a long wait; his was not considered to be an urgent case, because Alvin could see well enough. Not well enough to become a policeman, that was all.

Meanwhile Alvin liked to pretend he was a kind of trainee police officer. He was always on the lookout for matters that might draw him to the attention of his superiors. And he was intent on demonstrating that his eyesight wasn't that bad. He was, in fact, determined to prove that his sight defect should not prevent him joining the force, and that he was definitely made of the right stuff.

There was, of course, an alert out for Joyce's black Range Rover, as well as for the stolen blue Honda Accord in which it was believed young Fred Mildmay had been transported out of Tarrant Park. This was not something with which Alvin Nightingale was expected to concern himself when off duty. But such was his eagerness to impress, he remained vigilant long after his shift had finished.

He was assisted in this, albeit with little tangible success so far, by his place of residence. Alvin lived with his grandmother in one of the thirties semis lining the Portway at Sea Mills, coincidentally not far from Vogel's bungalow home. He had a bedroom overlooking the main road. And when he had nothing better to do of an evening, which was often now that he had given up swatting for police entry examinations, he would sit at his window, checking the passing traffic against a list of vehicles he and his colleagues had been looking out for that day on CCTV and ANPR.

When the Mildmay Range Rover passed that evening, Alvin had been at his window, for almost an hour, with binoculars, pen, notebook and mobile phone at the ready.

The make, colour and registration number of Joyce's vehicle featured in the list jotted on the back of his left hand

how could he read it if he was west Indian

in marker pen. He had already noted several large dark four-wheel drives which had attracted his attention until they passed directly beneath his gran's house, where a conveniently placed street lamp revealed them to be of the wrong make or colour.

Joyce's was the second black Range Rover to pass by in the direction of the city centre. Alvin used his binoculars to check and double-check the registration. It was the vehicle owned by Joyce Mildmay, the woman whose child was missing, and whose own whereabouts was currently unknown. There was no doubt about it.

Alvin stood up in front of his bedroom window and focused his binoculars on the Range Rover's windows, straining to see inside. The rear windows were tinted. He could see nothing though them. He could, however, see that there was a passenger in the front, and he was sure it was a woman. He could not see the driver.

That was good enough for Alvin. He punched the air delightedly. At last – a result! He couldn't wait to call in his information. He had found the Mildmay car. He may even have found the whole family. His suspect eyesight had surely proved to be up to speed.

Alvin called the main MCIT number straightaway, and was diverted to a duty officer. The duty officer then called Vogel.

Vogel was sitting in the lounge bar of the Royal Marriott Hotel, where Nobby Clarke was staying. After two hours at Southmead Hospital, they had finally given up hope of extracting any information from Henry Tanner that night. If indeed at all. The man appeared to have suffered a relapse. Or, as Vogel suspected, he was faking it to avoid their questions. But the hospital staff did seem concerned about him, and they were unlikely to allow the police anywhere near him until the morning.

Uniform dispatched a constable, who was put on sentry duty outside Tanner's room. He was there partly to provide protection, and partly on a watching brief. Clarke and Vogel wanted to know at once if there was any change in Henry Tanner's condition. The two officers also wanted to know whether or not he had any visitors aside from Felicity, who had returned to her husband's bedside shortly before they left.

Clarke, with the help of sat-nav, had driven them to College Green, where she parked the CID car illegally right in front of the Royal Marriott.

'C'mon, Vogel, we need a drink,' she said.

It wasn't an invitation. More of an order.

'What about the car?' Vogel asked, somewhat tragically he thought, even as he spoke.

'Vogel, since when have you become a bloody jobsworth? Parking tickets are for making paper airplanes with.' She sighed at him wearily. 'Don't worry, I'll get uniform to send someone to pick it up later on, and they can take you home too.'

Vogel hadn't thought it politic to remind the DCI that he did not in any case drink.

As they made their way into the hotel through the downpour, he repeated a question he'd already asked during the drive over, one which Clarke had dodged, or so it seemed to Vogel.

'C'mon, boss, tell me about this Mr Smith,' he demanded. 'Who the heck is he?'

'For your information, Vogel, Mr Smith is a woman,' Clarke corrected, deadpan.

'You know this is getting ridiculous, boss, don't you?'

315

'A woman at the moment,' Clarke continued, to Vogel's greater confusion.

She put him out of his misery then.

'Mr Smith is the generic code name given to Henry Tanner's government-level controller,' she explained. 'It's always been Mr Smith, ever since the beginning when Henry's father and Maxim Schmidt set up Tanner-Max. Apparently the first Mr Smith really was called Mr Smith. So for simplicity they carried on with the name.'

'For simplicity?' responded a bemused and irritated Vogel. 'Boss, I don't believe this nonsense. Codes and controllers? Smith and Schmidt? It's the stuff of spy stories.'

'Well, you'd better believe it, Vogel,' remonstrated Clarke. 'Because it's not a story. It's real. Now shut up and get me that drink.'

They sat together at a table beneath a window down which raindrops dripped relentlessly. Vogel ordered a soda and lime from a smiling waitress who had no idea what a bad mood he was in. Nobby Clarke ordered a large malt. No ice. Splash of still water.

Vogel paid. The Marriott charged London prices. He was still trying to make sense of the whole Mr Smith thing, whilst idly wondering what chance he had of claiming the drinks back on expenses, when his phone rang.

'Get uniform on to it,' he barked. 'I want that vehicle caught up with and apprehended immediately.'

He ended the call and turned to Clarke.

'We gotta go, boss,' he said, already standing up and heading for the door. 'It's Joyce Mildmay – her car's been spotted heading into the city centre along the Portway. That's just down the hill. If we move fast we should be able to head 'em off. C'mon. Let's go.'

Normally Clarke would have reminded him that she was the one who gave the orders. But not in this situation. She rose at once and followed Vogel without so much as a backward glance at her abandoned whisky.

The pair of them raced out of the hotel and into the CID car. Clarke set lights flashing and siren wailing, manoeuvring the vehicle at speed around College Green and in the direction of the Portway, as instructed by Vogel.

'You know, Joyce and Molly could have been diverted for reasons we do not know. They could now be heading for the hospital as originally planned,' Clarke suggested.

'And it's taken ten hours from Tarrant Park, has it?' snapped Vogel, forgetting she was his superior officer and nearly biting her head off. 'In any case, they're going in the wrong bloody direction for Southmead. They were spotted at Sea Mills, where I live. They've already gone past the damned turning. Even I know—'

'That's enough, Vogel,' interrupted the DCI.

Vogel was on a knife edge, and he knew it. This wasn't how he usually behaved.

'Sorry, boss,' he muttered. 'It's just that we don't know what's happen—'

He stopped speaking when his body was flung forward against his seat belt as Nobby Clarke executed a flawless emergency stop.

'What the fuck?' began Vogel.

He looked ahead. The traffic was fairly light, but several vehicles in front of them had also stopped suddenly, forcing Clarke to do the same. Some of the passengers were getting out of their vehicles and hurrying towards the waterside. Then Vogel noticed the buckled railings ahead at the harbour edge.

'Shit,' he cried.

In a split second he was out of the CID car and running. The offices which overlooked the harbour along that stretch were in darkness, but a few local residents had emerged from their waterside flats and were also running towards the scene. Vogel pushed through everybody.

'Police, police, make way,' he shouted.

Then, automatically, he added: 'Did anyone see what happened?'

'Yes,' came a male voice out of the small crowd gathered by the railings. 'This bloody great Range Rover swerved straight across the road, hit the railings and catapulted over. I was right behind, I saw exactly—'

Vogel didn't hear any more. He could see something in the water. A head emerged. The head of a woman. He stared, willing his eyes to become quickly adjusted. Quite a lot of light was shining on the water. There were street lamps, the beams of car headlights, and shafts of light from the windows of buildings. It was not, however, enough to allow him to see the woman's face clearly. But he was certain it was Joyce Mildmay. It had to be. The following motorist had said the vehicle was a Range Rover, and Joyce's Range Rover had already been spotted heading this way.

The weather was terrible, worse than it had been all day. There were actually breakers in the Floating Harbour. The woman gasped for air. A substantial wave rolled over her. Both her arms came up and she disappeared again beneath the surface.

'Shit,' said Vogel again.

He was suddenly aware of Nobby Clarke, having presumably illegally abandoned the CID car for the second time that evening, by his side. He turned to her.

'I can't swim,' he said.

Clarke didn't seem to be listening. Neither did she hesitate. She pulled off her ankle boots, shrugged her way out of her jacket and jumped in.

Vogel felt not only helpless but pathetic. He was physically so inept. All he could do was watch as his DCI, performing an impressive crawl in extremely choppy conditions, powered her way out to the spot where the woman had last been seen. He did, at least, also call in the incident on his mobile and request all emergency services. Soonest.

But it didn't occur to Vogel to look for a lifebelt or a lifeline along the quayside. Fortunately a young man in the crowd did just that. He arrived at Vogel's side with a lifebelt as Nobby Clarke, kicking her heels smartly in the air, duck-dived into the depths in search of Joyce Mildmay and whatever else she might find down there.

The young man was Alvin Nightingale. As soon as he had finished phoning in his sighting of Joyce Mildmay's vehicle, Alvin had rushed out of his gran's house, boarded the pre-loved 100cc Yamaha motorcycle he kept in the front garden, and taken off in hot pursuit, pushing the bike as fast as he could along the Portway. Alvin was going to show 'em. He really was.

'I can help,' he told Vogel. 'I'm going in. I'm a trained life-saver.'

He thrust the lifebelt into Vogel's arms. 'Throw it in when I bring someone up,' he ordered.

Then, perhaps sensing that Vogel was no action man, he added: 'And don't forget to hang on to the line.'

Vogel nodded. It was not police procedure to encourage civilians to take part in potentially dangerous rescue missions, and Vogel had no idea that Alvin Nightingale was employed by the Avon and Somerset Constabulary. In any case he was still a civilian. But there could be children in that sunken car, and Vogel's senior officer was already risking her life.

Alvin Nightingale didn't give Vogel time to think that through. He dived into the water as DCI Clarke resurfaced clutching the woman Vogel assumed to be Joyce Mildmay.

Alvin turned in the water and called above the noise of the rain and the wind for Vogel to throw in the lifebelt. Vogel did so. With the belt over one shoulder, Alvin swam out to Nobby Clarke and the woman she had rescued. He helped Clarke put the belt around the rescued woman, then began to swim with her to the shore, leaving Nobby Clarke to follow.

But the DCI had other plans. Up came her feet again as she made yet another dive. It was clear she was attempting to return to the submerged vehicle below.

Alvin reached the shore. Willing hands grabbed the half-drowned woman and pulled her out of the water. Vogel joined in. He saw at once that the woman was Joyce Mildmay, and that she wasn't breathing. At least he had managed to complete a first-aid course, and he thought he was reasonably well-versed in emergency life-saving techniques. He was certainly trained in cardiopulmonary resuscitation, or CPR, although he'd never before had to execute it for real. He began chest compressions at once, rhythmically, and it seemed effectively, pumping Joyce's chest. Gratifyingly, she spewed up sea water and, although barely conscious, began to breathe.

Meanwhile Alvin had returned to the site of the submerged vehicle.

He and Nobby Clarke made several more dives before

coming up with another prone victim, this time a man, and bringing him to the quayside.

'There are at least two people in the back,' Clarke called up to Vogel. 'One of them could be the daughter. We can't get her out. She's trapped. And the boy. I think he's there too. Also trapped.'

Clarke was gasping for breath. Her face was grey with shock, and probably with exertion too, thought Vogel.

The fire brigade arrived as the DCI spoke. And a police emergency dive team.

'We'll take over now. Everybody stand back,' someone shouted authoritatively.

Strong professional arms helped haul Clarke, Alvin Nightingale and the prone man on to the quayside.

The man, of whose identity Vogel had no idea, appeared to be dead. Nonetheless one of the paramedics on the scene started to go through the motions of revival.

Vogel's attention was attracted by two other paramedics preparing to load the still prone but breathing Joyce Mildmay into an ambulance.

He hurried to her side. She had recovered consciousness. Her eyes were glazed but open.

'Joyce, Joyce, who's the man who was with you?' Vogel asked.

She focused on him. Just about. But she made no attempt to answer.

'My children,' she murmured, her voice quivering. 'My children.'

There was no query. Vogel thought she already knew the fate of her children. She had been there. She had been in the submerged car. And she had tried to dive down again to rescue them. She knew better than anyone that there was no hope. All the same, he lied to her. He felt he had to. At that moment anyway.

'We're still trying,' he said. 'We have divers here. Is there anyone else still down there, apart from the children?'

She shut her eyes, as if trying to shut everything out.

'My children,' she said again, weakly.

Vogel was getting no further.

He repeated his earlier question: 'Who is the man?'

'What?'

'Who is the man?' Vogel asked for the third time. 'They've brought up a man.'

'Charlie?' she murmured. 'Charlie?'

There was puzzlement in her voice, as if she couldn't understand why Vogel needed to ask her the question.

Joyce was obviously in pain. She was bleeding heavily from cuts on her face and arms. She must be in a state of the most horrendous shock. Vogel wondered if she were delirious.

'Charlie, your husband Charlie?' he queried.

Joyce managed a slight nod and suddenly opened her eyes again. They were bright with anguished fury.

'The fucking fucking fucking bastard,' she wailed, as the paramedics completed their lift. 'He drove us into the water . . . straight into the water . . . he has murdered his own children . . .'

The wailing became incoherent.

Vogel stared at the closing doors of the ambulance. He was still staring as it pulled away in the direction of South-mead.

Hadn't Charlie Mildmay died six months ago? Yet, according to his wife, he had been the driver of the Range

Rover. Had Charlie Mildmay deliberately caused the death of his own children? And had he then also deliberately attempted to cause the death of his wife?

The whole thing could have been a tragic accident, of course. Joyce may have got it all wrong. But she didn't appear to think so.

'He drove us into the water,' she had said.

And the one eyewitness Vogel had spoken to so far seemed to back that up.

Vogel's thoughts were interrupted.

'We've got a pulse!' shouted one of the paramedics crouching over the prone body of Charlie Mildmay. 'Keep up the CPR.'

Twenty-six

Predictably Nobby Clarke refused to be taken to hospital to be checked out. Wet and shivering, she sat slumped on the quayside, coughing and spluttering, but still giving orders.

'Will somebody find me a blanket? I'm bloody freezing,' she said.

Vogel was at her side filling her in on the information he had so far gleaned.

'Whilst you've been playing hero, boss,' he said with a ghost of a smile.

She grunted.

'Right man, we have work to do,' she said, when he'd finished. 'I need to get back to the Marriott for a change of clothes, then we should get ourselves to Southmead to talk to Joyce Mildmay as soon as possible. And her husband, if he survives. And somebody has to make the death call. Think it had better be us. I reckon Henry Tanner might be a little more forthcoming now, don't you? And we have to see him tonight, regardless of his condition.'

Vogel agreed. Telling people of the death of loved ones was one of the worst jobs in policing. Vogel dreaded giving the news to Henry Tanner's wife. But the man himself was somehow a different proposition. Vogel remained convinced

Henry was at the heart of it all. There seemed a sort of cruel justice in his being made to suffer. The dreadful news he and Clarke were about to deliver might lead to them learning whatever Henry Tanner knew that they did not. And both police officers believed that might be a considerable amount.

Clarke commandeered a uniform to rescue the CID car she had earlier abandoned in the middle of the road, and told the PC he would be driving her and Vogel to the hotel and on to Southmead.

To Vogel's surprise, she seemed to recognize that it might be unwise for her to attempt to drive for a bit. She was shaking from head to toe. And Vogel didn't think that it was simply because she was cold.

'Think I may have to take a quick shower,' she muttered to Vogel through chattering teeth.

Nobby Clarke was in her room at the Marriott for less than ten minutes. Then she reappeared looking the same as she always did, and wearing another of her sharp suits. Vogel was impressed. He couldn't stop looking at her as they were driven to Southmead. She seemed as in control as ever. Her wet hair was about the only visual indication of what she had been through.

At Southmead the two detectives were told they could not yet see Joyce Mildmay, which Clarke accepted. And Charlie Mildmay remained unconscious. But the DCI would not be put off making the necessary visit to Henry Tanner by anyone. At the very least the man and his wife had to be told the tragic news.

Henry Tanner was asleep. Or looked to be. He had been given another dose of morphine following his earlier seizure.

Both for the pain, and to keep him calm. It was by now getting on for 11 p.m., way past hospital bedding-down time.

Felicity was sitting by her husband's bedside. PC Dawn Saslow, who had earlier been re-directed to the hospital as she remained the family liaison officer and there was little or no family to liaise with anywhere else, was also in the room, sitting over by the balcony windows.

Felicity wished the young woman would go. But Saslow had said she was under orders to remain, as, apparently, was the young uniformed PC on sentry duty in the corridor. Felicity did not have the energy to protest about the presence of either officer. She wished she too could sink into a morphine-induced sleep. Indeed she wished that she could sleep for ever.

Instead her mind was racing, trying to come up with some explanation for the disappearance of her daughter and grand-daughter. She dreaded to think what might be preventing them from answering her calls, or making contact to let everyone know that they were all right. Had they been abducted, like Fred? But by whom? And why?

Felicity picked up her phone again and dialled Vogel's mobile. She had no intention of using PC Saslow as a go-between, although she suspected that was what she was expected to do. Presumably, if the detective inspector had any news, he would have called her. But she had to do something.

There was no reply.

Felicity sat for a few minutes more, watching and envying her sleeping husband, then tried Vogel's number again. There was still no reply. PC Saslow continued to sit quietly by the window.

A minute or two later, the door to Henry's room opened softly. DI Vogel, DCI Clarke and a ward sister entered.

Felicity had only to look at their faces to know that they were the bearers of bad news. Very bad news, she feared.

Clarke's face was grey and her mouth was set in a grim line. Her hair seemed to be wet. Felicity wondered vaguely why. Vogel also looked pale. But perhaps he always looked pale? She thought he probably did. This was something else though. Clarke's hands were trembling. So, Felicity thought, were Vogel's hands. His eyes were red-rimmed. Felicity wondered if he had been crying. Surely not, she thought. Policemen don't cry, do they? No, it was just stress and weariness, she supposed.

The two officers approached Henry's bed. The nursing sister hovered behind them, unsure what to do.

PC Saslow stood up. She looked questioningly at the two detectives. They both ignored her. She seemed to know better than to speak. Felicity wondered obliquely whether learning when to stay silent was part of the training for police liaison officers.

Henry remained in his drug-induced sleep.

'Mrs Tanner,' said Clarke, 'you'd better wake your husband, if you can.'

Felicity felt the icy fingers of foreboding run down her spine. She didn't argue. She didn't even utter a cursory why. Instead she reached out and shook her husband's good arm.

'Henry, Henry,' she called to him, her voice loud and unnaturally high-pitched.

Her husband took a while to stir. Then he opened his eyes suddenly. Vogel and Clarke were standing at the foot of his bed, directly in his line of vision. They were the first people he saw as he began to re-enter consciousness, a state from which he might soon wish he could escape. Like his wife. For ever.

Henry's drug-affected eyes opened wider. He glanced to his right, looking for and at Felicity.

She looked away from him, at Vogel and Clarke, who were standing in silence as if waiting for the right moment.

'Tell us,' commanded Felicity. 'Just tell us what you came to say. Is it Fred?'

'Perhaps – we're not sure,' Vogel fumbled.

He glanced at Clarke. It was a glance that said, go on, you're in charge. Anyway, you're the woman, women are best at this sort of thing. This is down to you. Not me. You're the senior officer. You do it.

Felicity followed his glance. She focused her gaze on Clarke.

'Please, just say what you've come to say,' she repeated.

DCI Clarke took a deep breath and began.

'Mr and Mrs Tanner, I am afraid I bring some serious news,' she said.

Henry stretched out his good arm, seeking to hold his wife's hand.

Felicity ignored him and kept both her hands firmly in her lap. Henry had been her husband for almost fifty years, the patriarch of her family. She could not imagine she would ever stop loving him. But she felt sure that he was in some way involved in this bad news that she was about to hear. That he would be the one who should bear the ultimate responsibility. And if that were to prove to be the case, she suspected she would never be able to forgive him.

She instinctively withdrew from the man who had been the centre of her universe for so long. One thing Felicity knew for certain was that she didn't want him to touch her. And she wasn't sure if she would want him to touch her ever again.

Henry let his arm fall on to the bed.

'There has been an incident involving your daughter's vehicle,' Nobby Clarke continued. 'Her Range Rover is believed to have veered off the quayside at Hotwell Road into the harbour. I am afraid it is still submerged, and we are unsure—'

'I-is she dead? Is Joyce dead?' Felicity had to interrupt. That was surely the news they were bringing.

Almost immediately a second thought occurred to her.

'And M-Molly? W-what about Molly? Was she in the car?'

'Joyce is alive,' replied Clarke. 'She is already here in A & E in this hospital. She ingested a lot of water and is very weak, but I understand she is expected to make a full recovery—'

'And Molly?' Felicity interrupted again. 'What about Molly?'

'I am afraid we believe that Molly was also in the car, and . . . at any rate, when we left the scene . . .'

Clarke glanced towards Vogel, then continued to speak, choosing her words with care, as Vogel had done earlier when speaking to Joyce.

'When we left the scene, Molly had yet to be recovered.'

Henry seemed suddenly to be wide awake.

'No, oh no,' he gasped.

Felicity gave a little cry, a kind of low moan. She didn't even try to speak.

Clarke took a deep breath.

'On the way here we heard from the leader of the dive team now at work at the scene that there are actually three other people still trapped in the car,' she said. 'Two young women, one of them very young, and a child, a boy. We understand that all three are believed to have drowned.'

Felicity could barely take it in.

She supposed she was in deep shock. She was devastated but she could not cry. Felicity remained dry-eyed. She felt empty of everything. Henry began to weep. Felicity heard him sob then saw big tears rolling down his cheeks. She had never seen her husband cry before, not even when their only son had been killed. He reached out to her. Again she avoided his grasp. She knew he was to blame for it all. She just knew it. One way or another, Henry would be to blame. At that moment she hated him.

Eventually she found her voice. Barely. 'Oh my God,' she whispered.

Clarke ploughed on: 'Your daughter referred to her children being still in the car, and told us that she had found Fred—'

Henry interrupted this time. Loudly. Calling out desperately through his tears.

'No,' he shouted. 'No. It can't be. It can't.'

Nobby Clarke didn't stop. She couldn't stop. She had to tell them everything straight away.

'We therefore have reason to believe the boy is probably your grandson.'

Felicity still couldn't take it in.

'But Joyce is always such a careful driver,' she said.

She knew as soon as she heard herself make the remark that it was silly. It was the first thing that had come into her head. Joyce was a careful driver.

'How could something like this have happened?' Felicity continued. 'How could she go off the road like that?'

'Mrs Tanner, we do not believe that your daughter was driving the vehicle when it went into the Floating Harbour,' said Vogel. 'We believe a man was driving.'

Felicity was bewildered. 'A man? What man?'

'We believe that the driver was your son-in-law, Charles, Charlie, Mildmay.'

Felicity could barely believe her ears. She was incapable at first of comprehending. She was aware of Henry, trying to pull himself, as much as he were able to, into an upright sitting position. She couldn't read the expression on his tear-stained face. He was shocked and distraught, yes. But there was something else.

Suddenly she felt that she understood. That she was aware of what his expression meant.

'You knew, Henry, you bastard,' she said. 'You knew Charlie was alive.'

Twenty-seven

After her outburst there was a brief silence in the room. Henry remained sitting upright, but closed his eyes again, screwing the lids tightly shut, as if in so doing he might make the world, to which he had been so cruelly reintroduced, disappear.

Vogel had to feel sympathy for him, as well as for his wife. These were two broken people. A man and a woman reeling from the shock of having been told that they'd lost two grandchildren, and whose entire family life now lay in total ruin.

It was DCI Clarke who broke the silence first.

'I am so terribly sorry to be bringing you this terrible news,' she said. 'Is there anyone you would like us to call, anyone you would like to be here with you?'

Eventually Felicity found her voice again. 'Th-there's our eldest grandson.' She stopped, realizing what she had said. What the events of that day meant. 'Mark, our only grandson,' she continued quietly. 'He was here earlier. He went looking for his mother and his sister. I don't know where he is. But I can call him. Oh my God, he doesn't know. I must call him. I wouldn't want anyone else to tell him.'

'All right,' responded Clarke. 'Look, Mr and Mrs Tanner,

we have a lot more questions for you which may help us piece together what has happened here. Most of it can wait, but there are a couple that can't.

'As DI Vogel has said, we believe the Range Rover was being driven by Charlie Mildmay, your daughter's husband. Your daughter told us that. Now, he was registered as missing, presumed dead in January, was he not? And I understand an inquest scheduled for later this year was expected to declare him officially dead?'

Felicity was staring at her husband, who looked every bit as shocked and surprised as his wife did. Vogel wondered if Henry's reaction was entirely genuine. He suspected that the older man might be a good actor.

As if reading the DI's thoughts, Felicity turned on her husband: 'Henry, what do you know about this? Did you know Charlie was alive? I'll bet everything I've got left in this world that you know something. You always bloody do. So why don't you just tell it? All of it. Now. Or so help me, God, I promise you our marriage will end this minute.'

Felicity's voice had grown in volume. She seemed to have little control over it. And she didn't look as if she cared one jot.

Henry reached out to her again. Again she pulled away from him.

'Darling, I promise you, I had no idea Charlie was alive,' Henry said. 'If he is. Or I mean, if he was until today.'

He turned his head slightly to focus on Nobby Clarke.

'That's the truth, Detective Chief Inspector,' he said. 'In fact I had reason to believe Charlie had killed himself . . .'

'You bastard, Henry,' Felicity interrupted. 'You always said, when we all wondered how Charlie, such an expert sailor, could have died in that sort of accident, that you had no reason to suspect he would have committed suicide. Why would he? That's what you said. Why would a man with everything to live for want to end his life?'

'I was trying to protect you, Felicity,' said Henry. 'Like I always do. There were things it was better you didn't know about. There still are.'

'How can you say that, Henry?' she demanded. 'How the hell can you say that right now? Half your family has been wiped out.'

Felicity turned to face Nobby Clarke.

'The man you think is Charlie – is he dead now? Or has he survived this . . . this terrible accident, or whatever it was?' she asked.

'Yes. He has also been brought to this hospital.'

'Is he conscious?'

'I am afraid I have no details of his medical condition,' Clarke replied.

'My God, he has some explaining to do,' muttered Felicity, turning back to Henry.

'As do you, Henry,' she continued. 'And why don't you start by explaining why you thought Charlie was a likely candidate for suicide? Come on, Henry, break the habit of a lifetime. Try being honest.'

Neither Clarke nor Vogel said anything. They were both happy for the moment to let Felicity do the questioning. They just stood at the foot of the bed looking at Henry.

The older man sighed and then, as if resigned to his fate, began with the same question he had asked on their previous visit:

'DCI Clarke, you and DI Vogel know all about the, uh, covert activities of Tanner-Max, do you not?'

'More or less,' replied the DCI.

Vogel grunted. Rather more less than more, he thought, but he supposed he knew enough. He'd grasped the gist of it.

Felicity frowned. 'I bloody don't,' she snapped.

'You must have picked up some idea over the years,' said Henry.

'Not enough to think that it might lead my son-in-law to want to kill himself. Or to come up with some elaborate scam which has led us to believe all these months that he is dead. Not enough to think that it might end with two of my grandchildren dying so horrifically. Two of my grandchildren being murdered, Henry. My daughter lying in a hospital bed still fighting for a life she isn't going to want now. And what about William? Maybe his death wasn't an accident, either. Oh, Henry, Henry. What have you done?'

Felicity shouted the words then seemed to collapse. She sat slouched forward, holding her head in her hands. Her shoulders began to heave. Vogel could no longer see her face. He didn't need to in order to realize the state she was in.

'It wasn't the business, it wasn't anything we did at Tanner-Max that made me think Charlie had killed himself,' said Henry quietly, addressing no one in particular. 'I found out that Charlie had gone independent. It seems that what the family and our business provided for him was not enough. He was doing deals with gangsters, for God's sake. I discovered that he had diverted stock from a number of the international deals we brokered and he'd been selling weapons destined for our overseas clients to a London gang. He was involved in organized crime—'

'Henry, are you saying you are an arms dealer?' Felicity cried. 'You deal in arms? I always knew there was something going on at Tanner-Max, something more than sending whisky all over the world. But not this. Is it true?'

Henry inclined his head slightly.

'In the service of the British government,' he said rather pompously. 'And we are brokers, not dealers.'

'You are monsters,' responded Felicity, horrified.

'Would you go on, please, Mr Tanner,' interjected Clarke. 'You were telling us about the criminal activities you believed your son-in-law to be involved in.

'Yes.'

Henry glanced anxiously at his wife before continuing. She was not looking at him.

'I found out about it the day after he disappeared off his boat. I think he was afraid of the people he was dealing with. I still think that, even if he staged his death rather than killing himself. Maybe he knew he hadn't covered his tracks well enough. He would certainly have known that I would be furious. But I don't think for one moment he was afraid of me. No, he was out of his depth. He was afraid of the criminals he'd got himself mixed up with. It seems he had good reason to be. After he was gone, they started to put pressure on me. I believe they were behind the shooting. Who else would send a gunman to kill me?'

'You said yourself that the work that you have done over the years could have made you a target,' responded DCI Clarke. 'Is it not possible that you were shot by members of some terrorist organization, for example?'

Henry shook his head. 'I don't think so,' he said. 'Mr Smith has been looking into that side of things since Fred disappeared. He and his people hadn't come up with any evidence to suggest—'

Felicity interrupted again.

'Who the heck is Mr Smith?' she asked.

Henry made no attempt to reply.

Vogel too stared at the older man. A rooftop sniper was likely to be a professional, that was for sure. But Henry was only wounded, shot in the right shoulder, away from the heart. A professional with a sniper's rifle did not often mess up. If the intention had been to kill Henry, then Vogel would not expect him to be still alive. So maybe that hadn't been the intention.

Tanner continued to ignore his wife.

'Here, take a look at my email,' he said suddenly.

Henry reached for his iPhone on the bedside table and tossed it across the room towards the two police officers.

Nobby Clarke's physical reactions were better and quicker than Vogel's. But then so were almost anybody's. She caught the phone with one hand and brought up Henry Tanner's email account.

Vogel studied the screen over her shoulder.

Third on the list was an email from an innocent enough hotmail address, Marlon8920@hotmail.com.

Vogel was a crossword freak. There was something about that email address that was crying out to him. But, for the moment at any rate, he couldn't quite get it.

The message was simple and to the point: *You have been warned. Please reinstate our order.*

'So what do you believe this to mean, Mr Tanner?' enquired Clarke.

Henry leaned back in the pillows. Again he seemed to be willing the whole scenario to disappear.

'For fuck's sake, will you answer their bloody questions before we have any more deaths?' barked Felicity.

Henry did so.

'When I found out what Charlie had been doing I put a stop to it at once. I let the people he was dealing with know they would receive no more arms from us. They didn't take it well. They were in the middle of a transaction with Charlie and there was money outstanding. Not a fortune – about £10,000. I offered straight away to repay it. But that wasn't good enough.

'They said a deal had been done. They didn't want the money, they wanted the goods. As arranged. They kept insisting, and I kept saying no. I suppose I was calling their bluff. I mean, I couldn't believe they would do anything. Then when Fred disappeared . . .'

Felicity screamed. She actually screamed. Once. At the top of her voice. Stopping Henry in his tracks. It was a shrill, sharp sound cutting through the claustrophobic atmosphere of the hospital room.

Yet when she spoke her voice was quiet. Dangerously quiet.

'Are you saying that when Fred disappeared you thought he had been taken by these people, these evil, dangerous people, that you thought they would use him to threaten you?' she asked. 'And yet you told nobody about any of this. Not the police or your family. Henry, you are despicable.'

Henry flinched. 'Look, I asked them if they had taken Fred,' he said. 'They replied that they weren't child molesters. That's all. They weren't child molesters.'

'Mr Tanner,' said Vogel. 'How did you find out that Charlie had been dealing with criminals?'

'From his email. After he disappeared from his boat it seemed a good idea to check out his email account. At first we didn't have any idea what might have happened to him. We thought his email might give us some sort of clue. And it did. As soon as we read all this stuff it seemed obvious that Charlie had reason to kill himself. I knew he lived on a knife's edge. I knew he relied far too much on prescription drugs. Of course I knew. But as long as he held himself together I wasn't going to do anything about it. When I came to believe that he'd ended his own life, naturally I wished I had.'

'You didn't consider that he could have staged his own disappearance?'

'Actually no, it didn't occur to me. That's the stuff of fiction, isn't it?'

Vogel persevered. 'Who exactly is this "we" you keep referring to?'

'Me and Stephen Hardcastle,' said Henry.

'So Stephen also knew about the illicit arms dealing?'

'Yes. He was as shocked as I was. Charlie was Stephen's closest friend, but he hadn't confided any of it to him.'

'I see. And how did you break into Charlie's email?'

'He'd left a laptop locked in his safe in the office. He had a brand-new one, which he must've taken with him, but when we looked in the safe we found the old one.'

'His personal safe?'

'Yes.'

'So you and Stephen Hardcastle had access to it.'

'Janet kept a spare key.'

Vogel nodded. He glanced at Nobby Clarke. She seemed content to let him lead the questioning.

'Wasn't it password protected?' he asked. 'His email would have been, surely?'

'Yes. But we have a chap who does IT for us, sets up our accounts. I contacted him. Charlie had never bothered to change the passwords this chap used to set the whole thing up for him in the beginning.'

'Didn't you think that was sloppy for a man involved in

illicit arms deals? I mean, wouldn't you have expected him to destroy an old laptop? He doesn't even ensure that he has a password nobody else knew about, and he leaves a laptop containing incriminating information in a safe to which other people have access. Didn't you think that was unbelievably sloppy?'

Henry shrugged. 'It wasn't out of character, given the way Charlie had been behaving. Besides, if he was planning to kill himself, what would it matter? Even if he were planning to stage his own disappearance and create a new life for himself, as you now seem to think might have been the case, it wouldn't have had any impact on his plans. Besides, Charlie was hopeless at computer stuff. One way or another, it didn't strike us as odd that he had left his old laptop in a safe.'

'And you used the email addresses Charlie had on his machine to contact these people and cancel all arms deals, is that correct?'

Henry agreed that it was.

Vogel was still looking at the screen on Henry's iPhone. He did some quick mental arithmetic, using the fingers of both hands. Suddenly he got it.

'Mr Tanner, didn't you think that the Marlon email address was a little . . . prosaic?'

Henry looked blank.

'Marlon, as in Marlon Brando, *The Godfather*,' said Vogel. 'Numbers 8, 9 and 20. They represent the letters of the alphabet: H, I and T. HIT. As in hitman, perhaps?'

Henry still looked blank.

'Maybe, but what difference does it make?'

'It could be an implied threat,' said Vogel. 'You were maybe supposed to work out that the email address was telling you it was from a hitman of some sort.'

'I didn't even come close,' said Tanner. 'I can't see how you worked it out so quickly, either.'

'He has that sort of mind,' remarked Clarke.

She didn't make it sound as if she was paying Vogel a compliment.

Vogel paid her no attention.

'Mr Tanner, did you at any stage have dealings with "Marlon" or any of these people through any other means than email?' Vogel asked.

Henry said that he hadn't.

'So you've never met any of these people, you've never spoken to them on the telephone?'

'No,' said Henry. 'I tried to when Fred went missing. I gave them my phone number. I told them to phone me any time day or night. I told them I was prepared to do anything, give them anything, even the arms they wanted so much, anything to get my grandson back. I wasn't entirely convinced, you see, by their denials. I still reckoned it was possible they were holding him to ransom. I kept thinking they would call sooner or later. I kept waiting for them to call. Nobody called.'

Vogel had more questions but was interrupted by the arrival of a uniformed constable, PC Mick Perkins, who had been instructed to keep a watching brief on Joyce Mildmay.

'They told me you were here, ma'am,' he said, addressing DCI Clarke. 'And they wouldn't let me use my phone in intensive care. There's something I thought you should know straight away.'

He leaned closer to Nobby Clarke, speaking into her ear in little more than a whisper. Vogel could not hear what the PC was saying. He looked at Clarke questioningly.

Henry Tanner took the opportunity to reach out again to

his sobbing wife. A glutton for punishment, thought Vogel. He had rarely seen anyone as angry as Felicity Tanner. Again she leaned away, rejecting him. And tough, strong Henry looked about to break down himself.

Clarke touched Vogel on the arm.

'C'mon,' she said.

Turning back to the bed, she addressed Henry and Felicity: 'Mr and Mrs Tanner, we're going to leave you now. Although I am afraid we will need to speak to you again later. Meanwhile, I would like to say again how sorry we are for your loss.'

The Tanners, both overwhelmed now by their own misery, seemed not to hear her.

'If there is anything we can do to help, please tell PC Saslow,' Clarke urged them as she opened the door. 'That's what she's here for.'

Clarke then led Vogel from the room, with Perkins following.

'PC Perkins says Joyce Mildmay's wide awake now and the medics have given us the go-ahead to question her,' said the DCI, as soon as she had closed the door to Henry's room. 'But it's not going to be easy, that's for sure.'

Twenty-eight

Joyce had been in a merciful daze ever since her admission to Southmead Hospital. Following her brief moment of dreadful lucidity on the Floating Harbour quayside after being pulled from the water, she had become hysterical. In the ambulance, en route to the hospital, she'd had to be restrained after banging her head repeatedly against the metal frame of her stretcher, and grabbing pieces of the paramedics' medical equipment, including an inadequately secured oxygen tank, which she had proceeded to pound against the sides of the ambulance. She had also attacked the paramedics, scratching and kicking out at them.

She continued to repeatedly bang her own head against any adjacent hard surface in A & E, and to attack staff who tried to remonstrate with her. Ultimately one of the duty doctors had prescribed a heavy sedative, partly for her own protection, and partly for the protection of hospital staff and property.

She had been checked out as much as possible then moved to intensive care, because she was still considered to be at risk, and possibly to be a risk, although she did not know that.

The effects of the sedative were only now beginning to

wear off. And she could remember little of the last few hours.

She knew that both her younger son and her only daughter were dead. Of course she knew that. She had seen their poor dead faces. But her brain had not quite accepted it. She also knew that their own father had killed them. Her children had been murdered by their father. There was a name for it. Patricide. Charlie had committed patricide.

It couldn't have happened, though, could it?

She thought maybe she was going mad. Like Charlie. Even madder than Charlie. She didn't mind. If she was mad then it could mean that Fred and Molly might still be alive. Couldn't it?

She knew better.

And what about Charlie? How mad had he become to do what he did, to deliberately drive the wife and children he purported to love so much into the deep water of the harbour? And the young woman who'd been duped into believing that he wanted to start a new life with her, she'd been in the car too. Monika, whom Joyce had considered part of her household. Not that it mattered. Not that any of it mattered.

It mattered that Charlie had survived. She'd been aware of him arriving in A & E. For some reason she did remember that. Clearly. Everything after that was a blank. Perhaps she had been medicated. Later – she had no idea how much later – once she'd begun to come round, she'd asked a young nurse how he was. Medical staff had been buzzing around her like flies, as concerned about the state of her mind as of her body. But she had felt calm. Icily calm. She just wanted to know about Charlie. Straight away. He was her husband, after all, and it was possible that the nurse was not aware of the circumstances which had led to Charlie and Joyce being admitted to hospital. Nonetheless the nurse had told Joyce that she had no information about Charlie's condition. But that was enough. It was enough to tell her that Charlie was still alive. And she found that fact unbearable. Her children were dead and the man who had murdered them, a man she had once loved so much, the man she had married, who had now totally destroyed her every bit as much as he had destroyed their children, was still alive.

She wondered where he was. She tried to think where he might be. It was hard for her. She was still not functioning fully. But then, she didn't expect to ever again function fully. And this was important.

She looked around her. She was in intensive care. So would Charlie be, wouldn't he?

She lay still. She concentrated on appearing calm and peaceful. She pretended to fall asleep again. Eventually the concerned nursing staff drifted away, having come to the conclusion that she was no longer a threat to herself or anyone else. Which had been her intention.

After a while she opened her eyes cautiously, and peered around the ward. There were nurses in attendance at a bed across the way. But nobody seemed to be taking any notice of her.

Joyce disconnected the two tubes attached to her arm. She had no idea what they were or what they did. Or what disconnecting them would do to her. She didn't care.

She pushed herself into a sitting position, swung her legs over the side of the narrow bed and stood up. Overcome by dizziness, she had to lean against the wall until it passed. Then she set off down the ward, moving slowly and deliberately, looking from left to right, checking out the other patients. Nobody seemed to notice her. Not any of the staff, anyway. Or if they did they didn't react. Strange, because a short while earlier they had been fussing over her, anxious about how she might behave. Perhaps there had been a change of shift. Perhaps the new staff on duty had not been told that they should be concerned for and about her. Maybe, if they'd noticed her at all, they thought she was going to the toilet. Were intensive care patients supposed to go to the toilet on their own? She had no idea. She realized her brain was all over the place, her thoughts incoherent.

However, her sense of purpose was absolute. It didn't take her long to find Charlie. He lay in a bed close to the door. His eyes were shut. She assumed he was unconscious. In fact, although she didn't know how or why, she was positive he was unconscious and not merely asleep. But that wasn't good enough. She wanted him to be dead. He wasn't dead.

She studied him for a moment. Various tubes and leads connected him to an array of hi-tech medical equipment. His chest was rising and falling rhythmically. He definitely wasn't dead. Not yet.

She had no idea what Charlie's prognosis might be. Maybe he wouldn't pull through, whatever she did or didn't do. On the other hand, he could recover consciousness at any moment. People did, didn't they? Sometimes when they were not expected to. People came out of comas after months and sometimes years.

Joyce wasn't prepared to risk that. She couldn't. She wasn't prepared to give Charlie any sort of chance, however slim, of living, when her children, her precious children, had died at his hands.

Charlie had to die. He had to die now.

Joyce stepped forward. She wondered if she dared switch off the machines that were helping to keep Charlie alive. Or pull out the tubes that were feeding him. Feeding the man she now thought of as an incarnation of pure evil. The fiend, the ogre, the beast she had married.

But surely someone would notice. In television dramas any such action was invariably followed by alarms bleeping and a major alert. In any case it was possible that Charlie might survive even without being connected to the equipment that surrounded him. No. Joyce decided that she would have to be more proactive than that. There was one narrow pillow beneath Charlie's head. One pillow would be enough.

How quickly can you smother someone? she wondered dispassionately as she reached out to grab the pillow, pull it from under Charlie and take it in her hands. How long does suffocation take? How long would it take for the vile creature to die?

She had just grasped the pillow when she felt a firm but gentle hand on her arm.

'C'mon, Mrs Mildmay, I think we'd better get you back to your bed, don't you?' said a voice she recognized.

It was David Vogel.

Vogel had known immediately what Joyce intended to do. He glanced at Clarke. The DCI's expression was deadpan.

Like him, it seemed, she had decided not to notice.

In any case there should have been a police presence with her. PC Perkins had, perhaps a tad over-excitedly, chosen to leave Joyce Mildmay unattended in order to give Vogel and Clarke the news of her return to consciousness. He should not have done so. He should have waited for a replacement.

This was the kind of cock-up which could lead to shattered careers. Not to mention, in this case, yet another violent death.

Joyce returned to her bed meekly enough and by the time

347

Perkins rejoined them, having excused himself to go to the toilet on the way back to intensive care, Clarke and Vogel had found a nurse to attend to her.

Neither officer passed comment on what may or may not have happened in PC Perkins' absence, and Perkins himself was to remain blissfully unaware of the career-threatening incident.

Vogel looked down at the stricken woman lying on the bed. Was she relieved to have been stopped from fulfilling her intention? Was she in fact thankful to have been prevented from killing her husband?

Vogel thought not. He thought it more likely that she wished she had completed the act. He doubted that she would care about the consequences. Why should she?

Nobby Clarke asked a nurse to pull a curtain around the bed. It wasn't much of a privacy barrier, but it at least gave the illusion of seclusion. In any case it was way past visiting time, and none of the other patients in intensive care looked to be in any condition to eavesdrop.

While Clarke apologized for disturbing her, Joyce stared unseeingly into the middle distance. She looked deranged, thought Vogel, but then who wouldn't, given what she'd been through that day? He glanced at Clarke, who gave a brief nod to indicate that she wanted him to lead the questioning.

'We need you to tell us exactly what happened when you were proceeding along the Hotwell Road alongside the Floating Harbour, Mrs Mildmay,' he began without further preamble. 'You told me earlier that your husband, Charlie, was driving. Is that correct? Can you tell us how your vehicle came to leave the road and be submerged?'

Joyce focused her newly mad eyes on Vogel.

'I told you that too, didn't I? I told someone, back on the

quay, he wanted to kill us all,' she said. 'He tried to kill us all. My children are dead. And Charlie did it deliberately. Oh my God, yes. He slammed his foot on the accelerator and drove at the railings as fast as he could.'

Joyce, it seemed, needed no official confirmation of the death of her children. She had been in the car with them when it went under. She had probably watched them drown.

'Can you tell me how you all came to be with your husband in the Range Rover?' the DI asked. 'I know this must be unbelievably hard for you, but can you please tell me, starting at the beginning, everything that happened from the moment you and Molly left the house to come here and visit your father?'

Joyce looked blank.

'Mrs Mildmay, if you want justice for your children, please help us now,' interjected DCI Clarke.

'Justice? What good is justice?' Joyce snapped.

She closed those mad eyes. For a moment Vogel feared she was going to clam up and they would learn nothing. Then she opened her eyes again and proceeded to speak in a voice that was quite calm, albeit distant. She seemed to be at least trying to tell them everything she could, continuing at length in the same dispassionate manner, and in surprising detail. It was as if, Vogel thought, she was telling a story about somebody else, or even reciting a piece of fiction.

She told the two detectives about the texts to Molly, the drive to Exmoor, the barn in the wood, about her shock at finding out that Charlie was alive, about Monika and the affair with Charlie, and, perhaps most significantly of all, about Charlie's explanation for having staged his own disappearance.

'He said that he and my father worked for the government, brokering arms deals. He said he'd been seduced into joining the business by my father . . .'

She broke off then, lost in her own thoughts. Awful, soul-destroying thoughts.

'My father has always been persuasive,' she continued sourly, her voice rising in anger. 'He's always been able to get people to do exactly what he wants. To bend their wills to his own. Damn him. Damn him to hell.'

Then, suddenly calm again, she carried on with her dark tale.

'But it all went stale for Charlie over the years, he said. He came to regret relinquishing his ideals and allowing my father to take over his life. When Dad started trading in chemical weapons, Charlie said he was disgusted. But the final straw for him was when he found out that Dad was siphoning off arms and supplying them to criminals.'

Vogel glanced at Clarke. She raised an eyebrow, in that quizzical way that she had.

Oblivious, Joyce continued: 'Charlie said my father turned against him as soon as he challenged him over the chemical warfare thing. Charlie threatened to go to the authorities, but Dad talked him out of it. He didn't dare challenge Dad about supplying weapons to criminals. He said it would have been too dangerous, and anyway he'd given up trying to talk Dad round. He was planning to go to the police without saying anything, or so he said.'

Joyce sounded unconvinced.

'But Dad found out. Charlie thought he might have been hacking into his computer. He said my father was planning to put a contract out on him. That's when he decided to stage his own death and run away to start a new life. I thought it was all too far-fetched to be believable. Now I don't know. I don't know what to believe about anything any more.'

The two detectives continued to press her further on the matter of illicit arms dealing. Joyce continued to cooperate to the best of her ability. Or certainly she appeared to.

'Charlie blamed everything on my father,' she said. 'He glossed over his sordid little affair with Monika as if that didn't matter. Not that it did really. Or it doesn't now. He blamed my father for ruining his life.'

Clarke cut in with a question: 'Charlie was quite clear that your father was the person who was trading arms with criminal elements, was he, Mrs Mildmay?'

'Yes. Absolutely clear. Who else? My father *is* Tanner-Max, whatever anyone else might think. He had access to the sort of people who kill for a living. "On a daily rate." That's what Charlie said.'

An idea was forming in Vogel's head.

'Mrs Mildmay, did Charlie say how he'd found out that your father was involved in illicit arms deals?' he asked.

Joyce shook her head.

'Did you ask him how he found out?' Vogel persisted.

'No. I was too busy trying to take in what he was telling me.'

'So he gave you absolutely no idea about that.'

'No. I suppose he must've found an email or something. That he'd hacked into Dad's email . . . Only, no, it was the other way round. He said Dad had hacked into his computer. Or got somebody to do it for him. Neither Dad nor Charlie have ever been very good with computers.'

Vogel asked whether she had considered that Charlie could have shot her father. She nodded, then repeated what

Charlie had told her about being miles away on the moors with Fred at the time.

'In any case, he wouldn't have known how to handle a gun, even if he'd got hold of one,' she volunteered. 'Or at least, I don't think he would. Right now I'm not sure that I ever really knew Charlie at all. Or my bloody father.'

She looked directly at Vogel.

'He was out of his mind, completely out of his mind,' she said. 'And he'd brought it on himself, like he always brought everything on himself. For years I suspected he was addicted to prescription drugs. Then I found out that, since going missing, all those months he was living with that woman, he'd been smoking skunk. Day in and day out, she said.'

'Skunk,' repeated Vogel thoughtfully. 'So do you think he had become psychotic?'

'Maybe. What does it matter?' asked Joyce. 'He killed my children.'

Vogel returned to his previous line of questioning: 'Did Charlie express a view about who might have shot your father?'

'He said he didn't even know Dad had been shot until I told him. Then he said it must have been the criminals Dad was dealing with. That Dad had been playing with fire. Maybe Dad hadn't delivered what he said he would, or fallen out with them . . .'

She stared at Vogel with those disturbing eyes.

'What does it matter?' she repeated. 'My children are dead. Their lives are over. My life is over too.'

Vogel forced himself not to look away. Joyce's eyes were so unnaturally bright. She really did look mad, he thought. Nobody ever said that any more. He supposed it wasn't considered politically correct. But it happened, surely. That events in people's lives were so devastating that they simply lost their minds. Even if in the modern world you called it something else. Vogel had no idea that Joyce had thought the same thing about Charlie. And that she had told Charlie so.

Suddenly Joyce slumped back on the pillow, closed her eyes, and seemed to shut Vogel and Clarke out, not responding to their voices, whatever they said.

It was apparent they were not going to get any more out of her for a while. If at all, thought Vogel.

Would she ever recover? he wondered. Could anyone fully recover from what she had experienced?

'Time to go, Vogel,' said Clarke, interrupting his reverie.

She turned to Perkins: 'Do not leave Mrs Mildmay's side, Perkins,' she said. 'Not for anything. You took a risk earlier, you know.'

Perkins coloured slightly. But he was never to know how great that risk had turned out to be.

'Yes, ma'am,' he said.

'Right,' said Clarke. 'I'm getting another officer in on a watching brief over Mr Mildmay. So there will be two of you here. I expect there to be one of you on duty at all times. If you want a slash, you go one at a time. Is that clear?'

'Yes, ma'am,' said Perkins again, puzzled by the DCI's forcefulness.

On the way out of the ward Vogel and Clarke noticed a young female doctor attending Charlie Mildmay, and stopped to ask her what the latest prognosis was.

'I'd say he's got a fifteen to twenty per cent chance of some kind of recovery,' said the doctor. 'But if he does recover I would not like to try to predict to what extent that might be. He stopped breathing for far too long.'

Clarke thanked her, then turned to Vogel.

'Let's go grab a coffee,' she said, steering Vogel out of the ward and along the corridor in the direction of the coffee shop.

'We need to work out what we're going to do next to clear up this mess,' she continued, as they walked. 'If what Joyce told us is the truth, and we have no reason to doubt her, then both Charlie Mildmay and Henry Tanner have claimed that they believed the other was involved in selling arms to criminals.'

Vogel didn't reply. Clarke glanced towards him.

'Vogel, I can see the wheels turning. What are you thinking?'

'I'm thinking maybe there was no illicit arms dealing. Maybe neither Mildmay nor Tanner were involved in any such thing.'

'Vogel, you're talking in riddles,' said Clarke.

Vogel stopped in his tracks. 'Look, boss, there's one more question I want to ask Henry Tanner. Forget the coffee. Let's go back and see him.'

Clarke stopped too, and turned to face the DI. She raised that quizzical eyebrow again.

'I don't reckon we'll get much more out of him tonight, nor his wife come to that,' she said. 'He's not superman, you know. Looked in total shock to me. Wiped out, I'd say.'

'Let's try, boss, please,' said Vogel.

But he wasn't really asking for her permission, or even her approval. Before he'd finished the sentence he had already turned on his heel and was heading back towards Henry Tanner's room.

DCI Nobby Clarke, shaking her head in resignation, followed.

Twenty-nine

Henry lay still. He looked wiped out, as Clarke had predicted. Dawn Saslow remained with him. She was sitting, as she had been earlier, on an uncomfortable-looking hard chair by the balcony windows. Uncomfortable or not, Vogel thought she may have been asleep when he opened the door; she had the look about her of a woman who had just woken up. Apart from the police officer, Henry was alone. Felicity Mildmay had left the hospital. Vogel wasn't altogether surprised. Felicity had made it pretty clear she wanted little more to do with her husband. That might change. But not for some time, Vogel didn't think.

Henry's eyes focused blearily on Vogel. He made no attempt, at first, to speak.

'Mr Tanner, we don't wish to intrude further at this time, nor to add to your distress, but I'm afraid there is one point I must ask you to clarify,' Vogel began. 'Whose idea was it that you check out Charlie's email after he disappeared from his yacht?'

Henry looked blank. His mind was somewhere else. Probably reflecting not only on his terrible loss but also on the ruin of his whole carefully constructed existence, thought Vogel.

'Please, Mr Tanner, this is important. Whose idea was it that you check out your son-in-law's email?'

With tremendous effort Henry hauled himself, at least partially, back to the here and now.

'I told you, Stephen Hardcastle and I thought it might throw some light on things . . .' Henry's voice drifted off.

'But which of you first suggested it?' Vogel continued doggedly.

Tanner looked bewildered. 'Does it matter?' he asked, just as his daughter had whenever Vogel persisted in any line of questioning.

'We are trying to find out what, and who, was behind the chain of events which have engulfed your family,' Vogel persevered. 'And, however you feel at the moment, there will probably come a time when you will want to know that too. When it might matter.'

Tanner shook his head slightly. Vogel assumed that the other man could not imagine anything ever mattering again. Like his daughter. But Henry did answer the question.

'It was Stephen,' he said. 'It had to be Stephen. I didn't even know Charlie had a new laptop, let alone that his old one was in the safe.'

Vogel was aware of that familiar tingling sensation at the back of his neck that told him he was nearing a breakthrough on a case.

'You didn't know the laptop even existed,' he murmured, almost to himself.

'No,' responded Henry.

'Mr Tanner, do you remember if the email exchanges you presumed were between Charlie and his gangland connections were online, or stored on the laptop itself?' Vogel continued.

Henry looked as if he didn't understand a word Vogel was saying.

'I mean, did Charlie use Outlook Express, or similar software, which actually takes emails off the net and downloads them onto a specific computer?'

'Yes, we both did. Outlook Express.'

'So those emails weren't online in his server mail? They were in his Outlook Express?'

'I suppose so,' said Henry. 'Look, I neither know nor care. If you think any of this is important, why don't you check out the damned laptop? It's still in Charlie's safe, as far as I know.'

'As we speak, that should be happening. I was just hoping—'

'It's too late,' Henry moaned. 'It's too damned late now.'

There were tears in Henry's eyes. Vogel was embarrassed. He so much preferred his interviewees to be feisty. Although he neither liked nor respected Henry Tanner, it gave Vogel no pleasure to see him reduced to this state. Nevertheless he was determined to persevere with his questions until he had the answers he needed.

'You have told us that you believed Charlie was supplying arms to criminals, Mr Tanner. But are you absolutely sure he did so? Are you sure arms were diverted from their destinations, that they actually went missing whilst in the possession of Tanner-Max, from your bonded warehouses or elsewhere?'

Henry moaned more loudly. The tears were now rolling down his cheeks. However, through those tears he still managed to shoot Vogel what could only be described as a withering look.

'Of course I am sure. After we found those email exchanges I checked and double-checked everything. Didn't I make that clear when you asked me about it before? I went back over all the records and contacted our sources overseas. Because of the nature of our transactions, sometimes those sources are not clear on the precise quantity of items they will receive. Nobody had raised the alarm because the paperwork had been altered and everything matched up. But once I knew what I was looking for, I was able to see discrepancies. Over a period of about a year there were several instances. Nothing much – some small arms, a few rifles. Not whole cases of weapons, or anything like that. That would have shown up. This was more at the level of pilfering, except the nature of the goods being pilfered made it a serious matter.'

'Any specific make of rifle?'

'The Dragunov SVU – Soviet-developed, widely regarded as the best lightweight sniper rifle in the world. Three of those went astray from three different consignments, one at a time . . .'

Henry Tanner stopped in mid sentence. He remained a quick-witted man, even in his present condition.

'I suppose you're going to tell me I was shot by a Dragunov, are you?' he enquired.

'Quite possibly,' agreed Vogel.

He and Clarke had both received an email a little earlier giving a preliminary list of weapons the bullet removed from Henry Tanner's shoulder could have come from. The Dragunov was top of the list.

'Did Charlie shoot me?' asked Henry.

'We don't think so.'

'His bloody gangster pals then, as I thought all along. Charlie has wiped out half my family though. And my wife holds me responsible. I expect my daughter does too.' He raised his voice. 'It's not my bloody fault! None of it is my fault. I only ever did what I thought was best for my family.'

He wiped the tears from his eyes and looked directly at Vogel. 'Will you just go,' he said.

'One last thing,' persisted Vogel. 'It is likely that the third person trapped in the car, now confirmed as drowned, was Monika, the young woman who was working for both you and your wife and your daughter. Joyce has told us that your son-in-law was having an affair with Monika, and that he lived with her following his staged death. Do you know anything about that?'

Henry shook his head. He looked stunned.

'Of course I don't,' he shouted. 'I don't know anything about any of that. Look, I have nothing more to say. You must go. And I don't need your damned nursemaid, either. You can't insist she stays, can you? I haven't been accused of anything. I'm not a bloody criminal. Leave me alone will you, all of you.'

The outburst seemed to weaken him.

'OK, Mr Tanner, we will all leave you alone,' said DCI Clarke. 'We may need to speak to you again soon, but for the moment that's it, and thank you for your help.'

The DCI put her hand on Vogel's shoulder. 'C'mon,' she hissed at him as she turned and headed for the door.

This time it was Vogel's turn to follow, along with Saslow, whom Clarke instructed to take up sentry duty outside Henry's room. Just in case.

The young woman PC did not look particularly enthusiastic. She was tired, thought Vogel. They were all tired. And he was also frustrated.

'Boss, I think you're going soft,' he said, once he and

Clarke were both outside the room and out of earshot of PC Saslow.

'That's as maybe,' muttered the DCI. 'At risk of sounding sanctimonious, Vogel, that old bastard in there is as near as you're going to get to a bloody patriot nowadays, and I doubt any of this stuff would have happened if he hadn't spent his life doing what he has for our bloody government.'

Vogel wasn't impressed.

'Feathered his own nest too, from what I've seen,' he said.

'It's none of your dammed business, Vogel. Just tell me what's going on in that devious mind of yours.' She fixed him with a shrewd gaze. 'You think there's been a set-up, don't you?'

'It's the only thing that makes any sense, boss.'

'And who, might I ask, do you think is behind this set-up?'

'There's only one person, as far as I can make out, in a position to play Henry Tanner and Charlie Mildmay against each other. One person with the knowledge of both the business and the men. And the motive.'

'Which is?'

'The motive? Why, money and power of course.'

'And the guilty one?'

'Who do you think, boss?'

Clarke smiled. 'I think, Vogel, that you reckon Stephen Hardcastle's our man. He's the one who suggested to Tanner that they check out Charlie Mildmay's email account, where they conveniently found so much incriminating information. The one who was best placed to manipulate the family – including Tanner, who probably thought nobody would ever dare take him on at his own game. The one Charlie Mildmay thought was his best friend. Yep, it's Hardcastle, isn't it? That's what you think.'

'I sure do, boss,' said Vogel.

Thirty

Stephen Hardcastle arrived at Henry Tanner's bedside minutes after Vogel and Clarke had left.

PC Saslow had not been instructed to apprehend any visitors, merely to monitor them. She called DCI Clarke at once.

'Thank you,' said Clarke. 'But do nothing except keep an eye and an ear out, and call again when Hardcastle leaves. Don't suppose you can hear anything, can you?'

'Sorry, ma'am. I did try to have a listen, but the door's shut tight.'

Inside the room Henry stared at Hardcastle through bloodshot eyes. He uttered no greeting.

'I am so, so sorry, Henry,' said Stephen.

Henry merely nodded, almost imperceptibly.

'I came as soon as I heard. Janet called me. She's with Felicity now. And Mark. At the house.'

So they were together then, his wife and his grandson. Mark hadn't returned to the hospital to see his father or grandfather. Henry was not surprised. Felicity had made her feelings clear to him. She would no doubt have made them clear to her grandson too. And he felt pretty sure that Mark would take his grandmother's side. No doubt the boy felt the same way. Henry was even more bereft. It seemed he had lost his entire family.

Stephen moved close to the bed, pulling up a chair. He sat down and leaned forward, so that his face was only a foot or so from Henry's.

'I don't think they're coming in,' he said, his voice little more than a whisper.

Henry didn't react. He'd already come to that conclusion.

'Not tonight. Probably not tomorrow. Who knows when? If ever.' Stephen's voice was light. Inappropriately light. He paused, looking down at his injured employer. Henry still did not speak.

'But I am here, Henry,' Hardcastle continued. 'I am with you. I will always be with you. You needn't worry. I will take care of the business. I will take care of everything. Like always. That is all I have ever wanted to do.'

At last Henry met Stephen's gaze. He had suffered a terrible tragedy from which he would never recover. A tragedy for which, it seemed, he might never be forgiven by his remaining family, the wife, daughter and grandson he truly loved. They held him responsible, even though he did not see how they could. He had merely conducted the business as he saw best, and for the greater profit of everyone concerned, as he'd always done. It seemed to Henry that he was being betrayed. He was in pain still. He felt old and bereft.

But none of this had turned Henry Tanner into a fool. He'd realized exactly what David Vogel had been getting at as soon as the detective had started questioning him about Stephen's involvement. And he'd thought of little else since. It made sense. It made terrible sense. Stephen was behind so much of it. Stephen had known that Charlie was still alive, that was for sure; he'd probably helped him, and that little bitch he'd been shagging, stage his death. Perhaps it was Stephen who had put the fear of God into Charlie. Perhaps it was Stephen who had pushed him to the brink, pushed Charlie so far that he ran from it all, abandoning his old life. And perhaps Stephen had planned and executed all of it. Stephen had presumably wanted Charlie out of the way for his own ends. Even though Charlie was his alleged best friend.

As he lay nursing his wounds in his hospital bed, Henry hated Stephen Hardcastle more than he'd ever hated anyone in his life, except perhaps Charlie, because of what he had done that day. And before. But he understood Stephen. Stephen wanted the business. Stephen wanted the power that came with it. The extraordinary power and kudos that came courtesy of its covert activities.

Henry wondered what fate Stephen had planned for the only remaining adult male, his grandson Mark. And indeed for Henry himself. He still didn't know who had shot him. That was the biggest question that remained unanswered. He would have thought it more likely that Charlie would have wanted rid of him than Stephen. But he couldn't imagine that either man was capable of handling a precision sniper rifle like the Dragunov SVU. Unless of course he had been the victim of a lucky shot. Or an unlucky one, for the shooter, depending on how you looked at it.

Henry stared hard at the lawyer. Stephen was more like him than any member of his own family, he reflected grimly. Henry knew exactly what made the younger man tick. For some time now he'd been observing the way the handsome Zimbabwean looked at Joyce before and after Charlie's 'death'. The prospect of Stephen taking his involvement with the family to another level had not worried him. Not then.

But that was before the cataclysmic events of the last few days. Now it worried him. Or it would have done, if he thought his daughter would ever again be capable of having a relationship with anyone.

'I'm here, Henry. I will always be here,' repeated Stephen softly.

Henry remained silent. Hardcastle appeared to be building up to something; Henry was curious to find out what it was.

'It's been hard for me over the years, you know,' Stephen remarked conversationally. 'You've never let me into the fold, have you? Despite the fact I have done everything you ever required of me, given my all – to you, to the business, to the family. You were the family I always wanted. You were the father I always wanted – you must know that. I never had a father. My mother took me away from my father and brought me to England. The man she married here had no time for me. Oh, he sent me to Eton, he provided for me after my mother died, but he barely came near me. I thought with you I had found a father. But I was doomed to be forever the outsider, wasn't I? You would never fully accept me. After all, how could you?'

Henry was goaded into speaking. 'You'd better not be trying to say that I wouldn't accept you because you're black! Is that it, Stephen? Are you playing the race card, you damned fool?'

'Still hurling abuse at me, eh, Henry? I just suck it up, don't I?' Stephen Hardcastle gave a hollow laugh. 'No, not that, Henry. I don't think you take much notice of colour, any more than you worry about caste or creed. Not if people are useful to you. For you, Henry, the world is divided into family and non-family. Throughout my many years of service

I have always remained non-family, an outsider. And that hurt. You promised to make me a partner in the business, but year after year you invariably came up with a reason for putting it off. Charlie – weak, pathetic Charlie – was a partner right from the start. Then last year you made that spoiled brat of a grandson of yours a junior partner as soon as he joined the firm. Only then did you admit to me that, although you valued me, I would never be a partner. Not in your family business. And you had the nerve to try to fob me off with a rise in salary to make up for it! How could you, Henry?'

Henry narrowed his eyes.

'Did you shoot me, Stephen?' he asked abruptly.

'No,' replied Stephen quickly. 'Why would I do that? Why would I want to hurt you?'

Henry didn't know the answer to that. But he reckoned he had answers to some of the other questions that had been bothering him over the past few days:

'You did all the rest of it, though. Staging Charlie's death – he could never have pulled off that charade without help. You knew damn well he was still alive, shacked up with that little slut Monika.'

'Monika?' queried Stephen.

'Yes, Monika. You must have known about that.'

'No, actually, I didn't know about Monika. Well, not specifically. I was aware there was someone Charlie wanted to start a new life with. And I thought he'd have the sense to leave the country and begin afresh with his new woman, never to be seen again. I had no idea he'd come back here, to Bristol.

'Naturally, I did wonder, when Fred disappeared, whether it might be down to Charlie. I didn't have a phone number or an email address for him – we'd agreed it would be best if there were to be no further contact between us. So all I could do was hope I was wrong. Like everyone else, I hoped that Fred would turn up safe and well and there would be a simple explanation. I never expected any of this to happen, Henry. How could I? Yes, I helped Charlie bugger off. He'd turned into such a pathetic excuse for a man, I thought we'd all be better off. Me, obviously, because you would have to turn to me, rely on me. And that's exactly what happened. You may have made Mark a partner, but he's just a kid. I was the only one competent to take Charlie's place. I thought you'd be better off too. And Joyce. I didn't know he was going to come back here, murder two of his children and damned near kill Joyce, for God's sake! How was I to know he'd gone from being a bit unhinged to a full-blown raving bloody lunatic?'

'What about his alleged arms deals with gangsters?' asked Henry. 'Charlie told Joyce that *I* was the one trading with criminals.'

'Well, you know that's a lie: you did no such thing. But we both know that weapons went missing – we checked the records together. If not Charlie, who else? No doubt it was Charlie's gangster associates who were behind the shooting. The moment you put a stop to the trade he'd been doing with them, that's when you became a target.'

What Stephen was saying made a kind of terrible sense. The more Henry thought about it, the more plausible it sounded. And besides, Stephen Hardcastle was taking a huge risk in confessing all of this to him.

'What if I go to the police, tell them everything you have told me?' Henry said. 'What do you think would happen to you then?'

Stephen shrugged. 'Not a lot. I'm not sure that I've committed any crime worth mentioning. I haven't even handled the distribution of Charlie's estate, because he has yet to be officially declared dead. As for helping him stage his own death . . . As a lawyer, I have to say it would be pretty hard to prove.'

'Unless Charlie lives and gives a statement to that effect.'

'He's a proven liar, an addict and a double murderer. Who's going to believe a word he says?' Stephen shrugged again, then leaned towards the bed. 'Henry, I still want to be at your side, running the company for you, until you are better, until you are on your feet again. And you know I will do it how you would want. I didn't do anything that I thought would harm you, Henry, and I never would. It was Charlie who did all the damage. Even if Charlie lives, he will go to jail for a long time. Charlie's gone. Your surviving grandson blames you for what happened to his younger brother and sister; he's gone too. But I am still here. I am still here for you, Henry.'

Henry wanted to lash out at him. He didn't dare. He didn't dare lose Stephen too. Henry had called Mr Smith again just before the police had returned. As usual he had left a message on an automated answer service. As usual he had waited for the call back, from an encrypted phone, he'd always presumed, which usually came within ten or fifteen minutes. He was still waiting. Mr Smith would know by now all about Charlie, back from the dead, driving his wife and children, and the woman with whom he was having an affair, into the harbour. Henry's son-in-law had murdered three people and very nearly a fourth. That was going to attract a considerable amount of public and media attention. Mr Smith did not like anything that attracted attention. And Mr

Smith would be unlikely to be swayed by the plea that Charlie's actions had nothing to do with Tanner-Max's work for HMG. Henry feared he might really be alone now. Without even Mr Smith to turn to.

Stephen was watching Henry closely. Gauging his every reaction.

'I'm all you've got,' Stephen said.

Henry knew that. Only too well. Stephen had echoed his own thoughts uncannily. At last Henry spoke. His voice was strained, but his speech was clear and deliberate.

'I know,' he said.

And he reached out with his one good hand to grasp Stephen's.

The hand of the man who was both his most bitter enemy and the only friend he had left. The man he considered to be his only conceivable saviour.

Stephen was euphoric when he left Southmead.

He knew how much Henry must have suffered over the last couple of days. He had seen first-hand how devastated his employer was by the loss of his grandchildren and the destruction of his family. But no matter how distraught, Henry had a brain like a bacon slicer. That was how he had been able to keep all his myriad cards in the air for so long. It was inevitable that he would have turned his powers of deduction to unravelling the role that Stephen Hardcastle might have played in the recent chain of events.

That chain of events had taken several unexpected turns, so far as Stephen was concerned. He had been genuinely shocked and even at times distressed by what had happened, but that hadn't stopped him cynically taking advantage.

After years of coveting Charlie Mildmay's ludicrously elevated position in Tanner-Max, not to mention his wife, Stephen had exploited his alleged friend's increasingly fragile mental state to the full. A succession of near accidents had been enough to frighten poor, vulnerable Charlie into believing that he was being targeted. Not that he was ever in any real danger. Stephen wasn't a violent man. Or he never had been in the past, anyway. He hadn't set out to do serious harm to Charlie – much as he wanted him out of the way, Stephen wasn't capable of murdering someone in cold blood. His aim had been merely to unnerve him, to persuade him that it was time to disappear. Of course, being Charlie, he couldn't just do a runner. He had to go through an elaborate charade, faking his own death. Stephen had been only too happy to help.

And with Charlie gone, who better to fill the void than Stephen? He had the business acumen, the nous, the guile to be Henry's second in command at Tanner-Max. Unlike Charlie, who would never have lasted in the company, let alone made partner, had it not been for the fact he was married to Henry's only daughter. Even so, there had never been any affection or even regard between the two men, whereas Stephen admired everything about Henry Tanner. It hurt him deeply when Henry used him as his personal whipping boy, which he did frequently. Yet in spite of that, Stephen looked upon Henry as the father he'd never had.

His biological father, a prince of the Mahlangu royal family, had married his mother, Ayanda, when she was only fifteen, though the ceremony would not have been considered legal under international law. She had given birth to Stephen nine months later, after which his father had lost interest in her, even though Ayanda grew into a beautiful young woman.

His father had more important things on his mind. Even his first name, Busani, meant 'rule'. That was what Stephen's father believed he had been born to do. And Busani Mahlangu saw his destiny as being far more important than either his young wife or his son.

The Mahlangu were of the Ndebele tribe. As was the legendary Joshua Nkomo, leader and founder of the Zimbabwe African People's Union, ZAPU, which had been banned by the white minority government of his country, then known as Rhodesia. Busani Mahlangu had fought alongside Nkomo through the years of civil war and political struggle which preceded the notorious Robert Mugabe coming to power. In 1982 Mugabe unleashed his infamous fifth army in a genocidal campaign against the Ndebele, slaughtering up to 20,000 civilians. Nkomo fled the country, but Busani would not leave. He did, however, arrange for his wife and son to travel to the UK, where they were taken in by a distant relative.

Not long after her arrival in London, Ayanda caught the eye of a hedge-fund manager, high on tequila slammers, at the Brick Lane bar where she'd found work clearing tables. Ayanda knew that neither she nor her son had any future in Zimbabwe, or with Busani. She decided to use all her wiles to ensnare her suitor, who was both a high earner and the eldest son of wealthy parents. She wouldn't let him near her unless he married her. Somewhat to the surprise of all concerned, not least Ayanda, and against the wishes of his family, James Hardcastle eventually did just that. It was he who insisted Stephen should take his surname, and change his first name. In his circles, it simply wouldn't do to have a stepson called Nyongolo Mahlangu.

So Stephen Hardcastle was invented and promptly sent away to Eton, where he learned to speak with a public-school

371

accent and to lord it over those who didn't. He was a survivor. And like his father he'd been born to rule, hadn't he?

But then, a couple of years after her second marriage, Ayanda died in childbirth. Stephen rarely saw his stepfather after that, although James Hardcastle continued to provide for him, paying his school fees and making sure arrangements were made for him to be cared for during the holidays.

Stephen dreamed of creating his own family. But he had never come close to marriage, or even to building a lasting relationship with a woman. Instead he lusted after Joyce, the wife of the man whom he had honestly once considered to be his best friend. Most of all he sought total acceptance from Joyce's father, the patriarch of the clan. He wanted to be everything to Henry. He wanted Henry to be forced to rely on him alone. And he thought that night at the hospital he may have come close to achieving that.

As he drove home from Southmead, he even found himself wondering when he might dare make an approach to Joyce again. She had survived it all, thank God. Perhaps she would turn to him, now.

Stephen had taken a calculated gamble with Henry, but it seemed to have paid off. It had been a risk, admitting to colluding with Charlie in his disappearance, but a flat-out denial would never have washed with Henry. As it turned out, the half-truths he'd told seemed to satisfy the older man.

Stephen had gambled on two things. The second had been the big one. Stephen had gambled that Henry would accept that he could not survive without Stephen. That he would see Stephen as his only possible saviour, the only one who could steer Henry and Tanner-Max through the troubled times which undoubtedly lay ahead.

And Henry had fallen for it. Hook, line and sinker.

Vogel was right. Neither Henry Tanner nor Charlie Mild-may had engaged in arms deals with criminal organizations. That had been an invention of Stephen's. A double bluff aimed at causing fear and distrust all round. It had been a considerable success too.

The subterfuge had been helped by the fact that Henry knew little about Stephen's private life. He may have been vaguely aware of Stephen's reunion with his natural father and his two elder brothers a few years previously, and of his African holidays. But he had no idea that Busani Mahlangu was now the leader of ZIPA, the Zimbabwe People's Army, a breakaway arm of Zimbabwe's official opposition party, the MDC, Movement for Democratic Change. Nor, of course, was Henry aware of Busani's great pride in the educated son who was occasionally able to deliver to ZIPA, through complex and rather clever lines of supply, a small number of exceptional weapons.

And Henry would have been utterly astonished to learn that during his African holidays Stephen attended ZIPA training camps, where he was tutored in the use of those weapons by battle-hardened mercenaries.

Although he had proven to be something of a natural marksman, Stephen had never expected to make use of that training, nor of the Dragunov SVU he had kept for himself, concealed in a box beneath his bed, for reasons he could not quite explain. Just in case, he had told himself. Or maybe, simply because he could.

And ultimately he had not hesitated to use the Dragunov on Henry Tanner in pursuance of his aims. He'd trusted in his ability as a marksman, confident that he could inflict a non-fatal wound on the man he so revered. It was an act, as Stephen saw it, of damage limitation, made necessary by the fallout from Charlie's psychotic attempts to reunite his family.

It did not occur to Stephen that most observers would regard his own behaviour as deranged.

Stephen was pretty pleased with himself.

At last, and under the most extraordinary circumstances, Henry Tanner seemed to have realized how much he needed Stephen.

Indeed, that Stephen was all he had left.

There remained only one lurking concern: that policeman, Vogel. The one with the intelligent eyes behind thick spectacles. He seemed a cut above the rest, Stephen thought. He was a planner and a thinker. A plotter. And Stephen knew one of those when he saw one.

He felt sure, as he had indicated to Henry, that it would be impossible to prove a case against him. He had covered his tracks every step of the way.

But would Vogel see through his carefully contrived smokescreen? Stephen wondered.

He did not know, of course, how close Vogel was to seeing through everything.

Thirty-one

Immediately after their discussion in the hospital corridor, Vogel and Clarke returned to Kenneth Steele House. It was almost midnight. They were both oblivious to the hour, and well past weariness.

PC Bolton had come to collect them. He had also lost count of the hours he had been on duty.

Stephen Hardcastle was now the focus of the investigation. Vogel and Clarke needed to know everything about his past.

'Whoever did that shooting knew how to handle a high-powered sniper rifle,' said Vogel. 'That calls for specialist training. From what we've been told, Hardcastle is not ex-military, nor was he a member of any shooting clubs or teams at school or university. On the other hand, I suspect there is an awful lot about Stephen Hardcastle that we don't know.'

While Vogel set to work digging up information on the Internet, Clarke began double-checking Hardcastle's whereabouts over the past few days and looking into every possible aspect of his behaviour. She was assisted by Bolton, who needed the overtime.

The duty IT man was called in to go over Charlie Mildmay's abandoned laptop, and to be ready to examine the computer equipment which they were expecting to bring in from Stephen Hardcastle's home as soon as a warrant had been obtained.

'Not that I expect there to be much on there,' Vogel had said. 'Our man is clever. He will have covered his tracks. He's good at working on computers too. Probably better than he lets on. He will have used Charlie's computer, not his own. And if he needed to use another one, I reckon it would have been a laptop that he's now got rid of.'

Vogel's Internet searches also revealed the fact that Stephen Hardcastle owned a powerboat, which was moored at Instow marina – the same place Charlie Mildmay had moored the *Molly May*. He asked PC Bolton to check it out.

Having raised the marina boss from his bed, Bolton was able to report that Stephen Hardcastle had in the late summer and autumn of 2013, just before and around the time of Charlie's supposed death at sea, professed a previously unknown interest in night fishing.

'So if he took his boat out at night it didn't look unusual,' said Bolton. 'The marina chap didn't know whether he went out at the time Charlie staged his disappearance, but he says nobody would have made anything of it if he did, because Hardcastle was known to go night fishing. There's more too. He took his boat out yesterday afternoon, first time this year. He arrived at Instow about one o'clock, saying he fancied a quick spin, wanted to make sure she was ready for the summer, and he was out for about an hour. It's a top-of-the-range Goldfish. A beast. Cost a pretty penny and goes like stink. I reckon Hardcastle steered straight out to sea, then dumped the gun and anything else that might incriminate him over the side, don't you, boss?'

Vogel thought exactly that. 'Good work, Bolton,' he said.

Meanwhile, his own enquiries soon revealed the bare bones of Stephen Hardcastle's early life in Africa and subsequent near reinvention in the UK. Once he discovered the Zimbabwe connection, Vogel wasted no time in contacting people who knew all about the militant Zimbabwe People's Army and the involvement of Hardcastle's father, along with his half-brothers, who were Busani Mahlangu's first lieutenants in ZIPA.

He also learned that there had been a recent attempt on the life of a senior member of the Mugabe regime by a sniper armed with a Dragunov SVU, the same kind of rifle which had been 'pilfered' from Tanner-Max, and had almost certainly been used to shoot Henry Tanner.

Furthermore, Hardcastle was a frequent visitor to Zimbabwe.

At about two in the morning Vogel's research was interrupted by a phone call, initially taken by PC Bolton.

'It's Frank Watts, DC at Barnstaple,' said Bolton. 'He and a uniform are with Charlie Mildmay's parents. They've been breaking the news to them. Watts says he thinks you should speak to them straight away.'

Wondering what the Mildmays could have to say that was so urgent, Vogel took the telephone receiver from Bolton's outstretched hand.

'Yes,' he said.

Frank Watts told him he was putting Mr Bill Mildmay on the line.

Charlie's father sounded distraught. Hardly surprising, in light of the news he'd just been given about his son and grandchildren.

Bill Mildmay had insisted on speaking to someone

connected with the investigation because he believed he had crucial information to impart.

'I don't know if you are aware that my wife and I adopted our son Charlie,' he said.

Vogel was not aware of it. Neither did it seem to be relevant. But he allowed Bill Mildmay to continue.

'We adopted Charlie when he was seven years old. He came to us after both his parents were killed in a motor incident. First of all we fostered him, then we adopted him. He was a sweet little boy . . .' Bill Mildmay broke off, his breathing coming in short, sharp gasps. A moment later he resumed: 'We never had any trouble with Charlie. He seemed to get over it all quite quickly. So we never talked about it. He was clever at school. He sailed through everything. Then he married Joyce. There was that beautiful house, an excellent job in the family business. It was as if he had a charmed life. And the grandchildren, those beautiful beautiful children . . .'

Bill broke off again. Vogel could hear a woman, presumably Charlie's adoptive mother, sobbing in the background.

'Please go on, Mr Mildmay,' Vogel encouraged.

'Yes, well, we knew he could be a bit moody. But can't we all? We never thought there was anything wrong. Not really. Not enough for us to upset Charlie, to remind him of terrible things we hoped he'd forgotten. We should have done though. We know that now. We were heartbroken when we thought he'd been lost at sea. But this, this is worse, much worse. We blame ourselves, you see. If only we'd told him all of it. Maybe he could have got help. We blame ourselves now for what's happened. It's our fault that Molly and little Fred are dead. Our fault.'

Vogel could hear Bill Mildmay stifling a sob.

'Why do you blame yourself, Mr Mildmay?' he asked.

'How on earth can it be your fault that your grandchildren are dead?'

'Charlie's parents died the same way,' replied Bill Mildmay in little more than a whisper. 'Their car went off the quayside into the river at Bideford, when the tide was in. Charlie was in the back. He got out – we never quite knew how. The police said there was one window open and they think Charlie scrambled through it and floated to the surface. They said an adult would have been unable to make it. But this was a seven-year-old boy, Detective Inspector, desperate to survive. Think what he must have experienced. He never spoke about it. It was as if he'd blanked it out. We thought it was for the best – people didn't talk things through back then like they're taught to now.'

Again Bill Mildmay struggled to compose himself. Vogel remained silent, waiting for the other man to speak.

'His mother was driving,' Mildmay continued eventually. 'Charlie's mother drove her car, with her husband and son inside, into the River Torridge at high tide. We knew that the police always suspected she did it deliberately, but they couldn't prove it. You see, Charlie's mother was schizophrenic, Mr Vogel. Seriously so. She'd been in and out of hospitals all her life. And we never told Charlie. My wife and I now think he must have been ill. How else could he have done what he did? We think he inherited his mother's schizophrenia, Mr Vogel. And we never told him about it, never told him he might be at risk, never gave him the opportunity to be medically checked, to be given the right medication. Looking back, we ignored all sorts of signs. Charlie was always so changeable. Look at his life: one minute he was a hippie leftie, the next he was part of the establishment, a successful businessman. We told ourselves it was all just Charlie. Our loveable

Charlie. We wanted everything to be all right, so we told ourselves that it was, and we told Charlie nothing. That, Detective Inspector, is why we blame ourselves for the death or our grandchildren.'

Vogel was thoughtful when he ended the call. It didn't make any difference now whether or not Charlie Mildmay had been suffering from schizophrenia, but what Bill Mildmay had told him made terrible sense. It explained why Charlie had become so vulnerable. And if Vogel's assessment of the sequence of events leading to this dreadful night was correct, it explained why he'd proved so susceptible to the manipulative trickery of Stephen Hardcastle.

'I'm damned sure that bastard is the real villain, boss, and we have to make sure he doesn't get away with it,' he told Nobby Clarke after he had filled her in on his telephone conversation with Bill Mildmay.

At the same time another lead was being explored by the technical department. Henry Tanner had called Stephen Hardcastle on his mobile shortly before being shot. The tech boys had now been able to pinpoint where Hardcastle had been when he took that call.

He had not been in his home overlooking the harbour, as he had maintained when questioned following the shooting. Stephen had either been in Traders' Court or adjacent to it. Vogel was of the opinion that his precise location had been on top of one of the buildings overlooking Traders' Court.

This evidence established that Hardcastle had lied, and that he had been at the scene of the crime shortly before Henry Tanner was shot.

'We've got enough to arrest him now, surely, boss,' said Vogel excitedly.

DCI Clarke agreed.

At 4.30 a.m., Vogel, Clarke, Bolton, and a team of uni-forms, including an armed response unit, arrived at Stephen Hardcastle's Bristol waterside apartment. Given the close association with firearms Hardcastle was now known to have, Vogel and Clarke were taking no chances.

They were admitted into Conqueror House by prior arrangement with the caretaker. Hardcastle's flat was on the first floor.

'Go on, Vogel, you take the honours. It's your collar,' said Clarke.

Vogel led the way, taking two stairs at a time. This wasn't something he would usually do, but he couldn't wait to arrest Stephen Hardcastle. He thought the man was despicable. And arrogant with it.

Vogel hammered on the door of number 15. There were two armed response men right alongside him. They told him to stand to one side of the door. Behind them lurked a team carrying an enforcer, the heavy steel battering ram used by UK police to force entry if necessary.

It wasn't necessary. Although, it did seem a long time before Vogel heard Hardcastle unlocking the door from the inside. He had been on the verge of ordering the two PCs carrying the enforcer to break it down.

The door opened slowly. Hardcastle was standing in the hallway looking bleary-eyed. But if he had been taken by surprise, as surely he must have been, he made a pretty good fist of concealing it.

'Can I help you, Detective Inspector Vogel?' he asked pleasantly.

Hardcastle was wearing only a pair of white boxer shorts, which, contrasting with his ebony skin, helped show off his muscular physique. He made no attempt to cover himself.

'My my, both of you,' he remarked in his Etonian drawl, registering the arrival of DCI Clarke. 'And you've brought some of your friends too. How lovely. But I'm afraid you're a little early for breakfast.'

This was some cool customer, thought Vogel. But he too kept his cool as, stony-faced, he began the customary caution.

'Stephen Hardcastle, I am arresting you on suspicion of having perverted the course of justice, theft, and the attempted murder of Henry Tanner,' Vogel declared. 'You do not have to say anything. But it may harm your defence if you do not mention when questioned something which you later rely on in court. Anything you do say may be given in evidence.'

Hardcastle remained smiling. If a little stiffly.

'Prove it,' he said.

Epilogue

Vogel and Clarke proceeded to do just that. It took time. There were a number of fruitless interviews with Hardcastle, who barely gave an inch at any stage.

And during this period, whilst on police bail, Stephen Hardcastle finally achieved his ambition. Henry Mildmay, ~~Tanner~~ now unable to remain in charge himself, made Hardcastle a partner in Tanner-Max, or what remained of it, and handed over the running of the company to him.

This incensed Vogel, who became more determined than ever that Hardcastle be brought to justice.

The weapon used to shoot Henry Tanner was never found. Neither were any computers carrying information pertaining to illicit gun dealing, other than the laptop owned by Charlie Mildmay. However, records were found of Hardcastle having purchased through Amazon the previous year a laptop which could not be accounted for. It wasn't much, but it was something. The laptop was still under its manufacturer's guarantee. Hardcastle claimed he'd lost it. He'd left it on a train. It hadn't been insured.

The IT boys did their wizardry on Charlie's laptop. Using advanced techniques now available, they were able to ascertain, from pressure on the keys, that Hardcastle had frequently used it. The problem was, he had never denied doing so. Both he and Henry had admitted to hacking into the laptop in order to check up on Charlie after his disappearance.

The police had more luck with the powerboat. They now knew that Hardcastle's Goldfish had left Instow on the night that Charlie had set off on his supposedly fatal voyage the previous November, thanks to the emergence of a witness who had initially been reluctant to come forward. Once given assurances that his wife need not hear about his extra-marital adventures at the marina on the night in question, he had given a statement.

And it was already known that Hardcastle had taken the vessel out hours after Henry had been shot.

Forensics were able to prove that the envelope containing Charlie Mildmay's fateful letter to his wife had been opened before she received it. Both the letter and its envelope bore the fingerprints of Stephen Hardcastle and Henry Tanner.

Most of the evidence was circumstantial, but eventually the CPS made the decision to charge Stephen Hardcastle with all the offences for which he had been arrested, namely: perverting the course of justice, theft and attempted murder.

Eight months later, in January 2015, Stephen Hardcastle stood trial before Bristol Crown Court.

Vogel had been able to ascertain beyond any reasonable doubt, after meticulous dissection of all available records and a certain amount of intercourse with criminal contacts, that no arms or defence materials of any kind had been siphoned off from Tanner-Max and sold on to any criminal elements within the UK.

It was, however, possible to prove that a number of firearms that had been in the custody of Tanner-Max, including at least two Dragunov SVUs, had found their way to ZIPA in

Zimbabwe. And Hardcastle's family links with ZIPA were also easy to prove.

Tanner-Max records showed that a third Dragunov could not be accounted for. The prosecution argued that this was the weapon Stephen Hardcastle had used to shoot Henry Tanner, and that he had disposed of it by taking his power-boat out to sea and throwing the rifle overboard.

Hardcastle denied that he had ever been in possession of the rifle, and he also denied that he had ever received any training in the use of firearms, even of the most unsophisticated nature.

But police in Zimbabwe, anxious to discredit ZIPA, had supplied tangible evidence that Stephen Hardcastle was a regular visitor to their country and had undergone such training with the militant breakaway group.

The prosecution sought to prove that Hardcastle had both opportunity and motive. Janet Porter was a witness for the prosecution. She told the puzzling story of the letter, from the allegedly dead Charlie, which had been withheld from Joyce Mildmay.

Mark Mildmay also gave evidence for the prosecution. He claimed that he had known nothing of the arms brokerage activities of Tanner-Max, over which his grandfather, father and Stephen Hardcastle had presided. His mother had told him that his father had claimed these arms deals were a covert activity on behalf of the British government. He said that did nothing to alter his opinion that the international sales of arms by sovereign nations was morally repugnant. Such was his disgust with all aspects of arms dealing, particularly with regard to chemical weapons, that he had relinquished all claim to Tanner-Max and had now moved to

London, where he would, in the near future, be embarking on a new career in banking.

The defence dismissed Mark's references to covert activity on behalf of the British government as being merely fanciful, and the judge ruled inadmissible as hearsay any reference to it, in terms of Mark's mother having related to him what his father had allegedly told her.

Charlie Mildmay could no longer speak for himself. A week after his near drowning, and without ever recovering consciousness, he had suffered an aneurism, brought on by his brain being deprived of oxygen when he had stopped breathing. And this time Charlie Mildmay was definitely dead.

Joyce Mildmay was unable to be called to give evidence by either the prosecution or the defence, whether she might have wanted to or not. She was a broken woman who had spent the eight months since the violent death of her daughter and her youngest son in and out of various clinics and mental institutions.

Her doctor was called to the stand as an expert witness, to give evidence on the mental state of both Joyce and her mother Felicity. Felicity was almost as ill as her daughter, and had taken up residence in a Bristol nursing home. On the basis of the doctor's testimony, neither woman was called to give evidence.

Henry Tanner did take the stand. Since the shooting and the destruction of his family he had lived alone at the Corner House, rarely going out, and with only Geoff Brooking, the driver DCI Clarke had always suspected as being rather more than that, in occasional attendance.

Stephen Hardcastle had been banned from personal contact with Henry, as a condition of his bail, until the impending legal proceedings were concluded.

Henry was incoherent, resolutely vague about the nature of the Tanner-Max arms brokerage, and seemingly unable to remember anything. He even claimed he couldn't remember whether or not he had seen Charlie's letter before it was ultimately delivered to his daughter.

He was a terrible witness. Vogel wondered whether it was yet another performance. Perhaps his last performance. Desperately maintaining a lifetime's discretion regarding the covert activities of his company.

Henry might not be the man he was, but now that his family had abandoned him, Tanner-Max was all he had left. Perhaps he remained determined that his legacy should survive. Which meant he needed Stephen Hardcastle – now the boss of Tanner-Max and the one man who could keep the business going – to be cleared of the charges against him.

To the annoyance of Clarke, Vogel, and the whole Operation Binache team, the attempted murder charge against Hardcastle was reduced to grievous bodily harm.

Hardcastle was found guilty by majority verdict on that and the two other remaining charges, and sentenced to eight years in jail.

For Vogel, the best thing about the trial and its conclusion had been the look of absolute surprise on Stephen Hardcastle's face when the guilty verdict was read out by the jury foreman.

Vogel had no doubt that the man's self-delusion was such that he had believed he would get away scot-free.

Throughout the proceedings, both prosecution and defence seemed content to allow the involvement of Tanner-Max in the international brokerage of defence materials to be presented as a transparent part of Britain's thriving and legitimate armaments industry. Only Mark Mildmay even attempted to suggest anything other, and his evidence was struck from the record.

There was no further mention in court of British government involvement, of encrypted phone calls, of covert deals and counter deals, of shipments of arms being dispatched to secret destinations worldwide in such a way that no one would ever know who dispatched them. Neither was there even the slightest whisper of Mr Smith.

DCI Clarke, still officially stationed in London, had, when necessary, commuted to and from Bristol throughout the proceedings, sometimes staying overnight at the Royal Marriott. On the last day of the trial, after Hardcastle had been sentenced, she insisted Vogel return with her to the Marriott for a large drink.

The guilty verdict was a result, and Hardcastle's immediate reaction had been most satisfying. But both officers were dissatisfied with the sentence that had been meted out.

'You're not going to stick to bloody lemonade or whatever it is you put away after that, Vogel, are you?' Clarke asked as they walked into the same bar they'd been in when the news had come through about the tragic incident at the Floating Harbour.

Vogel shrugged. He didn't even like the taste of alcohol. And he doubted it would take away the anger he felt at Hardcastle's punishment, or lack thereof.

'Eight years – that means the bastard'll be out in five,' he grumbled. 'After all that work to get a guilty verdict! I'm seriously brassed off, boss.'

'Aren't we all, Vogel,' murmured Clarke laconically.

She didn't seem to have a lot to say. She had a different way of dealing with her disappointment.

'Get me another drink, Vogel,' she instructed.

He did so. Then continued to grumble.

'It's been yet another damned cover-up, barely a mention of what lay behind it all: the shady goings on of our bloody government, and your flippin' Mr bloody Smith.'

'She's not my Mr Smith,' said Clarke.

'Well, he, she or it sure as hell ain't mine.'

'Oh grow up, Vogel,' instructed the DCI.

She knocked back four large malts in quick succession whilst Vogel looked on in amazement. He knew she liked a drink, but he'd never seen her drink like this before. He was so gobsmacked he didn't even make a move to leave.

Clarke got drunk quickly. More quickly than Vogel had ever seen anyone get drunk. But, he thought, if you pour whisky down your throat at that speed, something is bound to happen.

'Know what, Vogel, if you weren't shuch a boring old happily married fart, I'd take you upstairs with me – I would, honest,' Clarke said, her words not entirely clear.

Vogel blushed and began blinking furiously behind his spectacles. He so wished he didn't do either.

'Would you?' he asked, not sure whether she was joking or not.

He'd been going to address her as boss, like he always did. Under the circumstances, though, that didn't seem right. But he could never call her Nobby. How could any man address a woman like her as Nobby?

'Ma'am,' he added lamely, and immediately wished he hadn't.

Her eyes narrowed.

'Yep,' she said. 'I would.'

She leaned forward conspiratorially.

'But only if you'd call me "ma'am" in bed. All right?'

Vogel's blush deepened. His blink rate increased. In common with most of her colleagues he knew next to nothing about DCI Clarke's private life. The rumour, based on her being spotted by one of the biggest gossips in her old MIT unit strolling through St James's Park with an arm across the shoulders of another woman, whom she had also been seen with on more than one other occasion, was, of course, that she was gay. And this woman was clearly her life partner.

'Aren't you spoken for, ma'am?' he asked, more directly than he'd intended.

'Yep,' she replied, grinning wickedly.

Vogel found more courage. The boss was drunk, after all. He could probably get away with saying anything.

'And you share your life with a woman, don't you? Aren't you gay?'

'Ah ha!'

Clarke leaned close to him.

'Only on Mondays, Wednesdays . . . oh, and weekends,' she said.

'Right.'

'And today is Thursday.'

'So it is,' said Vogel.

He didn't know what else to say.

Nobby Clarke's grin widened.

'I'm joking, you bloody fool!' she said. 'You didn't think I was that drunk, did you?'

Vogel had a feeling he should be insulted. Mostly he was relieved.

'Of course not, boss,' he said.

Acknowledgements

Grateful thanks to:

Former Avon and Somerset Constabulary Detective Inspector Stephen Bishop, Incident Room Manager of the Bristol-based Brunel Major Crime Investigation Team; former Avon and Somerset Constabulary Detective Sergeant Frank Waghorn; and Pip Hall, of the Maritime and Coastguard Agency.

Plus, of course, Wayne, Anne and all the team at Pan Mac, Tony, and Amanda. As ever.

extracts reading groups
competitions books new
books discounts extracts extracts events
competitions extracts reading groups discounts
books new extracts events reading groups
events books extracts discounts reading groups
extracts new titles reading groups
interviews events new
events extracts extracts
books discounts new books events events
events new extracts
discounts extracts discounts

www.panmacmillan.com

extracts events reading groups
competitions books extracts new